RETURN POLICY

Also by Michael Snyder

My Name Is Russell Fink

RETURN POLICY

A Novel by
Michael Snyder

ZONDERVAN®

ZONDERVAN.com/
AUTHORTRACKER
follow your favorite authors

ZONDERVAN

Return Policy
Copyright © 2009 by Michael Snyder

This title is also available as a Zondervan ebook.
Visit www.zondervan.com/ebooks.

This title is also available in a Zondervan audio edition.
Visit www.zondervan.fm.

Requests for information should be addressed to:

Zondervan, *Grand Rapids, Michigan 49530*

Library of Congress Cataloging-in-Publication Data

Snyder, Michael, 1965–
        Return policy : a novel / by Michael Snyder.
            p.   cm.
        ISBN 978-0-310-27728-6 (pbk.)
        1. Conduct of life—Fiction. I. Title.
    PS3619.N938R48   2009
    813'.6—dc22   2008049747

Interior design by Beth Shagene

Printed in the United States of America

09 10 11 12 13 14 15 • 23 22 21 20 19 18 17 16 15 14 13 12 11 10 9 8 7 6 5 4 3 2 1

In loving memory of my big brother, Rusty
To Sherry, Jessica, Ashley, and Beth

Bottled up my hope, before it got spread too thin
I threw it in the ocean and then I jumped right in
All my heroes disappeared just like déjà vu
But I am a strong swimmer and I swam right into you.
Jonatha Brooke, *Steady Pull*

* * *

Your memory is a monster; you forget — it doesn't.
It simply files things away. It keeps things for you,
or hides things from you — and summons them
to your recall with a will of its own. You think you
have a memory; but it has you!
John Irving, *A Prayer for Owen Meany*

* * *

Love stinks! Yeah, yeah …
J. Geils Band, *Love Stinks*

Willy

Once a year, my senile aunt tries to kill me.

Her name is Mavis and she's really my great-aunt, my grandmother's sister. And although she may not be trying to murder me, it darn near works every September. These days Mavis remembers very little besides names and birthdays, so every year for the last six years, she's sent me the same card: on the outside, the words "Happy 30th Birthday," and on the inside, "Embrace the Zero."

I cannot begin to express the terror this simple act of kindness evokes in me.

At fourteen years of age, someone had to die for me to live. I felt guilty before my surgery and have felt that way every day since. Several days after they opened my chest, removed my diseased heart, and installed its donated replacement, I overheard a conversation between the surgeon and my mom. My mom was terrified the new heart wouldn't take. "Not to worry, Ms. Finneran," the surgeon said, "William's procedure went swimmingly well. If we're lucky, we just added another decade and a half to his life."

I often picture the ticking in my chest as an old-fashioned alarm clock, wrapped in pink pumping flesh and set for some unknown hour in the not too distant future. According to the Internet, the average life expectancy of transplant survivors is eleven very short years. I was never very good at math, but I believe my surgeon's estimate puts my expiration date at about age thirty.

Yesterday I turned twenty-nine.

I spent the better part of a decade trying to figure out who to blame. Was it God for knitting together such a weak heart in my mother's womb? My mother for smoking through two out of three trimesters? My father for driving my mother to the nasty habit in the first place?

The donor for not eating more vegetables and shunning elevators and Twinkies? At some point I decided to blame them all equally, then abandoned my accusing ways altogether. Instead I turned my attention to my list, officially titled: "Things to Do before I Die." It's not a bad list. It just needs one more item: "Stop wallowing and actually do something about the list before you die."

When I can't bear to look at Aunt Mavis's card any longer, I push back from the kitchen table, causing frothy espresso to lip over the edge of my World's Worst Teacher mug, which now appears to be shedding dirty tears in mourning.

I enter my bedroom and rummage through my underwear drawer till I find my grandfather's lockbox. Then I dump this year's card inside with the rest of Aunt Mavis's identical birthday wishes.

Before I close the lid I catch a glimpse of my first novel. It's a shiny library copy of *The Handyman*, the first in my series of detective novels about Ralph I. Handy (my unlucky one-eyed, one-handed repairman-cum-sleuth). The cover reveals the sleeve of a tan overcoat emerging from the shadows, a revolver protruding like a vacuum cleaner attachment from where the hand is supposed to be.

I've scrawled my to-do list on the dedication page, in pencil under the words: "For Walter, my brother, mentor, and friend. I miss you now more than I ever thought I could." My brother had few talents — namely, finding trouble, accidentally breaking the hearts of gorgeous women, and stoking the unshakable devotion of his kid brother. Legend has it that by the time he was four, my parents swore off ever having another child. I appeared in my first (and only) ultrasound eight years later. By then my parents were ready to retire from the child-rearing business altogether.

I remember the day I came up with my list. I was just young enough and dumb enough to think that the act of jotting down a few goals would somehow magically produce the internal fortitude necessary to accomplish them. I study it now, mentally crossing off the few items I've managed to do already (buying my grandparents' house, writing my "serious" novel, riding in a helicopter) and scoffing at the rest. One item, scratched out and rewritten numerous times, makes me groan aloud. "Fall in love ... for real this time."

Then it dawns on me. What good is a list when I have no real intention of following through? It's like a giant Post-It note reminder of my most glaring inadequacies.

I snap the book shut, grab my stack of birthday cards, carry them all to the kitchen, and toss them in the sink. I should have done this years ago. I root around in the junk drawer, finding every candle that Lucy left behind but not a single match. Then I remember my grandfather's pipe rack. They're lined up, bowls down, like prehistoric golf clubs, each one eliciting its own quiet memory. I pause to inhale the aroma of wet tobacco, then snatch my grandfather's favorite flip-top lighter and hurry back to the kitchen, wondering if this is a purging or a sacrifice. I hold the copy of my novel aloft, then flick the lighter open. I spin the flint wheel once, twice, then it ignites. My thumb goes numb as I touch the flame to the edge of the dangling book cover and wait.

Nothing.

Yellow tendrils flirt with the edge but refuse to catch. I let the pages flutter, hoping the resulting breeze will fan the flame. Then my thumb starts to burn and I have to let go of the lighter.

I stare at the book, stupidly, wondering if it's been treated with some secret flame retardant to prevent libraries from burning down. I gather up my stack of birthday cards and flick the lighter into action again, holding the edge of Mavis's death notice to the flame.

It catches. I alternate my gaze between the growing flame and my demented fun house grin reflected in the belly of my teakettle.

That's when the smoke detector goes off. A shrill, piercing chirp that literally stops my heart. I drop the lighter and the burning card, then grip the edge of the sink with both hands. I'm not typically one for omens, but I decide now to do something *else* about my list.

* * *

It took the better part of an hour — and a dozen hands of solitaire — for the turbulent pounding in my chest to subside. The only casualties of my botched arson attempt appear to be one blistered fingertip and a relentless tingling sensation along the length of my scar.

I place the nine of spades on the ten of diamonds, then resume turning cards over and ignore the sound of my telephone ringing. After a long beep, I hear the habitual throat clearing of my literary agent. His voice sounds like a drowsy Muppet, his bored monotone more despairing than normal, if that's even possible.

"William ..." (Sigh.) "We need to talk ..." (Elongated nasal breathing.) "Soon ..." (Bigger sigh.) "And in person ... so please call me." (Medium sigh, but with feeling.) "I have news."

The word *news* is bloated with meaning, conjuring the image of a grim-faced soap opera doctor — *I'm sorry, Mr. Finneran. We did everything we could ...*

I asked him once if he was getting enough sleep. He simply said, "The world ... is too giddy for my tastes."

"And you think your gloomy outlook is somehow going to stem that particular epidemic?"

"I'm no hero, Willy. I'm just doing my part."

Despite Stan's perpetual grogginess, he's a real animal when it comes to business dealings. This proved invaluable when my books were actually selling. But I haven't heard from Stan in months, not since the last puny royalty check arrived. He didn't even bother with a Christmas card this year.

I take another sip of espresso — a vile beverage — and place a red jack on a black queen. When I draw the ace of hearts, it's as if Lucy is staring right back at me. Years ago I took the *real* aces out of my deck and replaced them with the following:

> An index card with Doug's cell number on it — *Clubs*, because we used to play nightclubs.

> A photograph of Lucy celebrating our first anniversary — *Hearts*, for obvious reasons.

A severely cropped greeting card I found tucked between the pages of Song of Solomon in Lucy's Bible — *Spades*, for digging graves.

The receipt for Lucy's espresso machine — *Diamonds*, still not sure why.

Lucy's been gone almost five years now, and what I hate more than the loneliness is the fact that I've lost her scent. I used to stand in our closet and sniff the sleeves of her shirts and the necklines of her best dresses. But it's her skin I miss most — the sight of it, the warm touch, and especially the smell.

One night I got the bright idea to stuff Lucy's favorite pj's with sweaters and balled-up sheets. I just knew I couldn't suffer another night of waking up at two in the morning and weeping at the sight of the empty spot beside me. She didn't own any wigs so I resorted to a volleyball and a new mop I found in the garage. It didn't have to be perfect, just passable, since Lucy always slept with her head under a pillow. I washed the mop with Lucy's shampoo, then doused it with perfume and lotion and tucked it between the covers. With the lights on, my handiwork resembled a Lucy scarecrow. I still woke up at two a.m., but the only difference was my screaming in fright before the sobbing started up.

I've gone thirty seconds without a play when my homemade ace of spades appears. I place it in the first foundations position and pause to study it. The card was from a guy named Alvin. On the outside it said, *Thinking of you*. Folded inside was a printed version of a back-and-forth email with conflicting versions of what transpired between Alvin and my wife. He used words like *bliss* and *affair* and *love*. She called it an "emotional hiccup" that could have led to a "physical disaster" that should be "filed under *Things Best Forgotten*." This last bit should make me feel better, but it doesn't. Every time I read it I feel my borrowed heart nudge sideways a fraction of an inch, like when a stranger squeezes into the seat next to you on the subway.

The phone rings. I ignore it and perform an illegal search for a black three. A few moments later the answering machine clicks on in the bedroom. I crane one ear toward the familiar voice. It's Alistair "the Dean" Langstrom, my boss, and he doesn't sound pleased. He rarely does though. My latest infraction, it seems, was my homogeneous approach to grading students. I do have a vague memory of giving my entire freshman comp class A-minuses.

Three grimacing swallows later, I rinse my cup and change my shoes for a trip to Wal-Mart to pick up more espresso mix. That's when Doug shows up, letting himself in with the key I keep hidden in plain view on my front porch. He's a big man, not fat so much as thick, bulging like a pincushion. His chubby cheeks and enormous hands make him look like a giant toddler. Once inside, he tosses a giant stack of mail in the middle of my cards and croons, "Avon calling!"

"I thought you saved that prissy burlesque routine for the dean, who, by the way, may have just fired me."

"Hah. Not on my watch." Doug plants his fists on his thick hips like an effeminate superhero; a move his wife finds adorable, yet strikes mortal fear in our boss.

When Dean Langstrom inherited the current Edwards University English Department he was more than a little dismayed to find a hack genre writer (me) and an outspoken born-again homosexual (Doug) on his otherwise esteemed staff. Blatantly ousting either of us would only trigger Doug's unbridled social activism. He once staged a sit-in to protest the Girl Scouts preying on the obese and elderly when hawking their chocolate devil wafers.

So with cries of discrimination only a breath away, Langstrom employs alternating strategies of either shaming me or bullying me into resigning. He scrutinizes my work, talks down to me, and peppers me with trivial questions about obscure literary figures at faculty meetings.

Doug, however, is tenured, both as a professor and friend. The only thing he loves more than his wife is Jesus. He claims to have undergone a period of sexual *disorientation* in college, which ended on a blind date with Maggie, another sojourner of nebulous sexuality. They made a pact, more spiritual than carnal, and the result was a modern day arranged marriage, complete with the first of their two-point-six kids on the way.

"So," I say. "How's Maggie?"

"Fat and grumpy and more beautiful than ever. At least the morning sickness is behind us." Doug refers to his wife's pregnancy in plural possessive, owning inasmuch as possible his share of the pain and suffering. I have to admit, he does an admirable job. In fact, their love is so complete and endearing and sickeningly idyllic, it depresses everyone in its soupy green wake.

"Won't the arrival of your bouncing baby boy tip Langstrom off to your rampant straightness?"

"Nah, it'll confound him more. But enough chit-chat. Why didn't you answer your phone?"

"I don't know. I'm busy."

"Should I check the tub?"

I look up, blinking. The last time he dropped in on me I was filling the bathtub with all things Lucy, not just clothes and perfumes and shampoos, but also her hair dryer, laptop, and espresso maker — all plugged in through a network of extension cords. He assumed, of course, I was preparing a place to die. I'm too scared to ponder what I was *really* doing.

"What's this?" he says, pointing to the stacks of paper opposite my array of playing cards.

"Oh, that. Just some schoolwork."

Doug walks to the end of the table for a closer look. I resist the urge to crawl under my chair. He squints at the stacks, angling his big head for closer inspection. His eyes alternate between a stack of mail and a pile of assigned short fiction I was supposed to grade and return to my fall semester students. In a fit of frustration I guess I reversed the process.

"You gave your electric bill a C-minus?"

"Well, look at it. The sentence variety is atrocious. What few verbs that appear are either passive or soulless. And I find the omniscient voice condescending, intrusive, and blatantly authoritative."

"No argument here." Doug studies the stack of papers I was grading, a grim look clouding his face. "But do you think it's a good idea to write personal checks to your students?"

"Compare the prose, Doug. You tell me who's more deserving."

"Look, I'm not here to hold your hand or interrupt your wallowing. I need a favor."

We both know I owe him dozens. So I do the mature thing and ignore him, sorting my new mail into piles: junk mail, bills, and personal correspondence. The stack of bills is smaller than the junk mail, but much more daunting.

"I'm not taking your sister out."

"Fair enough."

"Or Maggie's sister."

"She'll be devastated."

"Or any pathetic souls from your church."

"You do realize you're wearing pajamas and a pair of galoshes?"

"Shut up."

"What is it this time, Will? Lucy? Your secondhand ticker? Writer's block?"

I don't know what it is exactly. My birthday? Missing Lucy? This nasty espresso coating my tongue?

Finally I say, "I thought you needed a favor."

"What I need is a guitar player for Saturday night."

Doug is a remarkable writer who wants desperately to be a real musician. I'm an alleged guitar prodigy bent on becoming a better writer. It's these kind of odd intersections that define our friendship. I avoid conflict at all costs where Doug goes looking for it. I found Jesus early, then lost him whereas Doug found him late and makes sure everybody knows about it.

"I don't know," I say. "Jazz?"

"Class reunion."

I groan, but it's mostly for show.

"Come on, Will. You need this."

He's probably right. For the first time in a long time, the thought of acting as a human jukebox to slobbering drunks actually appeals to me.

"I swear we'll play some tunes you actually like. We can squeeze in some Miles and Monk and Coltrane, maybe some Springsteen and Radiohead covers. And our patented Steely Dan medley."

"Will Bernie the Bass Player be there?"

"Yeah, but don't sweat it. He doesn't hate you anymore."

"How do you know?"

"I checked."

"I don't know, Doug."

"Absolutely nothing in E-flat. I'll see to it personally."

"I can't believe I'm—"

"Excellent. Rehearsal's tomorrow night at eight. Dinner's at six, if you think you can muster a shower between now and then."

When Doug leaves, I stare at Lucy's espresso machine, finger my scar through my pajama top, and wonder whatever happened to my toothbrush.

Ozena

Sometimes, if I squint just right, Reggie doesn't look so bad. Especially when the fluorescent tubes in his office turn dark and flicker. Still not what you would call handsome, or at least not what *I* would call handsome. But the combination of my slitted gaze and the poor visibility make his acne scars dissipate, give his lazy hairline hope, and almost make the wattle of flab under his chin look like a pink ascot.

Almost.

I'm midway through wondering whether you could buy special

contact lenses to maintain this effect, when Reggie grips the wide end of his striped necktie to corral a violent sneeze. He revolves a half turn to acknowledge the chorus of *bless yous* and *gesundheits* from the cubicled underlings in his charge. That's when he catches me, peering cross-eyed over my coffee mug (strategically positioned to block his potbelly and wide, girlish hips). He holds up one finger, signaling he'll be with me in a minute.

I glance at the clock on my computer — 9:53 — exactly seven long minutes till my scheduled smoke break. I don't actually smoke, but Javatek, Inc.'s antiquated employee handbook mandates that management allow two fifteen-minute breaks per day for any and all workers afflicted with the nicotine habit. So I've been carrying the same war-torn pack of Virginia Slims for a little over two years now, strictly for emergencies such as this one. The handbook says nothing about the mandatory lighting and/or puffing of said cigarettes.

Reggie finally breaks away from his unreciprocated flirting with Sheila (the only other single girl in our department) and heads my way. He clearly prefers her to me. Or at least he should. She's younger and prettier and just ditzy enough not to pose a threat to Reggie's tenuous authority. I try to be grateful for my consolation prize status — second choice is still a *choice*, after all — but I'm more concerned with the bank of green lights on my multiline telephone, dark and idle.

I mutter a nominal prayer of forgiveness as I slip my hand into my purse, grope around for my cell phone, then thumb the digits of my direct line at work. Timing is critical as I calibrate my boss's footfalls with the pressing of the Send button. I release my grip on my cell just as Reggie's tasseled loafer squishes into my personal berber (not quite gray or tan, but rather some queasy mix of the two) and my office phone shrills to life.

After mouthing a quick *Sorry* to Reggie, I turn in my chair and say, "Thank you for calling Javatek. This is Ozena. How may I assist you?"

I realize this little ploy flirts with dishonesty. But my strategy is as simple as it is brilliant. The only thing more crucial to Reggie than finding a suitable mate is his commitment to excellent customer service. I do admire his principles; I just wish he would floss more. But instead of wandering off to let me deal with my pretend customer, he just stands there waiting. I hadn't planned for this contingency — and I'm not that good an actress. Instead of waddling off, Reggie stays put, casting a long shadow on my computer monitor. As I sit and listen to the bloated silence in my headset, Reggie creeps forward and squats to admire the glossy four-by-sixes tacked to my carpeted walls. He grunts approvingly at my pretend husband, three imaginary children, and one make believe basset hound. I refer to them as the Grinning Whiteheads. The pictures were the result of an alphabetical mix-up at the 24-hour photomat. I got the wrong snapshots. So this exceedingly photogenic family ended up with thirty-six exposures of my son's graphic artistry (shot after shot of enflamed poison ivy inching its way up from my ankles and over my knees) and I got this great fake family to keep me sane from nine to five. Of course, Reggie has access to my personnel file and knows full well that I'm legally divorced (although I doubt the words *willful desertion, abandonment,* or *quite possibly dead* are in there) and live with my son, Lloyd Jr.

When I can't think of anything to say to my pretend caller, I hang up.

"So," Reggie says, "have you given any more thought to my suggestion?"

Since company policy strictly forbids fraternizing between employees, going so far as to insinuate that superiors pursuing subordinates is tantamount to sexual harassment, Reggie must stop short of technically asking me out. But he can, and often does, *suggest* that we get together after hours to discuss creative methods to improve the processes and morale of the customer service department.

"Yes, and I couldn't agree more, Mr. Limpkin." I realize I actually *could* agree more, but I don't bring it up. "We really should limit personal phone calls to authorized break times."

"Not *that* suggestion." Poor Reggie has no clue what licking his chapped lips does to a girl's heart. "My idea about getting together later for, you know, a business dinner."

"Oh, that ..."

"I have a couple of things I need to discuss with you."

"Well, as much as I'd love to, I don't think I could get a sitter on such short notice."

"We could order in? The three of us?"

"Sorry, I forgot. We're getting fumigated tonight."

Reggie is terrified of insects, a fact I discovered the day I found him perched on all fours atop a break room table, tossing peanut M&M's at a platoon of spiders carting off a mostly dead cockroach. And lest anyone think I'm lying about the fumigation thing, my kid brother is an exterminator and lives in my building.

"Again?"

"I know, I know. But those spider larvae are just the darndest things."

This is not technically a falsehood either, as I really do believe, that of all the darn things in this world, that spider larvae *are* the darndest, if in fact there is any such thing as spider larvae. I make a mental sticky note to explore Wikipedia between putting Lloyd Jr. to bed and begging Eugene for an emergency house call.

"Well you can't possibly stay there during fumigation. So why don't we have Javatek treat us all to dinner? You, me, and Lloyd?" I'm not sure why it bothers me so much to hear my boss use my son's name. "What do you say?"

I open my mouth, prepared to utter whatever lame excuse my brain offers up. But I'm interrupted by the blessed sound of my phone ringing. I shrug helplessly at Reggie and turn back to my computer monitor.

"Thank you for calling Javatek. This is Ozena, how may I assist you?"

The man's voice cracks when he says, "I have one of your machines that won't die."

Willy

When I can't bear to look at it any longer, I try running over it with my SUV. But the machine's rounded Buddha shape makes it impossible for my allegedly all-purpose tires to gain any sort of traction. All I end up doing is knocking the espresso maker all over the driveway, scarring its once shiny finish.

My next-door neighbor hears the commotion and ambles out to see if he can help, which I'm sure he could if I weren't too embarrassed to ask. Ronnie Cheevers is a retiree with too much time on his hands. He rests his flannel-clad arms on the open window, close enough for me to inhale his woodsy pipe smells.

"You okay, Willy?"

"I decided to give up caffeine."

"Cold turkey, eh?" We swap grins, his gentle and knowing, mine probably wary and a little unhinged. Ronnie is like my grandpa, much wiser than he likes to let on. "I'm sure you'll let me know if you need a hand."

"Maybe you could come by later and freshen the place up with your pipe?"

"Glad to, Willy." He claps one hand on the window frame and makes his way across my lawn toward, oddly enough, his wife's house — which begs for explanation.

I knew Ronnie and Gladys as neighbors growing up, then later as widows when I was in college. But by the time I moved back into my childhood home they had decided to get hitched, only they forgot to hammer out a few important details first. Each assumed the other would sell their house once they were married, but neither one did. They tried cohabitating in spurts, alternating weeks, then months, before stopping altogether. Apparently they now eat all three meals together, help tend each other's gardens, attend the same funerals and weddings, but live in separate homes.

Once inside my own house, I debate calling the tire manufacturer to encourage them to adjust their marketing claims down to "most-purpose." But I'm sure they would just hang up on me. I plug the espresso maker in and it fires right up again. So I haul it up to the attic for some target practice, hurling everything at it, from my broken toaster to unopened cans of Spam (left over from the Y2K scare) and an entire butcher block full of knives. The net result is a giant mess and one very sore shoulder.

The decal on the machine includes an 800 number and the words: *Problems? Questions?* Since I have some of each, I decide to call Javatek customer service.

Her name is Ozena and she doesn't sound happy, which may be entirely my fault. Nor does she sound much like an Ozena. After a pause to digest my story, she says, "Let me get this straight. You're calling to complain that your coffee maker still works?"

"It's an espresso machine. And yes, that's exactly what I'm doing."

"I'm afraid I don't get it."

"The owner's manual explicitly states that submerging the unit will cause severe damage. Not *may* cause or *could* cause, but *will*."

"I'm still not sure I follow."

"Look, I tossed the whole blasted machine into a tub of bubble bath and let it marinate for about an hour." Actually, it was a witch's brew of Lucy's greatest hits — several bottles of obscenely expensive perfumes and bubble baths, and a few love notes from our dating days. "Then I pull it out and plug it in, and it still works!"

"And that's a bad thing?"

"It's like, I don't know, false advertising."

"Technically, an owner's manual is not the same as advertising. Two different departments."

"Either way, it's misleading and I want remunerations."

"So you're saying you want your money back for something that's not broken?"

"Not exactly."

"What exactly, then?"

"I want to know how to destroy this thing."

"Well couldn't you just snip the wires?"

"That would be cheating."

After a moment's silence, Ozena says, "I'll have to talk to my supervisor. Please hold."

The on-hold music is a collection of lite-rock favorites, no doubt selected for their calming effect on angry customers. It has the opposite effect on me, making me dread the class reunion gig I agreed to do. After three-and-a-half minutes of sticky falsetto and insipid synthesizers, Ozena comes back on the line.

"Thank you for holding. I'm afraid the best we can offer is this: you can return the working model—you pay the shipping, of course—and we can send you another one."

"A broken one, I hope?"

"I don't think we have any of those in stock." I groan, part frustration and part resignation. But before I can say anything else stupid, Ozena says, "But I'll see what I can do."

I love her for that, if only for an instant.

* * *

The UPS man delivered Lucy's espresso machine one rainy Tuesday morning nearly three years ago, when I was "working" from home as a so-called full-time writer. Since it was addressed to my wife, I placed it on the kitchen table and poured myself another spot of tea. But every time I needed to relieve my bladder or forage for another snack in the pantry, the parcel seemed to loom larger on the table. Once I thought I heard it whisper to me. When Lucy called me on her lunch break to remind me to thaw the chicken breasts, I took the opportunity to ask her about the mysterious package. (I was too paranoid to ever call Lucy at work. She worked as a 9-1-1 operator, and although she assured me I was just being obsessive and unreasonable, I couldn't help imagining one of my banal calls somehow blocking a real emergency. My conscience couldn't take it.) Of course, knowing her inability to delay gratification, I knew she'd want me to open the package. At her prompting, I used a steak knife to break the seal. As the packing peanuts fluttered groundward I said, "It appears to be a fancy coffee maker of some sort."

"Huh, wonder who'd send us a coffee maker?"

I was already bored with this endeavor, but since I'd piqued her curiosity, I felt obliged to follow through. I mustered a playful radio announcer voice and said, "Not just *any* coffee maker either, but an espresso machine, a Javatek 3000."

"Oh."

"And wait, here's a note." It was smallish, khaki-colored, and written with what seemed to be deliberately masculine strokes. I cleared my throat, affected a haughty tone, and read aloud: "Love, Shawn."

Lucy chuckled on the other end of the line. In retrospect, I'm sure that my mind was filling in the blanks. But I'd swear now that her ragged laugh was laced with relief.

"He's such a nut," she said. "I'll have to call him and thank him. Now don't forget the chicken."

"Yeah, right," I said. "The chicken."

I returned the note to its place and padded down the hallway. I dug Lucy's address book out from under a pile of magazines and looked up her brother's address in Cleveland. One look at Lucy's loopy handwriting and I knew. Her brother spelled his name S-E-A-N.

I almost broke my rule about calling her at work. Almost.

* * *

I decide to take Ozena up on her offer, that it must be fate. In the attic I find the original Javatek box. The Styrofoam packing materials are missing so I have to improvise, using a combination of mostly popped bubble wrap and an assortment of small pillows Lucy started sewing for Christmas presents but never got around to finishing. I seal the box with entirely too much packing tape, carefully script the return autho-

rization number and *Attention: Ozena* on all six sides, then end up paying sixty bucks to guarantee next day shipping back to the factory.

It doesn't dawn on me until I get home from the post office and
plug the tracking number into my computer that Javatek, Inc. has a
Nashville address. I could have driven by there, asked for Ozena, and
hand-delivered the stupid thing.

I find that this idea simultaneously thrills me and makes my stomach hurt. I try to conjure an image of Ozena based on her voice. But all
I can come up with is a vague, featureless version of Lucy.

Shaq

My collection of unfiltered stumps makes a galloping sound as they
thud around the inside of the shoebox. Tires squeal and horns honk all
around me as I run into the street and retrieve a smoldering cigarette
butt, then toss it into my box on the run. My feet slap the pavement,
aching inside shoes two sizes too big. My lungs burn from too much
oxygen, yet I still manage to huff out, "The world is not your ashtray!"
as I run. I know I look and sound ridiculous. And I'm sure I used to
care about stuff like that. Someday soon, I hope I will again.

The battered panel van is forced to stop at a red light. I watch the
bald man's eyes go wide in his sideview mirror. His window is still part
way down. I'm yelling, "Hey mister" over and over.

The faded red letters — *Manny's Plumbing* — barely register as I finally pull even with the door. The man cranks the window down and
says, "You got a problem?"

His face distracts me, but only for a second. He looks foreign to
me now, and doggedly apathetic, not at all like I remember him. "I
have something that belongs to you." My voice is ragged from all that
running.

"Yeah?" He revs the engine and the nice parts drain from his face.
"So spill it."

I do. The whole shoebox. Right in his lap.

"I believe these are yours," I say like a lunatic. He stares at the dozens of chomped and discarded cigarette butts in his lap, his white painter's pants and wife-beater undershirt dotted with ash. When he opens the door, two things happen at once. I end up on my scrawny butt with the rest of the wind knocked out of me, and the van lurches forward. Manny is halfway out of his seat when he realizes the van's still in gear. In one quick motion he stomps the brake, jams the lever to park, and is cramming a handful of cigarette butts past my clenched lips.

He punches me hard once in the stomach, then again. This unhinges my jaw and I can immediately taste ashes and pavement and grime. I manage to sit up, gagging and spitting and trying to remember to breathe through my nose. Then he's pounding the top of my head with my flimsy shoebox. He's still raining powerfully impotent blows down on me when I see Father Joe limping our way.

His large beefy hand grips the back of the bald man's neck. Manny's eyes roll back and he yelps. He flails his elbows and fists wildly behind him, cursing his unseen captor. With barely any effort, Father Joe spins the man around and smiles, still squeezing the back of his neck.

"You about done here?" Father Joe's voice is low, seemingly benign, but riddled with pent-up things. Scary things.

"Get your hands off me."

"In due time." Joe's forearm clenches and I almost feel bad for the poor guy. "Now drop the shoebox."

Manny does as instructed. Then Father Joe, still gripping the man's scruff, hoists me to my feet. I know what's coming next and can't help but smirk a little.

When I finally catch my breath I look at Manny and say, "Who do you think picks up your litter?"

"Hobos like you, that's who."

I look to Father Joe for help. But he shakes his head once and says, "Shaq, do you need to apologize?"

"No," I say, mustering as much defiance as my soiled throat is able. I think I swallowed one of the butts. "Manny does."

"Who?" The bald guy alternates his wary gaze between me and the giant man gripping his neck.

Joe looks at me hard and says, "Do it anyway."

I know better than to argue. And I know what's expected. I turn to face the litterbug and say, "I apologize for dumping your filthy rotten litter in your lap."

Manny's wary expression ping-pongs between Father Joe and me, then he says, "Yeah, well, just don't let it happen again."

"Nope," Father Joe says, applying even more pressure, oblivious to the honking cars piling up in either direction. "You need to forgive him."

"Are you outta your freakin'—?" The man's knees buckle and he yelps again. He looks like he has tears in his eyes now. Judging from the way that vein is pulsing in Joe's wrist, I know I would. "Okay, alright. I forgive you. Just let me go."

"Not me," Father Joe says. "Him."

"Okay, I forgive you, alright? And stop calling me Manny. My name is Philip."

"How about you look him in the eye and say it again ... with feeling."

"I forgive you already."

Father Joe releases his grip and the man massages his neck.

"Okay," I say, and open my arms wide. "Might as well get this part over with."

Manny looks more frightened now than before. He shoots a questioning look at Joe and says, "No. No way, man. I ain't huggin' that freak."

Father Joe makes a grabbing motion at the man's neck. Then all at once I'm embracing my old friend—who now feels like a total stranger—in the middle of Lafayette Street. A couple of winos I know from the shelter applaud. Manny breaks free and wipes his body with his hands as if he's been contaminated.

"You've changed, Manny," I say. "And not just your name either."

He looks at me the way most people do these days, then climbs back into his van. Father Joe leans on the open window and says, "This thing got an ashtray?"

"Yes sir."

"Then I suggest you use it."

The van pulls away. Father Joe waves apologies at the stalled traffic and guides me to safety. This is not the first time he's saved me. Probably not even the first time today. Sometimes it's hard to remember.

Willy

I'm on the stage of the swanky ballroom of the Harington Hotel and having second thoughts. And of course my guitar won't stay in tune.

"You about ready?"

It's Doug. He's grinning, always grinning his incessant grin. If only he could somehow figure a way to bottle and sell the joy he finds in playing music, a good two-thirds of John Lennon's imaginings might come true.

"Yeah, give me one sec. I put new strings on today."

He twirls his drumstick, winks at me, and says, "Play pretty" in the valley girl voice usually reserved for the dean and me. Then he turns and picks his way through speakers and cables en route to his rightful place atop his drum throne.

I tweak the G-string one final time and mutter, "Close enough for schlock and roll." Then I hear the familiar click of wood on wood. I turn to see Doug; he oozes glee like a punctured oil tanker as he counts off the first tune. The rush of adrenaline surprises me. After the second click my sticky fingers find their spot on the fret board. Blinding stage lights ignite on click number three. I close my eyes, savoring the infinitesimal space between click number four and the first grungy chord of Nirvana's "Smells Like Teen Spirit."

Other than a few obnoxious whoops, the crowd responds with neither a roar nor a whimper. My '69 Stratocaster feels good in my hands and sounds even better. In spite of myself, I surrender to the music. Sure it's cheesy (the circumstance, not the song). As a creative writing instructor, a modestly successful novelist, and a slightly-better-than-average jazz guitar player, I have no real business prancing around the stage of a rented ballroom with my old band. But gauging by the idiot grin I feel on my spotlit face, I'm loving every cheesy note of it. I remind myself to try and enjoy it, that it won't last.

Nothing good ever does.

But when the first set ends I remember the part I hate about doing these gigs. The combination of greasy nostalgia, embarrassingly bad dancing, and witnessing the mass inebriation of an entire roomful of people old enough to know better, makes me long for simpler things—a good book, some mindless TV, nestling down in my very own bed in my very own house.

These are my thoughts as I roam the back halls in search of an employee restroom, adopting a bit of a swagger to keep the suspicious looks at bay. The wait staff is clad in cheap, asexual formalwear—polyester tuxes sans jackets and all manner of dingy footwear. They all look frazzled and bored and in dire need of a cigarette. Just when I spot the symbol for unisex restrooms, the handle of an enormous banquet cart slams into my middle. The pain is so rich and immediate I nearly soil myself right there. The blue-haired girl pushing the VW-sized cart rolls her eyes, never breaking stride as she runs the back caster over my foot.

I hobble toward the restroom with literally no time to spare, grasping the knob and turning. It's locked.

I knock politely, pacing in place and searching for a wall clock. A man calls from inside: "Someone's in here." I find his attempt at anonymity amusing, as if the poor guy has forgotten his own name. Or maybe it's misplaced shame. I'm sure they covered this in freshman psych, but I must have slept through it.

Eventually I go in search of yet another out-of-the-way restroom. What I find instead is the retreating form of Lucy, my dead wife.

Ozena

Eugene shows up with three ice cream sandwiches and a canister of toxic bug spray. He inherited all the good Webb genes and wears them well even into his third decade—tall and lean with a tenacious hairline of amber curls. A soggy toothpick rests in the corner of his mouth. He swaggers into my kitchen and says, "You got bugs? Or did you drag me out of bed to appease your conscience again?"

"There could be bugs."

"What I figured." He pops the top on the bug spray and releases a short blast under my kitchen table. "Feel better?"

"Well, actually …" I feel like a complete dork as I take the can from him and read the label. "This is spray, right?"

"Yeah, so?"

"I told Reggie I was getting fumigated."

"You're kidding, right?"

But we both know I'm not. His knees pop as he hauls himself up and out and across the hall. Minutes later he uses his thumb to underline the word *fumigator*, then peels the foil wrapper back. "You know you're not supposed to breathe this stuff?"

"I know, but we're not going to use that much."

He rolls his eyes but doesn't argue. He sets everything up, adds water, then waits for the first few tendrils to rise up out of the canister. I pull the collar of my T-shirt up over my nose and count to ten. Then I nod and he recaps the canister and sets about disposing of it. When he's done, he grumbles, "What a waste."

But he doesn't complain when I slide the twenty-dollar bill across the table—eleven for the bug poison and nine for his trouble. He knows better.

"You ever considered just going out with what's-his-name?"

"I consider it daily."

"Let me guess. He don't measure up to your whatchamacallit? Your love diary?"

I made the mistake of confiding in Eugene at a family reunion when I was fourteen and he was twelve. An innocent English assignment turned into an obsession. In a hundred words or less, we were to write a metaphor for love. I have no idea what I turned in, but my diary became an endless string of *Love is ...* phrases. Eugene had just been dumped by Lisa, his eventual wife — they've since married and divorced each other twice — and asked my advice to win her back. I immediately opened my journal, combing the lines for some nugget of literary brilliance to share with my downcast brother. I believe I told him "love is a new coloring book, mostly blank and rife with potential, but in dire need of people to come and color the life into the pages." He claims it worked, but he's never stopped teasing me about it. In fact, he came to me for what he called a tune up after each divorce. Each time I wanted to tell him the truth (as I knew it) that *love is simply a waste of time.* But I couldn't do that to him.

If he asks again, however, I'm going to tell him that, in his case anyway, love is a mild case of hemorrhoids. The pain and discomfort will keep coming back. But a little daily care and tending might quell the itching, swelling, and burning, might even prevent surgery. (Okay, so I'll never win a poetry contest. But that's not the point, now, is it?)

I ignore him and motion for an ice cream sandwich. He peels the wrapper before handing it over, then peels another and begins carving a vanilla canal around the perimeter with his tongue.

"Sorry you missed Lloyd." I pause to lick cold cream from the corner of my mouth. "He would love to have seen you."

He taps the third wrapper, then slides it toward me. "It'll keep. And the boy needs his sleep. Just make sure you tell him where it came from. From Uncle Levi."

"Levi?"

"My new nickname." My brother tilts his body in the chair and cocks his thumb at the little red flag on the hip pocket of his jeans. "Lloyd cracks up every time he says it."

"Your wardrobe really could use a little diversity."

"You know, I'd love to watch him for you so you could go out."

"Thanks, but where would I go?"

"Out. Like maybe some shopping? Dinner and a movie? A real date?"

Eugene bites a third of the sandwich off and chews. When he grins at me, his teeth are stained with gooey chocolate wafer.

"No thanks."

"Oh, come on. You'll regret it one day when you're moldy and arthritic and look more like a raisin than a grape."

I bat my eyelashes and clutch my heart. "How sweet ... I've never been called a grape before!"

"You know what I meant. Right now you're still cute, but your clock is ticking."

"My clock runs on batteries. And I think they're mostly dead."

"Nah, they just need a little recharging." He wiggles his eyebrows seductively, neither of us able to keep a straight face. "And I'd be happy to give you some pointers."

"I'll think about it."

"No you won't. Come on, don't you ever meet anyone interesting at work?"

"You have black cakey gunk on your teeth."

He scrubs his teeth with his finger while I stare at my ice cream sandwich and wonder if it will go straight to my ankles. Then I wonder if a guy obsessed with killing off his espresso maker counts as *interesting*.

Hours later when I should be sleeping, I remember my offhand comment to Reggie about spider larvae. I kick the covers back, fire up my computer, and browse Wikipedia long enough to satisfy my inner moralist. It turns out that spiders do indeed have larvae. Their days inside the egg start out as bald and blind, munching on yolk and eventually on their more "disadvantaged" siblings. Eventually I shut down my computer and contemplate popping a few sleeping pills to keep from dreaming about hairy spiders. Integrity can be such a drag.

Willy

I first met Lucy on my front stoop. Her eyes looked too big for her face, too pretty to harbor such anguish. She hugged herself, all tight and fidgety, as if stranded in a cold drizzle. But it was a sunny eighty degrees out, which made her bulky man-sweater that much more curious. She had dark unruly hair, pale freckles on either side of her nose, and smelled fresh out of the shower. Not quite a damsel, but definitely in distress.

She rang the bell; I answered. Then she stood there, staring and aggressively unspeaking.

"Can I help you?"

She scrutinized my face, found something, then looked away and massaged her own arms. "Your name Willy?"

"Depends. Are you friend or foe?"

She barked out a humorless laugh. "I took the call."

Several thoughts romped through my brain, none of which made any sense. The clueless look on my face seemed to further agitate this already uptight stranger.

"The call, Willy. As in *The Call*?"

"Look, I'm sorry. Who are — ?"

"The call from Walter? You do have a brother named Walter, right? I mean, you *did* have a brother named Walter?"

The sound of my dead brother's name put me on edge, as if I'd tipped too far on a stool and was windmilling to keep from falling. I took two clumsy steps back only to find I was locked out. With the doorknob stabbing my kidney, the madwoman began tearing at the buttons on my shirt, all frantic and ghoulish. Then her finger found the scar. That was the first time she made it tingle.

Lucy spent that night on the couch, then every night after for two weeks. Despite the guilt sloshing around inside me, it was all very above board and platonic. It took weeks to lose that panicky feeling in my chest.

Now it's back.

Logic would presume it's impossible for me to see Lucy in the back hallway of a downtown hotel. But my heart would know that languid gait anywhere. By the time I find my voice she has already disappeared back into the noisy ballroom.

I turn and sprint down the hall after her, mostly ignoring my sluicing bladder as I burst into the ballroom.

Once inside, I scan the room in a panic, searching for a woman with medium-length brown hair and a black dress — which ends up being every other woman in the room. Just when I convince myself that I was merely seeing things, I catch Lucy's profile bathed in pink stage lights. I call her name again and begin elbowing my way through the crowd. But she's gone, and Doug's kick drum is calling me back to the stage. I pick my way through the crowd of eerily familiar faces — flabby jocks, former cheerleaders who never grew out of it, nerds who did, and some truly bad dancing. Occasionally a name will pop into my head, then right back out again.

I scale the steps, strap on my guitar, and join my bandmates mid-song. Then it hits me. The roomful of familiar faces makes sense now. Odds are, they didn't all marry kids from the same graduating class. I walk to the edge of the stage and read the upside down letters of the banner hanging there — Andrew Jack Welcomes Class of '95.

Finally I turn toward Doug, sweat streaming into the corners of his omnipresent smile. He recognizes the look on my face, laughs at me yet again, and mouths the word *clueless*.

This is not just any class reunion. It's mine.

* * *

I glance at the set list as I slip my guitar strap over my head. The next song is a Michael Jackson number with a heavy guitar intro. Doug counts it off as I flip my amp off standby and press the volume pedal to the floor, praying I'm still in tune.

My bladder sends up a quick and painful reminder that it is less than pleased. I ignore it and focus on playing the intro, flawlessly I might add. Relief nips at the heels of my inner artist as I realize I've made it. Sixteen bars of me and my guitar, perfectly in tune. Now I can coast through another set, hopefully without wetting my pants.

The musical train wreck occurs on the downbeat of bar seventeen, the part where the rest of the band enters in the *correct* key.

In that single instant my mind is able to process the following:

1. I have begun the song in E, just like it was on the original recording.

2. Apparently Bernie the Bass Player changed the key from E to E-flat, probably so Clifford wouldn't have to strain on the high notes.

3. Because of a bizarre, post-transplant medical condition, it will take every molecule of determination I can muster to keep from nodding off during this song.

4. Musically speaking, this is a disaster.

For the next few seconds every eye in the crowd lifts in unison, searches the stage for the source of the cacophony, then follows the collective gaze of my bandmates to the spot on the stage where I am standing. The expressions range from horror to confusion to strangely familiar. Only the handful of musicians in the crowd seems to be amused.

I make the one-fret adjustment, bringing sweet repose to the musical bedlam I have just created. When it's safe to look up again, I meet Doug's gaze. His eyebrows arch, the left one laughing at me, the right one warning me that Bernie the Bass Player might decide to jam his guitar down my gullet if I don't get my act together soon.

Somehow — probably just my embarrassment — I manage to finish the song without nodding off.

(Ever since my heart transplant, I've been afflicted with a specific, and very rare, form of narcolepsy. So rare, in fact, that I have my own entry in a medical journal — which, on a lark, I bought, autographed, and gave as stocking stuffers one Christmas. No one thought it was funny but me. The point is, whenever I hear a song in the key of E-flat, I fall asleep instantly.)

The rest of the set is pure torture. I hate the songs, hate my playing, hate standing on stage and watching people who never really liked me that much to begin with use me as a glorified CD player.

Mostly I hate the fact that I can't find Lucy anywhere. Every time I think I see her in the crowd I lose focus on the music and screw something else up.

I keep scanning the room, but Lucy's gone now. I can feel it. Just like the day I came home and found her half of the closet empty. I knew it before the hinge on the screen door squeaked. The house felt like a crime scene from the moment I stepped inside. I wandered around for weeks afterward, noticing more and more things that were missing, little things, like her favorite coffee mug and the long hairs in the sink and the orphaned socks stretched over the bedpost until their twins were located and, of course, the espresso maker, which I'm convinced she left behind to somehow *prove* to me that it didn't mean anything.

And my toothbrush.

That was my first inkling that our marriage was in trouble. When Lucy first arrived she slept on the couch, kept her clothes in a battered suitcase, and stored her toothbrush in a makeup bag. Eventually we shared the same bed, the same closet, and the same red plastic cup suspended over the bathroom sink. This seemingly insignificant detail tweaked something inside me. If I could allow my toothbrush to nestle into hers (for hours at a time *and* with the bristles touching!) then maybe, just maybe, I could survive this. Despite the fact that I was the one who invited her to stay in my house, it was still my home, my sanctuary, and her presence there felt a bit like an invasion. I'm not proud of that fact.

My routine consisted of brushing, spitting, and rinsing, followed by a haphazard toss of my brush into the red plastic cup. As far as I could tell, Lucy's was the same, at least in the beginning. I don't know which came first — her precision or my paranoia. I thought it was just my imagination. But careful examination revealed that she really was strategically positioning our toothbrushes.

It was subtle in the beginning. She would simply make sure the bristles weren't touching. I assumed it was just another of her odd quirks. But then I would wake to find the brushes meticulously staged, back-to-back, facing opposite directions like angry lovers. We never really talked about it. But around that same time, I began waking to an empty bed, only to discover she'd moved to the couch in the middle of the night. One week she moved her toothbrush out of the holder. The following week she moved out.

The crowd has now thinned down to a handful of old crushes (in various stages of rekindling) and several drunk divorcees on the brink of making a mess of their lives if they don't sober up and leave soon — alone.

The band is sleepwalking through our final number — a mercy killing — when someone screams. The shrill sound sets off a chain reaction of scattering dancers and more screaming. A wide circle of onlookers all point toward the center of the dance floor where an oversized, pointy-headed rodent in a red sweater is waddling from spot to spot, pausing occasionally to sniff and twitter and lick his fearsome-looking claws.

Of course we all recognize him as Rufus the Lightning Badger, the school mascot of our most hated rival, Jefferson High School. There are a few tipsy, half-hearted attempts at capturing Rufus, but he scurries under a table and out of sight as we end our last song.

The rest of the band congratulates each other while I hurriedly start packing up my gear. I convince myself that Lucy will be waiting out by my car, but only if I can get there quick enough.

Of course I know in my recycled heart that I didn't really see her.

"Nice set, man." It's Doug, right in my ear. "Sure was great playing together again."

Bernie snorts and shakes his head as he peels black duct tape off his guitar cable.

"I don't know, man. I felt kind of distracted tonight."

Doug waves me off, still beaming. "So who was it that you kept staring at?"

"You saw her too then?"

"You kidding? I bet Derrick ten bucks it was Lucy's mom. Looked just like her."

Before I can catch myself, I nod, as if he deduced exactly right and had more than earned all ten of his dollars. I wish I hated dishonesty as much as I hate conflict. But I tend to put truth on a sliding scale, which basically means I turn it into a lie I can live with.

Doug says, "She looked sad too." I try to remember exactly what I've told Doug about Lucy. But that's the problem with half-truths. I can never remember which half I've told. "Probably still mourning her loss."

I nod again, mentally kicking myself, wishing I had a beard to stroke thoughtfully.

"So, you're going to Waffle House with us, right?"

Ingesting greasy carbs after a long night of music is a long and storied tradition among bands of all shapes, sizes, and musical genres. The dejected look on Doug's face when I shake my head could make me cry if he weren't somehow still grinning through it.

* * *

It's after midnight when I pull out of the hotel. The speed bump at the end of the drive reminds my bladder to scream at me. I decide that

that's Lucy's fault for making me temporarily forget I had to go, and I vow to stop at the first gas station I see.

The last address I had for her family was fifty miles north of Nashville, somewhere near Clarksville, the last stop on the Tennessee/Kentucky border. It's been a year or more since the last time I drove by her house, parked at the end of the block, and waited for my eyes to well up. It was daylight then. And I had directions.

I pick up my cell phone again and dial the seven digits that would connect me to Lucy. But I can't bring myself to hit Send. I just don't know what to say. Sure I want to bug her about why she left me. And apologize yet again for all my failings. And yes, even try to convince her that I never stopped loving her — or at least caring a lot. But what I really want to know is why she took my toothbrush and left that cursed coffee maker behind. Not the kind of conversation I think she'll be up for at two a.m. Still, I can't help myself.

I stare at the undialed number.

The black ribbon of country road unfurls in my peripheral vision as I allow my thumb to hover over the Send button. I'm just about to press it when the phone erupts in my hand. I nearly drive myself and the Land Rover into a field of sleeping cows.

"Willy? You still up?"

It's Doug. I can almost hear the grin, along with the mindless chatter, clanging forks on dishes, and sizzling griddles in the background. "Yep, just driving around."

"Uh-huh. Not doing anything stupid, are you?"

"Like what?"

"Like looking for ghosts." He pauses long enough for me to hear George Jones trying to ironically convince Waffle House patrons that he does not, in fact, still care. I can relate, sort of.

"What kind of ghosts?"

"Ones named Lucy."

I recognize a familiar turnoff and take it. I can't tell if I actually recall the terrain or if it's merely the combination of the ungodly hour, my mutinous bladder, and a large dose of wishful thinking. But then I see it, the old two-story home handed down through three generations of Sharpes.

"Willy?" Doug says. "You still with me?"

"I have to go, Doug. I think I'm lost."

Shaq

The mission is deserted this morning, but not quiet. And if you ask me, it's not eavesdropping if you can't help but hear. Besides, the walls in this place are like pizza delivery boxes, thin and greasy and sour with old man smells. I suppose I should be grateful that I have walls at all. But I don't care what anybody says, leftovers and hand-me-downs get old quick. At least my underwear is fresh out of the wrapper. Father Joe sees to that. If not, I don't know if I could get up off my stained mattress every morning. Anyhow, it's not the crying so much, but the way he calls her name like that. Guess that's what I get for bunking down right outside Joe's room; my lame attempt to protect him, I suppose. When I can't handle the sound of his crying anymore, I slip out the back, propping the door open with a blue sneaker from the lost-and-found box. Downtown Nashville is mostly deserted at this hour, at least this part of town.

The knurled texture of the basketball feels like a million tiny pebbles. I dribble it a few times, right handed, then left. The ball makes a tortured wheezing sound every time it strikes the pavement. I stare up at the rim, backlit by a bluish streetlight, and wait for my eyes to adjust. The rim is rusted, bent forward, the chain net glinting like tinsel. I make my way to the spray-painted free throw line, bounce the ball twice while eyeing the front of the rim, then launch the ball. It feels good coming out of my hand, but clanks once on each side of the rim before plummeting impotently toward the blacktop. I retrieve the ball and make my way back to the foul line, allowing my mind to sort itself out and make a few connections. I've sunk three in a row, Seven more and I'll have my answer.

I've all but forgotten about Joe and his quiet sobbing when he appears in the doorway, still snuffling, eyes rimmed red, and his thick lips clenched.

"What are you doing shooting at this hour, Shaq?"

"Couldn't sleep."

"I know the feeling," he says, rubbing his eyes and biting back a yawn. "Sorry, you know, if it was me that kept you up."

I accept with a shrug, pretending not to watch Father Joe watching me. After I arc an ugly shot off the back of the backboard, I glance in his direction. His nod is barely perceptible in the dark, but his hands are hard to miss when they rise in invitation for my bounce-pass. He spins it in his hand once, then again, then makes a twenty-footer. I snatch the ball on one short hop and send it back to him.

After a dozen or so shots, he says, "You okay, Shaq?"

"From the sound of things, maybe I should ask you the same thing."

He says nothing, just keeps his eye on the rim and lofts the ball toward it.

Finally, I say, "Would it help if I said I was sorry?"

"Might if you had something to be sorry about." I see his eyes flick to my waistband, then away.

"I *am* sorry." He'll never admit his crying is my fault, like he's got too much pride or something. I'm starting to think his memory is as bad as mine. I want to promise him I'll make it up to him, that I'll find Patrice for him, for both of us. But that conversation never ends well.

I guess he's reading my mind again though. "Let it go, son."

That's what he used to call me — *son*. Back before the mission, before the mental ward, before the accident. Joe says I have credibility issues. The truth is that I have blank spots on my memory, or maybe one big spot, like a window. Things float by sometimes, usually when I'm between sleeping and waking, and I'll lean way out and grab for whatever happens by. Occasionally I'll grab hold of something and it'll help complete the picture of me, give me some clue about who I am and where I came from and the name I was born with. But mostly things float by unmolested and I end up with more not knowing. When the memories do come, the reliable ones anyway, I get this glassy feeling under my tongue. If it's really strong it's followed by that funny bone sensation in my lower back. And a crushing headache.

I tried telling my shrink about the window, but she just gripped her pen too tight, clicking it open and shut real quick. She thought I was crazy, but the state eventually had to let me go. That's when my memory kicked in, when the meter started running. And that's when I met Joe, about eight years ago now. He knows about my two years in the nuthouse, probably even talked to my shrink about it. But whatever else he knows about my past and our connection, he's not telling. One day — one of my oldest memories — I worked up the nerve to ask him why he was crying. It was the middle of the day and nobody was around, just like today. He told me about his daughter that he only ever met once, when she was eleven. How she grew up while he was in prison, how he's been looking for her ever since they let him out, about his routine visits to hospitals and morgues in a futile search for his grown-up baby girl. All he had to go on was the memory of one stilted visit and a single photograph. Her mother remarried while Joe was in prison, which meant he didn't even have a name to go on. Joe described his daughter in detail that day. And that's when my headaches started, when I reached out through the window and grabbed my first memory — I was married. And her name was Patrice, Joe's lost daughter.

At first I didn't have the heart to tell him. I searched for weeks for Patrice — on the streets, on the Internet, and the inside of my brain. Finally, the guilt and the frustration collided and I made my way to this free-throw line. That was the day I earned my nickname — my only name, I guess — and the first time Father Joe had to save me.

When I tried to explain myself, all the guilt and shame, he just looked at me with that pathetic look he has, like one of us is crazy, maybe both. I couldn't tell if he was trying to protect me or protect his own heart.

He's looking at me like that again right now, in fact.

"Library called again, Shaq."

"Overdue book?"

He shakes his head, all fatherly now.

"Computer's down again?"

"Nope. They say you been smelling the women again."

"No law against it," I say, hiding my embarrassment by staring at the backboard.

"Maybe not. But it's my library card that's gone get revoked if you keep it up. So how about you knock it off?"

"It's research, Joe."

"I know, Shaq. That's what you always say. Just try and keep it under control."

I stop mid-dribble and glare at him. "Why do you do that to me?"

"Do what to you?"

"Patronize me, like I'm some child." I should know better than to raise my voice at a man nearly three times my size. Just can't seem to help myself. "It's like you don't trust me at all. Or like you're ashamed of me."

"You know better than that."

"Then you should at least yell at me. Or maybe take a swing at me."

He finds that amusing. Joe doesn't smile much, but when he does it's infectious. "You're not the easiest guy in the world to argue with, Shaq."

"Well stop agreeing with me when you don't mean it."

He puts his enormous hand on my head and ruffles my hair, again like I'm some runty kid. It's a hard thing owing your life to a man when you know you're the cause of all his misery, especially if he

~~thinks you're crazy. But all that's in God's hands now.~~ My job is to keep looking for Patrice.

On the way back into the mission, Father Joe says, "Don't suppose you going to tell me what you was shooting for this time?"

I mean to shake my head, but I'm not sure it worked. Joe knows about my ritual. Some people flip coins or draw straws; I shoot free throws. Ten in a row. And he knows better than anybody that the last time I did this was almost the last time I did anything ever again. Before we part ways, he lifts the hem of my flannel shirt and tugs on my waistband. Satisfied I'm not wearing a belt, he nods and goes to his room.

Willy

I stare at Lucy's childhood home through unspilled tears.

I keep staring until the gray brick house before me morphs into a tombstone. Fresh tears emerge, shoving each other over the side of my eyelids. Finally, I put the car in drive and head home, and it occurs to me that my gas tank is empty and my bladder is still full.

When I see the neon glow of a convenience store, I park in front, toss the phone onto the passenger seat, and ease myself out of the car.

I glance around the deserted parking lot, shrug, and waddle inside with my thighs clenched together. The men's is blessedly vacant. I emerge five minutes later lightheaded and relieved. Next I fill a Styrofoam cup with thick black coffee, snatch up a pack of powdered donuts, and wade into an invisible cloud of Old Spice and stale tobacco.

"Know something, partner?" the toothless cashier says in fluent redneck. His eyes and mouth are pinched and crowded around a large, sprawling nose. "If they'd let me charge for that there healing chamber, I'd be a rich man."

"Healing chamber?" I glance over my shoulder, afraid I'm missing something obvious.

"Yessireee. Every night I watch cripples limp into that there toilet.

And miracle of all miracles, if they don't come strutting out grinning like idiots. All upright and healed."

He cackles till he coughs. Ignorant of how to respond to this rural humor without offending, I allow my gaze to wander. My writer's eye notes the incongruence of the antique cash register positioned below the video surveillance cameras, the unfiltered cigarette burning in the ashtray despite the proliferation of No Smoking signs, the way the old man stares at me without really seeing anything, then averts his eyes as if he somehow sees everything. When he collects himself, he clears his throat and says, "You gonna need some gasohol to go with them snacks?"

"Yeah, I suppose I will. Be right back."

Save for the hint of gasoline, the cool night air seems to have a cleansing effect. The hold-down clip is missing so I have to pump by hand, watching the numbers on the aging pump scroll by like a groggy slot machine. Through the Rover's window, I notice my cell phone light up. For a moment I dare to believe Lucy is calling. I squint through the window and see Doug's cell number. I consider answering it, but only until the gas pump clicks off and simultaneously splashes cold gasoline all over my right hand.

After muttering a few things that would have offended both God and my mother, I replace the dripping nozzle. I dip my hand in a bucket of window washing fluid and grab a handful of stiff blue paper towels, then forage in the back of my car for antiseptic hand wipes or sanitizing gel or maybe even a paint scraper — anything to get that nasty smell off my fingers.

Unable to resist the temptation, I sniff my fingers, my eyes welling up immediately as the putrid fumes burn my eyes, nose, and throat.

I'm wiping my hands and cursing under my breath as I make my way to the counter again. The old geezer is holding unscratched lottery tickets up to the light and studying them through a magnifying glass.

When he sees me, he says, "Gotta watch that pump. It'll splash you for sure."

"Thanks. I'll remember that." I stifle the urge to fling my powdered donuts at his knobby nose. "So am I still in Clarksville or what?"

The old guy seems to recoil, narrowing his eyes and working his flaccid lips together as if physically chewing up whatever offense I've levied. The ice cream freezer's compressor clicks off, filling the dingy convenience store with strained silence. Finally, the man says, "You trying to start something, mister?"

"No, I'm trying to find my way back to Nashville."

Without warning, the old man rears back and cackles again. He smacks the fractured linoleum repeatedly, causing the giant pickles and pig's feet to slosh in their respective juices.

I shove my purchases toward the ancient cash register and remove my money clip. Of course my muse is devising ways to torture this old guy in my next Handyman novel, wondering which attachment Ralph Handy would use. Blowtorch? Reciprocating saw? Giant squirt gun? "Alright, I'm glad you're having fun at my expense. Can I just pay for these and be on my way?"

"Sure thing, boss," he says through dwindling ripples of laughter. He punches a few oversized typewriter keys, then pulls a lever. "Lemme see. Eighty-two fitty for the gas and a buck twenty-nine for the donuts. Coffee's kinda stale so that's on the house."

"Gee, thanks."

"And here," he tosses an air freshener in the shape of a Christmas tree onto the pile, "might help with the gas smell."

I surrender my American Express. The old man frowns through a loud sigh.

He licks his fingers to separate the carbon paper and loads it into the manual imprint machine. There's no carriage on the machine, so he retrieves a rubber mallet from beneath the counter and pounds out his own impression. It takes another two full minutes for him to find his reading glasses and transcribe the info into the requisite boxes before requesting my signature. When he's finally done, he screws up his face and says, "This is no good. You're gonna have to pay cash."

"The sign on your door says you take credit cards."

"Guess the sign's wrong then."

"But it's your sign. And you just went to all the trouble to take my card and make an impression. You know, that whole routine there with the mallet."

"Well it didn't work. Computer's down or something. Happens all the time. So you have to pay cash."

"But I don't have any cash."

"So what are you saying? You need a loan or something?"

"No, I'm saying your sign says you take credit cards and that's all I have."

"Well we got a problem then."

"Look, you have my credit card number and my signature. I'm sure when your manager comes in, you can figure out how to charge me."

"I am the manager. Fact, I own the place. So what do you have to say about that?"

"Congratulations?"

"You trying to be smart, mister?"

"No, I was trying to be congratulatory."

He chews the inside of his cheek some more. Finally, he says, "Gimme your license."

"Good idea," I say, handing it over. "We'll swap names and addresses and I'll mail you a check."

"Dang straight you will," he says, dropping my driving permit into his breast pocket. "And I'll hang on to this here till the check clears."

"Wait, you can't just keep my license. I need that."

"We all have needs, son."

He grips the mallet again, pounding it softly into his palm. We stare at each other as long as I can stand it. Finally, I scoop up my refreshments and turn to leave. When the bell dings over the door, the old man calls out, "I'd point that fancy truck of yours back down the other way if I's you."

In spite of every instinct to the contrary, I turn. It was something in the man's tone.

"Nashville's the other way, boss. You in Kentucky."

* * *

I put the car in gear and my mind in neutral. I'm tired of thinking so I queue up some Miles Davis to help blow the clutter from my mind. But it's not working; Miles must be using a mute.

Between the thickening fog and the sharp curves, I may not have to worry about my heart giving out from natural causes. The high beams don't help, somehow reflecting in the fog and blinding me. I slow the truck down, scanning the horizon for road signs, anything that points me back in the right direction. Some unknown time later, I've taken enough correct turns to find myself back in Nashville cruising through familiar neighborhoods. I'm idling at a stoplight and staring across the street at the Harington Hotel where I last saw Lucy a few hours before. When it finally dawns on me where I am, I snap out of my stupor and apply my blinker.

A squad car cruises by, both cops staring at me a little too long. I hesitate a moment longer, then hit the gas. That's when I hear a sickening thud, feel the front of the Rover leap off the payment, followed by another thumping and screeching sound.

I slam on the brakes.

My phone tumbles into my lap before thudding against the carpeted floorboard. I turn in the seat and stare through the billowing steam, searching in vain for the carcass of the dog or skunk I'd just flattened. Actually it felt more like a grizzly bear.

My heart threatens mutiny as I scan the road behind me. I watch the steaming pavement for another half minute before turning and trying to catch my breath. Part of me knows I should go back and investigate. But the thought of waiting around on the local game warden to answer a slew of inane questions (especially at this hour and without having my driver's license) steels my resolve. I release my death grip on the brake. A final glance in the rearview reveals the most bizarre image, most likely a trick of my overtaxed mind, but something that resembled a colorful toboggan hat cartwheels out of the steamy fog in slow motion. It's bright red. And I would have sworn it had a big letter *J* on it.

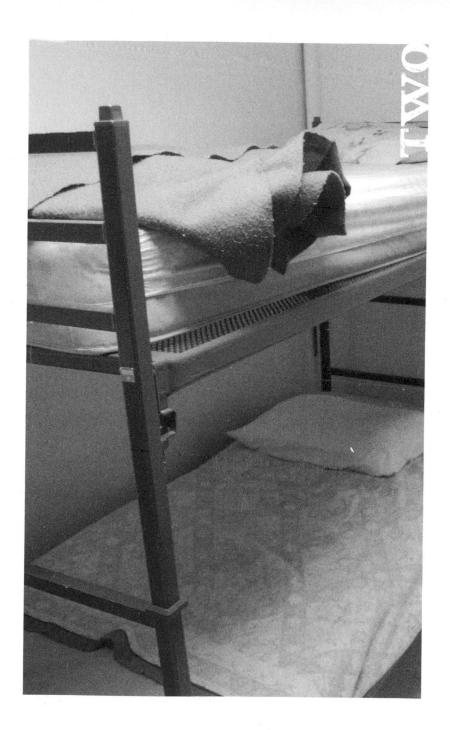

TWO

Willy

I squint at the tiny window of my cell phone … 10:18 a.m. For the briefest moment I think that Lucy is back and sharing a bed with me. I can almost feel the ring on my finger, the one that was never there in the first place. I must have been dreaming about alarm clocks (Lord knows I could never *own* one) and that Lucy's the one silencing it. But then the phone rings again and I realize my error. A dull throb pounds from the back of my skull to some indiscriminant spot behind my eyes. My mouth feels pasted shut, my teeth covered in little mittens. A violent yawn rips through me when I open my mouth to speak. Once the spasms subside, I grab the phone and manage to croak out a greeting.

"William? Is that you?"

"Doug?"

"Who else, babe?" Doug has reverted back to his ridiculous femme fatale voice. "Time to rise and shine."

I hear another voice — one eerily similar to mine — mutter something unintelligible before collapsing into another yawn.

"You okay, William? You sound … well, rather horrid, actually."

"Gee, thanks."

"You do realize you missed your eight o'clock?"

I cringe, then swallow another full-bodied yawn.

"Well anyway, I covered it for you. But Langstrom was fit to be tied. At least until I told him about your mother's funeral."

"My what? That was three and a half years ago."

"Well I didn't say *when* it was."

I swallow another yawn. "Obviously you failed to consult your *What Would Jesus Do?* bracelet this morning."

"You forget that I specialize in creative non-fiction."

"What if Langstrom checks the obituaries?"

"Newsprint makes his hands dirty."

"He could make a few calls and find out easy enough."

Doug's run-on sentences continue. "You'd better get your tush in here, and quick, because you know I can't possibly cover your eleven o'clock and teach mine too, and I almost forgot, your agent called, what a zombie, anyway, I guess I couldn't be trusted with the really super important message, which basically amounts to the fact that he wants you to call him back pronto."

"Thanks, Doug. I owe you one."

"Good thing you have guitar to fall back on."

"Why's that?"

"Your math stinks."

I dial the shower up to one notch below scalding. The billowy steam cleanses me from the outside in, opens my pores, allows my brain to breathe a little. I keep thinking I hear the doorbell, but it's probably just my ears ringing from the gig last night. Or the lack of sleep. Or the bizarre memories of the crotchety old cashier and whatever I mowed down in the road. Or the dread coursing through me at the thought of running into Dean Langstrom.

While toweling off, I pause to stare in the mirror, at the reflection of the raised, pink tissue of my scar. A bead of water trickles the length of it, as if my heart is weeping silently. Then I hear the meaty sound of a fist on my front door. Something tells me to stay put.

Minute later, I part the curtains just enough to notice the police car in my driveway. Two cops—one in uniform, the other in civvies—are inspecting the tires of my Land Rover. The uniform hands the plain-clothesman some tweezers, then glances up at the window. I drop the curtain and retreat into the shadows and think about calling in sick. I even pick up the receiver and start to dial. But that's when I notice the empty spot on the counter where Lucy's Javatek 3000 used to sit. So instead of dialing the English department's administrative assistant, my index finger taps out the familiar toll free number.

"Thank you for calling Javatek, this is Sheila ..."

"Can I speak to Ozena please?"

"May I tell her who's calling?"

"Tell her it's Willy."

"Just Willy?"

I almost hang up. There's something in Sheila's voice besides a desire to serve her customer well. An almost giddy quality, as if she's holding back a punch line. I imagine a gaggle of customer service girls clustered around a break room table sipping diet colas and laughing about the guy who wants to murder his coffee maker. But my Ozena wouldn't do that, I'm sure of it.

"Willy Finneran."

After forty-five seconds of on-hold music, Ozena is on the line. Her voice confirms what I already suspected. She's not the making fun type.

Ozena

Sheila announces that Willy Finneran is on line four. The name sounds familiar, but it's that forlorn voice that reminds me this is the guy with a vendetta against his coffee machine. I've been using his UPS parcel as a footstool all morning.

"Did you get the package I sent?"

"It came yesterday afternoon. I'm afraid I haven't gotten to it yet." I have to resist the urge to apologize.

"I don't want to be a pest or anything, but do you have any idea when I can expect it back?"

"That may take some doing. As you already know, we make a pretty durable little machine."

He chuckles politely, but it dries up as quickly as it came. "Can I ask you something?"

"Sure, I don't see why not."

"I'm sure you must think I'm crazy."

"Technically, that's not a question."

"But you almost have to, right? I mean, you'd be crazy not to."

I feel like I'm back in customer service training again, when the only thing scarier than silence on the line was the sound of my own shaky voice, the drone of chattering voices and clacking keyboards from neighboring cubicles reminding me that everyone in my orbit was better at their job than me. And now I'm adding to the silence on the line, allowing poor Willy to draw his own conclusions. Finally I blurt out my answer like a crazed game show contestant. "Passionate."

"Excuse me?"

"I read once that the dividing line between passion and lunacy is filament thin. That one man's crazy is another man's passion." Of course I don't realize until after I've said it that the place I read it was my own journal.

"Yeah?" He actually sounds relieved.

"Well I'm not sure I'm qualified to diagnose your mental stability over the phone."

"Are you saying you could do it in person?"

"Um, well, no ..." My radar goes off here. He *could* be calling from an asylum. Maybe he's planning a breakout and wants me to be his getaway girl. He is trying to murder his coffee maker, after all. Finally, I say, "Is there anything else I can assist you with today?"

"I'm sorry," he says. "That probably sounded creepy. I didn't mean anything by it. I should let you get back to your customers. And I'm running late for work myself."

Good, at least he has a job. Although I guess it could be cleaning toilets or peeling potatoes at the neighborhood lockup for the criminally insane. But then I catch myself. Why do I even care if he has a job? How could that possibly affect me? Unless he really is crazy? And if he needs to let me get back to my *customers*, what does that make him? Before I even realize it, I'm googling *William Finneran + Nashville* — with him still on the phone. The top five entries all refer to a local mystery writer. Just for fun, I click on the first link, an old article from the *Tennessean*, and although I doubt it's the same guy, at least the one in the picture has a wife and a job teaching college. And this Willy Finneran is kinda cute too, in a sort of earnest, forlorn way. Then I catch myself again.

"Are you still there?" Willy says.

"Yes, I'm sorry. I was just checking something on my computer. I'll get right on our little project as soon as we hang up."

"Thanks, Ozena."

Willy

As a rule, I avoid the faculty parking lot, mainly because my newish Land Rover seems pretentious amid the sea of antique Volvos, Subaru wagons, and whatever the plural of Taurus is. And I don't even like the stupid thing. I bought it for Lucy with the only good royalty check I ever received, simply because I knew she adored them. But she took one look at it, rolled her eyes, and called me an idiot. She never put the first mile on it.

I have no choice this morning, however. I've already missed one class, so cruising the men's dorms for an inconspicuous spot is not an option. Besides, some reconnaissance is in order. I need to liberate my lesson plan from my office without running into Dean Langstrom.

The English department is mostly deserted when I duck into my cubicle. After dialing the department voicemail, I secure the receiver between my ear and shoulder, then sift through piles of manila folders on my desk. The first message is from Langstrom himself, a *please see me in my office at your earliest convenience* reprimand. Next in the queue is the sultry student voice of Beverly Ray, suggesting a private meeting to work through her latest manuscript. A diabolically pretty fifth-year senior who insists on writing everything in second person, Beverly has a blatant and insatiable crush on me. One that I try to ignore, but that always makes me blush. The last message is from my agent, Stanley J. Jenkins, again informing me that he has urgent news and that I should call as soon as I get this message. He sounds more despairing than normal, if that's possible.

"Hah," I say under my breath. "If you want to dump me, you'll have to find me first."

"Found you!"

The receiver bounces off my thigh, then onto the floor when I throw my hands up to defend myself — from what or whom, I have no idea. My heart stutters to a stop as I turn to see Professor Doug Turko, batting his eyelashes and preening like a silent movie drama queen.

"Who's dumping you anyway? You got a new woman in your life you're not telling me about?"

"How many times have I told you not to startle me like that?"

"Nonsense, it's good for your heart. Like exercise."

"Great, my agent is trying to depress me and my best friend nearly scares me to death."

"You know, most writers love hearing from their agents. Maybe he's sold something and wants to send you a big check." Doug's smile breaks even wider, allowing an impish giggle to come spilling out. "You could get a Hummer this time."

"I'm sure he just wants to know how many remaindered copies I want before another Handyman novel goes out of print."

In the publishing world, "remaindered" is a cross between a Dear John letter and getting impeached. The publisher asks me to marry them, but the voting public gets together and issues our divorce decree, or rather, forces an annulment on the grounds of willful neglect. To milk the last few drops out of this metaphor, it means I'm now undateable and don't get paid anymore. Based on last quarter's sales figures of my Handyman novels, I'm slightly less popular these days than the guy who invented the enema.

I continue rifling through piles of homework and unlabeled folders before searching my briefcase for the third time in two minutes, thankful that my heart is throttling itself back to idle. But still no lesson plan. "Hey, what time is it anyway?"

"Five till." Doug stretches the two syllables into six as he pulls a folder from behind his back. "Looking for this?"

"As a matter of fact …"

I reach for the folder but Doug pulls it back and says, "Not so fast, tough guy. It's going to cost you."

I follow Doug through the maze of cubicles and filing cabinets until we find ourselves squinting at the sun and wading through a stream of backpacked and caffeinated coeds. When I spot Langstrom using one of his trademark silk handkerchiefs to wipe a smudge off the hood of his shiny new Mercedes, I duck behind my enormous friend and try to blend in with a gaggle of neuvo-bohemian students.

Once out of Langstrom's purview, we break off from the pack and duck into the west entrance of the humanities building, opting for the stairs.

"Now that we've agreed you're indebted to me, how about Sunday? All the donuts and coffee you can eat?"

My groan is lost amid our echoing footfalls. Doug first recruited me into his band, then into teaching English. I guess I should just be thankful he skipped making me rush his gay fraternity and is only harassing me about church. "I thought proselytizing was illegal on campus."

"Come on, man. I know what you're thinking — a bunch of misfits and wackos, holding hands and singing 'Kum ba Yah,' right? But we're just normal people. Well, you know, for the most part. And I swear to you, Will, I'm the only Fruit Loop in the cupboard."

"You do realize you're not really gay, right?"

He shrugs and says, "As far as you know."

"I'll think about it, Doug."

We top the stairs, and Doug lumbers off toward his classroom. I enter mine and shuffle a few papers around, pretending to study my lesson plan. The assignment had been to compare and contrast selected short stories of Flannery O'Connor and Graham Greene. But I'm in no mood now to referee another sophomoric debate where the net result would be to reduce my two favorite authors to punching bags. Instead I decide on a timed writing exercise followed by discussion groups. The announcement is greeted with loud groans and sighs, all except for Beverly. She welcomes any chance to weave her subtle, quasi-erotica into even the most tedious assignment. She even had the audacity to come to my office once to ask about the plausibility of her assigned short story. "Do you really think you …" She paused to fake a giggle and allow her hand to rest on my thigh. " … I mean *my character* would really have so much restraint in the face of such lustful temptation?"

My reverie splinters when I hear someone knock on the classroom door. I turn to see a grim-faced Dean Langstrom enter, hands folded in front of him, followed by the two cops from this morning, one uniformed and one in a cheap suit. I sigh dramatically and ask the class to excuse me for a few moments. It's the most interested they've looked all semester.

Once in the hallway, I notice that Langstrom seems dour, delightfully so.

"William Finneran?" the bigger cop says, the one in the suit. Good news never follows the phrase *William Finneran*.

"Yep, that's me."

"You're under arrest."

"What … what are you talking about? For what exactly?"

Words collide in my overwrought brain, words like *hit-and-run, failure to report*, and *aggravated assault*. But they seem to do their damage and bounce right off. Nothing about this conversation sticks.

My knees go weak, but Beverly Ray, apparently eavesdropping, is the one who actually faints.

Shaq

The sound of the phone ringing in this place makes everyone jumpy, or at least the regulars. Even the twins sit up and take notice — they're our resident potheads, nearly identical with matching beards and body odor. They drift between downtown shelters and supposedly act as middlemen for the real drug dealers. No one can tell them apart, and their names are always changing. I don't need their names to distrust them.

As soon as Father Joe answers his phone, the main room is steeped in silence. Small talk ceases, cards stop mid-shuffle, all humming and coughing and demented mumbling withers. Even the cots stop squeaking while we all wait to diagnose the bad news. Is it the morgue calling? Or one of the local hospitals to report a new Jane Doe? I catch myself silently praying it's simply a parole officer checking up on one of his charges.

The next sound from Joe's room is a strange one. I swear it sounded like he laughed, then sort of coughed to cover it. But it's been so long since I've heard him laugh, I'm not sure I recognize it. That's when the flock of homeless exhales together, each one absently resuming whatever trivial activities mark time. I keep my ear craned toward Joe's open door, but two cots down from mine there's a violent ripping, no doubt the sound of Velcro. It's the burly guy we call Prophet, shirtless as usual and mumbling crazy talk at the dozens of black adhesive strips he hoards in a tattered knapsack. He's so hairy it's impossible to tell where his beard stops and his chest hair begins. He nods a greeting at me, flashing brown teeth and a peace sign with his fingers.

Father Joe is quiet, probably listening to whoever called. Then he says, "Shaq? Bring me the paper."

"What section?"

"How about all the sections I paid for?"

I unfold my half-completed crossword, then refold it and smooth the creases out before stuffing it under the sports section. After I drop it on his desk, I do my version of turning invisible — two loud steps toward the door, followed by two quiet ones. Then I stop just outside the door and listen.

"Rufus?" Joe says, again with that weird trace of hilarity in his tone. "You got to be kidding me."

" ... I'm sorry, you're right, it's not funny ..."

"Sorry, Judge. Just seems like he ought to have been a little quicker than that. Seein' as he was a *lightning* badger and all."

The word *judge* triggers that glassy feeling in my mouth, followed by a tiny spark at the base of my spine. I used to clerk for Justice Robert Reynolds in the early days, which he seems to have completely forgotten. He's still kind of a hero of mine, even if he did forget I ever existed. Regardless, he's the man responsible for springing Father Joe from prison and trying to clear his name.

In 1957, the judge held every meaningful record on the Jefferson High School football team—rushing, receiving, and touchdowns in a single season. The records held until a bulky freshman named Joe Carter arrived on campus twelve years later. As the team's equipment manager I watched from the sidelines as he obliterated all the judge's precious records. Joe graduated with every conceivable award, then started in on setting new records at the University of Tennessee the next fall. That's when he was convicted of raping a senator's daughter. I don't know if the judge was trying to salvage Joe's legacy or his own, but he made Tennessee history in 1987 by using DNA testing to exonerate Father Joe. Eventually the girl fessed up, but by then Joe's career—and in a lot of ways, his life—were already over.

Father Joe asked me one time how I could remember every detail of his trial, all his records and highlights, but couldn't even come up with my own name. Sometimes I can't tell if he's teasing me or if his memory is as bad as mine. Maybe it's contagious.

"Says here it was an accident ..."

" ... hit and run? Come on, Judge. It's the school mascot, not the principal ..."

" ... he ain't even dead yet ..."

"You throw the book at this guy and send him to me? And I'm supposed to make him sleep next to addicts and work him like a dog, right? Sorry, Judge, no more. I'm too old for that nonsense ..."

" ... but the trial ain't even over yet, Judge."

" ... fine. You do what you gotta do. I'll babysit him if I have to, but if you want to abuse him, you can come down to the mission and do it yourself ..."

Eventually Joe goes out for his afternoon walk and I sneak the newspaper out of his room. That's when I catch the twins in action. One of them is distracting Prophet by asking patronizing questions about his Velcro collection while the other one is messing with the man's knapsack. I clear my throat and all three men look up. I glare at the twins, shifting my gaze from one to the other until they drop whatever it is they were up to and slink off to their cots in the far corner. Ever since their last arrest I've suspected them of stashing their drugs in other people's stuff. Just haven't caught them yet.

I read the article Joe circled about William Finneran and his mishap with a badger, but can't seem to get interested in it. So I work on finishing my crossword.

Willy

Day one of the trial reminds me of my one and only trip to a nudist beach. Not quite boring, but nothing compared to the hype. The over-bright chamber is scantily clad in threadbare carpet, stark white drywall, and faux wood furnishings. Fluorescents buzz over a pair of rickety lecterns and rigor mortised flags. The effect is more pedestrian than the hallowed halls of justice seen on TV. Save for the armed guards, dark suits, and the official state seal of Tennessee, it feels more like a classroom than a courtroom.

Yet here I sit, facing reduced felony charges, a hostile judge, and the very real possibility of going to prison. The particular badger I mowed down was indeed Rufus, the beloved mascot of the Jefferson High Lightning Badgers — the *judge's* alma mater.

After much pomp and circumstance the trial officially begins with the most unremarkable opening remarks in history.

Day two, the absurdity of standing trial for mowing down an oversized rat in a letter sweater continues. We get to hear a fairy tale.

After Rufus's trainer takes the stand and tells everyone what a smart little badger he is, how kind and intelligent and giving, he then launches into a local legend of how Rufus saved a little girl who'd fallen into a well. The longer he prattles on, the more his thin whiskers and severe underbite make him look like a badger.

With a plotline ripped right out of a *Lassie* screenplay, he regales the courtroom with every detail of Rufus's heroic rescue. Somehow, the little critter managed to scale the stony wall of the well, offer some sort of rodent-like assurance to the girl to not give up hope, then scurry off to town and perform some charades-like version of the little girl's ordeal so the townsfolk could rush out in droves and save her.

* * *

Day three begins with the attorneys crowded around the judge, their murmuring and angry whispers indiscernible. Then the jury is brought in and seated. After another twenty minutes of wrangling and lega-lese, the DA calls his final witness — the geezer from the antique gas station.

Decked out in a canary yellow leisure suit, white loafers, and gleam-ing dentures, he bends his lanky frame into the witness chair like a wooden fold-up ruler. A brief and shocking biography ensues. John Edgar Hooper, known to his colleagues and constituents simply as *Jed*, emerged from the coalmines of West Virginia through two decorated tours in Viet Nam before he was elected mayor of Ewing, Kentucky, in 1980. His journey from politician to cashier is left to the imagination. When asked to describe his interaction with the defendant, he squints at me and says, "Well I know'd he was drunk the second he come stag-gering in my store."

Despite my attorney's repeated warnings to remain placid, I nearly come out of my chair. Derrick forearms me back into my seat and shouts, "Objection!"

Judge Reynolds glares over his bifocals and mumbles, "Overruled." I'd swear I caught a glimpse of his letter jacket under his robe.

On cross, Mr. Hooper grudgingly confesses that he can't recall selling Mr. Finneran any alcohol. Nor did he witness Mr. Finneran actually imbibing anything stronger than a sip of coffee. In fact, there was not so much as a bulge in his pocket that would indicate a flask. "So do tell, Mr. Hooper," Derrick says. "How could you possibly know if my client was, as you say, drunk?"

"Takes one to know one, sir." His tone is confident, unwavering, and dripping with good ole boy charisma. The most damning thing about his testimony is the sincere look he gives me when he repeats, "Takes one to know one."

A handful of jurors nod their solemn approval.

Finally it's my turn to take the stand and tell my side of the story. But my performance lands way south of stellar. Things start out well, just like we rehearsed them. Derrick poses familiar questions and my confidence mounts with each measured response.

The trouble comes on cross-examination. The DA manages to dredge up all the times I've been pulled over for driving drowsy. I try to explain it was my heart transplant that caused the odd form of narcolepsy, how it took years to realize that a certain musical key makes me insanely sleepy. I know it sounds absurd, even when Derrick reads my case study directly from the *New England Journal of Medicine*. He then argues that there's no law against driving drowsy, but the DA (with a little help from the judge) makes me sound like a menace behind the wheel.

The DA makes me recount my run-in with Rufus in excruciating detail, and although I know better, the more the DA probes, the more defensive, argumentative, and downright hostile I become. I realize I'm making it all too easy for the jury to imagine me knocking back a few six-packs, then mowing down poor Rufus with a gleam in my drunken eye. But I can't seem to stop myself. The shrill stammer in my voice reeks of duplicity. And every syllable out of the DA's mouth is an accusation.

"Why, Mr. Finneran, if you had nothing to hide, did you not stop at the scene and investigate?"

"I don't know."

"I mean, it was obvious you hit something, right?"

In a rush to fill the incriminating silence, I blurt out the first thing that comes to mind. "I don't know, I thought it was a skunk or something."

"A *skunk*, Mr. Finneran?" He pauses, feigning surprise and playing to the gallery. "I'm curious, sir. Are you telling the court you find it morally acceptable to run down skunks in cold blood?"

"Of course not."

"Ah, I see. Then you must be implying that poor Rufus is nothing more than a smelly rodent. No further questions, Your Honor."

Derrick does an admirable job on redirect, but the damage has already been done. Our expert witness, a tenured veterinarian from the University of Tennessee, is dismissed as "hostile" before uttering a single word of testimony. The DA peppers his closing argument with references to my fateful skunk remark. "Ladies and gentlemen of the jury, as Rufus lay dying on the side of the road—"

"Objection," Derrick says. "Inflammatory. The badger is not even dead yet."

"*Yet?*" the DA shouts.

"Sustained," says Judge Reynolds, fingering his class ring.

But the DA is on a roll. "It sounds to me like the defendant and his attorney are assuming, nay, *hoping* for Rufus's ultimate demise."

The judge says lazily, "I said 'sustained,' counselor."

"Pardon me, Your Honor. While Rufus lay *suffering* on the side of the road, our not-so-good Samaritan plowed his luxury SUV over him. And what's his excuse? What sort of commiseration does he offer the grieving student body, alumni, and Rufus's trainer of nearly a decade?" He sweeps his arm toward Rufus's trainer, who then dabs at his eyes with the sleeve of his flannel shirt. "I thought it was a skunk," he repeats, having worked himself into a sarcastic lather. "*It? A skunk?* Ladies and gentlemen, the defendant may not have killed Rufus, but the gross negligence and abject lack of dignity on display here appalls me. It should appall us all. We need closure. We need to pick up the pieces and move on from this horrific and untimely tragedy."

The DA sighs deeply, then approaches the jury in slow, measured steps. His voice pitched just above a whisper, he says, "Who really knows?" He pauses thoughtfully, then adds, "What we do know is that the defendant — driving without a license — stole gasoline and groceries along the way, then ran down Rufus in his luxury SUV. One eyewitness you heard claims Mr. Finneran paused to examine his handiwork, then attempted to back over the dying animal before driving off. I contend that if William Finneran had the decency to stop, maybe Rufus would have recovered more quickly. Surely he wouldn't have suffered so much. Maybe he'd be there for opening night against the Truman High Hilltoppers?"

Derrick shouts his objections; the judge even sustains a few, but only after allowing the incriminating waves to lap the shores of the crowd's collective ire one last time.

* * *

The verdict is in and I'm about to learn my fate. Spectators are decked out in school colors and Rufus the Lightning Badger T-shirts. There's even a handful of cheerleaders and players in jerseys as well. The jury has just been seated for the last time.

Finally, the bailiff bellows, "All rise." A half-second later the judge's chamber door swings open and the Honorable Judge Reynolds stalks toward the bench. After situating his robes, adjusting his glasses, and shuffling some papers around, he scowls at me.

The gavel bangs and all of Derrick's earlier assurances now seem thin and pointless. He declared victory early and often and somehow convinced me that there really was nothing to worry about. Or that we at least had a shot at it. But any confidence I did have now seems like an ill-fitting pair of bowling shoes.

"Has the jury reached its verdict?"

A squatty man with thick glasses and a *Members Only* jacket stands and addresses the top of his shoes. In a hoarse whisper, he says, "Yes, Your Honor."

"Speak up, son!"

"Yes, sir. Sorry, Your Honor, sir."

The bailiff steps forward, grim-faced, and nods reassurance at the now trembling jury foreman. With a waddling version of military precision, he delivers the folded slip of paper to the judge for his review.

The judge studies it, frowns, nods, then appears to read it again before passing it back. My stomach flips. I wonder if throwing up on the table would maybe garner a little sympathy for the sentencing phase.

"Now," the judge says. "Mr. Foreman, please enter it into the record."

"Excuse me?"

"Read it," the judge says, clearly frustrated at the lack of aptitude and decorum.

"We the jury—"

The bailiff pretends to cough, loudly. The Honorable Judge Reynolds slams his gavel again and says, "Would the defendant please rise?"

My legs turn to rubber. I half expect Derrick to yank me to my feet. But my attorney has turned ashen and appears to be leaning on the table for support.

"We the jury find the defendant, one William J. Finneran, guilty."

I'm mostly numb, only vaguely aware of the commotion. There's a dramatic wail behind me followed by a dull thud. I'm pretty sure Beverly Ray just fainted again.

Ozena

The hum of rental skates on the wooden floor sounds like one endless gutter ball. I thought having lunch at Super Skate World might bring back a few fond memories. Now I'm not sure what I was thinking. My BLT sandwich tastes like the giant pickle that came on the plate. My fries taste like a cross between onion rings and the grayish hotdog that appears every thirty seconds on its Ferris wheel rotisserie cooker. My Dr. Pepper tastes way too much like Dr. Pepper. The only memories this experience conjures so far are all the stomachaches and pimples from my youth. And the rink's deejay is not helping either with his penchant for nineties hair bands.

And to think I had to turn down two separate invitations for lunch today. Not because I really wanted to, but because Reggie asked first. Not two minutes later, Minnie DeLong popped her head into my cubicle and asked if I had plans for lunch. Minnie's been the head of our Human Resources department since her last boss ran Hengle's Supply into the ground. She's mousy but sweet, the kind of girl I think I would really like if I ever got to talk to her away from work.

"I'm sorry, Minnie. I'd love to, but I brought my lunch today."

"Oh, don't worry, my treat." She was so earnest, so upbeat, it broke my heart to turn her down.

"It's not that. I just hate to see good food go to waste."

"Oh," she said, dropping her eyes to her kneading fingers. "I see."

But she didn't see, not really. Minnie turned and scurried off before I could explain. I really did pack my lunch today. And I really do hate to see good food go to waste. But of course now she thinks I'm lying. I can only imagine her working up the nerve to come down and invite me to lunch, then how lame my excuse must have sounded. But the sad reality is, as much as I really did want to go with her, that would be like lying to Reggie. And what if we ended up at the same restaurant and Reggie saw me with her? So I climbed into my Civic — alone with my brown bag and guilty conscience — then dialed up a ridiculous talk radio show about relationships, only to discover the Swiss cheese on my turkey sandwich was tinged blue.

It was too late to catch up with Minnie. So to keep from looking like a stuck-up, lying hypocrite, I was forced to find someplace to eat where I wouldn't be recognized. Now I'm thinking I should have gone with my first instinct and just had popcorn and a candy bar in the break room.

I force myself to swallow another bacony bite and pretend not to listen to the ladies working behind the snack bar counter. But it's nearly impossible. I stare over my shoulder into the shadowy expanse of the rink itself. A disco ball scatters a dizzying array of pinks and purples and blues. There's a busload of field-tripping preteens horsing around, a small girl trying unsuccessfully to teach herself to skate backwards, and a familiar-looking woman about my age in a long skirt making figure-eights and elegant pirouettes. The playful murmuring between the snack bar attendants grows more intense.

"Now you listen to me good." It's the younger girl, bleached and pierced and oozing with redneck authority. She's sitting on a counter loudly flipping pages in a magazine. "Dr. Dennis on the radio? He says that sometimes dee-vorce is the onliest option."

"Tell that to my mother," the older of the two says, veins bulging in her arms as she scrapes charred remains off a blackened griddle top.

"But you didn't *ask* Freddy to take up with Lorraine and those dual air bags of hers, did you?"

The older woman doesn't answer. Instead she brushes her bangs out of her eyes with the back of her wrist, then keeps on scraping. The sound makes my teeth hurt.

"You listen here, Linda. Cuz I'm only telling you this one more time, you hear? You are not going to hell for serving that two-timing son-of-a-gun-runner with papers. I don't care what your momma or your preacher or that sorry excuse for a husband says. You hear?"

"All I hear is the voice in my head saying, 'God hates divorce.'"

I'm tempted to leap over the dirty counter and hug poor Linda, and not just to make her stop all that scraping. I want to tell her I hear that same voice. I'm not sure if it was God who actually said the thing about hating divorce, but I don't doubt it's true. For the record, I hate it too. But I'm pretty sure God also hates drunkenness. And abandonment, betrayal, and the injustice and cruelty of watching part of his own creation stunted and retarded by the careless acts of someone who should know better.

I'd spent the first year sulking and the second filling diaries. I chronicled in excruciating detail the pain of abandonment and Lloyd Jr.'s lack of progress, of my search for a job and suitable daytime care for my handicapped son; I wrote about my bad marriage, about my first Al-Anon meeting, even the humiliation of having my ob-gyn explain how a monogamous housewife contracts venereal disease from her unfaithful husband; I wrote about Lloyd's ridiculous investments, a string of failed attempts to prove his business acumen to his perennially unimpressed father, how his fickle temper sabotaged a promising coffee shop venture with an old high school buddy; I wrote about having to divorce *in absentia* a man I hadn't seen in years just so I could qualify for better insurance and a little help from the state. I've never gone back and reread the entries. And why would I? It's bad enough to watch hope die. Who needs a blow-by-blow description? That's a lot of misery packed into a few hundred pages. If I were smart I'd just burn them.

The scratchy voice of the deejay says, "Okay guys, grab your ladies and cozy up for a couples skate!" He then queues up a synthesizery song I recognize from an oldies station. The sound of metal scraping metal ceases. I venture a glance at Linda, who is hunched now, shoulders heaving. The younger girl jerks a nonchalant thumb at the now sobbing woman and says dully, "Her and Freddy's song." The young girl shrugs and flips the page in her magazine.

The guy crooning through the PA system talks about his heartache and pain before pondering, "I want to know what love is . . . I want you to show me . . ." That's the same worthless question I've been asking my

71

journal for years. Maybe that's all love is anyway, just a diary, a place to load up all the pain and hurt, sorted and stacked with the labels facing out, like some emotional kitchen pantry. Some of us work our love out on the page while the lucky ones get to share it with actual humans, like fine wine, French loaves, and heaping bowls of pasta.

The sappy love song ends with help from a choir, the older woman perks back up and resumes her scraping, and the deejay spins another relic about some chick singlehandedly responsible for giving love a bad name.

Now that's more like it.

I grab a napkin from the holder and a pen from my purse, certain I've hit upon what love really is. It's a stray bullet through the living room window, random and unexpected, able to wound or maim or simply sail right into the drywall. An extremely lucky shot might bury itself in the heart. In the final analysis, love makes about as much sense as a drive-by shooting. And if you're in the right place at the wrong time, it can kill you.

Or maybe I'm as crazy as I feel, hiding out in a skating rink snack bar on a Tuesday afternoon, waxing philosophical with Bon Jovi and overcooked hotdogs as inspiration.

I tuck my scribbled musings back into my purse, then grab a fresh napkin to dab grease from the corners of my mouth. After scooping the crumbs onto my red plastic tray, I dump my trash. As I turn, I see Minnie DeLong putting her billfold away, forehead beaded in sweat, with a pair of pom-pommed skates slung over her shoulder. That's why that shadowy pirouetting figure skater looked so darn familiar.

She sees me seeing her, her eyes pink and watery, but too proud to look away. I manage to seal my gaping mouth and swallow hard. I can still taste the pickle when I say, "Minnie, wait. It's not what you think."

She scoops her fountain drink off the counter and pushes past me. Sunlight streams in through the door as she disappears into the parking lot. I turn toward the snack bar, the young girl shaking her head pitifully at me.

I hate having to apologize. Not that I'm not sorry about stuff, just the opposite. I'm too sorry, if that's possible. But it's the actual apology I stink at. I freeze up, get tongue-tied, end up worrying so much about sounding sincere that I end up sounding anything but.

I feel my mouth popping open, the need to explain to this total stranger that I did not lie, that it was all Reggie's fault, that it was all just a big misunderstanding. Her sneer is half-hearted as her gaze drops to her magazine and she snaps another page.

Willy

Derrick's only victory in my case comes at the end. After a long and pitiful display of begging and pleading and citing numerous legal precedents, he manages to reduce my sentence of eighteen months' incarceration to a mere two thousand hours of community service.

He tries to spin it like it's really good news, but I'm not buying it. He's trying too hard.

"What does that mean exactly?"

"It means you don't have to go to jail."

"But I'm still doing time, right?"

"No, I mean, well, sort of, yeah."

"That doesn't sound very lawyerly."

"Instead of jail, you're going to serve your sentence at a place called Mercy Mission, under the watchful eye of a guy named Father Joe Carter."

"So it's like prison without the bars."

"If you want to look at it that way, sure."

"Can't I get time off for good behavior or something? Maybe wear one of those electric dog collars around my ankle instead?"

"Funny you should ask. I'll be filing my appeal in the morning. In the meantime, you be a good soldier, stick to the judge's recommendations, do whatever this Father Joe guy tells you, and I promise we'll get the sentence reduced. Maybe even cut in half."

"So if he tells me to break rocks all day or pick up garbage or be the towel boy in the community showers, I have to do it?"

"It won't be that bad, Willy."

"I suppose," I say. "At least I get to sleep in my own bed at night."

"Well ..."

"What is it, Derrick?"

"Not unless they let you bring your own mattress to the mission. I guess I could check into that."

"Wait, I have to spend the night there too?"

"Judge's orders. It's a condition of your sentence, a tradeoff for actual jail time."

"Are there any other *conditions* I need to know about?"

"Just keep your nose clean. No speeding tickets, parking violations, or loud music after hours. Something as trivial as jaywalking could land you in the slammer."

"You have to do something, man. I mean, I just can't ..."

"Just trust me. And try not to worry."

"That's what you said about the trial, Derrick."

I can tell I've hurt his feelings, but I can't muster the energy to care much. I should shake his hand and thank him and try to be grateful. But all I can think about is not spending the night in my own house.

"What's this place called again? Mercy Chapel?"

"Mercy Mission, downtown."

"Sounds like a homeless shelter." His silence is all the answer I need. "Oh, God in heaven, please tell me I'm not living in a homeless shelter."

After a brief eternity I realize we've made a silent pact. He's not answering and I'm not meeting his eyes. Eventually I hear him mumble, "I did the best I could, Willy."

Then I hear him shuffle his feet down the hall.

Derrick failed to inform me that the judge also revoked my driver's license. But the cop who pulls me over on the way home from the courthouse tells me. Then he too acts like he's doing me a big favor by only citing me for driving too fast. I guess all the grateful bones in my body were crushed when I realized I only had a few days in my house before swapping my sanctuary for a cot in a soup kitchen. Derrick doesn't understand. No one ever understands, not even Lucy. But the thought of not living in my house hits me harder than the verdict itself.

Ozena

I'm digging through the garbage in the break room when it occurs to me—a perfect metaphor for marriage—the skating rink.

Prior to your first trip, the anticipation seems so romantic, rife with music and mystery and carnal knowledge, from the snack bar delicacies to budding romances culminating in a sweaty-palmed couples skate. But eventually the novelty gives way to a series of sad realities—burnt popcorn, sweaty feet, blisters, and watching Tommy Newsome ask two *other* girls for a romantic spin around the rink. Eventually the lights come back on. The room is dingy and cavernous. The dull pain in your legs reminds you how much work is involved. And you realize you've been going around in circles the whole time.

Okay, so it's not a perfect metaphor, but I blame it on the fumes from the garbage. And it might not even be worth transcribing into my journal. But at least it took my mind off the disgusting task at hand. I finally locate my turkey sandwich right where I left it, at the very bottom of the break room trash can. Of course it looks like a failed science project, or maybe an exhibit on one of those forensic dramas on TV. But it should still prove my point.

Minnie's door is open, but I knock anyway. She's smiling when she looks up, but her face flatlines when she sees me. I keep the baggie concealed behind my back.

"I hope you're happy."

I can tell by her tone she hopes I'm not. "About what?"

"Reggie took your little suggestion about personal calls at work and is about to implement a new policy ... thanks to you."

It takes me a second to remember. "But I didn't really mean that. It was just a throwaway line to keep Reggie from ... you know, asking me stuff."

She mumbles something that sounds an awful lot like, "You know, Sheila was right about you."

"Excuse me?" I say, determined to do what I came here for and not let this devolve into a petty argument.

"What can I do for you?"

"Well, I wanted to apologize." I hold the baggie up and watch her stoic expression droop into a ghastly frown.

"What is that?" she says. "And why is it in my office?"

"It's proof, Minnie."

"Of what? Or do I really want to know?"

"I told you I brought my lunch from home. See? I had to throw it away, and that's why I went out to the skating rink. The cheese is blue. I had to dig through the garbage to get it. It proves I had to throw my sandwich away, just like I said. Why else would I go to all this trouble?"

"If I accept your apology, will you get that thing out of here?"

"Yeah, sure. I'm sorry. I didn't mean to upset you. I just, you know, didn't want you to think I lied or anything."

"What difference does it make what I think?"

"It makes all the difference to me."

She nods, then looks away.

"Anyway," I say, "I'll let you get back to work."

Willy

I meant to spend the evening packing a duffel bag for my new home. But it proved more difficult than I first imagined. By the time I pack, unpack, and repack a half dozen times, my entire chest of drawers has been cleaned out and cycled in and out of my suitcase. Finally, I dump it all out on the bed again, put the teakettle on (I realize I actually miss Lucy's lover's espresso maker), and deal a hand of solitaire. Then another, and a few more after that.

Walter would know exactly what to pack for the mission. He could tell me how to act, who to trust, and who to avoid. His instincts were impeccable, both for finding trouble and for making sure I stayed out of it. Once he broke parole, my overprotective grandparents forbade me to correspond with Walter. So when he wanted to talk to me, my big brother would have his girlfriend of the month call from some out-of-the-way motel and ask to speak to me, claiming she was a classmate, then hand him the phone once I was on. I wasn't crazy about the dishonesty, but I loved the idea of being in on one of Walter's scams. I endured his opening gambit of *do as I say, not as I do.* Then I would sit enraptured at all his doings, the things I was strictly forbidden to emulate, but that he was so proud to tell me. Eventually he would catch himself, realize the bad influence he was imparting, then corral our collective fervor over his exploits into a sort of benediction. Once again, I would be exhorted to study hard, obey my elders, and stay away from drugs, loose women, and stupid people. It took me years to realize that most of his antics were either for show or for spite. Only the robberies were out of necessity. At his core, Walter Finneran was kind and articulate. He read great books, often calling me in the middle of the night to recite his favorite passages from Dickens or Steinbeck or Graham Greene. I'm a writer today because of Walter.

But more than that, I'm *alive* today because of Walter.

After I finally win a hand of solitaire without cheating, I wash my face and brush my teeth. But I'm not sleepy.

So I break down and do what I've wanted to do all night. I call Ronnie Cheevers. When he doesn't answer, I call his wife's house, feeling more than a little guilty about interrupting whatever it is they do on the rare occasions they hang out after dark.

"Everything okay, Willy?"

"Yeah, everything's good."

We listen to each other not talk for almost a minute.

Finally he says, "I'll be right over."

"Thanks, Ronnie."

I meet him at the door and he follows me to the TV room. I sit in my grandfather's recliner and watch Ronnie finger the small assortment of pipes. I sometimes wonder if his belaboring is all for show, a small gift to me to add some profundity to the moment so I won't feel like such a sap for asking. He selects the bull pipe, the one I bought as a gift with my lawn mowing money the summer I found out my heart was bad. Ronnie roots around in his pocket and retrieves a small pocketknife. He uses the butt of it to tamp the velvety sweet tobacco. With the stem tucked into the corner of his mouth, he angles his head and flicks the lighter into action. He puffs and squints and puffs some more, then eases back on the couch and allows the smell of my childhood to waft over me. I lean the recliner back and lace my fingers over my scar.

It's time for the tradeoff; I got what I needed, now it's Ronnie's turn. Odds are two to one that he'll go with the war story. It's an okay story about his single tour in Viet Nam as an Army photographer. But Ronnie has something else on his mind.

"I'm thinking of leaving her."

"Who?"

"Gladys. Who else?"

"But you just did."

"I mean permanently."

I picture his long, slow trek, suitcase in hand as he walks across my yard, a sad string quartet dirging in the background. I fake a cough to keep from grinning, then wonder if it's my fault, if somehow I've *literally* come between them.

"You mind if I ask why?"

"I don't know. It's just not working out. And I don't see it getting any better anytime soon."

"Well how bad can it really be? I mean, you don't even really live together."

We share a look, more of a silent pact. Neither of us has much room to criticize anyone else's dysfunctional marriages.

"You have no idea what it's like, Willy."

"Is this about your cigars?"

He shakes his head. "Those dang cats. I swear she loves them more than me."

"So you're jealous?"

He looks at me like I just made a pass at him.

"Sorry," I say. "I'm just trying to keep up."

He puffs Grandpa's pipe, either thinking deep thoughts or about to nod off. Finally he says, "I don't think she finds me attractive anymore."

"Are you kidding me? Have you not seen the way she watches you from her kitchen window when you're out talking with the neighbor ladies?"

"What neighbor ladies?"

"Mrs. Jenkins timing her mailbox runs to coincide with yours. And how Miss Jakovich does all her power walking on *our* side of the street."

His wet lips flirt with a smile and his birdlike chest inflates a few fractions of an inch. Then he looks at me sharply. "You're just messing with me, aren't you?"

"No, sir. If you ask me, *she's* the one who's jealous. You just need to use it to your advantage."

"You think so?"

"I know so. If anything, she's just playing hard to get."

He's quiet now, his brow clenched as he cleans the bowl of Grandpa's pipe. Then he shakes his head and says, "Maybe you're right. Maybe I got it all wrong. Her cats aren't really *that* bad. You think I'm just being stubborn?"

"Could be."

"Sorry to puff and run, Willy." His knees pop as he stands. "Time to turn the charm back on, like in the old days."

"Wait, where you going?"

"To call my realtor."

Now I'm the one who's jealous.

When Ronnie leaves I feel worse instead of better. Solitaire's no good either because I end up winning the first game, fair and square. Then I make the mistake of stretching out on the couch with a John Irving novel. I wake up nearly eight hours later with refracted sunlight streaming through the blinds, a sharp pain in my neck, and an insatiable need to check on my espresso maker.

The outgoing Javatek loop is midway through announcing that all customer service reps are busy assisting other customers when the switchboard operator cuts in. I'm too startled to catch her name, something like Avon or Mary Kay. In the silence directly following her last question mark, I say, "Can I speak to Ozena?"

"Oh, you must need some parts and accessories then. Am I right?"

"Sure, yeah, parts. And accessories."

"I'll transfer you."

A mere half ring elapses before Ozena is on the line.

"Oh, hey Ozena. It's me, Willy."

Ozena

I had every intention of spending a few minutes in the breezeway this morning, inhaling my coworkers' secondhand smoke and jotting a few ideas in my journal. For weeks now I've been wrestling with the idea of exorcising my love-defining obsession by turning the spotlight on my own life. Conjuring impersonal metaphors about my brother's failed romances or the on-again-off-again relationship of celebrities is just too easy. And doesn't really help. So I print the familiar "Love Is ..." heading at the top of an otherwise blank page and wait for some cathartic inspiration.

I stare at the page, willing some idea — any idea, even a bad one to raise its hand from the back row of my brain. The smattering of smokers stubbing out is my cue that break time is over. In a terrifying bout of controlled fury, I bite the cap off my pen and carve out the letter *N*, an apostrophe, and the letter *T* after the word *is*.

It's not very poetic, three simple syllables followed by three tiny dots. It's devoid of insight or literary leanings. But at least it feels good. Finally I rip the page out of my diary and touch one corner to a smoldering cigarette. It begins to burn but fizzles out before it gets to the letters. I can't decide if it's more pathetic to leave my musings there for any passerby to read or to actually reach into a nasty, rusted ashtray to crumple up the piece of paper. But before I can react, a small breeze lifts up my two-word cogitation and carries it across the parking lot. My only shot at catharsis now is if a bird poops on it.

On my way back to my cubicle, I pause outside Reggie's office door and covertly spritz his hinges with a small bottle of hairspray I keep in my purse for emergencies. With his office a mere thirty feet from my desk, the warning sound of his shrieking hinges allows me plenty of time to come up with legitimate excuses for his advances.

My phone is ringing before my butt hits the chair.

"So are you the same Willy Finneran that writes books?"

"*Used* to write books is more like it." He sounds embarrassed for some reason. "Why? Are you interested in writing?"

"No, but I can't seem to stop. Maybe you can help me. Why did you stop?"

"My books did okay in the States. They had just enough of a cult following to talk the publisher into more and more sequels. Then my agent sold the rights to a Japanese publisher and international sales just took off."

"I have to say, Willy, I don't really see a downside yet."

"Well, the problem was with the translation."

"No good?"

"Too good."

"What does that mean?"

"The guy they hired to do the translation was brilliant and funny and basically took my character and completely rewrote everything else in the story. He turned my pedestrian one-armed detective novels into a raging comedic success. A big production company in Tokyo started making movies, and there were talks of spin-off comic books and TV shows and lunchboxes."

"So what happened?"

"A lot of lawsuits."

"I take it you didn't win?"

"Not even close. He changed the character's name, location, occupation, and most of the major plot points. By the time this guy was done, there was so little resemblance to the original material that my agent and I had no legal ground to stand on. It seems that having a one-armed, one-eyed detective that can slap attachments onto the end of his arm to foil criminals and solve crimes is not all that original an idea."

"So you just stopped writing altogether?"

"Not really. I started work on my serious novel."

"Serious, as in not funny?"

"I guess they call it literary. It was about people and life and love and stuff. Nothing blew up and no one got shot."

"Sounds intriguing. Why don't you work on finishing that one?"

"I can't."

"Writer's block?"

"No, I lost it."

"You're telling me you lost an entire novel?"

Willy Finneran's willingness to sit in his own silence is unnerving. Or maybe he just nodded off. Finally he pitches his voice to a happier place and says, "The switchboard lady said you're the one I need to speak to about ordering some accessories. Got any recommendations?"

"A better segue for starters."

He paused. "Sorry, something about that lost book terrifies me."

"Fair enough. What kind of accessories did you have in mind?"

"I don't know. One of those tamper thingies maybe. Something to make the espresso less bitter? Just anything like that."

"For the same espresso machine you asked me to destroy?"

"I may as well be prepared."

"For what?"

"I still don't believe you can break that thing."

"Is that some sort of challenge?"

"If that's what it takes, sure. I dare you to break it. Double dare you."

"Well in that case ..." I had no clue how I was going to end that sentence. But thankfully two more lines light up before I have to try. "Sorry, Willy. Duty calls."

"Well if anyone else is requesting a demolition, tell them to get in line."

"I'll remember that."

The first call is a wrong number and the second is some guy looking for Sheila. I take out my journal, flip to the first blank page, and write: *Love is a broken coffee maker.*

I stare at it, waiting for some flash of inspiration to complete the metaphor, to fill in exactly *how* love is like a wrecked appliance. But the best I can come up with is a question mark at the end of the sentence.

Willy

It's Monday morning and I have forty-five more minutes to kill before it's time to call the taxicab to ferry me off to what I now refer to as prison lite. I run my finger across a bright yellow refrigerator magnet for a taxicab company. I used to tease Lucy about the magnet since she'd never once ridden in a taxi. Turns out, that's the last number she dialed from this house before leaving for good.

I know I should be doing something important, some poignant last ritual before stepping out of my home. Naturally, I wander from room to room, using my writer's eye to log away memories to keep me company during my upcoming incarceration.

The living room is bookended by archways. Against my grandmother's wishes, I spent hours every day jumping and trying to reach the highest point in the arc. She claimed she was worried about my heart. The day my incessant leaping finally paid off just happened to be the same day I found and ruined one of my grandfather's fountain pens, which made it easy for everyone to remember my triumph. Grandma went ballistic and insisted I either clean up the inky black smudges or repaint the entire hallway.

The first and only time I saw my grandfather stand up to his wife was in my defense.

"Liddy, the boy finally made his jump. We are *not* cleaning it. And we're not painting over it either!" When she stormed off, I felt a conspirator's elbow in my ribs. Grandpa had knelt down and was pointing up. "Wouldja looky there? Even Deputy Fife could make those prints out."

This was the closest I ever came to a manly rite of passage. It was my bar mitzvah, my confirmation, my baptism and graduation. To this day, I still reach up and touch my tiny fingerprints whenever I pass under the archway.

Lucy claimed my fascination with the house was an attempt to recapture something, and that I could never be happy until I figured out what. She hypothesized aloud about romantic notions of a lost childhood and trying to reunite with my parents or Walter or maybe even Jesus. I'm sure she had a point. But what she didn't get — couldn't possibly understand — is that this is the only place I know where the pulsing in my chest turns to background noise. It pounds away, unobserved. I don't have to think about it, or count how many beats it has left.

Before I know it, thoughts of Lucy have directed my steps into the bathroom where I aimlessly run my fingers around the lip of our toothbrush holder. A knot forms in my throat and I have to leave before glimpsing the sad man in the mirror.

Thanks to Ronnie, the den still smells like my grandfather's pipe.

Grandpa's prized leather recliner still faces the blocky console TV that works to this day. The only time it saw action was during wars, elections, and the World Series. I come from a family of readers. Or maybe it skipped a generation. I can only assume my parents know how to read. (I don't say much about my parents because I know so little of them. And what little I know, I don't think is true. Suffice to say that they married too young and possessed only scant tolerance for their offspring — neither the elder hellion nor his puny kid brother. Father loved every woman but the one he married. Mother loved the stage, but I can find no real evidence that she spent much time on it. Or at least not the center of it. The last I heard, she was stage managing off-off Broadway productions in the northwest.)

I was fourteen when the house, *my* home, was sold out from under me. A week after the big stroke, Grandpa died and went to heaven. A week after his funeral, Grandma followed suit. At the funeral home I begged my parents to keep the house. But they refused, wanting to get whatever money they could out of it and go back to their regularly scheduled lives. The remainder of my teenage years were spent with my Great Aunt Mavis's family where I was forced to sleep over corpses. They owned and operated a wildly successful discount funeral home. Between the mourners, the sad organ music, and the heavy rotation of the unliving, I found every excuse to spend time away from home.

My epiphany came in college. I woke in the middle of the night with possibly the best idea I'd ever conjured. It was so good I dragged myself out of bed and wrote it down. My roommate yelled at me for waking him, but I would not be dissuaded. The empty beer can made a wooshing sound in the dark before it dinged against my forehead and stained the paper I was scribbling on. I remember exactly what I wrote:

Graduate in May, then buy my grandparents' house.

A simple and brilliant plan, and what would eventually become the first draft of my infamous To Do list. I finally had a goal, one that made sense even.

My reminiscing now has me staring at a blank spot on the wall behind my grandfather's reading chair. The convulsive urge to hang a picture there overcomes me like a seizure and I'm tugging the attic's ripcord down and bounding up the steps in search of a hammer, some nails, and something to hang.

I'm already prickled with sweat by the time my foot lands on the plywood floor of the attic. Another five minutes of searching produces an even sheen of perspiration. After sifting through boxes of family photos and an old footlocker from college, I decide on a framed black-and-white poster of Miles Davis. In all the years of living in this house, I've never once tried to make it my own. Now that I'm being exiled I'm suddenly desperate to force the issue, to make it my home instead of the house I grew up in, moved out of, then moved back into.

My grandfather's toolbox has the gentle reek of axle grease and old wood. The hammer is scarred and the nails thin, but more than adequate for picture hanging. I pluck one tiny nail from my pinched lips, position it on the wall, then tap lightly with the hammer.

Nothing happens.

I tap harder, but instead of watching the pointy tip of the nail disappear, I see a chunk of plaster tumble to the hardwood below. The nail is now poised in a small crater. I strike the nail again, harder still, and watch scraggly fissures form along unseen fault lines. A small cloud of dust joins the freefalling flakes of plaster. The tip of the nail is still in full view, mocking me. I continue to pound the nail until it bends. The crater is now an inch deep and two inches wide. I wonder how long it would take to knock the whole house down this way. It doesn't dawn on me how futile it is to drive a one-inch nail into a one-inch crater until I have the hammer cocked and am about to slam it home. That's when Doug lets himself in.

"Simmer down there, John Henry." Three long strides later he's by my side and easing the hammer from my grip. "You do realize this is plaster?"

"Yeah, so?"

"And your thumb's bleeding." I have to see the blood seeping under my nail for the pain to register in my brain. "Got a power drill handy?"

"Nope."

"No pilot hole then. Any more nails?"

"Just more like these."

"Grab me a couple, along with some masking tape and dishwashing liquid."

I do as instructed, sucking on my sore thumb, wondering if the taste in my mouth is from the nails or the blood. I hand them over and say, "What are you doing here anyway?"

He bows ceremoniously. "Your car awaits you, sir."

"I told you I was taking a cab."

"Nonsense." He rips and applies a few strips of masking tape a couple of inches above the sinkhole I created in the wall. "You're not driving yourself to prison. That's just too pathetic somehow. Besides, I thought you could use some good news."

"They changed my sentence to the firing squad?"

"You're going to be a godfather!"

"So what's the good news?"

His profile swivels my way and I can tell at once I've hurt his feelings. But he shouldn't be surprised either. We've had this conversation a dozen times. It's not that I really hate kids, I'm just flagrantly selfish.

Doug is all business now, coating the nail in slimy green liquid and wiping the excess on his dark sock.

"I'm sorry," I say. "Tell Maggie thanks for me. I really am honored."

Doug centers the nail in the patch of masking tape, pointing it at a severe angle. Three short taps later, the nail disappears and Doug is ripping the masking tape off the wall. "There you go."

"Man, that's annoying ... and thanks."

"Hand me the picture and I'll treat you to Starbucks on the way."

I do a quick scan to make sure the appliances are all turned off and the AC is off. When I return to the living room with my suitcase, Doug is admiring my new artwork. It fits the room like a white tablecloth in a bowling alley. He's too polite to say anything, but that doesn't keep him from pointing at my luggage and laughing.

"You do know you'll be the only guy in prison with a shaving kit and slippers, don't you?"

"It's not prison, Doug. More like a soup kitchen."

"I'm sure it's not the Hampton Inn either. Why don't you just take the necessities and let me bring you clothes on my morning commute?"

"It's thirty miles out of your way. That's way too much trouble."

"Not for the godfather of Doug Junior."

"What if it's a girl?"

"We'll name her Finny, after you." He snaps the toolbox shut and checks his watch. "Let's get going. You don't want to be late for the ball."

When I open my front door, I nearly run over my dead wife.

* * *

I can't believe how different she looks — too thin, her skin pleated around the eyes and lips, more like forties than thirties, her lustrous black hair ceding ground to hints of gray.

Doug waves at Lucy, then excuses himself to his idling Volvo. For such an imposing figure, he always seemed a bit terrified of Lucy. If I could actually tear my eyes away from her I'm sure I'd see him hunched over the wheel, squinting in our direction, trying to read our lips.

"So how are you?" I say.

"Pretty good, thanks …" I indulge myself one shallow breath. Maybe this won't be as bad as I feared. Then she adds, "… for a dead woman."

"Look, I never really said —"

"You never really say much of anything, do you? Not if it might make your life a little more complicated. Life *is* complicated, Willy." I open my mouth to respond but she waves me off. "I was hoping you'd learned that by now."

"That's not fair, Luce."

"You think it's fair to let people think I was dead so you wouldn't have to admit I left you?"

"I never once said you were dead."

"Exactly."

I move my suitcase from one sweaty hand to the other. As usual, she's right and I'm wrong, which always leaves me speechless. In my defense, I was a terminally sick kid with little hope of any real future. So keeping my "present" peaceful was a pretty huge deal. The present was all I had. That's why it's so easy for me to allow assumptions to pass by uncorrected, things like letting my neighbors assume my wife was dead.

"Aren't you going to invite me in?" Lucy asks.

"I'm kinda running late for something."

"Suit yourself. But when Gladys pops over with a plate of brownies, I'll let you explain my resurrection."

My gaze swivels toward my neighbor's house. I was already in the emotional crapper the day Lucy left. That's when Gladys Cheevers forced herself and her nutmeg cookies on me (she used the key that Lucy gave her to check our mail when we went on vacation, which we never did). I had no intention of lying. I just wanted to get rid of her.

"Yoo hoo?" she said. "Anybody home? I made cookies."

I was pasted with sweat from ferrying Lucy's belongings from various points in the house to a steaming bubble bath. "Oh, um, hi. Now's not really the best time."

"Not a good time for cookies? Nonsense."

"I'm just a little upset is all." And it was true. I *needed* to get Lucy's new Dell laptop into the bubble bath in just the worst possible way.

"Is this about Lucy? Are you kids having issues again?"

"Lucy is ..." It didn't dawn on me until much later that a bead of sweat had plummeted from my eyebrow to my cheekbone, making it appear as though I was crying. What I meant to say at this point was, "Well, Lucy's gone." What I said instead was that she was "no longer with us."

And of course a few real tears began chasing my pretend ones.

Gladys Cheevers dropped her entire plate of cookies and scurried to my side. "Oh, you poor, poor dear." She wrapped me in a long hug. And other than the Aqua Net smells and the crusty feel of her goiter on my neck, it was rather nice. "Tell me how it happened, William. Oh dear, tell me it wasn't a car wreck." Car wrecks were her default disaster since her first husband died in one.

I managed to shake my head.

"Was she sick? I'll bet she was sick."

I simply nodded, my chin rhythmically digging into her shoulder with each successive drop. Then, in an admittedly puny attempt to make things right, I said, "No, nothing like that. She did it herself."

Gladys reared back, crossed herself, and stampeded her way through a pile of nutmeg cookies on her way out the door to run home and call everyone she knew and spill the bad news of her neighbor's suicide. For some odd reason, I vividly remember sliding to a sitting position on the floor, staring at cookie shrapnel, and knowing this would all come back to haunt me.

So it's not as bad as Lucy makes it sound, or at least not from my vantage. I like to blame my confusion and grief. But really, it was just easier to let Gladys think what she wanted so she would leave. I didn't hear the rumor for almost a week. By then, I was ready to believe it myself.

Lucy snaps her fingers in front of my face, then pitches her voice like a reporter and says, "Mrs. Finneran is survived by her husband of three years, their faithful beagle Walter, and a plethora of heavy-hearted neighbors."

It turns out Gladys's eager nephew worked as an intern for the local paper. His premature and mostly fabricated obituary ran four days later. I'm pretty sure Gladys helped him write it.

"Well?" Lucy sounds more hurt than angry. "Did I miss anything, Willy?"

"Gladys saw me crying and assumed the worst. That I was grieving the death of my wife."

"There you go again. I'm not your wife. I never was your wife."

"You know what I mean."

"Just another one of your sins of omission. You didn't even correct your own publisher." Lucy mimes reading from the back flap of my third Handyman novel. "Willy Finneran resides in Nashville with his beautiful wife, Lucy."

I'd argue if I had a leg to stand on. My mother had been telephoning a lot, threatening to come and visit me. Lucy answered once when she called at seven in the morning. I panicked and snatched the phone. My mother mockingly wanted to know about the strange woman answering my phone. While I tried to think of a plausible response, she said, "You didn't up and get married, did you? Then forget to tell your very own mother." I responded with an exaggerated, "Well …"

And before I knew it, my mother was shouting congratulations in my ear. I really was going to correct her, but then she started weeping and telling me how happy I'd made her. That this was the happiest day of her life.

The truth of the matter wasn't all that different. I'd already asked Lucy to marry me and she'd already said yes. I just never got around to making it legal.

Now she's still staring up at me when I feel my borrowed heart start to wobble and thrum.

"Lucy … look, I really do have to run. It's … well, kind of a legal thing."

"Fine." She looks so tired and old. I can't help thinking that is somehow my fault too. "Just go."

"Why are you here? I mean, I'm glad and all. It's just sort of unexpected."

She stares at me, then through me. Finally, she says, "Nah, we'll talk later. When you have more time."

"I'm sorry."

"If you say you're sorry again I'm going to scream, Willy. I mean it. I really am."

"It was good seeing you again, Lucy. Really good."

She nods, then bites her lower lip in that way that always made my knees turn to applesauce. As she turns to leave she says, "See you around."

That was the last thing Lucy ever said to me before she left the *last* time.

Ozena

I hate board games. But I play them anyway because I love my son and love that he loves playing them.

I'm especially antsy tonight though, so much so that I keep catching myself staring at the telephone, actually hoping it will ring. Anything to break the mind numbing, card-flipping, space-counting tedium of Sorry! Just ten minutes of idle conversation with Eugene. Or Reggie calling to ask me out, or even Minnie to cuss me out. I could call Patti and make up some question about Lloyd's health. But the last thing I want to do is alienate my son's favorite person with my neediness. Besides, I'm sure she's busy. Patti's still young and actually has a life.

Lloyd Jr. stops in the middle of counting out twelve spaces and announces he has to pee. I stand and stretch, which makes me yawn. I'm scooping decaf coffee grounds into my own Javatek machine when Willy Finneran pops into my head. It makes me wonder what he does in the evening. But that thought strikes me as … unprofessional, or irrelevant, or maybe a little naughty. There's more to the guy than this ritualistic sacrifice of an inanimate appliance. But whatever that is is not necessarily directed at me. He doesn't know anything about me. He doesn't know if I talk during movies or drool when I sleep or openly discuss bathroom habits over appetizers. Not to mention my mentally handicapped son and my disgustingly fat ankles.

I snap the filter into place, press the start button, and make a mental note to get Spencer in engineering to work on destroying Willy's espresso maker.

"Okay, Mom," my son says. "Stop stalling and come take your medicine." He learned this phrase from my brother, along with the sinister mad scientist way he rubs his hands together.

At Lloyd Jr.'s third birthday party, Eugene delivered a Candyland game gift-wrapped in funny papers. My son has been nothing short of obsessed with board games ever since. Anything with bright colors or spinners or buzzers, and the more complicated the instructions the better. At first the sheer variety of games kept me sane, but there are just so many times you can roll dice, discard, spin, and move your game piece around a board before madness takes root. Especially with a ten-year-old boy who drains the love right out of you with a single smile, but who's unable to write his name or fully control his bladder. And I have come to believe that board game lunacy may just be terminal, so even though I may end up with a reduced life expectancy or wiling away my golden years in a nuthouse, I do indeed roll, deal, spin, tabulate, and shuffle game pieces every night from the end of dinner until bedtime for Lloyd Jr. How could I not?

He draws a seven and counts his little blue man into the home position. He applauds his good fortune and rocks violently in his chair. I clap along with him and cast a furtive glance at the phone — I'd even settle for a telemarketer or a political campaign recording. I draw a four, move my green piece backward four spaces, and wonder what it would be like to talk to Lloyd Sr. on the phone. What would I say? Would I really be able to sustain my anger? Would he even be able to answer the only real question — *Why?* I doubt it.

Lloyd Rogers was my high school sweetheart, shy and lanky and predestined to take over his father's garbage collecting service, despite the fact that the only thing he hated more than the waste removal business was his father. I encouraged him to pursue the things he loved — making movies and creating magnificent stained glass windows for area churches. But his domineering mother, a misguided sense of loyalty, and an insatiable desire to prove the unprovable to his dying father (namely, that he *could* run the family business without running it into the ground) propelled Lloyd into owning a company he despised.

The debate never changed. The father took enormous pride in the fact that he made a small fortune doing what others thought they were too good to do. Lloyd wanted to add consulting services, broadening their customer base and increasing revenues by implementing waste management and recycling strategies instead of merely collecting and disposing of refuse.

"Admit it." Lloyd's father would say, his tone tinged with ridicule and bourbon. "You're just ashamed to be the son of a garbage collector."

Lloyd would try to explain that he simply wanted to expand the business, that there was more to it than just picking up garbage and burying it.

That's when his father would look at anyone in the room but his son and say, "Was my money — garbage collecting money — that sent this boy through college. I banked on a number cruncher and ended up with a tree hugger."

Lloyd's father agreed to retire after his first heart attack, but never really let go of the company reins. Within weeks of taking the helm, not one but two out-of-state competitors arrived on the scene, both promoting solution-based and environmentally sound approaches at a lower price point. Undaunted, Lloyd went on the offensive, implementing the very strategies his father had so staunchly ridiculed. But it was too late. Lloyd lost the company's three oldest customers in the first month.

Two things happened as a result.

One, Lloyd's father came back. Lloyd's failure was all the rehabilitation the old man needed; he returned to his old office, looking a good decade younger, and promptly fired his son.

Two, Lloyd started drinking again.

That was at noon. By dinnertime, I suppose he was getting tipsy. But I was too preoccupied to notice. I'd stationed him by the tub, where Lloyd Jr. was splashing in a few inches of warm water, and tiptoed into the kitchen to call my mother-in-law. If the two men could just sit down and talk, I thought, then all would be forgiven and they could figure out a way to salvage the family business together. But this would require the blessings of the matriarch, Darlene Rogers. She controlled both the purse strings and the apron strings in the family. I was mid-way through making my case when I heard the sounds that will forever torment me.

The noises barely registered at first … A gasp followed by a splash-ing thud … Footsteps, lumbering at first then speeding away … The sound of water gurgling down a drain … A madwoman screaming … The panic in that same woman's voice as she shouts at the 9-1-1 opera-tor … The sirens, stern voices, medical banter … The doctor's soft voice assuring the hysterical woman her boy's been stabilized … A mother sighing in relief until the doctor speaks again, this time about brain damage … Then the nothingness sound of the inside of a faint.

Lloyd Sr. had disappeared; the sum total of his efforts to save his drowning son was to pull the plug on the drain and leave. If you want to know what it sounds like when a baby's brain is gasping for oxygen, come visit me in my nightmares. I couldn't begin to explain it. It's the only sound more insufferable than spinners, buzzers, or tumbling dice.

Willy

I don't really get nervous until I see the Nashville skyline. This foreign world outside Doug's car window moves in silent slow motion, like war footage or a world hunger ad. The surroundings are more sad than scary, more abused and neglected than menacing — windows barred, sidewalks buckled, graffiti in full bloom on every available surface, and lots of people that don't look anything like me. A dreadlocked man in a tank top shares a laugh and a bottle with a skinny middle-ager. A pregnant teen pushes a wobbly stroller, head held high. Children jump rope or toss a football in the street, some simply sit and stare. These are not just poor people or black people or fill-in-the-blank people. More like a whole population of survivors and realists, people who've learned to trudge against the undertow, an invisible current of violence and oppression that makes the sum of this community greater than its blighted parts.

"Man." Doug's voice startles me. "This had to be a safe neighborhood at some point, didn't it?"

"Probably before we were born."

"You scared?"

"You have to ask?"

Doug slows and begins veering toward the curb. I glance down at the directions then up to verify we're in the right spot. But my view is obliterated by an enormous black man.

"Must be your guy," Doug says. "You said he was a football player, right?"

"I thought he'd be older."

"You want me to wait around?"

"Nah, you might slip into your Tinkerbell shtick and get us killed. But thanks for offering … and for the ride."

We shake hands. He pops the trunk so I can grab my suitcase and meet my new landlord.

"Are you Joe Carter?" I ask when I step out of the car.

The man blinks once, then appears to size me up with equal parts curiosity and disdain. His eyes pause to ponder my shoes, my watch, my leather suitcase, then he nods his head slightly.

"Okay, good. I'm Willy Finneran, reporting for duty." Still nothing from the big man but another hard stare.

"Well," I say. "Is there someplace to put my things?"

I'm just about to tap on Doug's idling Volvo and beg him to come hold my hand when he finally puts it in gear and drives away. The giant man watches him go, then takes a look at my suitcase and says, "You wait here. I'll do it for you."

His voice is pitched a good octave higher than his body would indicate, but still sounds rusty and sharp.

"No, that's okay. I can manage."

That's when he tilts his head and glares. "I said wait."

His ease in hefting my bags is frightening. The guy is strong as a dump truck. While I stand mute and wait for my next instructions, I'm accosted in quick succession by two panhandlers and a prostitute with false teeth. I lick my trembling lips and look longingly at the door of the mission. Just when I decide to disobey orders and go inside, the door opens. Yet another black man emerges, a tad shorter, a decade or two older, but every bit as enormous. He says, "You must be Willy?"

He extends his hand and squeezes mine hard enough for me to see my musical future pass before my eyes. I nod, more than a little afraid of what I know will be his next words.

"Name's Joe Carter."

"That's what I was afraid of."

"Problem?"

I make a confusing gesture toward the door. "There was another guy, about your size. And he just made off with my luggage."

"Luggage?"

He's smiling, but only with his eyes, that are now darting from my face to a spot over my shoulder. His cheeks are pebbled, his dark skin littered with nicks from a dull razor. And he smells clean too, like hotel soap. I don't mean to stare, but the odd combination of grace and power is unnerving. Even his limp is intimidating. My peripheral vision picks up a familiar blur as I hear tires screeching on pavement. Doug's car is still rocking as he leaps out and begins dragging the original Joe Carter out into the street with one arm and my suitcase with the other.

"I just caught this very large man running down the sidewalk with your bag."

"Luggage," Father Joe says again under his breath, shaking his massive head.

The guy who stole my bag simply blinks at his shoes. Finally he says, "I'm sorry, Father Joe."

"Nope, not me, Darnell." Father Joe jerks his thumb at me. "Him."

"Sorry, mister."

He sounds so sincere too, like a little kid. "Don't sweat it," I say.

There's an awkward silence, then the giant man pushes his glasses up his massive nose and whines, "He ain't doing it right, Joe."

Father Joe looks at me and says, "You need to forgive him."

"Oh, okay. I forgive him."

"Not me," Father Joe says, clearly exasperated now. "*Him*."

I look the man in the eye and see he's at least as uncomfortable as I am. "I forgive you."

Then Darnell-the-suitcase-thief leans toward me, smiles, and lifts me up off the ground. He hugs me. He has tears in his eyes when he finally puts me down.

"Guess I'll be heading out now," Doug says.

"Hold up." Father Joe is talking to Doug but looking at me. "You might ought to lose the suitcase. This ain't the Hampton Inn."

"I tried to tell him," Doug says.

I remove a fistful of clean underwear and socks, a pair of jeans, a dog-eared copy of *A Good Man Is Hard to Find*, my first Handyman novel with my To Do list inscribed inside, and a Ziploc bag of toiletries.

My heart thumps a tad quicker at the sight of Doug leaving. Call me stingy, but at roughly one hundred beats per minute, I have somewhere in the neighborhood of 464,000 heartbeats remaining until my thirtieth birthday. I remind myself that I can ill afford to waste any on fear. But it doesn't help.

My hands shake slightly as I situate my stuff under one arm, but

I keep dropping things. I notice the nearest sidewalk crack filled with shards of broken glass, the wail of sirens fading in the background, the pounding of machinery from a nearby body shop, the sloshing of a bottle tipping one way, then the other. Someone shouts nonsense behind the door of the mission. And all I can think about is the sirens, how I wish they were approaching instead of fading.

* * *

Father Joe shows me to my so-called private room.

"It's called the honeymoon suite," he says, his voice devoid of irony. "I put the new guys in here to get acclimated, have a little privacy. And the women too, but we don't get many of them."

The "suite" consists of a rickety cot in the corner with a Caribbean-themed shower curtain strung together with two bungee cords. The bed is made up with military precision, the top blanket pulled taut over bright sheets visible through a series of tears in the fabric. My first thought is bullet holes as I absently finger one of them. I realize they're cigarette burns when Father Joe says "Smoking's not allowed no more."

I place my belongings on the foot of the bed, stare at them for a long moment, then pile them up again near the pillow, using my books to barricade my clean underwear from potential intruders. I wish now I'd brought thicker books. And maybe a deck of cards.

"Bathroom's this way."

There's another shower curtain in the doorway, but none on the actual showers. The room is solid concrete, a yellowy charcoal with hairline cracks and fissures. At least the toilets have stalls, but apparently no locks.

"Can't seem to keep latches on these doors." He points to a grungy flap of duct tape hanging from the inside of the stall. I peer inside, pleasantly surprised to see a normal (and surprisingly clean) commode. Toilet paper dangles from inverted paint rollers.

I pinch the duct tape, checking for stickiness. "I suppose we have to check our modesty at the door, eh?"

"You'd be surprised. Folks pretty much stay out of each other's way."

There's a lone bar in the soap dish hanging beneath the showerhead. It has a hair on it. Makes me wonder the longest I've ever gone without a shower, which then makes my skin itch. Finally I ask, "Is there hot water at least?"

"Usually, yeah. And downright scalding when somebody flushes."

Father Joe shows me the kitchen, by far the brightest room in the building. The cooking equipment is a combination of residential and commercial, all hand-me-downs and in varying stages of disrepair. That's when it dawns on me that the whole place is like this. Everything in the building is dented, scarred, scuffed, shoe-strung, and coat-hangered together. Every surface is either stained, dimpled, or chipped. But there's an understated dignity to the place, as if somebody's trying.

"Don't suppose you can cook?"

"Does cereal count?"

He seems to consider this, then offers the first trace of what might be a smile. "You're hired."

We stop in the main room and Joe points to a pay phone on the wall. "I'd bring my own quarters if I was you, but not too many at once. If you got a calling card, best memorize the numbers. And turn your back when you dial, just in case. If somebody tries to sell you a card, just smile and say no thank you."

I'm considering the wisdom of bringing my cell phone with me when he says, "One more thing." He taps a homemade poster board sign with his fingernail. The paper is scarred and faded, the letters upright and stiff like perfect grade school script:

No smoking, no drinking, or drugs.
No fighting, gambling, or swearing.
No loitering and no sex and no pets.

"No sex?" I say. "Or pets?"

"Like I said, you'd be surprised."

I don't ask him to elaborate. "So that's it?"

"Almost. Don't take anything from anybody, even if they offer it. The last thing you want to do is owe somebody something."

At first I thought it was a rule: a few short minutes after breakfast the men pack up their meager belongings and head out, all but some skinny bearded guy, Father Joe, and myself. I grab my Flannery O'Connor volume, then sit inconspicuously and wait my turn to get kicked out. But no one bothers me. Father Joe putters around and mumbles to himself. The skinny guy wanders in and out, barking orders at the last few stragglers on their way out. The place smells vaguely now of body odor, spilled beer, and someone else's cigarettes.

Through the shower curtain I watch as Father Joe kneels beside a snoring man, shakes him awake, then drops a handful of pills from his cupped hands into the man's upturned mouth. The intimacy of the moment is unsettling. Father Joe holds a paper cup to the man's lips. Then his eyes flick upward and find mine through the slit of the shower curtain. I look away first, feeling like an intruder.

When I turn around, Joe is gone.

It doesn't take long to realize that as intimidating as Father Joe can be, it's even scarier when he's not around. Thankfully, he's not that hard to find. I pause in the doorway of what appears to be his office, living room, and bedroom, then knock on the door frame.

"Yeah?" he says, his voice thick with boredom. "You need something?"

"No, I guess I'm fine."

"You plan to stand there much longer?"

"I hadn't really thought that far ahead, I guess."

"Then why don't you stand someplace else while you figure it out?

I'm not real fond of people loitering outside my cage and staring. Reminds me of prison."

There's no real threat in his voice. But that doesn't keep me from feeling it. "Sorry about that."

"Yeah ... but you're still standing there."

"What am I supposed to do here all day?"

His shrug is muscular, daunting. "Whatever you want."

"Aren't you supposed to boss me around and make me feel miserable about my crime?"

"Good point. Why don't you go clean the toilets then?"

There's a hint of something in his eyes. I just hope it's a smile. "I don't know. They look pretty clean from here. Besides, I'm allergic."

"Allergic?"

"To anonymous germs."

"Suppose I could scrounge up the names and social security numbers of most every man who's ever missed the rim and peed on the floor. But only if you think it'd help."

"I think I'll pass. Anything else?"

"Yeah, keep an eye on Shaq."

"Which one is he?"

"The one who likes to reminisce."

"Does he know me from somewhere?"

"I'm sure he does. But you won't know him."

"I don't get it."

"Don't worry, I'm sure he'll find you soon enough. Just keep him out of trouble for me."

"What kind of trouble?"

Joe thinks about this much too long, as if he's narrowing down a long list. Finally, he says, "He's got a bit of a temper."

Great, just what I need. To babysit some seven-foot, three-hundred-pound, basketballing homeless guy.

Then Father Joe adds, "And he likes to smell the women."

Shaq

May as well get this over with. It always helps to set the tone early with the new guys. I work my way through the maze of cots, then rip the shower curtain back and stare at him hard.

"You must be the badger killer." I say this much louder than necessary, pleased to hear a few of the regulars pipe down, still pretending to mind their own business.

"He's not dead," the newcomer says, defiant but still scared.

"You mean he's not dead *yet*."

"He's in intensive care, actually. And besides, it was an accident."

"Right. An accident." Anyone with half a brain knows there's no such thing as accidents. Father Joe taught me that. I used to think that whatever landed me here was an accident, or at least a coincidence. But Father Joe claims it was God, and that it happened for a reason, what he calls the greater good. And I guess I have to believe him. But I don't see much "greater good" in this new guy. "You know, prisons are just chock full of innocent men."

"I'm sorry," the man says, extending his hand. "My name is Willy Finneran."

"I know. I read all about you in the papers."

"I'm not looking to cause trouble."

His hand is still hanging there. And I almost shake it, but catch myself just in time. He looks more confused than annoyed, then says, "You think you could do me a favor?"

"Actually, that's why I'm standing here." I meant this to sound scary. But either this guy doesn't get it or I'm losing my touch. Or maybe I'm distracted because he looks so familiar. He's not a regular — his clothes fit too good and he's still naïve enough to be hanging on to his pride. He's humbled, but not broken. I'll figure it out eventually. I always do.

"You think you could point Shaq out to me?"

"What do you need with him?"

"Father Joe says I'm supposed to look out for him."

"Is that right?"

"Yeah, it was weird." He pitches his voice low, conspiratorial. "Made me wonder, is the guy crazier than most of the regulars?"

Before I can answer, I sense the twins creeping up behind me. Together they smell like the inside of the Grateful Dead's tour bus. They stare at Finneran with identical expressions, conflicted and amused, both dressed in army surplus greens. The pungent cloud of marijuana helps mask their mingled odors of spoiled milk, smelly feet, and the inside of a dumpster. Finneran alternates his gaze amongst the three men standing by his cot, as if he's waiting for a cue. Eventually the twins wander off mumbling to each other.

"Be careful around those two," I say, pleased at the alarm in his eyes. "You could get high just shaking hands with them."

"Thanks. I'll remember that."

"So I'm guessing Father Joe set you straight earlier."

"Meaning?"

"About what's expected of you around here?"

"There weren't a lot of details, actually."

"I'll make it simple for you then," I say, pleased with the threatening sound of my voice and Finneran's wide-eyed expression. "Your number one job is to stay out of Father Joe's business. He's got enough to worry about without you hounding him about special favors and whatnot."

"Oh yeah? What's he have to worry about?"

"You just worry about you, not him. And keeping your own nose clean."

"Okay, fine. But just so we're clear, you mind telling me what *your* job is around here?"

"Same as yours, I guess. To keep my eye on *you* and keep *you* out of trouble."

"I'm sorry I didn't quite catch your name."

"I'm Shaq."

I enjoy watching him squirm. He stands up, like he wants to try and shake my hand again. I do my best to ignore him, but something passes between him and me, then vanishes like déjà vu or a piece of a dream you want to recall but can't. That familiar sizzle starts in my spine and spreads. The inside of my mouth is like porcelain now and the black spots in my head flicker with light. This one will definitely cause a headache. But at least now I *know* I know this guy from somewhere.

Willy

This Shaq guy couldn't weigh more than a hundred pounds. He's obviously practiced the tough guy routine, but it's more caricature than convincing, especially with all that squinting and the way he constantly wets his lips. I don't realize how short he is until I stand up. Even then, the guy just doesn't compute. His brown hair is a conservative business cut gone haywire, parted down one side, longish and mangy and fragranced with fruity shampoo. His beard is sparse, trying too hard, like everything else about him. It dawns on me when he absently pushes his glasses up onto his prodigious nose that he's like a bearded Woody Allen.

I have to admit I'm more than a little relieved that he refuses to shake my hand. When he turns to leave I notice a tattered *New York Times* crossword puzzle flapping in his hip pocket. The filled-in letters are carefully inked in all caps.

The whole encounter leaves me confused and more homesick than I thought possible. I don't know whether to laugh or cry. And I'm not about to go mingle with my new roommates, especially since there seems to be some sort of argument brewing in the main room. I stand to pull my curtains closed and spy the pay phone on the far wall. I touch my hip pocket to make sure my cell phone is still there. I don't dare use it. Since the power supply is still in my suitcase in the back of Doug's car, I promised myself I'd save it for emergencies.

I make my way along the scarred drywall to the pay phone, desperate to talk to someone from real life. Up close, however, the grimy receiver seems more like a sewer grate than a portal. I pat my thighs, listening for the rattle of change in my pockets while trying to ignore the escalating sounds of a fight breaking out behind me. There's an ageless man they call Prophet, grizzled and shirtless with a hearing aid looped around one ear. He's bleeding from somewhere, screaming accusations at a guy that could pass for his son. Apparently someone has stolen his Velcro.

I lift the receiver, pausing to wipe both the earpiece and mouth-piece with the tail of my T-shirt. I hold my breath and raise it to my face. I'd love nothing more than to call Doug and beg him to bring me a deck of cards. Or even dial home and replay the four-year-old message from Lucy on my answering machine. Heck, if the university had a toll-free number, I'd call and ask to speak to Dean Langstrom just to hear him make fun of me. But this phone requires quarters and I don't have any.

To minimize the risk of infection, I use the pinky on my left hand to dial the only 800 number I know by heart.

"Thank you for calling Javatek. This is Sheila. How may I help you?"

"Can I speak with Ozena?"

"I'm sorry sir, we're not allowed to take personal calls."

"It's not personal. It's business."

"Great, then how may I help you, sir?"

"By transferring me to Ozena."

"Might I remind you, sir …" It's subtle, but there's a menacing point on the word *sir*. " … that all calls may be recorded to ensure quality service?"

"Is that a threat?"

"No sir, merely a reminder."

"Look, I called the other day and Ozena was helping me. I just need to follow up on a few details."

"Great, do you have your case number?"

"No, I have a coffee maker that won't break and a progressively bad attitude. Now please transfer me to *Ozena*."

Everything goes quiet — not just the voice on the other end of the phone, but all the commotion behind me. I don't have to turn around to know they're all staring at the new guy, the crazy man who yells into pay phones about broken coffee makers. Of course this could prove to be a good tactical move — if they think I'm certifiable, my new room-mates might just leave me alone. Finally I hear, "Please hold for my supervisor …"

I slam the phone down and turn in time to see the grizzled man with a blistery sunburn take a wild swing at one of Shaq's cohorts. I retrace my steps along the outer wall, far away from the jeering and fighting, and back into the safety of my plasticine cocoon.

It seems Prophet's nickname carries as much irony as the rest of the names in this place. Otherwise he would have foreseen what would happen when you pick a fight with three guys half your age.

Ozena

I dial Spencer's extension and rehearse the oddball request in my head. Since he's an avid call-screener, I want my message to sound casual but firm, more like a challenge than a favor. After I fumble the first few words I hang up and decide to ask him in person.

I take advantage of the uncharacteristically quiet phones and pe-ruse my emails — all but the one from HR about personal phone calls (since that one's all my fault anyway). It does appear our former VP of sales tendered his resignation this morning, citing that he could "no longer contribute to the caffeine delinquency of irresponsible Ameri-cans and their insatiable lust for leisure." The word also came down that the outgoing VP's successor is none other than our man Reggie. I knew something was up this morning because his grin seemed to be widening in direct proportion to the sweat stains under his arms. Poor Reggie will never be sales and marketing material, but as the company's most tenured employee *and* as the nephew of the CEO, his title as VP of Something was a foregone conclusion. My guess is that he'll get a little more money, a much bigger office, and far less responsibility. But he'll just be happy that he gets to attend all the good meetings. Among other things, Reggie is a status monger. I know I shouldn't, but I actually feel bad for Reggie about this promotion. Or maybe I'm just afraid he won't be able to handle it. Nevertheless, the void of Customer Service Supervisor needs to be filled by someone. And this someone will be of Reggie's choosing.

I stare at the enormous printout on my desk and try to convince myself I was going to volunteer for this project anyway, that I am indeed *not* brown-nosing to improve my chances at promotion. But I can't even meet the eyes of the Grinning Whiteheads. When Javatek overhauled their computer software a little over three years ago, a tremendous backlog of files was lost in translation from the old system to the new. So the only way to recover this data in a digital format is for someone to manually pore over every single-spaced entry, then log all the pertinent information into the new computers. The project has been sitting dormant in a file box for years. I figured now's as good a time as any to prove my mettle for distasteful grunt work. I just need to make sure Reggie's watching.

I can't decide which sounds more pitiful, the fact that I *need* this promotion so bad or the fact that I think I really *deserve* it.

It's not like I'm poor. But my wardrobe needs updating, my retirement fund has been plundered to make ends meet, and I would love to someday own my own home. At least twice a week I take the long way home, cruising by the most adorable Tudor on Baker Street and lust after the For Sale sign. And then there's rent and utilities, and a son in need of constant care. His special needs school only runs half days and his physical therapy isn't getting any cheaper either. Thankfully I have Eugene, who's happy to come sit and play games with Lloyd Jr. (as long as I provide the beer), since he does most of his exterminating in the morning. Twice a week Lloyd's physical therapist, Patti, will stay after his one-hour session and babysit for us. Lloyd loves her and the feeling is mutual. She's dark and beautiful and brimming with more life than she'll have years to live it. Insurance covers the therapy, but this promotion could afford me the luxury of having Patti look after Lloyd every afternoon till I get home from work. And the poor girl could use the money as well, as she seems to be scraping by while waiting to get into nursing school.

It seems only natural that Reggie would choose either myself or Sheila to fill his vacancy. I mean, he chooses both of us daily with his constant and sophomoric advances. For a moment I catch myself wishing I'd finally gone out with Reggie, that maybe it would help my chances at winning his old job. But the thought makes me feel like I need a shower.

Reggie catches me staring and smiles. I flash him a thumbs up and mouth "Congratulations," which elicits another pink-faced grin.

"So that's how it's going to be, eh?"

I didn't hear Sheila sidle up to me, but I should have smelled her swanky hair products sooner.

"How what's going to be?"

"You're going to play on poor Reggie's affections to land his old job."

"What on earth are you talking about?" This doesn't come out very convincing. I can hear the backpedaling in my voice.

"I saw you flirting with him just now."

"I was congratulating him."

"Okay, whatever. I saw what I saw. I just find it a bit, um, *odd* that you continually throw ice water on Reggie's affections. But now that he has the power to promote you, you turn into the office flirt."

Me? A flirt? If I didn't find Sheila so incredibly annoying, this would probably cause me to laugh out loud. I want to point out that she's the one who primps and preens and prefers undersized blouses to accentuate her oversized boobs. But I can feel my brain sputtering, wondering if there is any truth to her accusations. The best I can come up with is, "You can't possibly be serious."

"I can and I am. And I plan to keep my eye on you. That little detail in the employee handbook about fraternizing with colleagues works both ways, you know. And we both know I'm every bit as qualified to run this department as you are."

My brain fires two thoughts at my tongue: *I'm not sure cleavage counts as a qualification* and *Qualified for Reg's old job or new girlfriend?*

Judging by the horrified look on Sheila's face, I'm afraid I actually *said* the first one.

Willy

10:15 p.m.

If I were to make a list of all my talents, item number one would be my ability to sleep in almost any circumstance. However, I fear my first night in the mission will be an exception.

Shaq just announced that it will be "lights out" in approximately fifteen minutes. That seemed like good news ... until Shaq reminded us all that when the lights go out, the doors get locked. Unless there's a fire or a hurricane or some other act of God, we'll be barricaded in here together like in *Lord of the Flies*. The words of King Lear waft through the cellar of my brain ... "As flies to wanton boys are we to the gods; they kill us for their sport."

If this were real jail, at least I'd have a sturdy set of iron bars between me and the nearest inmate, instead of a smelly plastic shower curtain with smiling palm trees on it.

10:42 p.m.

I hear someone whimpering. It takes several minutes to convince myself that the sound is not coming from me.

11:38 p.m.

I've tried every trick I know to settle my brain down and get to sleep —counting backwards from one hundred, deep breathing exercises, even reciting every Bible verse I ever memorized as a kid. But it's no use. Every intermittent cough, snore, or rustling sheet makes my whole body tense. The fans on either side of the room swivel, pushing liquor-tinged halitosis from one side of the room to the other and creating an occasional crosswind that makes my shower curtain shimmy like a spirit. It doesn't help that the twins keep taking turns passing gas and giggling.

I try humming a few bars of "Summertime" in E-flat when some-one, likely the grizzled Prophet with the Velcro fetish, unleashes a cata-clysmic scream. All the snoring stops, the ensuing silence broken by a few whispered threats. Then the man screams again, louder and more chilling than the first time.

I need to find a few private moments tomorrow to call Doug on my cell phone and beg him to bring my iPod. I'm fairly certain this quali-fies as an emergency.

After readjusting my covers a few times I resort to an old sleep-inducing trick — visualizing all the many ways I tried to position my toothbrush next to Lucy's in the holder. It's like counting sheep, only with warped bristles and colorful molded plastic. Tonight it's particu-larly frustrating though. My mind keeps turning the bristles away from each other without my help. I simply cannot bring them together.

3:19 a.m.

I dreamed I forgot how to swim. It may not sound scary, but I had to bite back a scream of my own. At least that proves I slept a little.

3:22 a.m.

I fluff my pillow, resituate the covers, then roll over. I try to ignore the fact that my cell phone is stabbing me in the butt. But the harder I try to ignore it, the more I can't think of anything but that. I slip it out of my pocket and into a clean sock, then stuff them both into the toe of my shoe.

4:02 a.m.

My shower curtain is moving again. But this time it didn't move back.

I'm sure it's just my imagination, but I'd swear I can feel a presence

Willy

111

on the floor below me. Squinting doesn't help either. Now there's a rustling sound and I see the whites of someone's eyes flicking up at me, then back at the ground in front of him. By the time I realize exactly what I'm witnessing, I'm too horrified to react.

A pair of eyes belonging to a man I don't recognize in the dark has crawled into my personal space on his belly and is stealing my underwear, socks, cell phone, my Handyman novel, and my Flannery O'Connor book, right out from under my cot. At least I had the foresight to sleep in my jeans, one pocket loaded with wallet and keys, the other with my newest toothbrush.

I want to stop him but I'm too scared to move. On the way out, he never takes his wet eyes off of me.

Some unknown time after 4:02 a.m.

Someone (I can only guess it's the perpetrator) slides my copy of *The Handyman* back under the shower curtain.

I'm still too scared to move. Instead I lie there, wallowing in what could be my most devastating rejection to date.

People are milling about, talking in hoarse whispers, grumbling about the fact that the coffee's not finished percolating yet. Someone begins to play a sad melody on a harmonica. Must be in E-flat ...

Sometime after sunrise

Father Joe is towering over me, a steaming mug of coffee in each of his giant hands.

"Sleep okay?"

"Yeah, I think so. Before I was robbed."

He raises one eyebrow.

"Someone crawled in here and stole my toiletries, my socks, my cell phone. Even my underwear."

"You had a cell phone?"

I nod. "For emergencies."

"That wouldn't have lasted too long anyhow." Father Joe points to my wrist and says, "Looks like they got your watch too."

I rub my arm like a genie's lamp, waiting for the watch to reappear. My grandfather gave me that watch.

"I'm sorry. These fellas treat the place like one big lost and found box. If you ain't wearing it, it's up for grabs."

"But I *was* wearing it."

He makes a helpless, hands-up gesture.

"What? I'm supposed to wear four pairs of skivvies in my sleep?"

Father Joe just shrugs, then takes a loud sip of coffee. "Only if you want to keep them."

"So that's it? There's nothing I can do about it?"

He seems to really mull this over, then says, "I suppose you could steal 'em back."

I sit up and rub my eyes till they stop throbbing in their sockets. I accept one of the coffees but get greedy and burn my tongue. It still feels good going down.

"I had no idea you did breakfast in bed," I say. "But why do I sense there's a catch?"

"Need you to tag along with Shaq to the library."

"And?"

"Like I told you before. Just keep an eye on him."

Then he disappears through the shower curtain without saying goodbye.

Shaq

It's hard to think inside the mission. Too many people, too much noise, too many sad stories that try to crawl in my head and put down roots. So I take my coffee out to the curb where I can air out my brain a little better. The mission door creaks open behind me and I make the mistake of turning to see who it is.

"Good morning, Shaq."

"Badger-killer."

"Hope you slept better than I did," he says.

"I did okay," I say, waiting for the blurry colors in my head to zoom into focus. I catch him squinting at my wrist, then notice him massaging the pale ring around his own.

I follow his gaze to a spot in the street, just beyond the edge of the sidewalk. It's a candy wrapper, pasted to the ground by some melted remnant. It's faded now, flapping gently in the breeze of passing cars, an irrelevant scrap that's outlived its usefulness and is headed for the landfill. Finneran steps off the curb, plucks the wrapper off the street, and tosses it into a dented trash can. I have competing urges to thank him and to punch him in the mouth.

I ignore them both as the twins step out of the mission and one of them winks at me. While his back is still turned, I motion for whichever pothead it is to start walking. I'll catch up.

Finneran wipes his hands on his pants when he returns. "Guess that takes care of our trash detail for the day, right?"

He's smiling in that inviting way people do, like I'm just supposed to grin back and now we can become friends. Wherever I know this guy from, I don't like him. And I sure as hell don't trust him.

"Anything else on the docket?" he says.

"I was about to take a little walk."

"Mind if I join you?"

"Sorry, not in the mood for chit chat."

I look past him and watch the twins disappear around the corner. If I don't meet up with them soon enough, they'll end up striking a deal with the first guy who comes along with a bag of weed. So I need to ditch Finneran and get moving. But he's saying something I don't quite get.

" … who's the harmonica player?"

It takes a second for my brain to catch up. "Oh, that's me. I was a musician in another life."

"Yeah?" he says. "Me too. Still am, I guess."

When I realize I've allowed my pride to make me a little too chummy, I take a quick sip of coffee and say, "You got a problem with my playing?"

"No, nothing like that. Could I see it for a sec?"

"See what?"

"Your harmonica." He seems jittery, unable to meet my eyes, like he's guilty of something. "I was just curious what key it's in."

"What difference does that make?"

"Could make a lot of difference." He extends his hand, palm up. "Mind if I have a look?"

I stare at him hard. He's too curious, too friendly, too everything. And I can't help thinking he's nervous about something. Part of me wants to stick around and see what, but I need to catch up with the twins before they do anything stupid.

"E-flat," I say.

"That explains it then."

I can tell he wants me to ask what explains what. But I ignore it and push past him, putting a period on our conversation. I've made the loop around this very block a hundred times, know every sidewalk crack by heart, every blackened gum stain, every boarded window. The telephone poles too, although they usually depress me. I think it's the thousands of leftover staples from where the local rock bands put up flyers to promote their bands. The flyers eventually come down but the nails and scars remain, a sad reminder of what we're willing to nail to a tree for our flimsy self-promotion. But today the band flyers attempt to remind me of something else altogether.

When I notice the twins loitering a block ahead, I pause and stare at one of the poles. I run one finger over a cluster of corroded staples. My mind turns inward, focusing on one black spot on my brain. It makes the coffee taste better on my tongue and my blood gush just a little harder in my veins. The blackness shimmers in my mind's eye, filling with blurry colors. There's something about band flyers and telephone poles and harmonicas. Something about Willy Finneran and me from a long time ago. Something that won't come to me all at once, not now anyway. And that something tells me not to run him off or alienate him, but to get close to him instead. To know thine enemy, as the saying goes. He's obviously acting like he doesn't know me. And there's no good reason for that unless he's up to something.

I look up to see one of the twins glaring down at me.

"You got the stuff?" I say.

"You got *my* stuff?" the other twin says.

"*Our* stuff," the first twin adds.

I reach behind me and pull a thin volume from my waistband. It's a library collection of Emily Dickinson. I had to scrape the bar codes off to sneak it past the security scanners at the library. One of the twins fans his face with the pages, pausing in the middle to sniff luxuriously.

"Well?"

He untucks a crinkled paper bag from under his arm. I peer into the opening and take a quick inventory of Finneran's belongings — a baggie full of deodorant and toothpaste and such, socks and under-wear, and his cell phone.

I pocket the cell phone and dangle the bag in front of the twins. "You want these?"

They waste no time, scrutinizing, making quiet deals, tucking the booty into pockets. I fold the bag around the toiletries before slipping it into the still warm spot in back of my waistband and wait for the twins to disappear around the corner.

Alone now, I duck into the covered entryway of an abandoned auto body shop and lean against the cold cinderblocks. Finneran's cell phone feels familiar in my hands, although no concrete memories emerge. Still, I watch my thumb move deftly across the keypad, as if guided by its own instinct. I pause to study the Recent Calls screen, realizing at once this is what I was looking for. I'm not sure what I was expecting, but I'm surprised to see the same contacts over and over, as if he only knows six people, none of whom seem to have a last name.

I scroll back to the first number, labeled simply "Derrick," and wait for my nerves to subside. I peer around the corner of my alcove one last time, then sit back and hit the Send button.

With each ring my throat gets tighter and my mouth gets dryer. After the fourth ring, I hear, "Hello, this is Derrick Singer."

I croak out a hello of my own before realizing I'm talking to a recording.

" ... and you've reached my cell phone."

The rest is a blur. He mentions something about law offices and another number. My brain scrambles to put the pieces together before the beep. But it's no use. I'm trying to sort out whether he's a singer or a lawyer when I panic and hang up.

I take a few deep breaths, then frown at nothing in particular. Why am I so nervous? I'm calling strangers from a stolen cell phone. Once I learn what I need to learn about Finneran, I can just toss the thing in a trash can. After a brief mental pep talk, I highlight the next number on the list and hit Send again.

"I don't believe this." The voice is thick and groggy. "Willy Finneran returned my call."

"Hi, um, Stan?"

"Are you okay, Will? You don't sound like yourself."

"I'm not ... I mean ... I'm not Will. See, I just found this here cell phone and I'm trying to find who it belongs to."

Now the guy seems to be talking to himself. "Guess that explains why he hasn't called me back."

"Um, you think you could tell me a little about this Willy guy? Maybe I can help find him. You know, so I can give his phone back?"

"Wait, how did you know my name?"

"It was in the little window here on the cell phone."

"I have to say, I'm not comfortable talking about a client in this manner. If you do indeed find Willy, just please tell him to call his agent as soon as possible. I have something rather ... *urgent* to discuss with him."

I don't have to wait long for that funny bone feeling or the glassy feeling in my mouth. It all makes perfect sense now — the band posters, Finneran's sudden interest in my harmonica playing, the fact that he has his own agent. Obviously we have some sort of shared musical past, probably even played some gigs together. I wait for the specifics to invade my brain, but all I get is more dead space. When I feel my frustration building, I call the next number, somebody named Doug.

"Willy? Is that you, girlfriend?"

I don't think to cover the mouthpiece when a city bus pulls to a stop at the corner, its brakes gasping and screeching.

"Will, you okay?"

It's the same voice on the phone, but different.

"Must be a bad cell," the guy says. "If you can hear me, hope you're surviving. Call me if you need anything."

I stare at the phone, still unable to process what I'm hearing.

"Willy?" There's something about his voice I feel like I should recognize. It's not like I think I know him. It's more the tone of his voice. I think that's what friends are supposed to sound like. Finally he says, "Hang in there, pal. Later."

The line goes dead and I scroll down to the next entry. There's no name, just a toll-free prefix. After a single ring I hear the first syllable of a woman's voice, followed by three incredibly loud beeps in my ear. The screen flashes "Low Battery Warning" and goes black.

Ozena

Sheila stomped off yesterday before I could apologize. And it was a good thing because I'm not sure how I was going to manage apologizing without dipping into some form of dishonesty.

There's a saying somewhere that love means never having to say you're sorry. That's a ludicrous notion. It seems to me that love requires constant and equal supplies of contrition and forgiveness, and grace by the minivan load. I may not love Sheila, but I will indeed have to apologize at some point. And I just hate that.

I use today's smoke break to track down Spencer. The cubicle maze in the engineering department looks just like our own in customer service. The most notable difference is the smell, a combination of machine oil, man sweat, and the rickety sculptures of fast food bags littering every available surface instead of magazine perfume samples.

He's hunched over a capsized coffee maker, his thick fingers deftly alternating between the exposed wires of the machine and the beads of sweat making their slow descent down his bald and freckled head. If I actually had a social life, Spencer would be the only crossover between that and my professional life. He's not only Javatek's chief engineer, he's also the weakest tenor in my church choir (not to mention the guy who recommended me for this job when Lloyd took off). He's revered by his peers and subordinates alike for his brilliant mind and quiet confidence. If something needs to get done around here, Spencer is our go-to guy. The problem is that everyone is going to him all the time, so he rarely has a spare moment to help with pet projects like the one rattling around in my brain this morning. So I have to use a little creative persuasion.

I tap lightly on the frame of his cubicle. He swivels toward the sound, then tries to hide a cheeseburger behind his computer monitor when he sees me. His tic—a quick, upward nose scrunch that makes him look like he just caught a whiff of something unpleasant—grows more pronounced when he's agitated.

"Hey, Spence. I still need that favor."

"Sorry, you'll have to take a number."

"Come on, it's for a customer."

"You see this?" He holds up a sheaf of stapled papers and wags it back and forth. "This is my to-do list. Every item on it is for one of our customers."

"You'll love what I have in mind, I promise."

"What I'd love more than anything is to cross a bunch of things off this list."

I tap the corner of my own mouth a few times until Spencer gets the hint. He uses his wide thumb to wipe a fleck of onion and a glob of special sauce from his lower lip, then stares at it like a murder weapon. Spencer's only known fear is his wife (the strongest alto in our choir) and her crusade to rid his diet of junk food.

"It won't take long, I promise."

"I don't know, Ozena. I'm way behind on everything."

"Yeah, but this will actually be fun for a change."

When he still doesn't budge, I grab the mouth of a McDonald's bag and shake it lightly. French fries clatter like maracas. His face sags and he says, "Tell me what you need. But make it quick."

After I give him the thumbnail sketch his first response is, "It's simple, we just snip a few wires and it's dead."

"No, it needs to be more ... I don't know, symbolic or something. Think total devastation, but with a little structural integrity still intact."

"Sounds like we're making a totem pole or some kind of trophy." Spencer's tone is complaining but he's already making doodles on a sheet of graph paper. "Who is this guy again?"

"Like I told you, a customer."

We stare at each other. "I don't know, sounds a bit fishy to me."

But just as I predicted, he becomes infatuated with the idea at once. We spend the last five minutes of my smoke break brainstorming different methods of destruction. He promises to shoot me an email later with the final plans. I thank him for his help and am about to leave when he says, "Reggie was right. We really do all need to get together for a double date sometime."

"Who?"

"Me and my wife, Reggie and you. Kathleen would just love that."

I stare at him, quite certain I'm gaping. My heart is pounding its way up my windpipe, making my face hot. And likely very red. When I finally find my voice, I choke out, "Reggie said that? When? How long ago was that?"

"I don't know. A few months, probably."

I wait for some sign that he's teasing. When I can wait no longer, I blurt out, "Well whenever it is, I'm sure I'm getting fumigated that night."

"Isn't there a commandment about that?" His smile finally appears, accompanied by a wink.

"Yep, there is. And a deadly sin against *that*." I point at the greasy wrapper poking out from his computer monitor.

"Liar."

"Glutton."

On the way back to my desk, I take advantage of the mostly deserted hallway outside Reggie's *new* office (indeed a corner model three times larger than his old one, but still only about ten yards from where I sit) and douse his hinges with my spray bottle again. I'm quick too, like a drive-by shooting. It does feel naughty, but not dishonest. I simply remind myself that if Reggie ever asks, I'll tell him the truth. Either that, or drastically change the subject.

* * *

Now I'm faced with nearly six tedious hours of processing orders, fielding complaints, working up quotations, and handling all the grunt work our sales force is supposedly too busy to handle themselves. To combat all that, I decide to plunge headlong into the customer database printout. Hopefully that will keep me busy enough to not obsess about how slowly the clock seems to be moving.

I'm clicking through various screens on my spreadsheet when my phone rings. I let it ring again, then twice more before I glance at the bank of green lights on my phone. Looks like I am indeed the "next available customer service representative."

Before I even finish my sing-songy greeting, another call comes in. I ask caller number one to "hold please" and regret it at once.

It only took the two simple syllables to realize the second caller was Willy Finneran. Now I feel pressed to ditch caller number two before Sheila or one of the other girls picks up Willy and scares him off. I'm barely listening as the rheumy voice in my ear wonders aloud if her brother would prefer a black machine or a shiny red one. I quote her a price. I explain the difference between espresso and cappuccino. Then I do it again. I feel my leg bouncing in place and my eyes dragging themselves back to the blinking green light that signals Willy is still out there, waiting, unencumbered, and I'm anxious to tell him about my conversation with Spencer. I quote caller number two another price and agree that, yes, the orange model is a bit loud but quite popular with a lot of gung-ho college fans. This piques her interest, which then sends her into another ridiculous debate with herself. After the fourth time she says "Gosh, I just don't know what to decide" I breathlessly suggest she do some more reconnaissance and call me back. I'm not exactly sure what she was saying when I punched Willy's line.

"I'm sorry to make you wait. This is Ozena, how may I assist you?"

Nothing.

"Hello?"

I hear a muffled voice in the background, a few seconds later the Doppler effect of a siren passing in the distance, but no Willy.

"Willy? Are you still there?"

There's a dull thumping sound, followed by an elongated sniffle.

"Ozena?"

"Everything okay there?"

"Guess I nodded off."

I can't tell if he's pulling my leg or not. I've heard just about every variety of sarcastic grievance from customers who hate to be put on hold. But he sounds sincere, just like always. And still a bit sleepy. But then he quickly adds, "It's your on-hold music."

"It's not *that* bad, is it?"

"Nah, it's me. I have this medical condition."

"Maybe I was wrong about you before. Maybe you are a little crazy."

"My doctor thought so too. He even sent me to see a shrink about my weird brand of narcolepsy. It's this very rare and specific thing that developed after my heart transplant — whenever I hear music in the key of E-flat major, I fall asleep."

"You're serious?"

"Yeah. And it gets a little worse every year. What used to make me drowsy now knocks me out within thirty seconds. Dr. Shoemaker said something about selective psychosomatic sleep disorder and recommended a professional counselor."

"Wait, go back. Did you say heart transplant?"

"Yeah, when I was fourteen."

A dozen questions romp through my mind. But I don't want to interrupt Willy's story. "Sorry," he says, "you probably don't have time for all this nonsense."

"It's fascinating."

"Well, I talked pretty much nonstop through the first two sessions, typical shrink stuff about my fears and my childhood and all that. But in our third meeting she produced a small jam box and asked to see a demonstration. All I remember is the first eight bars of Mozart's E-flat Symphony. She did this four more times."

"Put you to sleep in her office?"

"Yep. She called them 'clinical observations.' Then she suggested we increase to two-hour sessions, claiming we were on the brink of a major breakthrough. I asked her what kind of breakthrough and she just smiled and handed me an invoice. For some strange reason I paid it."

"That sounds a little shady to me."

"That's what I thought. And since my insurance only covered half of the ninety bucks per one-hour session, I decided to act on my suspicions. I mean, what could she possibly be observing for forty-five minutes three times per week while I was napping on her sofa? So on the next session I wore studio quality earplugs and faked like I was asleep. That's when I discovered her scam. She'd put me to sleep and then ignore me to pursue her own passions — cribbing ideas from an enormous library of self-help books to create her own philosophy of self-improvement. She was so focused on her work that she never heard me sneak up behind her. She freaked. My earplugs dulled her screeching. But I got the gist of it. She cursed my unprofessionalism, calling me a fake and a fraud and pervert, then insisted I leave her office and never come back. Two weeks later I received another invoice, which I promptly did *not* pay."

I don't realize I've forgotten where I am and what I'm supposed be doing until I hear myself laughing. I abruptly cut it off and attempt to restore some semblance of professionalism back into my tone. "So was there something I can help you with today?"

"You already did."

I realize now I never got around to telling him about Spencer's plans for killing his coffee maker. Guess I don't want to ruin the surprise. Plus I think I just heard Reggie's hinges squealing.

"So what about you?" he says. "Do you have any good shrink stories?"

"Define *good*."

"Pretty much anything you can tell me that makes me feel a little more normal."

"Well, my guy wasn't a shrink, more like a Christian counselor that I couldn't seem to please."

"Meaning?"

"He steered every session toward trying to make me admit that I was blaming myself for something bad that had happened. A couple of somethings, actually. But I wasn't blaming myself. I was blaming God. But the poor guy was young and just didn't know what to do with that."

"So who are you blaming now?"

"You."

"Me?"

"Yeah, 'cause if you keep distracting me I'm going to lose my job ... unless I can interest you in a countertop cream dispenser or perhaps a variable speed grinder?"

Willy

I planned to use all my newfound free time at the mission working on ideas for a new novel. But it's not really considered free time when you're busy feeling sorry for yourself, fantasizing about escaping the mission, wondering if your favorite students might actually be missing your lectures, or obsessing about toothbrushes or coffee makers or talking to Ozena again. I'm staring at the heading on an otherwise blank page in my notebook when I sense Father Joe's looming presence just outside the shower curtain.

"Guess you ran out, huh?" Father Joe says.

I have no idea what he's talking about until he points at the two lonely words on the page that have been mocking me for the better part of an hour: New Ideas.

"It's hard to think in here." I don't mention that it's also nearly impossible to sleep, eat more than a few bites at a time, or to recalibrate my bladder and bowels to life in the mission.

"Maybe I can help." I try not to groan. I would never have guessed this guy to be the type to accost writers with all his awesome, can't-miss story ideas. "Got a little job for you."

"Oh?"

"You any good in the kitchen?"

"You already asked me that."

"Oh yeah? What did you tell me?"

"That I do okay with cereal and milk, as long as we're using disposable bowls."

"It's a start, follow me."

"Really—" I close my notebook, tuck it under my pillow, and follow Joe across the main room. "I'd be much better suited to sweep floors or maybe tutor some of the guys to get their GED or something."

Without turning he says, "Not a bad idea. Come back and see me when the dishes are done and we'll talk about it."

I make a mental note to aggressively avoid him when I get the dishes done. Maybe tomorrow I'll pack my stuff up and follow some of the other guys around the streets of Nashville.

But I know myself better than that.

Joe retrieves a soiled apron from atop a pile of dirty breakfast dishes. He flips the power switch on a rickety stainless steel dishma-chine. "Ever work one of these things?"

"Once," I say. "When I was researching a book."

"See? This'll be good for your creativity. Bet you'll have plenty of ideas for your little notebook once you work up a good sweat. What do they say? An idle mind is the devil's workbench?"

"Work*shop*," I say, failing to consider the wisdom of correcting a man twice my size.

He doesn't seem to notice or care, as he pulls a plastic dish rack from an overhead shelf and stations it at the mouth of the dishwasher. The overhead sprayer leaks and splashes all over his shirt as he rinses a few glasses and loads them onto the rack. "See?" he says. "Nothing to it."

The voice in my head says, *If it's so easy then, why don't you do it?* Father Joe narrows his eyes at me, as if reading my mind. Somehow I discover my real voice and say, "Looks simple enough."

He steps aside, a silent invitation to take over. When I don't move, he puts his massive hand on my arm and tugs. The first sensation is his warm and gentle touch. But that's quickly eclipsed by his power. Sometime between my third and fourth rack, Father Joe disappears. I do some quick math and realize I only have about a dozen more. When he comes back an hour later with Shaq in tow, I realize I do indeed have a job around here. It appears I'm now a part-time cook and full-time dishwasher. Before the last rack of dishes is dry I find myself chopping vegetables over a disfigured cutting board. I manage to nibble a full meal's worth of food while prepping the salad, baked potatoes, and chicken breasts. I watch the rest of the men eat from the doorway of the kitchen, trying to quell the pride welling up inside me against my will. I do not want to find a silver lining here. I want to simply do my time and get back to my life. Which, as it turns out, is all about washing more and more dishes. As soon as Shaq dispenses the last of the generic lemon cookies, he squints at me and says, "Better get busy. Dinner dishes don't wash themselves."

* * *

So this is my new existence. Shaq wakes me up every morning at six, then follows me around the makeshift kitchen barking orders at Darnell and me but refusing to get his own hands dirty. His idea of helping seems to be sitting and working crossword puzzles.

"Hey, Shaq, any chance I could get a pair of gloves for this job?"

"Darnell?" He yells this over his shoulder, his voice already riddled with laughter. "Pretty boy's afraid he'll get dish pan hands."

"Tell him we use Palmolive."

They share another laugh at my expense, then Shaq elbows me out of the way. "I'll finish up. You got a visitor."

For one exhilarating moment I think Lucy found me here somehow. But then I see Doug's bulky form by the main entrance. He's holding a small duffel bag, his trademark grin abnormally tight as he watches a handful of men pack up the sum total of their earthly possessions and file out.

It seems the average day of the homeless man is not primarily accosting strangers with panhandling scams, but rather a lot of walking and waiting and foraging. Some are in denial and some don't care, but they all seem to know what's coming—derangement, affliction, addiction, or some sad combination of outcomes. I was surprised to learn how many of these guys have jobs. Maybe it's the way Father Joe runs things, but I've yet to be approached by a single drunk or find any dirty syringes lying around. The mission serves breakfast for anyone who spends the night and dinner for anyone who plans to. Cots and bedding and heat and air conditioning are free. Rumor has it that Father Joe used to incorporate short sermons and prayers and even some sort of confessional from time to time. But so far he seems more interested in sitting by the phone and staring at the walls.

Doug extends his hand in greeting, but we end up in an awkward hug. That's when Prophet approaches Doug, rubs his chin thoughtfully, then shouts, "My Velcro! Have you seen it?"

Doug pats his pockets, pretends to look through the gym bag, then puts his giant hand on the man's scrawny shoulder. Doug looks the man in the eye and says, "Not today, but I'll keep looking."

"Bless you," Prophet says in awe. "You see, I've lost my Velcro."

"You'll find it," Doug says. "I'm sure you will."

Prophet narrows his eyes, then springs on Doug. He grabs a handful of Doug's shirt and pulls himself up, his bony arms bulging and veiny. With his face in Doug's and spittle gathering on his chapped lips, he screams, "You did it, didn't you? You're the one. You took my Velcro."

Doug peels the man's fingers back one at a time and holds him aloft by his ribs like an infant. He places him on the ground, never breaking eye contact and says, "No sir. I would never do such a thing. I swear it. Why don't you tell me what it looks like in case I see it?"

Prophet pans to me and shrugs, offering an incredulous *can you believe this guy?* expression. "It's Velcro, man. It's black. Half bristly, the other half with fuzzy stuff on it."

Doug cuts his eyes to the ceiling, as if committing these details to memory.

The man's face softens, as if Doug's small gift of dignity has restored his sanity once and for all. Then he screams something that sounds like, "*Sizzleshrimprustbucket!*" and hobbles out the door.

"So?" Doug says. "How's prison life?"

"Everything I imagined it would be. And more." Doug follows me to my special corner. He produces a plastic bag for my dirty clothes, then steps outside the shower curtain while I change into my fresh ones. I open the curtain and Doug steps back in to reload the gym bag.

"Here, I brought you some flip-flops for the shower. And some soap on a rope."

"Thanks," I say, masking the choked up sound of my voice with a fake cough. I still haven't worked up the nerve for an actual shower, opting instead for the occasional sponge bath at the sink. The very thought of being naked in this place could fuel a thousand nightmares.

"Anyway ... here's your mail. I figure you can sort through it while I'm here. Tell me what to pay and what to toss."

"Just bring me my checkbook and some stamps."

"Yeah, right." He looks at me like my eyelashes are on fire. "I am not, however, going to pay your students. That little stunt might be the one that gets you fired. Although it was a big hit with your students."

It takes me a second to figure out what he's talking about — my grading invoices and paying students. I guess I really did put those in the mail. I flip through my stack of envelopes; there are only a couple of bills, which Doug insists on paying and allowing me to reimburse him later. There is one bit of good news at the bottom, namely, my pay stub. But even that's short-lived, making me wonder how many of those I have left.

Doug says, "Anything else you can think of you need?"

"How about a deck of cards? And I could use a new cell phone too."

"Probably just get stolen again."

"Okay then, how about a book of crossword puzzles? Hard ones."

"I thought you hated those things."

"They're not for me. Oh, and if you can swing it, how about one of those tiny iPods with some E-flat songs loaded into it?"

"Not sleeping, eh?"

"Nope."

"Sorry, man. That's rough." He looks around the room again as if waiting for inspiration, or some answer that refuses to show itself. "I guess I'd better get to class then."

"Has the dean figured out a way to fire me yet?"

"He's making noise. And I hear he has his lawyers looking into it. But I'm rallying support. By the time he's ready to pull the trigger, he may have to fire half the English department."

"Thanks, Doug. But don't do anything stupid. Maggie will shoot you if you lose your job over me. Especially with the stork on the way to your doorstep."

"Speaking of doorsteps, the UPS man left a few delivery notices. From Javaland or some such nonsense."

"Really?" I hate the dreamy sound of my voice, but it's too late to bottle it back up now. Besides, Doug is already grinning at whatever it is he's about to say.

"For the record, Maggie will shoot you first, then me."

Shaq

This time I'm trying to eavesdrop. But all the men packing up and heading out for the day make it hard to hear. I watch Willy and his friend duck into the honeymoon suite, certain they're up to something, but not exactly sure what. So I stake out the front door, pretending to inspect the deadbolt for damage until it's time to make my move.

I have no doubt that whatever Willy is up to, it has to do with me. But navigating the cratered landscape of my memory makes it difficult to sort out what I might be forgetting. Willy's clumsy questions about my harmonica were a lame attempt on his part to see what I remember from our band days. The images that do come are murky at best. Although I'd never admit it out loud, my initial reaction to Willy was jealousy, or something close. Probably some latent fear I carry around that someone will take my place in Father Joe's eyes. But now I'm positive it runs deeper than that, something from our days on the road making music. He has the upper hand because he remembers and I don't. For now.

The twins squeeze past me, heading out for the day and remarkably reeking of pot even at this hour. It's obvious those guys are just taking advantage of Father Joe's good will—obvious to everyone but Joe. Whenever I point this out, that they're both brainless and lazy and have no intention of rehabilitating themselves, Joe says the same thing. As long as they're sleeping here at the mission, they can't be getting each other drugged or jailed or killed on the street.

They continue down the sidewalk, shoving each other and making rude comments at a pretty girl passing on the other side of the street. I squint at her hard, just to be sure. But it's no use. It's not her. That's possibly the scariest of all my black spots, the one that holds the image of Patrice, that I somehow won't recognize her when I see her. And it drives me crazy. Over time the real picture of Patrice has morphed into a shifting collage of ageless, colorless, and shapeless women.

Still, I know I'll know her when I see her.

I slide the deadbolt open then shut, again and again as I attempt to corral my wandering thoughts. Eventually I see an image of Willy in my aching head. He's younger now, his longish hair pasted to his sweaty forehead, drumsticks tapping a flurry of polyrhythms on his thigh, ogling the kaleidoscopic image of Patrice across a dingy dressing room. Of course he wanted her. Everyone did. But she wanted me. She was mine. Willy came along and confused her, just like he's trying to confuse me now. But why? Is he using me to get to her? Somehow he learned about Father Joe and the mission and tracked us down here, knowing I would never give up my search for Patrice. But then why would he go through all that hassle of getting himself arrested?

Prophet sidles up to me, breaking my concentration by whispering in my ear about his missing Velcro. I snap the deadbolt a final time and usher Prophet gently through the open door. Willy and his friend are still huddled around his cot in the honeymoon suite. I watch them talk, trying in vain to reignite the fading image of Willy and Patrice and me. But it's no use. All I can conjure now is more doubt that maybe I've got it all backwards, that maybe he already knows where Patrice is and it's too late for me.

Most of the men have cleared out now, reducing the noise to a low murmur. I glance over at the honeymoon suite again; Willy's friend is coming my way. He nods politely as he turns his big body sideways to squeeze between the open door and me. Once outside with the door shut behind me, I call out to him. "Excuse me?"

The man turns around, shading his eyes from the morning sun.

"Your name's Doug, right?"

"That's me." I recoil when he extends his hand in greeting; an open hand aimed at a homeless man too often ends in a slap. I brace myself for some odd memory of a past with this man, but thankfully it never comes. "And you are?"

"Name's Shaq. And, well, didn't mean to overhear your conversation with Willy. But, um …" I now realize I should have planned this better. I have nothing to say, but it's too late now. "Well I heard you ask him about playing a wedding gig. And was just wondering if you could use a sax player?"

"That's mighty generous of you. And I appreciate the offer, but I think we're covered."

"So you already got a sax player?"

"Not exactly, no."

"Then what's the problem?" This comes out harsher than I intended.

"Well, for one thing, we can't afford another member. The gig doesn't pay that well." He grins a big conspiratorial grin. I close my eyes for a beat, counting up to ten real quick, trying hard to hang on to my wits and not lose my temper.

"Look, I play really good. I can do jazz, pop, R&B, dance music, whatever you need."

"I'm sure you play just fine. But it's a bit more complicated than that."

"How is it complicated? You just think I can't play." I can feel my anger welling up like bile in the back of my throat. Somehow I manage to swallow it.

"I have no idea what you can or can't do, but I'm willing to take your word for it."

"Don't take my word for it. Just ask Willy."

"Look, I'm sure you're a dynamite sax man. But this is a band that doesn't even really rehearse. There's no way to work you in on this particular gig."

"Nah, I see. You think I can't play. Either that or you don't want a homeless man onstage with you."

He manufactures a dopey grin. "We do have Willy after all."

"Look, man." I take a step back. For one thing, it makes my neck hurt to look up at him. But mainly I need to control the rage boiling over inside me and not do anything stupid here. "I just want to sit in with you guys. You don't even have to pay me."

"I'm sorry, not this time, okay? I need to get to my day job before I get fired. See you around, sport."

Then he puts his big hand on my shoulder and pats once, then again.

That's when I lose it. "Don't you patronize me," I say through gritted teeth. Then I take a swing at his big stupid grin. But the big guy is faster than he looks. He bobs, then weaves, then his hands are up in front of him.

"Okay ... Shaq, right? Let's not do anything rash here."

"I said don't patronize me." This time I lunge for his middle, but he manages to step around me and plant his foot behind mine. The top half of my body windmills backward and I feel myself plunging headfirst toward the sidewalk.

I close my eyes, dreading the impact. But it never comes. Willy's giant friend has me by the hips, lifting. It takes a second for my ears to catch up to the commotion around us. I'm dangling, inches away from the sidewalk that nearly split my skull. And now there's a crowd of mission guys, a few strangers, Willy, and even Father Joe watching me swing like a pendulum in the big man's grasp. All those frowns look like smiles when you're swinging upside down.

"I won't forget this," I say, flailing my elbows with abandon, but missing badly.

"Yeah," he says. "Me neither."

"Put him down." I see the tops of Father Joe's shoes less than a foot away. "*Easy*."

"No problem," Doug says. He flips me over slowly, powerfully, then sets me on the ground. The surge of blood to my head moves the black spots from my memory to my vision.

"You mind telling me what's going on?" Father Joe sounds like he might like to finish what me and Doug just started.

"We were just having a chat about music. Our man here took an unfortunate spill, and I was just trying to prevent him cracking his head open." He pats me on the arm then, and I'm half tempted to bite him. "I understand Shaq is quite the sax man."

Father Joe looks from the big man to me, then back again. Finally, Willy chimes in. "He's on the level, Father Joe."

"Didn't say he was lying. Just that every time he shows up there's trouble. First Darnell, then Prophet, and now Shaq."

"Doug's a peacemaker, I promise. A real teddy bear."

I should know better, but judging by my lingering vertigo and the painful fingerprint indentions in my side, I mumble something about him being more grizzly than teddy.

Joe releases a long breath, easing most all the tension in the air. Then Doug extends his hand again. "Sorry man, no hard feelings, right?"

"I don't know, *maybe*."

"Shaq." Father Joe says.

"I'm sorry. Yeah right, no hard feelings." I take his hand and shake it.

"Willy," Doug says, "let's book this man for an audition sometime."

I swivel my gaze to see if he's serious, or if he really has the balls to patronize me again in front of all these people. But my gaze never makes it that far. I see *Manny's Plumbing* on the side of a panel van and a glowing cigarette butt bouncing down the street behind it. The irrational part of my brain runs roughshod over the discerning part. And by the time I realize I'm tearing off down the street, it's too late to do anything about it.

Willy

Shaq found me reading *The Handyman* on my cot just before noon and asked if I'd like to join him for lunch—his treat. He returned with tamed hair, matching dress shoes, a yellow button down, and a blue blazer that almost fit. It took me a full minute to realize what was so markedly different about him. His clean-shaven face made him look a good decade younger.

Conventional wisdom dictates that if it walks like a homeless man and talks like a homeless man, then it must be a homeless man. But this morning Shaq was walking and talking more like a disheveled computer nerd.

We're seated in the same swanky hotel that hosted my ill-fated class reunion. The irony crawls all over me, but I'm too hungry to protest. Especially since Shaq says he's treating. I'd spent the weeks between my sentencing and reporting to the mission imagining tin cups full of sticky gruel and discarded muffin stumps. But as much as I hate to admit it, I've eaten better in recent weeks than I have since Lucy left. At least the mission serves protein and veggies.

Shaq summons the waiter with two fingers. The tuxedoed youth appears with a look of well-rehearsed concern. "Is everything okay?"

Shaq makes a tsking sound and says, "Hardly. The bread is barely warm. My butter knife has more spots than a Dalmatian. And you may recall that I specifically requested exactly two cubes in my ice water?"

"Yes sir?" We all follow the waiter's gaze to Shaq's glass.

"That clearly looks like three cubes to me. Willy?"

This is an open-palmed volley, one that I'm supposed to spike back in total agreement. "Actually, it looks like one of them broke in half."

"Yes, sir," our waiter says. "I was very careful to only put two cubes in the glass. Just as you requested."

"Please," Shaq says, making a sweeping motion with both hands. "Just take it all away and try again."

The waiter looks to me for something. Camaraderie? Condolences? Shaq is eyeing me the same way, as if I'm supposed to pick sides now. I shrug.

"How about you, sir? Is your water, um, satisfactory?"

"As long as it's wet I'm good." Once he's out of earshot, I say to Shaq, "Don't you think that was a little harsh?"

"The service here gets worse all the time."

"So you eat here a lot?"

"Let's just say *routinely*."

With that, Shaq snaps his napkin open and drapes it across his lap with a sophistication I would never have dreamed possible. He picks a fleck of something off the sleeve of his jacket and deposits it into his breast pocket, then gazes around the room, nodding and exchanging confident half-smiles with other patrons, as if he's some kind of visiting dignitary. We sit in silence until the waiter returns with a steaming basket of bread and fresh glass of water containing exactly one set of identical twinned cubes of ice. Shaq takes several sips of his water, then orders a petite filet mignon with a finicky set of instructions on just how the meat should be rubbed, spiced, and sizzled, along with a glass of red wine. I order a plate of spaghetti and meatballs with a Dr. Pepper.

When I ask Shaq just how often, in fact, he eats here, he responds by launching into the extended biographies of every man at the mission, conveniently ignoring his own.

"So, Willy, tell me. How long has it been?"

"I'm sorry," I say. "Been since what?"

He smiles without teeth, then gives his water glass a series of quarter turns. Finally, he says, "Okay, I see how this is going to work. I suppose I have to give something to get something. Is that it?"

I say nothing, still marveling at his hasty metamorphosis from seedy pauper to raging sophisticate.

"Alright then. I admit it was the twins or at least one of them anyway, who broke into your quarters and stole your things." Shaq appears conflicted here, as if not sure what to divulge and what to save for later. So he takes his time buttering a roll instead. "I suppose I'm to blame, since I'm the one who put him up to it. I doubt you'll see the toiletries or the socks again. But I was able to intercept your cell phone."

He pulls it from his coat pocket and places it on the table, as if he's doing me some great favor or anteing up his opening salvo of a negotiation.

"What about my watch?"

"If he's not already fenced it, I'll see what I can do to retrieve it for you."

"Okay, thanks I guess. Why would you have somebody sneak under my shower curtain and steal my deodorant and underwear?"

Our waiter clears his throat, obviously as embarrassed by my question as I am in having asked it out loud in public. He deposits our food and another customized ice water, then waits with his hands folded in front of him for Shaq to signal his approval. Finally, he says, "Will there be anything else, gentlemen?"

"More wine," Shaq says. I realize now I never saw him drink the first glass.

The waiter swivels his gaze to me, eyebrows cocked. "Nope, I'm good," I say. Then he's off again.

Shaq's prowess with his utensils is nothing short of elegant. From the elbows down, he could be a professional model for a food network. But he chews like a cow. After his first noisy swallow, he looks at me and says. "To keep you in your place."

"Excuse me?"

"You asked why I'd send someone to pilfer your stuff and I'm merely confessing. I was going to pass it off as a ritual hazing on the new guy. But the real reason I sent the twins in to harass you is to help you realize your place here."

"I'm afraid I don't get it."

"Alliances form and fall away quickly among the homeless. They are a suspicious but oftentimes loyal lot. Some are loyal to people, but most all are loyal to their routines. As I'm sure you've noticed, I've attained a certain level of authority at the mission. Father Joe trusts me. And in turn, so do the men. But you and I both know he always liked you better than me."

"Always?"

"Of course. Who did he call when he learned his daughter had quit school and become one of our favorite groupies?"

"Me?"

"Well, certainly not me."

Something in his tone tells me not to push too hard here. That if I just pay attention I might learn something. Or at least avoid ticking off a crazy person and getting a steak knife jammed in my forehead. I can still see the look on Father Joe's face when he warned me about Shaq's temper.

"Those were some crazy times," I say.

Shaq laughs. "You were quite the addict as I recall." If not for the giant meatball stuck in my throat, I'm sure I would have told him to keep his voice down. "Anyway, enough of our glory days. I want to know why you're here. What possessed you to track me down at the mission after all these years?"

"I didn't track you down. I was arrested and sentenced to six months of community service. This is where they sent me."

"So I'm supposed to believe that wacky story about you hitting a badger, that this is all some big coincidence? Come on, Willy. That sorry plotline might work for Stan and your more loyal fans. But personally, I think you can do better than that."

Did he just say Stan? As in, my agent Stan? This conversation has gone from slightly amusing to surreal. Between Shaq's fancy rhetoric and the way he's co-opted my biography, I'm having a hard time re-membering what's real and what's not.

"But wait," I say. "Wouldn't Father Joe have to be in on it too?"

This seems to bring him up short. Before I can decide whether it's prudent or not, I toss out a trial balloon, just to make sure. "Well, you know us drummers. Practical jokers till the end."

"You never were very good, you know. At the drumming or the jokes."

I'm actually offended, although I've never played drums or been a fan of practical jokes. But if I had, I'm sure I would have been equally proficient at both.

"Guess you got me there, Shaq."

"It did take me a while to put it together, what with you putting on some weight and cutting your hair. I actually thought it was a coinci-dence. But then I do not put much stock in coincidences. So I have no other choice than to believe you've shown up after all these years for a reason. Either you've tracked me down and have some ulterior motive. Or maybe you're some instrument of God sent to test me, to distract me from my mission."

"Which is?"

He regards me like I'm a child, one who should know better than to ask such obvious questions. "I'll play along. Father Joe saved my life twice already. If not for him, I would be dead and on my way to hell. Because of him, I'm having lunch with you and at least have a shot at the pearly gates. So it's my turn to save him."

"How are you supposed to do that?"

"By finding Patrice, of course."

"The groupie?"

Shaq pounds the table with both fists, hard enough to rattle the china and cause a few heads to turn. "Are you trying to be coy, Willy? Or obtuse? I don't recall you doing *that* many drugs."

"Calm down, man. I'm just trying to keep up."

"Patrice is not just the groupie, she's the daughter of Father Joe. And the love of my life ..." Remarkably, he chokes up here, even dabs his eyes with the corner of his napkin. He mutters something else, something that sounds like "mother of my child," but the waiter appears again, making me wonder if there really is a waiter school where they teach them to show up at the most awkward moments. He's about to ask all his tip-inducing wrap-up questions when Shaq cuts him off.

"Make it one check please."

"Yes, sir," the waiter says producing our bill like a magician and depositing it on Shaq's side of the table. "Can I get you another glass of water?"

But Shaq ignores him. He scrawls something in the signature line, followed by what appears to be *Room #219*. Then he's up and headed toward the men's room.

The waiter takes the check and disappears again.

I keep watching but Shaq never comes back. Neither does my waiter. I stare at the spot where my watch used to be, considering a stealthy exit, but that's when I see the plump hotel security guard eyeing me from across the room. My waiter is whispering and gesturing cryptically in my direction.

Shaq's scribbling on the bill and his hasty retreat make sense now.

The security guard takes a step in my direction. The pre-incarcerated Willy Finneran would reason with the man, simply offer the truth in a calm and sensible tone. But now all I can hear is Derrick's warning to stay out of trouble with the law or else I'll end up behind real bars. So I do the mature thing and stare at a spot just beyond the security guard's right shoulder, then cover my mouth and gasp as if a real hotel guest is in dire need of the Heimlich maneuver. He looks away for a split second, but it's enough.

I push back from the table and bolt toward the kitchen. My crepe-soled shoes slip on the greasy tiles and I get a face full of steam from a giant kettle. The security guard gains on me and tackles me by the ankles. I'm surprised to catch myself visualizing one of Doug's fancy wrestling moves as I squirm around like a dying fish. At some point my foot slips free of his grasp and my heel smashes into his chin — my *bare* heel. His grip on my other leg loosens and I redouble my flailing.

When I finally break free, I limp toward an illuminated exit, fully expecting the wait staff or an assistant manager to drop kick me to the floor. But I'm able to burst into the alley unscathed. By the time I realize I'm about to run right off the end of the loading dock, it's too late. I have two choices — either plummet to the concrete below or angle my sprawling body toward the edge of a smelly dumpster and cling to the side of it.

I go for the dumpster.

My hands make it to the lip of the giant rusty trash can. But said lip is covered in something that feels like raw egg goo. The result is both knees smashing into the side of the dumpster before I crash to the ground, jarring both ankles and both knees a split second before bruising my tailbone on the scummy concrete below.

The security guard appears on the back dock, dragging one leg behind him and shouting into a walkie-talkie. I push myself up and hobble away toward the mouth of a nearby alley. My socked foot sinks into a puddle of some unknown liquid. It takes fifteen minutes of navigating more alleys to find my way back to the mission.

When I get to the street corner across from the mission, I pause to wait on the traffic light to change. As I stand there taking inventory of my injuries, both physical and those inflicted on my pride, I sense a stirring nearby. It's more than just feeling like I'm being watched. There's an intentionality about it, as if someone is trying to get my attention. It turns out they are.

"Mister? Over here." I turn to see a goateed youth hanging out of his passenger window, his tanned arm extended in my direction. "Dude, you deaf? Light's green, don't have all day here."

My sock makes a wet slapping sound as I take two muddled steps toward the man before I realize what's going on. He presses something into my hand, then drops back onto his seat. I open my palm and stare, feeling sick to my stomach at once.

The man says, "Cheers, brother." Then he says something to the driver about me being deaf *and* crazy as the car speeds away. I stare at the money in my hand, a greasy five-dollar bill wrapped around a few coins. I let it spill out of my open hand and cross the street. In my mind I hear, *If it walks like a homeless man and talks like a homeless man …*

All my fear and anger and frustration evaporate during my shameful walk across the floor of the mission and into the honeymoon suite. I'm mostly numb now, but I still feel the collective gaze of the career homeless, shaking their heads at their pathetic new recruit.

I try to nap but it's no use. Both knees hurt and my left foot still feels cold and wet. Reading is no good either. At some point I realize I'm trying to pray. But that feels like speaking into the mouth of a tin can, knowing full well the string is not attached on the other end. Instead it lays limp around my ankles.

I drag myself up and out of the honeymoon suite, making my way to the lost-and-found box outside Joe's door. The inside of the mottled cardboard smells like a wet dog. Keys jangle in the bottom as I paw through the contents. Three empty wallets, a dress shirt with no buttons, some bloodstained khakis, several pairs of dilapidated glasses, and exactly one shoe. It's a left shoe even. But it's at least three sizes too big and the laces look chewed and frayed to the breaking point. I lift the tongue and eyeball the inside, holding my breath. When I don't see any signs of life — or former life — I slip the shoe on. Now the only thing my shoes have in common is the matted suede. It's the first time I've felt like crying since I got here.

Back on my cot, I pick up my copy of *The Handyman* and flip to the author photo on the back flap. The guy who thought he could write, so clever and proud and full of promise. He knew he wouldn't live forever but didn't care. But not only was that guy wrong, he tricked me. *That's* why he's smirking. I bought his hype and now I'm sitting in a homeless shelter with my heart winding down its final year, thoroughly disgusted by the hardback version of what will no doubt become my legacy — a virtually unreadable fairy tale about a guy who relies on spare parts to solve the mystery and get the girl.

But I haven't solved anything and I don't have the girl. And my only useful spare part is the blue suede Puma sneaker dwarfing my soggy left foot.

Soon I'm staring at the handwritten words on the inside cover.

Things to Do before I Die

    √ Buy my grandparents' house.

    — Play the perfect guitar solo to "Round Midnight."

    — Find Jesus again.

    — Learn to smoke a pipe.

    — Write (and hopefully publish) a serious novel.

    — Fall in love.

    — Kill the espresso maker (pending).

    — Find my toothbrush and if Lucy took it, find out why (in case anyone reads this after I'm gone, I do indeed brush my teeth every day, I'm talking about the green one I lost about the same time I lost Lucy).

    — Fall in love ... for real this time.

    — Spend some meaningful time with a kid, see if you can actually learn something.

    — Find Jesus again and ask Him what He was thinking.

    — Figure out the difference between a walrus, a seal, and a sea lion without having to consult the Internet.

    — Get in an argument (on purpose) and win.

    √ Go for a ride in a helicopter.

    — Fall in love for real and get married?

   __ Never bungee jump, not even once.

   __ Never sell the house I grew up in.

   __ Never discover a "favorite TV show" and/or plan to watch it every week.

   __ Never own an alarm clock or play Hot Potato.

   __ Either start doing the stuff on the list or throw it away.

I consider scratching that last one off the list too. Instead I close the book, get up off my cot, and walk to the nearest bus stop. My foot slips and slides inside its new home and I have to concentrate on each step to keep from tripping. I take the first available seat and watch my city through the murky, tinted window. There are so many people, all moving, striving, pushing, pulling — and for what exactly? *More?* I have a sudden urge to climb up on top of the bus with a megaphone and warn them that *more* is an illusion because there's never enough, that the new car smell will eventually fade, and that there will always be a better mousetrap. What you really want, I would tell them, is what you already have. But I don't need a megaphone. I'm just homesick.

According to the digital clock above the driver, the trip takes fourteen minutes. I enter through the emergency room, maybe not the saddest room in the hospital, but definitely the most bleak. The trauma is still fresh, mystifying, undiagnosed.

The maze of corridors hasn't really changed in years. I hear the same footfalls, pass the same grim faces, hear the same medical chatter and intercom blasts, breathe the same antiseptic air, follow the same signs to the same hospital cafeteria. The plastic tray is still damp and the spoon's handle deformed, like the silhouette of a broken nose. I make my way down the serving line, ignoring the bored questions from the nice ladies. No, I don't care for an entrée. No salad or coffee or shepherd's pie for me. I would *love* some banana pudding, but I don't see any and she doesn't ask.

I make my way to the saucers of fruit Jell-O, small square slabs that jiggle when you move them from the stainless steel counter to the tray. That jiggling always makes me smile, even when I don't feel like it. Which, I guess, is every time.

The cashier stares at my mismatched shoes for a moment, then looks up in surprise, her gold tooth gleaming when she smiles.

"That all for you today? Seven plates of Jell-O?"

"That's all they had," I say fishing for my money clip.

"You want we should make some more? I can ask."

"No, thank you. Seven is plenty."

We swap paper for coins, then she meets my eye and says, "Feel better, okay?"

"I will."

Ozena

I should know better than to bring my Javatek work home. With a highlighter in one hand and a tepid cup of tea in the other, I'm staring at the enormous printout in my lap, but the lines just run together in a liquid haze.

Lloyd Jr. is at the table slurping hot cocoa. Every wet sip is like marking time. So rather than using what little time I have left before the next interruption, I end up focusing on my son — and, let's face it, resenting his complete emotional dependence on me. Lloyd stopped taking naps years ago — the death knell of free time for Mommy. Working on anything but board games or dinner is all but impossible around Lloyd. Anything less than my constant attention seems to further addle his already fragile psyche.

I drain the last of my tea and bite down on the heel of the yellow marker. It helps; the words on the page come into focus and I'm able to find three suspicious entries in a row. But before the ink has dried on the page, Lloyd says, "Mom?"

"What is it, honey?"

"My chocolate is gone."

"What did Mommy say?"

"You said we could play Monopoly today."

"I said we could play *after* I finished my work."

"Oh."

My tone carries enough threat to at least make him think twice about interrupting again. My goal isn't to scare him into behaving; I want him to learn. But now I'll be thinking about that instead of actually doing my work. I highlight another entry near the bottom of one page. But when I turn to the next, the rustling paper reminds Lloyd that he's alone on one side of the room and I'm on the other.

"Mommy?"

"What is it now, Lloyd?"

"Are you finished with your work yet?"

"No, Lloyd. Now please either work on your colors or your blocks."

"But I'm ready to play Monopoly now."

"Well I've already told you, I'm not!"

"Okay ... well, we could play Clue instead if you want."

I press the highlighter on the printout hard enough to dent the page. "Lloyd, would you please just sit there and do what Mommy asked for fifteen minutes?"

"Yes, Mommy."

As soon as I hear the tremor in his voice I know I won't be getting any work done. But I don't care. Despicable mother or not, now I just want to sit here in the cruel silence I created and feel sorry for myself. I recap the pen quietly, press my aching head into a couch pillow, and savor my ill-deserved peace and quiet.

It's no use. Lloyd has started rocking now. The low hum will follow shortly. After that he'll grow more and more agitated until I either engage him in play or he has a complete meltdown. For just one day, however, I would give anything to tap into the part of his brain that understands reason. I know it's in there, only that it's broken and beyond repair. I know it's selfish and pointless and borderline pathetic, but I want so badly for him to see and understand how close I am to melting down too. But he never will. And it's not his fault.

When Lloyd's rumblings grow more erratic, I slump further into the sofa. I close my eyes and try to pray for something, anything really. His humming and shaking are more intense now, their source indecipherable. I can't tell if it's just Lloyd, or if it's me or the walls or some agitated fault line snaking its way under the apartment building.

Then several things happen all at once, none of them good.

Lloyd calls my name again. I pretend not to hear, pretend I'm somewhere far away. My son then alternates between grunting and rocking his chair up on two legs. That's when I hear the voice of the crazy woman telling her only begotten son to please calm down, to leave her alone for just five minutes, to *Just. Shut. Up.*

Something inside my son breaks open and he begins to cry. He's weeping actually, like he did before the accident. I pull my wretched self up off the couch and run to his side. I stop inches away from him, my outstretched arms hovering uselessly in the space around him. Lloyd cannot bear to be touched when he gets like this. So I'm forced to stand at a distance, as if he's on fire, and try to comfort him with words. But it was my words that made him this way. And I can't take them back.

The next sound is metallic. A key in the lock and the hinges squealing open. My brother is by my side in an instant. When he puts his arm around my shoulders, I turn and melt into him. My weeping sounds like Lloyd's now, only sadder. Because this is all my doing. I've broken the heart of my already broken boy.

At some point, Eugene eases me down onto the sofa, then sits opposite Lloyd at the table, speaking to him in a soothing voice. His words are hushed, calm. They're exactly what Lloyd needs, but what I couldn't give him. I realize I'm calming down in direct proportion to my son and have slipped into some half-waking state. That's when I hear the shuffling, followed by the gentle proddings of my kid brother.

When I make my way to the table I see my son engaged in a game of solitaire.

"What is this?"

"Solitaire." Lloyd's voice is matter-of-fact, with no trace of the hurt I inflicted or the anger I deserve.

"Where did you learn that?"

"Levi taught me."

"Yeah," Eugene says. "Really calms him down, you know?"

All at once, the pressure comes roiling out from inside me again. I'm like a teakettle about to scream. "When were you going to tell me about it?"

"I don't know. I figured you already knew."

"You thought I knew?"

Eugene flinches. He raises one arm as if to fend off blows.

"What I know is that if I don't pay constant attention to Lloyd, he gets all rattled and crazy, which then makes me all rattled and crazy!"

"Is that really such a bad thing?" he says. "You put so much pressure on yourself to always keep it together. I think it's probably a good thing for you to flip your lid every now and then. Sure didn't do him any harm."

And my brother is right. Lloyd Jr. is rocking gently in his seat now, studying the piles of cards before him, his emotional collapse all but forgotten. The sight of my son entertaining himself ties a fierce knot in my throat and floods my cheeks with tears. When Eugene sees me crying, he rolls his eyes as only kid brothers can do.

I punch him in the arm, which he promptly exaggerates, using both hands to keep from toppling in his chair. Lloyd sees this and cracks up. He pounds the table and points at my wounded brother struggling to keep his balance.

It's contagious. Eugene is laughing too.

My reaction is a bit more hysterical. I'm a quaking mess, unable to tell where the laughing stops and the weeping starts.

Willy

I haven't slept more than fifteen minutes at a time since my first night here. It's been nearly a month now, but it feels like six. Every cough, scuffle, scrape, or murmur startles me awake again. The snoring is relentless, a tortured nasal refrain. My arm ends up cramping as I hug the pillow and squint through the crack in my shower curtain, convinced that someone else will crawl through and do something unmentionable to me. My greatest reprieve comes from Shaq's dulcet, E-flat harmonica serenades. But ever since he realized how therapeutic I find his music, he hardly ever plays anymore. So I do most of my sleeping during the day. Until today, that is.

Father Joe materializes outside my shower curtain with a funny look on his face. He parts the curtain and mimes a request to sit by me on the cot. I sit up and scoot to one side, not sure what to do with the oppressive intimacy of the man. Then all at once I know what's coming — the hotel security guard somehow tracked me down and now I get to leave here and go to real jail.

"So how you holding up?" he says.

"I'm getting by, I guess. I don't cry myself to sleep at night, if that's what you mean."

"Shaq tells me you ain't sleeping much at all nights."

"No, not much."

"What are you afraid's gonna happen? Most of these men are too scrawny and diseased to bother you much."

"Most, but not all."

He nods, still staring ahead at nothing. His lips seem to be working something out. "Tell me something," he says. "You think you belong here?"

"I don't know. I'm sure I deserve it."

"Nah, this ain't what you deserve. Not even close."

"Thanks."

He makes that snorting, bottled-up sound. But this time his laughter won't be contained. As weird and self-conscious as it makes me, I have to admit it's a good sound, thick and musical. Eventually he gathers himself and says, "You deserve much worse than this. What I was asking is if you think you *belong* here."

I'm still confused, but I keep that to myself. Finally, I say, "What do you think?"

"It's tough to figure. You do have all your own teeth and most of your marbles. So it's not like you look the part. But then again, you're about to sprain your ankle trying to keep me from seeing that clown shoe you found in the box."

I feel the heat in my cheeks at once. If he notices, at least he has the good taste not to mention it. "So you're saying that even though I deserve much worse, this is indeed where I belong?"

"What I think is that you're the only man in this place that doesn't think he's too good to be here."

I have no idea what to say to that.

"It's not a compliment."

"What was it then?"

"A warning. If you spend too much more time here, I'm afraid you're going to start believing it."

"Believing what exactly?"

"That you belong here. After that you'll start acting like it and that will eventually make it true. Then I'll never get rid of you."

He goes quiet then, at least on the outside. The light in his eyes has dimmed to a dull gray. He's sitting and staring now.

When I can't stand it any longer, I say, "Something on your mind?"

"You got a car?"

"Yeah." I have no idea why this scares me so much.

"How'd you like to sleep in your own bed nights?"

"The judge was pretty clear about —"

"Don't you worry about the judge. You don't belong here. And a man's got to get his sleep."

"Why do I sense there's a catch?"

He laughs, sort of. It's more like he pitches forward a bit and exhales roughly through his nose.

"From time to time I need a ride. So it's not so much a catch as it is plain old-fashioned bartering. You get in here in time to do breakfast in the morning, keep an eye on Shaq during the day, then after the dinner dishes you can head on home."

"I missed the bartering part."

"When I need you to, you give me a ride."

"Okay, I guess. As long as it's legal." He does that almost laughing thing again. "So you don't drive?"

"Never got my license. By the time they let me out, the world was moving too fast. I sleep here and take the bus if I need to get someplace else."

"You're sure you can clear all this with the judge?"

He waves his giant hand lazily and that seems to settle it.

Ozena

"Looks like Reggie's been shopping," I say to the Grinning Whiteheads, whose only response is more grinning. And who can blame Reg? If the rumors are even half true, his salary doubled when he got his new title and corner office. I can just imagine the mystified look on his face when the other big shots sat him down and explained that he'd have to trade in his short-sleeved button downs, squared-off knit ties, and do-it-yourself haircuts for a few Brooks Brothers suits and an occasional trip to the salon. But he looks good, or at least he will when he loses the awkward, self-conscious veneer.

I bite back a grin as I see him trying out his new executive swagger in my direction. Until Sheila practically leaps from her cubicle to intercept him. She pinches the fabric of his jacket and says something I can't hear, but whatever it is makes Reggie's ears turn red. A weird mix of emotions stirs inside me. The first is anger at Sheila for so blatantly assaulting poor Reg with her feminine wiles. The other emotion is something akin to jealousy. Not that I could ever really muster the passion to fall for Reggie, just the fact that he finds her as attractive as he used to find me.

But then, who am I kidding? Four out of five dentists surveyed would find Sheila more attractive than me. She's endowed in all the right places. The most voluptuous things about me are my ankles.

Reggie flicks his eyes at me, massaging his former hairline with what I perceive as worry. Worry that I'll view his hallway dalliance as a betrayal! Then I catch myself and the runaway romance novel traipsing through my aching head. I wink at Reggie, give him a thumbs up, and watch him disappear into his office. Then I turn and mumble to my imaginary family on the wall.

"I should be happy for him, right? I mean, there's a lot to love about Sheila."

The Grinning Whiteheads smile back. They're not buying it.

"And I don't really *need* this promotion anyway, right?"

Now they're squinting at me from their position in the sand.

"Well, either way. It's out of my control. My work can speak for itself."

My pretend husband offers a solemn grin, chin resting on his hands, filling me with confidence.

"And no matter what, I refuse to stoop to Sheila-like behavior for a few extra bucks."

Both of my pretend kids, faces painted bright colors and beaded with sweat, offer up goofy waves and expressions.

"Although I have to admit, it would be really fun to boss her around."

"Boss who around?" Reggie has somehow managed to sneak up behind me. Either he's oiling his hinges now or he came from the break room.

Now I feel *my* ears going hot, wondering how much of the conversation he's heard with the Whiteheads. Several white lies gather at the front of my brain, then fizzle. I simply ignore Reggie's question, staring up at him and blinking.

"Look, I don't have much time. On my way to a meeting." The way he puffs out his chest when he says this is adorable … you know, in a Reggie kind of way. "But I do have a couple of things I need to run by you. First, I think I may have found a loophole."

"A what?"

"In the employee handbook. It appears as though only managers are precluded from dating—"

An up-tempo synthesizer-and-drum-machine number ignites from somewhere nearby. I watch as Reggie fumbles a bulky PDA from his belt and into his sweaty hands. He narrows his eyes at the tiny screen, clearly confounded by the gizmo, but looking oh so important and proud.

"Sorry, we'll have to chat later. The meeting has been upgraded to 'emergency status' and it's starting in two minutes."

It takes three stabs to reholster his PDA. Then he straightens his jacket, pats his ring of hair above his ears and around the back of his mostly bald head, then swaggers executively toward the conference room. His swanky new wardrobe fits him like a spoiler on a bread truck and I can't help thinking that he really does need a woman in his life. I resist the urge to ask the Grinning Whiteheads about it though. They've been in an awfully affirmative mood this morning.

Willy

Now I know why they invented the word *homecoming*. I observe the reverse evolution of my neighborhood with fresh eyes. It's not so much old as aging, which is a nice way of saying it's decaying slowly. But then so am I, right along with every sagging gutter, unruly shrub, and fractured sidewalk. My house has never been more alluring, book-ended by the Cheevers and bathed in the combined glow of a bruised sunset and a flickering streetlight.

"Sure you don't need a lift in the morning?" Doug says as he runs his front tire up and over the curb and into my yard.

"Nope." I pause to swallow the lump in my throat. "Father Joe says I'm all clear to drive again."

"Are you crying, Willy?"

"Shut up," I say, rubbing the wetness from my eyes with the heel of my hand. "And thanks for the ride."

At the end of my sidewalk, I stop to smell the roses — literally. Of course there's no blooms this time of year. The porch steps are dimpled and peeling green flecks, my welcome mat soggy. I savor the shrieky greeting of my screen door's hinge and slip the key into the lock. The air inside is cool, but not so much as to mask the familiar smell of my home. I try to place the odor, to give it a name or at least search out its origin. But it's nameless, entirely mine. It's the smell of freedom. I breathe in a lungful, then nearly choke on my held breath when I see a dark figure in the corner wielding some bizarre weapon.

My second-hand heart revs, then throttles back as I recognize the two-dimensional intruder is the Miles Davis poster I hung before my exile to the mission. I'm across the room in two long strides. When I yank the framed poster off the wall it brings the nail with it, along with a powdery spray of plaster.

When my breathing returns to normal I step into the kitchen, allowing my hand to graze the pebbled plaster archway. The hardwood creaks underfoot, in all the right places. Even the sight of my tiny bathroom makes me smile. I turn to explore the final room. And that's when I see my wife again, sprawled in my grandfather's recliner. Only she really is dead this time.

Lucy is motionless, mouth gaping crudely, eyes slitted just enough to glint in the lamplight. I sit on the edge of a sofa cushion, anticipating the grief that will surely bury me. And wondering if it's somehow my fault for ever referring to her as my dead wife.

I take her cold hand in both of mine and raise it to kiss her fingertips. As my lips move from one fingertip to another, my sweet dead

Lucy makes an awful gasping snore. I'm certain it's the legendary death rattle. I've written about it, but never actually witnessed it before. It's more horrific than I'd imagined.

But then she snatches her hand away from mine, her legs fumbling with the recliner to work her way back into a sitting position. She stares at me, opens her mouth, and yawns. For the second time in five minutes I'm certain my heart is going to beat itself into oblivion. It doesn't, but my scar does start to tingle again.

"Huh," she says, "guess I nodded off."

"Guess so."

"What's the matter, Will? You look like you saw a ghost."

"Well …"

Her mouth makes an O, then she giggles into the pads of her tiny fingers. "You thought … ?"

"No, I did not."

"Serves you right!"

"It's not funny, you know." I tap my chest with one thumb and she laughs harder. I stare at Lucy, her grin crooked, bustling at the edges.

"So fess up, have you started and won any arguments yet? Found a kid to like? Fallen in love — *for real this time*?"

My mouth is moving in slow motion, but there's no sound, only a dry heat.

"That's right, Willy Finneran. I've read your list."

This information turns me into an hourglass, flipped upside down, with sand filling my chest and head. My mind scrambles to recall the most embarrassing parts.

"Don't look so mortified. It's a good list, just what you need. And it's about time."

"For what?"

"For you to stop waiting for your heart to give out. I always found that maddening."

"Oh." I sense a certain depth to her words, but keep moving before

I can get lost in them. "So what are you doing here, if you don't mind my asking?"

"Just wanted to see you one last time." I'm surprised how much this pleases me.

"Are you going somewhere?"

"Yeah, pretty soon. But I don't want to talk about it. Anyway, that's the only reason I came to the reunion. It's not like I actually went to school there."

"Yeah. But then you stopped by the house too. Right before … you know, that day I was in such a big hurry."

"Sorry about that. I was a little out of sorts that day." She eases the recliner back, wincing at some unseen pain, then settles in for what looks like a nap. "Anyhow, tell me about your day. Just like old times."

"Oh … well, believe it or not, I spent the day at a homeless shelter actually. I was working in the kitchen."

Her eyes open. "Good for you, Will. No offense, but I didn't know you had it in you. What's prompted this sudden goodwill?"

I'm offended, but only until I realize she has a point. I'm the most selfish guy I know. And if the judge hadn't forced me into it, I would likely have gone to my grave without once hugging a homeless man or doing his dishes.

"Just, you know, felt obligated I guess." I congratulate myself for the shred of truth in my words.

"I think that's really great. I'm proud of you. See? That list of yours is working already."

We settle into what used to be a comfortable silence. At least for me. Lucy looks peaceful, unhurried, like she could nod off again. I'm about to take a stab at small talk when she says, "How about some tea, Will?"

We adjourn to the kitchen, navigating the cramped tiled floor like retired dancers, obviously out of form but knowing all the moves by heart. I put the kettle on and prep the sugar and non-dairy creamer. Lucy pulls the mugs down and retrieves the spoons, slamming both the cupboard door and utensil drawer. She takes her seat facing the window and I mine at the head of the table.

Lucy asks about my list, my dreams, and my finances. I navigate this thorny terrain without resorting to an actual fib. Somehow I manage to relate my encounter with Rufus the Lightning Badger without mentioning trials or convictions or the Mercy Mission. When she asks about Jesus I use the whistling teakettle as an excuse to get up and change the subject.

Lucy still uses the string to wrap and squeeze her teabag. I take the more oafish approach, squeezing with my fingers, then licking the residue and wiping my hands on my pants. Then she winks at me and says, "You ever see yourself having kids?"

I nearly snort orange pekoe through my nose.

"Hey, it's a legitimate question."

"It's not on my list, no."

"Now that you seem to be growing up a little, thought maybe you'd add it in."

"Doug and Maggie are having one for me. Turns out I'm a godfather." She doesn't look impressed. "Anyway, I think I need a parent more than a kid."

"We could have had one, you know."

"Are you saying you wanted to have kids with me?"

"I'm saying we *could* have. We did sleep together seventeen-and-one-half times during our so-called marriage."

"You counted?"

"Sort of. I remember most of the dates by heart. But I've also been a bit nostalgic lately, reading my old journals and such. So yeah, I'm pretty sure, eleven times the first six months and five more after that."

"You said seventeen."

"No, seventeen *and a half*. Once we were interrupted by your mother calling from New York, and once by Gladys Cheevers letting herself in when we didn't answer the doorbell."

It felt great to laugh with Lucy again, even better to see in her eyes that she meant it.

"We're still missing a 'half' time."

"I wasn't going to mention the time you fell asleep."

I take a few sips of tea to hide my burning cheeks.

"Don't worry about it, Will. Was probably just the wrong song on the radio. Plus, you'd been up late every night working on your novel. The good one, the one I kept telling you was Pulitzer-worthy. Not that drivel about the one-eyed, one-handed flying purple people finder."

"He wasn't purple," I say, more ashamed of my wounded tone than the novel itself. "And he couldn't fly."

"Whatever happened with that one? I still think it's your best idea — in fact, I thought it was brilliant."

The fact that Lucy loved my serious writing still amazes and embarrasses me. But not as much as the truth of what I'm about to tell her. "I can't find it."

"Can't find what?" Genuine concern clouds her features.

"The manuscript. It disappeared about the same time as you ... well, you know what I mean." I use the awkward energy I've just generated to risk what I hope is a subtle hint. "I lost quite a few things that month ... my girl, my manuscript, my toothbrush ..."

"What? You didn't keep copies?"

"I assume you mean the manuscript?"

"Of course. Girls and toothbrushes are a dime a dozen."

I shake my head.

"Why not?"

"I don't know. Just seemed too personal or private or something."

"Don't you mean sacred?"

I nod, distracted. I'm dying to ask about things she obviously has no interest in, but I'd hate to ruin her good mood. Besides, I'm still a coward when it comes to conflict.

Lucy yawns once, then again, with her whole being. "Oh man, I'm tired. Guess I need to get home and get some sleep."

"So that's it then?"

"What do you mean?"

"I just figured there had to be some occasion for your impromptu visit."

"Yeah?" Her grin flirts with both sarcasm and trepidation. "Like what?"

"I don't know. Like maybe you're getting married or some other life-altering event."

She bites her lip, deciding something I'll never know. "Nope, Willy. Just regular old, garden variety, cookie-cutter life and death stuff. No biggie."

Now she's up, rifling through her purse for her keys.

"Wait," I say, surprised by how desperate I sound. "I think I need to ask you something else."

"Yes?"

"Were we a mistake?"

"Nope."

"Just like that? You don't even have to think about it?"

"I already did."

"So what makes you so sure?"

Now she does pause to think about it. "Sometimes you just know stuff, Willy."

"I was looking for something a little more concrete."

"Trust me, Will. What we had wasn't perfect, not by a long shot. But it ended up equaling more than the sum of our parts."

Then she does the most unthinkable, yet most organic thing I could ever imagine. She kisses me on the mouth. It may very well be our sweetest kiss ever. I'm surprised to see the pools in her eyes. The only time I've ever seen Lucy cry was the day I met her on the doorstep. I reach to wipe the lone tear that dared spill down her cheek. Lucy puts her head on my chest. My heart thumps. My scar tingles like mad.

When she pulls back we regard each other with watery gazes, laden with sadness but not regret.

She opens her mouth to speak, but I stop her.

"Please don't say 'See you around' this time."

Lucy studies me. She still looks confused when she finally shrugs and says, "I was just going to say goodbye."

Then she turns and leaves. I follow her to the screen door and watch her walk away, still amazed at how much older she looks.

I notice Gladys Cheevers closing her mailbox and returning with a bundle of letters under one arm. I'm only vaguely aware of her gaping at Lucy ... and of the implications.

She's midway through alternating her palsied pointer finger between Lucy's car and me when she collapses in her front yard.

* * *

Watching Gladys Cheevers wither and fold onto her lawn has the opposite effect on Lucy and me. Maybe it was her $9-1-1$ operator training. Or maybe she's just a better human being than me. In a matter of seconds, she retrieves a first-aid kit from her trunk, calls an ambulance, and barks a series of orders at me. I, on the other hand, surrender to my rubbery legs and sit down in my own yard. I'm cross-legged on the ground, yanking grass up by the roots when Lucy finally gets my full attention.

"Snap out of it, Will. Go fetch Ronnie and get back here."

"Fetch?"

"And see if he has any ammonia, or maybe some vinegar."

Ronnie answers the door at once, his tired smile faltering as his gaze follows my pointing index finger. I mumble some nonsense about ammonia and salad dressing until something clicks in Ronnie's eyes. He pats the breast pocket of his flannel shirt, nods once to himself, then brushes by me. "She's prone to fainting spells."

I matched his limping stride across my lawn and into Gladys's. Fascinated, I watched him pull smelling salts from his pocket, break the packet open with one hand and two teeth, all while cupping the back of Gladys's head with the other. With more grace than I thought him

160

capable, he revived his wife. She blinked recognition and they shared a smile, buoyant and familiar, and blissfully painful to watch. Two dueling sensations blossomed in my chest at once—hope and an abject sense of jealousy. I looked to Lucy to see if maybe she felt it too. But she just looked sad. If she harbored any hope for love lost, I was certain that it belonged to someone else. With that single glance, she released me from any guilt or obligation, liberated me from my transgression of not loving her well.

"She okay?" I asked rather dumbly.

"Looks like it," Ronnie Cheevers said, casting anxious glances at his formerly deceased neighbor. Finally, he said, "Good to see you again, Lucy."

"You too, Mr. Cheevers."

"I take it you're not really dead."

"Not quite yet."

Ronnie nodded, still all business, fanning his wife's face, brushing her hair off her forehead. As he doted on his wife, I couldn't even bring myself to look at mine.

"Look," I say. "I can explain ..." But when Ronnie and Lucy both turn to look at me, I realize I can't.

Shaq

It's never a good thing when Father Joe closes his door, especially when you're on the inside of it. It reminds me of the days when Joe would turn his office into a confession booth. He claimed telling our secret sins to some other human was good for the soul, that it primes the Jesus pump or something. He used to say a lot of stuff like that, but not so much anymore.

At least I'm not in here alone. Willy looks confused, but not nearly scared enough. Joe doesn't say anything at first, just sits behind his desk and inhales for what seems like a full minute. It doesn't dawn on me what this is all about until he finally exhales. And by then it's too late to warn Willy, to get our stories straight, to apologize if necessary.

"Got an interesting call this morning," Father Joe says. He makes the word *interesting* sound like a disease, a bad one. "Any ideas who that might have been?"

I sense Willy shaking his head. I keep still. Joe just looks at us. He has this uncanny way of staring at the space between people, but somehow making each one feel like he's looking right through them. A distant jackhammer breaks the silence, causing a memory to flash across my mind, one of a woodpecker outside a bedroom window. But it doesn't feel like one of my memories.

"I half expect this kind of thing from him." Father motions toward me with his broad chin. I'm surprised by how quickly, and thoroughly, this hurts my feelings. Even if I do deserve it. "He can't help hisself. But I expect better from you, Willy. You got to know you're on a short leash around here. One little slipup and you end up in real jail."

"Sorry, Joe," Willy says. "But I have no idea what you're talking about."

Joe ignores him, a very good sign, then turns his hard gaze on me. "The library's one thing, Shaq. That's annoying, but it ain't stealing."

Willy opens his mouth, something I sense more than see, then wisely closes it again. What he doesn't realize yet is that Father Joe doesn't want to know certain things, things like two grown men skipping out on a restaurant tab in broad daylight. Joe's had his fill of justice, almost like he's done served enough time for everybody. What he's interested in is mercy and grace, true repentance and a change of heart. He wants us to know that he knows, and that he's keeping an eye on us. But as long as Willy keeps quiet about it, Father Joe won't turn us in. He won't be responsible for that. But if he's convinced we stole lunch, he'll find a way for us to pay for it. With interest.

I cross my arms and pretend to look troubled. Finally I say, "Sorry, Joe. If I did something wrong, I sure apologize. I guess I just don't really recall what it is you're referring to." I know better than to look at him. And thankfully, Willy has enough sense to keep quiet too. "But I do apologize, for whatever it is I did."

Joe doesn't smile, but he does look relieved. "Fine, but the next time you two feel the need to share a meal together, eat here. Got it?"

"Yeah," I say. "Sure thing."

I glance at Willy. He swallows hard, then manages to choke out, "Yes, sir. I got it."

By the time Willy and I make it to the sidewalk outside the mission, he's visibly shaking. "How did he know that was us?"

I shrug it off. "He's like God. He knows a little bit of everything. And he can't relax till he makes us feel uncomfortable about it."

"I still haven't forgiven you for that, Shaq."

"Sorry, Willy." I do my best impression of myself, complete with the troubled look and everything. "If I did something wrong, I sure apologize. I guess I just don't really recall what it is you're referring to."

Willy stares at me, his suspicion mellowing into gentle apathy. Finally he says, "Hey, I've got something for you."

He unlocks his big black SUV and roots around in the backseat. Eventually he pulls out a thick book of crossword puzzles and gives it to me.

"What's this?" I say.

"Just something I had Doug pick up for me. Thought you might like them."

"Thanks," I say. I turn the book over in my hands, not quite sure what I'm looking for, but looking nonetheless. I remember Father Joe's warning from what seems like decades ago to never accept anything from anybody at the mission, that there's always a catch.

"Hope they're hard enough for you." I stare at Willy now, certain he's making fun of me. "So what are you up to today?" he says, trying to sound casual, but it seems forced. Even the laid-back way he slips his hands into the hip pockets of his jeans seems forced.

"I don't know, some research maybe."

"Research? What kind?"

"The kind where you look for things you don't already know."

"Know what I think?" he says.

"No, but I'm sure I will in about three seconds."

"I think you know a lot more than you like to let on, Shaq."

"Do you now?" I play along now, seeing if I can learn something. "Like what?"

"I can't put my finger on it exactly. Sometimes it seems like you're playing a role, pretending to be sloppy and forgetful, alternating between your lawyerly voice and that weak impersonation of a street punk. But I think you're smart, resourceful, probably college educated."

"Well, *I* think you have too much time on your hands to try and figure out things you don't have no business knowing."

"Maybe I'm doing research too," Willy says. "Just like you."

"Look, I have things to do. Why don't you go clean something? Or get some early prep work done on dinner?"

"I can't, I'm supposed to keep an eye on you, remember? Or you're supposed to keep an eye on me. Either way."

"Darnell can keep an eye on you while you're chopping vegetables."

And with that, I jam my hands in my pockets and make a wide berth around Willy Finneran. The weather is a cool sixty-five degrees, the sun lounging behind the clouds. A perfect day for a twenty-minute walk to the new downtown library. Until I hear footsteps behind me.

I stop and turn, clenching too many things at once. "I thought I told you to go work in the kitchen."

"I took it more as a suggestion."

"Fine, suit yourself. Just stay out of my way."

We walk the first ten minutes in silence. Then he says, "What's up with Father Joe? Why didn't he just bust us for skipping out on that lunch?"

"Maybe he likes forgiveness better than punishment."

"He doesn't seem all that religious to me. In fact, he acts like he doesn't even like God very much."

It dawns on me that I'm being too casual here, close to letting my guard down. Willy is obviously fishing for something, likely some-thing he can use against me. I take a deep, calming breath, just like Father Joe would do, then say, "Maybe that's between him and God."

"There's something between him and God alright," Willy says, but too familiar, like he's actually earned the right to criticize Joe. "And I'm pretty sure it's his kid."

Gears grind inside me, and before I know it I'm in Willy's face, seething, but somehow keeping my voice under control. I poke him in the chest, hard, and say, "You keep your mouth shut about Patrice."

He steps back and takes a swipe at my hand, but misses. He's off balance now, nearly toppling into traffic.

I keep my distance. But I'm shouting now, or close to it. "You think you can waltz in here like you know things when you don't. Father Joe and me have a history. I don't care what you think of me or my current living conditions, I've known Joe since his playing days. I was around when he was arrested, and later when they let him out. He and I are in this together. I owe him, *Finneran*."

He doesn't retaliate. He just looks at me, sort of sad and pitiful. "How old are you, Shaq?"

I hate that question. And not because I'm vain or worried about getting old. I hate it because I don't know. "What does that have to do with anything?"

"I looked it up. Joe is fifty-six years old. You would have been in diapers in his playing days, if you were even born yet."

Willy looks eerily like Father Joe now, regarding me like I'm some child incapable of doing simple arithmetic. But it's not my fault if the numbers don't work out. I just know what I know. I remind myself that this is not about Willy and me, not really. It's about me finding Patrice, preferably before Willy does.

"I have work to do." I say. "And I'd appreciate it if you'd leave me alone."

With that, I open the door and enter the cool, echoey foyer of the library. I begin browsing the aisles, my senses alert and hunting. I like to think of the black spots as one big connect-the-dots puzzle in the shape of Patrice. They say smell is the scent most closely related to memory, so all I'm trying to do is trigger something, maybe flip the headlights on one of my black spots. It's not like I think I'm going to just walk up behind some unsuspecting woman, take a whiff, and suddenly see her standing there. And I know it's demented — I get that, I'm not that far gone. I just don't know any other way. And now with Willy showing up at the mission, it feels like the clock is ticking a little louder, and quite a bit faster.

It helps to target ladies about my age, maybe even a bit older. The young girls all smell like mall colors — pink and purple and orange, all plastic and sterile, like they were conjured up in a laboratory. But not Patrice; she's as earthy and organic as a dandelion. Anything grassy is good.

Like a bloodhound, I catch a scent and follow it. It takes a few seconds — and a few long, deep breaths — to come up with it. Baby powder. I allow the aroma to meander around my hollowed-out brain until it finds a match. The notion is vague, but it's there.

"Um, excuse me!"

Looks like I've done it again, gotten all tangled in my own thoughts and snuck up to some nice lady and sniffed her.

"I'm sorry, I didn't mean ..."

Then there's another voice, a man's voice. And it sounds a lot like Willy. "I'm sorry, miss. My friend here didn't mean any harm, I promise. He's, um, spatially challenged."

"He's what?"

"Not so good with distances, you know, depth perception."

"No, I *don't* know."

"Shaq?" he's talking to me now in a pretend stage voice. And I think he might have winked. "Did you forget to take your allergy medicine again?"

"Oh yeah." It takes me a second to figure out what Willy is up to. "Yeah, I suppose I did."

Willy is beside me now, his hand on my arm. And despite how thoroughly I dislike the man, the warmth of his touch feels nice. He guides me away from the glaring woman, past a scandalized librarian, and toward the elevator. It dumps us on the third floor. As we step off and toward a bank of computer terminals, Willy says, "You want to tell me what's going on?"

"Like I said, just doing research."

"Let me give you a quick word of advice."

"What if I don't want it?"

"Then you can forget about it later. If it's a woman you're 'researching,' be careful. That's what landed me in court and eventually at the mission."

"So you're some expert on women then?"

Somebody shushes us.

"All I'm saying is you can't figure them out. And you can only find them if they want to be found."

The earnest look on his face brings me up short. I mutter some strange combination of syllables, an impotent combination of gratitude and sarcasm. He did just help me out of a jam after all.

I sign into the computer lab as "Joe Carter," prepared to produce his library card if need be, then take up my customary computer cubby on the end. I log into the Internet, then turn around to locate Willy. He's flipping through a magazine a good thirty feet away, glancing up at me like I don't see him. I take a deep breath and begin my search. The problem is I'm never sure where to begin, where it will lead me, or exactly what I'm looking for. But I do know my way around a computer. And I'm bent on finding my girl and saving her father.

I conjure up the baby powder smell again, then search through maternity records, birth notices, and adoption agencies. Is it possible we split up over a child? It doesn't compute, but I guess it's possible. The longer I search the less I find, but the more plausible it seems that somehow a kid came between us. And if so, was it ours or someone else's?

"Find what you were looking for?" Willy says.

I ask myself the same question and offer the most honest answer I can. "I don't know yet."

Willy

I have a vague notion of easing into the recliner last night, allowing the ticking in my chest to lull me to sleep.

I drag myself up and out of my grandpa's recliner, then put the kettle on in the kitchen and pad back to my bedroom for a change of clothes. I notice wrinkles on the bedspread in the faint outline of Lucy. She must have spent some time here yesterday afternoon as well.

I retrieve a fresh pair of jeans from the squeaky bottom drawer, but before I can zip up I hear a knock on the front door. It's Ronnie Cheevers holding an oversized brown carton boasting the familiar Javatek logo, identical to the one I opened for Lucy all those years ago.

"This came for you yesterday," Ronnie says, handing it over.

"Thanks." We stand in my open doorway, both staring at my welcome mat. "How's Gladys?"

"Good, but not happy."

"I really did mean to tell her, both of you. But I just … I don't know. I'm sorry, Ronnie. And tell Gladys I'm sorry too."

"I don't think so, Willy." At first I think he's rejecting my apology. And he may do that yet. But that's not what he meant. "You tell her yourself."

I carry the box toward the urgent shriek of my teakettle. I move it from the hot burner to an idle one, then grab a steak knife from the utensil drawer, slamming it shut, just like Lucy always did.

I tear into the package. Packing peanuts flurry down around my ankles. I try hard not to be disappointed when I see the familiar scrape on the top of my espresso maker. For a moment at least I fear they merely polished up my machine and sent it back to me. But as I hoist it up out of the box, my entire skeleton sizzles like one big funny bone.

The machine looks exactly the same, save for a jagged wooden stake driven through its core at a perfect forty-five-degree angle. I turn its squatty body around in my hands, observing it from every angle, until my arms ache from the weight of it. I place it on the table and stare at it until the phone jangles behind me. I turn slightly, intent on ignoring it. But that's when I see the orange glow of the still-lit burner. As I leap up to go turn it off, the answering machine clicks on.

It's Shaq and he's not happy either. Apparently I slept through breakfast at the mission.

I unfold a note taped to the stake in the heart of Lucy's lover's espresso maker. It's actually two pages together. The first is handwritten:

I sincerely hope you find this satisfactory. And if you'd be so kind to fill out the attached customer service survey, I'd really appreciate it. Yours truly, Ozena.

Is that why she's being so nice to me? Just to get high marks on an evaluation? I ignore this lapse in euphoria and read the P.S.:

And you don't have to mention the destruction part; not sure if that will actually help or hurt my chances for promotion!

I stare at the phone for a long moment, dying to call Ozena and thank her. But then it rings again and I have no doubt it's Shaq.

Ozena

I've never been big on competition, especially the undeclared kind. But to be honest, that's exactly why I'm still sitting at my desk at five fifteen when my work for the day is done. What I do know is that I'm still here because Sheila is still here. What I haven't figured out yet is the actual reason. Does this mean I've acquiesced and joined in her tacit rivalry? And if so, for what? The promotion? Reggie's affections? I have to say it feels more maternal than anything else, as if I'm trying to protect Reggie from Sheila. With my brain sufficiently scrambled, I dial my home number. Eugene picks up on the third ring.

"How's Lloyd?"

"Giddy. He's annihilating me in the game of Life."

"I know that feeling." I'm vaguely aware of my voice devolving into a thoughtful silence. But unless he's napping, my brother has a zero tolerance policy for stalled conversation.

"So, Zee, if you called to beg me to watch Junior for you tonight so you can go out on some steamy hot date, the answer is a resounding yes."

"I am running a little late, but not quite that late."

"Well maybe you should be. Who was that supervisor that used to ask you out all the time?"

"Reggie."

"Ah yes, Reggie. Does he have plans for tonight?"

"I'm sure I have no idea."

"Go ask him then. I'll wait."

"Even if I wanted to — and I don't — it wouldn't be appropriate."

"Oh yeah, something about office dating policies, right?"

"Yep, that's part of it."

"What's the other part?"

"That I have no interest in —" I half-stand in my cubicle until I spy the top of Sheila's blonde highlights. On my descent I glance at Reggie's office door — still closed with the light on. "Because I don't want to, that's why."

"But he still wants to, right?"

"I suppose. He does still get that look in his eyes. You know the one, all you guys do it."

"Sorry, enlighten me."

"I don't know, desperate, smarmy. Like you're trying too hard to muster whatever sort of bravado you think will either: a) impress the girl, or b) make you impervious to the rejection. Like you want her to know you care, so long as she says yes. But if there's any doubt, you still need to look cool and unflappable, just in case. I think you guys think it's suave or something."

"Yeah, how should we be then?"

"Sincere might be a good place to start."

"Easy for you to say," he says. "It's a lot of pressure on a guy. We assume all the risk."

"How about you risk preheating the oven for me then?"

"Okay, fine. You realize there's nothing wrong with trying to get a promotion? It's what people do."

"It's out of my hands. If I really deserve it, I'll get it. Otherwise, it wasn't meant to be."

"Excellent. It's in the bag then."

"Yeah? How so?"

"Sis ..." Did his voice just break? "I've never met a more deserving person in my life."

I feel a tear bubbling in the corner of my eye at once. Eugene doesn't do intimacy. So this heartfelt declaration is tantamount to a skywritten poem.

"Thanks, you."

"I mean it, Zee."

"You know, risking a little of that emotion on Lisa might just save your marriage once and for all."

"Sorry, I stopped taking advice from third stringers in high school."

"What's that supposed to mean?"

"You've got to earn it, Sis. You're still a bench warmer. So I'm officially tuning you out until you get in the game."

"Fine, just don't forget to preheat the oven."

"Got it."

"And remind Lloyd to go potty."

"Goodbye, Zee."

"Thanks." But he's already gone.

I hang up, knowing my work is done for the day. But I'm still sitting here in a murky puddle of indecision. I look to the Grinning Whiteheads for help. I try to convince myself again that I'm hanging around for Reggie, like a tower guard protecting the borders of Reg's heart. But even that feels like I'm spraining my few remaining ligaments of honesty. I think the Whiteheads agree.

Before powering my computer down, I click over to the UPS website, verify the tracking number again, then click to see if the status has miraculously changed on Willy Finneran's package. This is the thirteenth time today; I called the local hub twice. Nothing has changed. The parcel was signed for two days ago by someone named "Gladys Cheevers" and I can't help wondering if Gladys is the reason behind Willy's bizarre request, if somehow she'd driven him to the brink of such sadness, then decided to keep the package from him after she'd signed for it. (My mind draws a childish and unflattering caricature of a scowling woman with a giant nose, which I quickly erase.) I try to explain to myself that my motives are pure, that I simply want to make sure my customer is satisfied with the level of service provided by one Ozena Webb, customer service representative of Javatek, Inc. But even I'm not buying it. And neither are the Whiteheads.

My knees pop when I do the half-stand thing again, nearly blowing my cover. Sheila is up now too, the shoulder strap of her purse in mid-sling, glancing at Reggie's office before turning my way. I plop back down into my squeaky chair and hold my breath. She piddles around a few minutes longer, pausing to sharpen at least three pencils, as if the fiscal health of the company hinges on how finely honed Sheila's writing implements are first thing Thursday morning. Finally, she takes off, leaving just me in my cubicle and all the workaholic executives barricaded behind their brass-placarded doors.

The hinge on Reggie's door squeals at exactly five twenty-seven. I hear his own spray bottle, applying WD-40 to combat the effects of my routine watering of his hinges. With my purse on my shoulder, keys in hand, and chair facing the opening of my workstation, I flick off my desk lamp and bolt for the exit. If I time this right, Reggie will see the back of my head and call out a greeting as I cross the threshold. I will shout goodnight over my shoulder and practically sprint to my Honda Civic. But something happens that throws the entire plan into a tizzy.

My phone rings.

Is it habit or hope that has me reaching for the phone? I tell myself it's my work ethic, fielding one more call after hours. Of course I know better. But I'm midway through my canned greeting when I realize it could be Reggie calling from his cell phone, to make sure I don't slip out unnoticed.

It's a familiar voice, male even, but not Reggie. And it takes real effort to keep my professional veneer from cracking.

"Oh, um, hi." He sounds surprised, his voice fraught with insecurity. "I got the espresso maker you sent."

"William?" I hate the dreamy sound of my voice. Either Willy doesn't notice or doesn't care. Less than a minute into our conversation, Reggie strolls by my office. I feel myself bristle a bit, but am prepared to launch my rehearsed smile and helpless shrug, the subtext being, *I'd love to sit and chat with you after work, Reg, but I'm just too darned busy helping customers.* But he doesn't even slow down, just offers up a half-wave and keeps on walking. It takes a few seconds to realize my feelings are hurt.

Willy

When my stack of overdue bills reaches the same height as a box of Cocoa Puffs, I call my cousin and beg his voicemail for a job, just in case. His company sells burial plots and headstones, and it just so happens that their only salesman died recently. Since it's just a matter of time before Dean Langstrom actually fires me, I imagine my days peddling death trinkets and my evenings punching redial. Then I dial Javatek's toll free number, knowing full well that it's after hours, but more than content to listen to Ozena's recorded voice. According to my cereal flake abacus, this is my thirty-third after-hours call this week.

My vocal cords are not prepared for the sound of her voice.

I realize now that my incessant redialing had become a way to mark time — *Dial. Listen for Ozena. Hang up. Repeat.* It reminds me of the week I spent playing solitaire unaware that the five of clubs was missing. It required just enough concentration to keep from having to actually focus on anything, just enough mental activity to keep the delectably naughty thoughts of taking a bubble bath with a plugged-in espresso maker from taking a foothold. *Shuffle. Deal. Lose. Repeat.*

"Oh, um, hi. I got the espresso maker you sent."

"William?" Everyone calls me Willy, but I don't correct Ozena. Her voice is a small pebble in the pool of my heart, rippling toward the edges. While I try to find my voice, I fondle the wooden stake she'd driven through the belly of the replacement espresso maker. "You really did a number on the machine."

"Thanks." I can feel the heat of her blushing through the phone's earpiece. "Are you sure it's not over the top?"

"It's perfect. Just what I needed."

"I'm glad. You know, I had to call in a favor from one of the boys in engineering. He came up with the idea of freezing the chunk of wood. But the stake was my idea. Drove it in myself."

A lump bulges in my throat. We listen to each other sigh for a moment. Then Ozena clears her throat and says, "You know these calls are recorded to ensure quality service?"

"Oh, yeah. I forgot. You're working."

"It's not that. I just need to get home for dinner."

"Okay, well I ... um ... I'd really like to talk to you again."

"You have my number."

Willy

Father Joe is waiting for me by the curb this morning, a steaming cup of coffee in each hand. His clothes look sharper than normal but his face is blank. And I notice his hands trembling as he climbs in and hands one of the cups to me.

"Good morning," I say.

He nods, but just barely.

"Where are we headed?"

He juts his chin forward imperceptibly.

I take a tentative sip of the coffee, but it burns my lip anyway. "You mind putting your seatbelt on?"

He makes no visible movement, just keeps inhaling air through his nose. I have no idea what happens when he's fully inflated, but I know it won't be good. So I put the truck in gear and drive. Straight. The streets around the mission seem no less scary to me now, but no less sad either. Maybe more, in fact. And I don't think it's just the poverty and crime; it's the lack of anything to look forward to but more poverty and more crime.

Still, there's a quiet dignity to it all too, something you can't quite see with your windows up and doors locked.

I recognize the twins on the same corner, one flirting with a gaggle of teenage girls and the other engaged in a cryptic conversation that looks like a drug deal to my novice eye.

With the Nashville skyline looming in my windshield, I realize I'm gripping the wheel tighter and angling my body to pick up any signals from Father Joe. We're approaching a major intersection with lots of options, including on-ramps for Interstate 40, and I still have no clue where I'm supposed to be going.

Finally he mumbles the word, "Baptist."

"Oh, okay. Which one? First Baptist downtown or that new funky one in the converted nightclub?"

I realize I'm hoping he'll be impressed with my knowledge of the hip new religious establishment in his neighborhood (one of my students wrote a paper about it, actually), but instead he does that inflating thing again. So when the light turns green I forge ahead.

"The hospital."

"Oh, right. Baptist Hospital. Got it."

I sip more coffee, just to have something to do. Ten minutes later we're driving under the crosswalk that joins the parking garage to the main hospital. I put my blinker on to enter the garage, but Father Joe uses a thick finger to point to a spot marked, "Clergy." I do as instructed and pull in.

"Don't we need like a placard? Or maybe something to hang on the rearview mirror?"

I lock the doors and follow him inside. We navigate the corridors until we reach the emergency room. It's a mini version of the neighborhood around the mission, albeit with better lighting and higher wages. But it's no less despondent and peopled with those forced to barricade themselves against forces beyond their control. Like the streets, the faces are either scared or scary, inducing or reflecting fear in taut expressions.

Father Joe approaches the admissions counter where a pair of women in cheery nurse's garb look up in recognition. The stouter of the two manages a tight smile, then rivets her gaze on a spot beside me. That's when I feel the weight of a man collapsing on my shoulder. He's tanned and shirtless and reeks of sweat and something metallic.

Then I see the blood. The sight of it nearly topples us both. My instincts prevail and I wrap him up, managing to keep him mostly erect until a nurse scoots a wheelchair under him. Two men in scrubs burst through a pair of swinging doors, tend briefly to the man's swaddled hand, then whisk him away.

When the other admissions nurse motions Father Joe to follow her,

I don't wait for an invitation, but I do keep a safe distance and a watchful eye. With every step, the blood drying on my shirt freaks me out just a little more.

I hear the nurse whisper something about "Jane Doe," then Joe is marching again toward a bank of elevators. I climb in behind him, watching as he punches the number 5 repeatedly with increasing urgency until the doors finally close.

On the third floor, the staff seems to be waiting for him, like he's a rock star or politician. A rail-thin woman in a white lab coat and orange plastic sandals makes a sweeping motion with her arm, ushering us toward Intensive Care Suite #4.

I take one tentative step toward the closed door, but Father Joe simply approaches the glassed partition. Head down, he raises his hands as if in supplication and places them on the transparent wall dividing the mostly living from the almost dead. His palms squeak on the glass as they come to rest. Now he's making a tormented sound, quiet and breathy. I can't tell if he's praying or cursing or merely working up his courage to look. The lab coat lady watches him, arms folded, staring. Finally, Joe raises his head. I realize then that I've yet to look inside the room myself.

She's beautiful — or she used to be. But the beeping machines, the array of tubes, not even her forced gape can mask it completely. The girl is in her twenties and of some mixed race. Joe shakes his head once and lowers his gaze to the floor. I don't know whether to laugh or clap or cry, and apparently neither does the doctor. Finally, she says, "You sure?"

Father Joe nods once. "I'm sure. That's not my baby."

The doctor looks relieved, then immediately like she's running late for something important. Father Joe opens his mouth to speak, then closes it, then opens it again. "Thank you for your help. Now you run along. I think me and Willy are gonna pray for this girl."

I watch the doctor go and am instantly terrified. It doesn't help either when Joe wraps his beefy arm around my shoulder and rests his head on mine. I have no idea what's coming next, so I wait, breathing in our combined humidity, laced with coffee breath and failing deodorant. I listen as Father Joe mumbles and whispers prayers for the poor girl in ICU. When it's over, he unwraps me, looks me in the eye, and says, "Your turn."

For one scary moment, I think he wants me to emcee some prayer vigil for a girl I don't know. Then he adds, "Judge's orders."

When I still don't get it, he says, "Time to pay our respects to Rufus the Lightning Badger."

"He can't make me do that."

"Maybe not. But he can make me make you do that."

"I don't understand."

"Look, you want your license back, or don't you?"

"Wait, I thought you already cleared that with the judge."

He mumbles something to himself as we retrace our steps to the Land Rover, only to find a bright blue parking ticket under my wiper blade. I catch myself looking at Joe with an accusing scowl, not sure what I was thinking. "I'll take care of that for you." Then he makes it disappear into his breast pocket.

* * *

The animal hospital is only a few minutes south. We pass a couple of high-end coffee shops along the way. I stop at one and offer to buy Joe something, but he's content to sip home brew from his Styrofoam cup. It has to be cold by now.

While we wait for my coffee, I try to work up the courage to ask Joe something. But I've broached this subject with other "spiritual" men and it never comes out right.

I firmly believe that I met Jesus when I was nine. I believed in Him and He seemed to be mostly okay with me too. But everything changed after my heart transplant, from odd cravings to my weird form of narcolepsy to my eternal standing with God; Jesus had knocked on the door of my heart, I let Him in, then the surgeon pulled his medical heist, replacing the original with a replica and hoping no one would notice. If spiritual matters truly are a condition of the heart, and I don't have mine anymore, where does that leave me?

All this makes total sense in my head, but giving voice to it gets more complicated. I pay for my overpriced coffee and put the car in gear. After a couple of sips, I abandon my brooding and just blurt it out.

"You seem like a spiritual kind of guy, mind if I ask you a question?"

"I'd rather you didn't."

"Oh. Mind if I ask why?"

"Pretty much. But I know you'll keep pestering till I answer. Thing is, I ain't got much use for Him anymore."

"Who?"

Father Joe points skyward.

"What about all that back there with the praying? That seemed sincere. And, I mean, you run a homeless shelter for crying out loud. I'm sure you could do anything you want with your free time, but you help people instead. So how can you do all that and act like you don't believe in God anymore?"

"I didn't say He don't exist. I believe in romance novels too. But I don't have much use for them either."

So much for gleaning insight from the resident high priest of homelessness. I'm surprised by how irritated his attitude makes me. But then we're pulling into the animal hospital and I can sense Joe smirking at me.

"Something funny?" I say.

"Just you, that's all. On the wrong side of the judge."

He climbs out and I follow him into the second hospital of the day. The staff seems confused even after Joe asks to see Rufus, less so when he mentions Judge Reynolds. Then all eyes are on me, the sadistic tormentor of defenseless mammals. The blood drying on my shirt only adds to my malevolent aura. As we follow yet another medical professional down yet another antiseptic hallway, I stick as close to Joe as possible. There's no telling what these folks might do to me.

We round one corner, entering through a parted floor-length curtain. And then there he is: Rufus, laying on his side, eyes closed, breathing labored and disjointed. He's a beautiful animal and I say so out loud. The white stripes lining his face make him look fierce, yet playful.

Father Joe agrees. "Yeah, looks like the good Lord was having some fun the day He come up with that mask."

"You just said you didn't have any use for Him."

"Just giving credit where it's due."

Rufus twitches, his closed eyes fluttering dreamily, before going still again. A wave of guilt laps around my knees, then starts to rise. Intentional or not, I mowed this little guy down with my car. I really should have stopped and investigated instead of driving away like that.

"You crying, Willy?"

"Shut up," I say, regretting it at once.

Father Joe thinks this is hilarious. The man has a brilliant smile and a laugh that could split granite. He sobers me up in a hurry when the vet's assistant sticks her head in and asks if everything is okay in here.

"You excuse us, missy? My friend here needs to pray for poor Rufus."

"But I don't want to pray for Rufus," I say.

The vet's assistant turns red. "Good, because I'm not sure we allow praying in here."

Father Joe says, "You'd better run along and check then. We got no place to be."

When she turns to leave, Joe pats me on the back and says, "Better get cracking. That little atheist lady scares me."

"But I don't want to. I don't even know what to say."

Joe's stare is hard now, his grip on my shoulder crippling. "You always pray for the fallen, Willy. Always."

"But you just said—"

"You ain't me, Willy. Now hurry it up 'fore that testy little white woman comes back with a needle."

With that, he steps back, folds his hands in front of him, and bows his big head.

"Dear God," I say, not sure what's next. I open one eye and scan the room for inspiration. "Please help Rufus to feel better."

Then I hear the vet's assistant shrieking in the background for me to knock it off. Joe must be blocking the doorway because she keeps calling him a brute and telling him to get out of her way.

"So anyway," I continue. "I'm sorry I hit Rufus. Help me not to do stuff like that anymore. And help the people here help him get well soon." I hear footsteps approaching and add, "Please don't let the vet lady hurt us."

"You'd better *not* be praying for me, mister!"

"Amen."

Ozena

Despite the barrage of angry customer calls today, I haven't been able to shake the sound of Willy's voice since our last conversation. Admittedly, I haven't tried very hard either. *I'd really like to talk to you again.* Eight simple words, earnest and unassuming, vulnerable but not needy.

Of course the spell was broken when I looked up to find Sheila blocking the mouth of my cubicle, her arms folded and eyebrows arched in mock surprise. She stopped just short of tsking at me before marching off toward Reggie's office.

It's a little after three and I'm replaying Willy's words when he calls again. His voice is a welcome change from the angry voices on the other end of the phone. He marvels again at the damage inflicted on his coffee maker, but I can tell his heart's not all the way in it. More than anything he sounds like he needs a friendly voice. And I'm more than happy to provide one. That is, until Sheila shows up again pantomiming embarrassed apologies as she delivers a memo on Javatek letterhead. She takes her time leaving.

"Willy," I say, eyes alternating between my clock and the memo. "It's a good thing you called when you did."

"It is?"

His incredulity makes my arms all light and floaty, as if by sheer reflex they want to reach out and hug him. "Yeah, looks like we have a new policy at work. A rather inconvenient one, I'm afraid."

"An end to the corporately sanctioned destruction of returned coffee makers?"

"Worse, no personal calls at work."

"Oh … What about your cell phone?"

This sparks several other reflexes, none of them light or floaty. "Sorry, Willy, I don't think I'm ready for that quite yet."

"So what do I do when I need to talk to you?"

At the word *need*, another reflex grips the corners of my mouth and provides a gentle lift.

"Give me a day or two. I'll think of something."

Willy

Dinner at the mission is unbearable tonight. Or at least cleaning up afterward is. The instant mashed potatoes simply will not release their death grip on the dishes. No matter how much pre-scraping I do, they cling like paste. So eventually I give up scraping them by hand and run them through the dishmachine. Not only does that petrify any remnants left on the plate, but the machine manages to re-circulate the fake potato mix and spread a thin layer of white flecks all over the silverware, glasses, and the inside of the machine.

Eventually, between my fingernails and a box of Brillo pads, I manage to scrape and clean my way out of the kitchen with five minutes to spare before lights out. As I drag myself toward the mission door, the pothead twins step inside, blocking my access. Their normally passive expressions darken as I mumble a series of excuse me's and pardon me's.

The tall one says, "Say man, can you break a twenty?"

I replay Father Joe's warning in my head and say, "Sorry, can't help you."

I turn my body sideways to slip between them, but the more menacing of the two puts one hand on my chest. He's much stronger than he looks. And their cloying dope smell is giving me a headache.

"You sure about that?" he says.

"Sure I'm sure."

That's when I feel his groping hand in my front pocket. It tickles like mad until he yanks out my money clip and starts thumbing through the bills. I watch as he peels back a ten, a five, and a bunch of singles.

Shaq emerges from Father Joe's office at this point, barking orders about settling in for the night. Bone weary and desperate to sleep in my own bed, I decide twenty dollars is a small price to pay. They can just have it for all I care.

The potheads huddle around my money clip, counting aloud. When they get to twenty-eight, the tall one says, "Close enough for government work."

The mean one jams my money clip, along with the overly crisp twenty-dollar bill, down my pants pocket again. I make a mental note to douse it with Lysol when I get home. Shaq is on us now, saying, "Is there a problem here?"

"Nope, I was just leaving."

"You sure you don't want to stay?" Shaq says, clearly playing to the crowd. "I think the vacancy light is on in the honeymoon suite."

The potheads swap a few obligatory giggles and wander off. I push the mission door open much harder than necessary and practically run to my car.

* * *

In the dream my alarm is set for five thirty, but that's not what wakes me up.

It's the phone.

Someone has the audacity to call me before six in the morning. I consider dragging myself up, but the ringing stops before I can manage to wipe the sleep from my eyes. The machine never picks up so I re-fluff my pillows and go in search of slumber again, finding it almost at once.

I can't be certain, but I think I was dreaming of an alarm clock that only played songs in the key of E-flat when the phone rang again fifteen minutes later.

After my morning shower, I put the teakettle on and spend a few minutes admiring my dead espresso maker while I wait for the water to boil. That's when I see the light blinking on my answering machine.

The first message is from my agent, still drowsy-sounding, still searching in vain for me, still perturbed. I erase it. The next is from Doug; he's landed an afternoon wedding gig and promises he'll have me back at the mission in time for dinner. The third message is from someone named Nadine. It seems she's been looking for William Finneran for three days now. A nicer man than me would return her call and politely inform her she's looking for the wrong William. Instead, I erase that one too.

The last message is the most delightful ever:

"It's me, Ozena. And I hate to bother you at home. But I did some research and figured out a way around the new policy thing at work. The employee handbook does prohibit personal calls at work, but not on break times. The time frames are pretty strict though — two breaks, fifteen minutes each. So what that means is, you can call me on my direct line at either ten a.m. or three p.m. That is, you know, if you want to call me."

She ends the message by leaving the number of her direct line at work. I hit play again, wondering what kind of woman would go to all this trouble. Then I'm replaying her voice in my head and wondering what it would sound like in person. Surely there's more to her effort than just exceptional customer service.

That reminds me, I need to fill out the survey forms she sent.

I dig them out of my briefcase and stare at the questions. But I can't focus because someone starts pounding on my door. Instead of answering, I walk around the table and peer out the kitchen window. There is a nondescript minivan parked at the curb, with two silhouettes inside. But I can't get a good enough angle to see who's at the door. My teakettle starts to whine. I hurry around the table and move it to an unlit burner, trying hard to keep quiet, a prisoner in my own home.

Whoever it is knocks again. It may be the most annoying sound I've ever heard. My To Do list flashes before my eyes and the idea of picking a fight with someone and winning seems like a really good idea this morning. I make my way through the living room and interrupt another round of maddening knocks by flinging the door open.

"Your name Willy Finneran?" Everything about her is angry and uptight, from her polyester stretch pants to the mole twitching on her upper lip when she talks. I don't recall ever disliking someone so perfectly on such short notice.

"Who wants to know?" I say, trying my best to match her belligerent tone.

"The state of Tennessee, the law firm of Tyler, Billingham & Sneed, some judge named Reynolds, and a small boy named Michael. But for right this minute, just me."

"And who might you be?"

"Nadine Sharpe. Ring any bells?"

"You left me a message, right?"

"Guilty as charged. And several more on your cell phone. And another handful at your office."

"Sorry, but you've got the wrong guy. And if you call my house at five in the morning again …" But my threat melts on my tongue as it dawns on me who I'm talking to. "Are you *Aunt* Nadine?"

"That's right. And I don't really have all day to chit chat. So you hold tight and I'll get the boy."

"What boy?"

She produces a folded sheet of notebook paper. I recognize Lucy's leaning scrawl at once. But the words keep shifting in and out of focus. Nadine continues, "You now have legal custody of her sole heir, one Michael Jefferson Sharpe. But don't get excited, Lucy didn't leave any money behind, just bills."

When the reality of her words finally hits me, I grip the door frame with one hand and the doorknob with the other.

"You didn't know?" Nadine says.

I shake my head in response.

"Bad ticker," she says, thumping her chest. A trace of compassion seeps into her features, but she shoos it away before it can get too comfortable. "Just like you."

When I look up from the paper again, Nadine is walking toward the van as I ease myself onto the top step of my porch, trying hard to remember the last thing I ever said to Lucy, hoping it was "I love you" and not "Later 'tater." Then I see Nadine round the corner of the minivan with a miniature male version of Lucy, same unruly brown hair, full lips, and dark eyes. I scan his features in search of anything un-Lucy-like, or rather anything resembling Alvin. But since I've never seen the man, I find nothing I can use.

The boy pauses at the bottom step to look before planting his first foot, exactly like Lucy. A half-second later, Nadine says, "Michael, this is your new legal guardian, Willy Finneran."

He stops and stares. Nadine clears her throat, then taps her foot. "Shake the nice man's hand. Just like we talked about."

The boy is quiet, but not overwhelmed. Nor is he apathetic or willfully obstinate. He's not much of anything, come to think of it. And he's not about to take his hands out of his pockets.

"It's okay," I say. I sit down on the top step and pat the spot next to me. "Have a seat, big guy. We'll shake later."

Nadine looks even more perturbed as the boy sits by me and scans the street, blinking. She opens her mouth, likely to insist this poor kid shake my hand. But I glare at her until she rolls her eyes and begins rummaging through her purse. She retrieves another sheaf of hand-written notes from Lucy and drops them unceremoniously in my lap. "Here's the instructions."

Finally I say, "So what happens next?"

"Not my problem."

"Well you can't just leave him here."

"He's young, not deaf. Try and have a little compassion, would you? He just lost his mother."

"But you don't understand. This is a really bad time."

"Take it up with the state." I open my mouth to protest, then feel the little male version of Lucy lean against my rib cage and place his small hand on my thigh. He sighs through his nose, another Lucy-ism. It hits me that all I have to do is explain my situation, that I'm a criminal who hangs around a homeless shelter all day and who can barely make his house payment. I should make Nadine take him away until this misunderstanding can be sorted out and a proper home found for the boy. "But until then, you're the guardian. His only parent, if you will."

"Wait, at least give me your phone number. What if I have questions?"

"You already have my number. I left you at least a dozen messages already. But it won't do you any good though."

"Why not?"

"As soon as I step off your porch, I'm officially on my honeymoon."

Ozena

9:57 a.m.

My direct line rings. I check the caller ID and see that it's Willy. As much as I hate to do it, I let it go to voicemail. He doesn't leave a message. Instead, he calls back one minute later, then once more after that.

10:00 a.m.

I had no idea I was holding my breath until I opened my mouth to speak.

"You got my message?"

"Yeah," he says, practically grumbling. "I got it."

"Well, you don't sound very happy about it."

"I was thrilled, but it accidentally got erased by this kid that was, you know, over at my house for a while."

"You obviously wrote the number down correctly."

"It's not that. It's just, you know, I might have wanted to listen to it again later or something."

We nestle into a comfortable silence, not quite ready to admit that there's more to this than excellent customer service. But of course I'm being naïve. Willy passed that point long ago. I'm just trying to catch up.

"So," I say, weighing each word. "Do you think this will work?"

"What do you mean?"

"Whatever it is you're really trying to destroy?"

"It's just a coffee machine."

"I don't think so. You're too heavily invested."

"Why can't it just be the machine? Maybe I really hate the way the stupid thing looks. Or the way it ruins perfectly good coffee." He pauses, then adds, "Seriously, that's all we've destroyed here."

"I don't know. Sounds rather hopeless to me."

Willy goes quiet again. But this time it sounds forced, as if he's covering the mouthpiece. Finally, he says, "That's what Lucy always said. That I was hopeless."

The name rings a bell, evoking the grainy author photo of Willy I found on the Internet. "So are you? Hopeless, that is?"

"I guess I can be sometimes. Although it could just be a side effect of my transplant. I think they accidentally removed my spine."

"I don't know. You seem pretty bold to me."

"My bold streak is late onset, like Alzheimer's or some forms of diabetes." I think I diagnose his attempt at humor before he does — obfuscation. At least his tone applies an apology. "And it's not really cowardice per se, more like a failure to engage. I think I didn't want to risk looking forward to certain things. I just don't like to get my hopes up."

"And what about now? Are you looking forward to certain things?"

"Yep."

"Care to elaborate?"

"Well I haven't made a full recovery yet. Suffice to say, I'm done checking out, I'm ready for more than playing solitaire and overdosing on strong coffee."

"So is this Lucy's espresso maker?"

When this question left my brain it was innocent enough. But by the time it scampers off my tongue I realize I don't want to know, that there's no good answer. I suddenly feel like a plate spinning on a stick, starting to wobble and teeter, about to come crashing down around me. But thankfully Willy is the one holding the stick, balancing things with ease. And his answer reaches up and gives me another gentle spin, setting everything right again.

"It was. She's, um, well, she's gone."

I'm about to apologize for his loss, to offer some platitude about hoping she didn't suffer, when I hear some odd commotion in the background, followed by a rather whiny, high-pitched voice. That might explain him covering the mouthpiece. My overactive imagination conjures some too-young coed — nubile, exotic, and now jealous of Willy's whispered conversation about hope.

Then Willy is the one apologizing, asking if he can call again later, promising to explain things. It all happens so fast I'm not sure what to think.

"Is everything all right, Willy?"

"I don't know. I'm supposed to be babysitting. But I don't think I'm doing it right."

"Well I've done my fair share of babysitting. So if you have any questions, you can always call."

"Always?"

"Yeah, sure. As long as it's ten a.m. or three p.m. sharp."

Willy

My dear sweet Lucy. Can the woman I pretended to marry, tried to love, then pretended was dead really be gone for good? How did it happen? Did she suffer? When is the funeral? And what is it with this kid? Do I have to hold his hand by her grave and try to think of something memorable to say? And what is it with this kid? Can he talk? Feed himself? Take himself to the *bathroom*? And what was his name again anyway?

In the middle of all my musings I hear a tiny voice, squeaky with uncertainty and quite probably fear.

"You got any cereal, mister?"

"Sure, kid. Follow me."

I watch him spoon Lucky Charms into his mouth, saving the colored marshmallow pieces till the end, just like his mother. I have to bite my lip and keep telling myself not to stare like he's a museum exhibit, that I'll make him self-conscious. But somehow that doesn't seem possible. And I keep hoping if I look at him long enough, his name will pop back into my head.

"I'm going to make a call now." I realize I'm narrating, too loud and slow, as if reading a children's book to a large circle of slow learners. I lift the handset, then stare at my hovering thumb.

I have no clue what the phone number to the mission is.

I resist the urge to toss the phone at the espresso maker, not wanting to be a bad example to Junior. I could just wait for Shaq to call and yell at me for being late. But I'm afraid he'll turn me in to Father Joe or the judge and I'll end up spending nights at the mission again. Or worse, jail. Of course violating the conditions of my sentence might put me on the fast track to getting rid of this kid.

Finally, I sit across from the boy again and listen to him slurp down the puddled milky dregs from his cereal bowl. He eyes me over the rim and I say, "Would you like to go for a ride?"

"Better not."

"Oh yeah? How come?"

"Mommy said not to ride wiff strangers."

"That's one smart mommy you have there."

"Not anymore. She's dead. I miss her."

There's no emotion in his words, a good thing, because they make me feel like blubbering. "I know. I miss her too."

"You knowed my mommy?"

"Yeah, I knew her pretty good."

He stares at his empty bowl for a while, eyes narrowed and lips scrunched into a thinking scowl. Finally he clears his throat and says, "Oh yeah? What's her favorite color then?"

"Huh?"

"My mommy. What's her favorite color?"

"Oh, well, I'm not sure."

"But you said you knowed her. So how come you don't know her favorite color is yellow."

"Of course it's yellow. You just didn't give me time to answer."

"You tricked me though. What's her favorite number?"

I see him take the four fingers on his right hand and tuck them into his left, concentrating hard. Then he nods ever so slightly as he counts them in his head. It feels especially rotten to cheat, but these are desperate times.

"Four," I say.

"Wow, how'd you do that?"

"Like I said, I knew your mommy pretty good. So, do you believe me now?"

"Did you love my mommy?"

"I did my best."

"Then how come you didn't live with my mommy?"

"That's a really hard question."

"You can take your time, then."

"See, that's the problem though. I don't have a lot of time."

"Oh." He looks away now, first up at the ceiling, then down at his wringing hands.

"What's wrong?"

"That's what Mommy said the other day."

"What did she say?"

"That she didn't have a lot of time. Then she died. Aunt Nadine says she had a bad heart. Do you have a bad heart too?"

"Yes," I say, regretting it at once.

"Are you going to die now too?"

It's like a punch in the chest. I'm tempted to explain about Aunt Mavis's birthday cards and the expiration date on my borrowed heart, but I keep all that to myself. Instead I say, "Nope, not today. Not for a while now."

"Good. I didn't want to like you too much if you're going to die."

"Good thinking."

"What's your favorite game?"

"Hard to say." And it is actually, although I'm sure the irony would be lost on him if I admitted it was solitaire.

"Mine is Hot Potato."

My heart shifts uncomfortably. "Afraid I don't have that one."

He thinks about this and finally nods. "Okay, we can go now then."

"Are you sure?"

"Yeah, you're not strange anymore."

194

* * *

I call Derrick for some legal advice. But he's no help.

For starters, he keeps trying to congratulate me. Then while I'm wondering aloud about how wildly irresponsible it is for the state of Tennessee to leave Lucy's recently orphaned child on the doorstep of a convict, he counters with, "You'd be surprised, Willy. Doubt they even have a clue. And believe me, there's a lot worse parents out there than you."

"Thanks a lot, Derrick."

"That's not what I meant. I'm just saying, at least you're not on crack or something."

"Hey, if that's all it takes …"

"I'll make some calls, Will."

I'm thinking how unseasonably cold it is for October as I carry the booster seat that Nadine left behind and place it on the passenger seat of the Rover. I stare at the tiny armrests trying to figure out where the seatbelt is supposed to go. The boy crawls under my arm, up over the console, and into the backseat. I lift the booster up and examine the bottom. I get a little too proud of myself when I finally discover a moving part. But it's just a hideaway cup holder.

I hear giggling in the backseat, then, "You're funny, mister."

"Oh yeah? You think you're so smart, you do it."

I place the seat near him in the back and he expertly nestles it into position. Then he uses his chubby little hands to pull the buckle across his body and thread it through the armrest. He snaps it into position, then grins at me all smug and knowing.

I check to make sure he's secure. "Nice work, kid."

"Thank you. I'm still hungry."

"You like eggs?"

"Nope."

"I'll see if I can scrounge up a Pop-Tart or something then."

The streets surrounding the mission seem scarier this morning.

I'd grown accustomed to the barred windows and graffitied walls, the young punks and aging winos, the insidious tandem of dejection and fear. But until I sort this stuff out with Lucy's kid, I am still his legal guardian. And I'm not up to the task of *guarding* anybody, much less a tiny boy who has yet to fathom what life will be like without his mother.

Thankfully, I see Shaq loitering by the curb outside the mission. I pull alongside and lower the window.

"You're late." Before I can speak, he leans in and says, "And what's with the kid?"

"Long story. Where's Father Joe?"

"He's waiting for the morgue to open. Got tired of waiting around on you and had to take a taxi."

"Well, I just stopped by to let you guys know I won't be able to help with breakfast this morning. I have to sort out what to do with this kid."

"What's his name?"

"Never mind." I thought it would have come to me by now. "Just tell Father Joe what's going on for me."

Shaq pokes his head in the passenger window. "So where'd he come from anyway?"

"He belongs to my wife. Or he did. He's my wife's kid."

"Wouldn't that make him your kid too then?"

"Not exactly," I say. But Shaq is ignoring me now.

"Hey there, buddy. What's your name?"

I hold my breath, waiting for him to answer, since I really *can't* remember his name. But I catch a glimpse in the rearview of him shaking his head.

"You're a stranger."

"Not for long. My name is Shaq." He reaches into the backseat to shake hands. "So what's yours?"

The next sound I hear is Shaq shrieking in my ear, followed by a colorful string of stifled profanity. "The kid *bit* me!"

"All the more reason I need to get going. He may need a rabies shot."

I'm about to put the car in gear when Shaq lunges for the keys. He's halfway through the open window now and I'm slapping at his hand, his knuckles red and dented with tiny teeth marks. I'm marveling at just how strong he is when the car lurches to an awkward stop.

Breathless now, Shaq eases himself back onto the sidewalk and pockets my keys. "You already missed breakfast. Those dishes are still waiting on you. I suggest you get to them."

We glare at each other, Shaq breathless from exertion, me from my utter dislike of conflict and the crowd of homeless guys ogling us from the sidewalk. I'm not sure they actually smell blood, but they do indeed want to see a fight. Shaq's clenched expression is practically daring me to try something, as if he can't wait to show me and everyone else just how tough he is. And as much as I hate to admit it, I really am afraid. Not just of bodily harm at the hands of this crazy little man, but of what it might mean if I don't stand up to him. What kind of message does that send to the kid? Or to Shaq? And what does it say about me?

Thankfully, I don't have to answer those questions. From the backseat, the kid says, "Willy? I gotta go potty." It's the first time he's called me anything other than "mister," though it comes out sounding like "Wiwwy."

In the end I agree to work through dinner prep. But I make it clear that I'm not doing the dishes and I'm not coming back to the mission until I figure out what to do with this kid. And if Shaq has a problem with it, he can take it up with Father Joe, who can then take it up with the judge if he wants.

Of course, this all takes place in my head. What I do with my body is slip my dingy apron over my head and hold my breath against the pungent grease that has worked its way into the fabric. That's when I see the boy walking toward Darnell, his hands up in front of him like a zombie, reaching for the surface of the hot plate.

I lunge for his tiny body, but Darnell expertly bumps him out of danger with his hip.

"Hey, little brother," he says, talking to the boy but cutting his eyes at me. "Best watch yourself in here. Good place to get your little self hurt."

"But Mommy always let me help."

"Do I look like your mommy?" Darnell's toothy smile swallows his face, leaving no doubt he's just picking on the boy.

Lucy's little man considers this for a long beat, then says, "No, you're much taller. And browner. And she smelled a lot better than you too."

A stern fatherly tone wells up in my throat. But it's hard to correct a kid with any authority when you can't remember his name.

Darnell is unfazed. "How old are you anyhow?"

"This many." He holds up four fingers, lowers one, spreads his hand wide open, then uses fingers from his other hand to pin his thumb at a cockeyed angle.

Darnell clangs a stockpot into position under a faucet, then raises his voice over the din of splashing water. "How many is that exactly?"

"Four and a half. I used to be four and a quarter."

Darnell stirs a pot of rice while keeping one eye on the boy. "So what's your name, little man?"

I pause, craning my ear in that direction. But the sound of the boy's voice is masked by the splashing sizzle of chicken breasts landing in a greasy pan.

"That's a good name, son. Strong. I like it."

"Unbelievable," I say over the din of the kitchen.

"Problem, Willy?"

"No, no problem. Why don't you send the kid back to me? I don't want him around the ovens and stuff."

"Better listen to your pop," Darnell says. "Run on along."

I consider setting Darnell straight, reminding him that this is not my child, but rather the child of my formerly dead wife, who was neither really dead nor my wife, who is now dead.

But I just let it go.

The kid makes a zigzag toward me, stopping to run his pudgy little hand across every available surface. When he finally traverses the kitchen, I plop him onto a rickety stool. He picks at the stuffing poking out around the duct-taped cushion while I ferry the two pans of dinner rolls over to Darnell. When I turn back to the boy, I see that he's picked up a chef's knife by the handle and is moving it toward his outstretched tongue, preparing to lick a fleck of green pepper off the shimmering blade like it's a popsicle. I open my mouth to scream at him, but all I can manage is one long ragged gasp. I'm still a good eight feet away when Shaq materializes and gently places one hand on the boy's wrist, stopping it less than an inch from his mouth. Then he pries the handle from his grip and places the blade on the counter. He shoves it in my direction, either to get it away from the boy or in hopes that it will slide off the table and lodge itself in my thigh, penance for being such a lame guardian.

Shaq ruffles the boy's hair, then glares at me.

"You have to be more careful," I say, lifting him by the stool to cart him over to a safer spot by the walk-in cooler.

"More careful than what?"

"More careful than you were being with that knife in your hand."

"But I wasn't being careful at all."

"Just don't touch anything till I come back."

Shaq and Darnell are huddled together, whispering and casting reproachful looks my way, no doubt lambasting my pathetic caregiving skills. And whatever they're saying, I couldn't agree more. I glance back at the boy, still safely perched upon his stool, then gather up a pile of dirty dishes to begin pre-scraping them for the dishwasher.

Ozena

10:00 a.m.

I pick up in the middle of the first ring. "How'd the babysitting go?"

"The what? Oh, that. I guess it's still going."

"You okay, Willy? You sound down."

"I'm sorry. I probably shouldn't have even called today."

"Is this about Lucy?" His silence is so abrupt, so intense, it makes me wish I could take it back and just ask about the weather or if he has any other appliances I can help him destroy. "I'm sorry, I'm sure that's none of my business."

"No, it's not that. It's just—I mean, it's Lucy's kid I'm … How did you know?"

"You mentioned her last time we talked. Guess there was something in your voice."

"I did? Oh yeah, I guess I did."

"Do you want to talk about it?"

"Yes," he says. "And no."

The ensuing stillness is hard to read. I turn it over in my mind, like a Magic 8-Ball, until I sense a silent invitation revealed. I just hope I'm right.

"So I take it she's, um, deceased?"

"Yeah, but it's funny—I mean, not ha ha funny. Peculiar more than anything."

"How's that?"

"Just that you assumed she was dead. But I'm sure it's my fault. I have a habit of letting people assume things."

"So she's not?"

"No, she is now." Willy pauses for what seems like days. "I'm sorry, I know this is all very convoluted and weird. But years ago when she packed up her things, and my toothbrush, and took off, I guess I accidentally allowed my elderly neighbor to assume that Lucy was dead. But she wasn't. She just left me for some guy named Alvin."

"Probably felt like she was dead though."

"Yeah, it really did."

"Love can be really cruel that way."

"It's not like she ever really loved me anyway. It's kind of like …"

Willy pauses and I can hear his breathing dwindle back to normal.

"Like she somehow got it in her head that being with me could bring my brother back. I think I knew better, we both did. But I sort of went along with it because … well, for lots of wrong reasons. But at least I got to scratch one off my list."

"Oh yeah? What list is that?"

"Just some silly thing I started awhile back. I made a list of things I wanted to do before I die."

"What kind of things?"

"Everything from writing goals to my love life to killing that stupid coffee maker. It's mostly ridiculous and morbid and not worth talking about."

"So was Lucy in love with your brother?"

"No. She just felt like she should have been able to save him. Lucy was on the phone with Walter when he killed himself. I'm sorry, I'm sure this all sounds dreadful."

"Yep, it does. But believe me, I get dreadful."

"You do … ? Of course you do. You haven't hung up on me yet."

"No, but break time is over."

"So does that mean you're going to hang up on me now?"

"No, but unless you're going to place an order or lodge a complaint, then I guess we need to say goodbye."

"Wait, now that you mention it, I think I do have a complaint."

"Oh yeah?"

"Yeah, I do. Your break times are too short."

I'm pretty sure I'm blushing now. The word *goodbye* forms on my lips, but I somehow manage to alter the launch sequence at the last possible second.

"See ya later, Willy."

"See ya."

I ask the Whiteheads if my ears are pink. They grin in unison.

* * *

Minnie turned *me* down for lunch today—all three times I asked. So I spend my entire lunch hour in the front seat of my Civic, picking at my turkey sandwich, baby carrots, and a baggie full of stale tortilla chips.

I'm trying to concentrate on the Javatek employee handbook, looking for any ammunition I can find to let Reggie down easily. I'm running out of time to make my pitch for the promotion. But the only way to do that is to stop avoiding him and have a face-to-face conversation. But the only way to do *that* is to be prepared with a loophole of my own, preferably something right out of the rulebook, so as to dissuade him from asking me out.

But I can't seem to focus on the words. At least not the ones on the page. My brain insists on replaying the words of Willy Finneran. His wife left him, just like Lloyd left me. Then he let other people assume she was dead while I allow the state of Tennessee to assume my husband is.

At least I still have my brother. Poor Willy not only lost his, but is left to wonder whether it's somehow his fault.

The alarm clock on my cell phone shrieks to life, reminding me that I have a staff meeting in exactly twenty minutes. I know it's pathetic, but I can't help myself. I swing by my cubicle and grab the giant printout. I run a quick mental morality test and convince myself yet again that it's perfectly legitimate to show up for the staff meeting a few minutes early with a big pile of thankless, extracurricular (and hopefully career-enhancing) work in my lap. If Reggie happens to see me going the extra mile and feels the need to reward me with a promotion, so be it.

I resist the urge to sit on the front row, opting for an aisle seat on the second row. I flip to the Post-It note where I left off on the printout and attack the names with my highlighter pen. I'm looking for "dormant" accounts, those defined as any account with a total history of sales less than one thousand dollars and/or with no activity in the past six months.

In the midst of paper shuffling, Reggie strides into the conference room. I can't help but smile at him. He's presiding over his first meeting as the new Vice President of Sales. The conference room is crammed full of supervisors and team leaders from manufacturing, a platoon of salespeople, and the entire stable of customer service reps — all except Sheila. And this makes me smile even bigger, which of course makes me feel guilty, but not enough to straighten my face out.

It's hard to tell if Reggie is stalling because he's nervous or if he's waiting on Sheila to arrive. Either way, he can't seem to get enough ChapStick on his parched lips. He pulls his notes from his breast pocket, runs a shaky index finger down the length of the first page, then tries in vain to fit them back in his pocket. After several failed attempts he slaps them on the wooden lectern and clears his throat. The quiet chatter tapers into silence. All eyes are on Reggie now, who looks mortified. His ears are red, his knuckles white, and he seems to be trying to expel a massive air bubble from his chest. He opens his mouth and says, "Good morning, everyone."

A smattering of returned greetings resound and Reggie's first official meeting is successfully underway. He thanks everyone for coming, offers a few introductory words about the agenda, then launches into an earnest homily about how grateful he is to be our new vice president, vowing to always do his best and to never let us down. If it were anyone but Reg, his manic sincerity would be pathetic.

"My door will always be open," he says. "You know, figuratively. Because sometimes I like to work with the door closed." He pauses, eyes on the ceiling, then continues, gesturing hard. "But not because I don't want to talk to you. Or, like, hear your problems or whatever. Not that I suspect you'll have loads of problems. Anyway, if you have something you want to say to me, just knock and I'll ... you know, let you in and listen to your ... You. I'll listen to you."

Reggie grabs a glass of water from a shelf behind his lectern and gulps. His eyes are still clenched when the conference room door opens. I'm hoping it's the cavalry, or maybe even Reggie's boss coming to bail him out. But it's Sheila.

When his eyes finally pop open, Reggie attempts a smile, then barks, "Where have you been?"

It's obvious he regrets his insensitive outburst at once. He's just a frazzled, spastic mess.

"I'm sorry I'm late," Sheila says. "I was putting the finishing touches on the Grassland rollout." This elicits ripples of murmurs and even a few high-fives from the sales guys. "Then I had to send an email reminder to a certain someone to refrain from personal calls."

"But ..." Reggie says, visibly calming down now. "Don't we have a policy against that?"

"I know. And I've tried to warn her."

"Warn who?" Reggie says. He sounds more curious than condemning, as if he's so pleased with this distraction he wants to milk it.

"Now this is awkward, having to say it in front of the whole group like this." Sheila seems to take in the whole room with her eyes, everyone but me, that is. "But I've reminded Ozena repeatedly to get her boyfriend to stop calling here all the time."

Reggie does a bird-like double take, his wide eyes finding mine a split second before every other eye in the room.

Before my brain engages, I'm halfway out of my seat, practically shouting. "I don't have a boyfriend. You know I don't have a boyfriend. *Everyone* knows that."

Now the sales guys start to snicker. Reggie eventually regains control of the room and is able to muddle his way through his agenda, comforted I'm sure by the fact that he's no longer perceived as the biggest loser in the room. I stare at the back of Sheila's head, willing it to burst into flames.

Willy

When I finally decide to call the state's Department of Child Services, I ask Shaq to entertain Lucy's son for a few minutes. The last thing the poor kid needs is to overhear me telling some stranger what a terrible idea it is for him to spend another fifteen minutes with me. Enlisting Shaq was easy once the boy apologized for the biting incident. It was sincere and unsolicited and really sort of adorable. Whatever grudge Shaq might have been harboring thawed when the kid offered to kiss his hand to make it feel better.

Thankfully, Shaq settled for a handshake.

After scouring the blue pages in Father Joe's phone book for a half hour, I give up and call information. I jot down the number and the address, then sit and marvel at the sight of Shaq on the floor constructing a tower of unopened cans of soup and vegetables. He's a real natural with kids. Maybe if he weren't nuts, he could raise this one for me.

I listen to the voice recording, entering digits as prompted, but can't seem to get a real person on the phone. I drop two more coins in the slot and try again. This time I hit zero for the operator and ask to speak to the person in charge of returning unwanted children.

"What do you mean unwanted?" she demands.

"Well … it's just … he's not mine."

"Oh please …" The rampant irritation in her voice seems to stereotypically impugn all males everywhere. She then transfers me to someone else's voicemail. I hang up, out of coins and almost out of patience. I make my way over to the makeshift playpen, perking my ears to the sound of Shaq saying the boy's name aloud.

I know I should just ask him. I mean, he's only four. And a half. But I don't want to hurt his feelings and I don't want Shaq to look at me like I'm a creep. Which I probably am, I just don't want to be treated as such.

"Okay," I say, "let's help Shaq put the toys away. We need to go for a ride."

"Where to?" Shaq says, clearly disappointed.

"To visit the child services people, see if I can sort this out."

"You're not going to give him back, are you?"

I shoot a reproving look at Shaq, which he misses completely. The boy seems oblivious. "I just need to talk to the folks. To straighten some things out."

"Can't you just leave him here? We're having a good time playing."

"I don't think so. We need to go. Now you tell Shaq goodbye."

I realize I'm holding my breath so I don't miss Shaq's reply. Not knowing the boy's name is really freaking me out now. When he stands and turns, there's a giant snot bubble ballooning out from one nostril. I decide right then and there that if he touches me with that thing I'm simply going to drop him off at DCS with a note.

Shaq slaps him five and says, "Goodbye, little buddy."

Once I get him buckled in I make what feels like a funny face and ask, "Say, what was your name again?"

"Puddin' n' Tain," he shouts. "Ask me again, I'll tell you the same."

No matter how I pose the question — casual, stern, playful, borderline threatening — he does indeed tell me the same. Only louder.

I give up and watch him in the rearview mirror as we make the short trip into town, amazed at how much he resembles his mother.

The building is old and blocky and we have to park on the curb out front. I retrieve my last thirty cents from my pants pocket and ask the boy if he wants to drop the coins in the slot. He nods and I realize I have to pick him up and hold him there. He's heavier than I would have thought; my fingers digging into his tiny ribs terrifies me. He fumbles with the first coin and I realize I'm holding real flesh and blood here. There's a heart beating inside this little person, a brain firing off signals to his clumsy little fingers. By the time he inserts the first nickel, my arms are burning from the strain. The readout indicates we have eight minutes to do our business.

"You need some help there?" I say, trying to make "help" sound like fun.

"No thanks, I like doing this."

He has the quarter now, turning it over in his hand and squinting at the picture on the back. My arms are shaking as he finally aims it at the biggest slot. But instead of disappearing into the meter, the coin clinks off the metal housing and tumbles toward the ground.

"Oopsy!" the boy shouts as the coin bounces once, then disappears into a sewer grate.

We now have six minutes. And no more coins.

I take his clammy hand and we make our way to the lobby. Our destination is on the seventh floor and I let the boy push all the buttons. It dawns on me that I should have him wash his hands at some point. Then I'm seized by a more urgent realization.

"Do you need to use the bathroom?" I whisper.

"Nope," he says, pleased with the echo his voice produces. We're flanked now by a burly cop in uniform and a pretty twenty-something fiddling with the buttons on her cell phone. "Not yet."

"Okay, good. And can I ask you another question?"

"Sure, as long as it's not math."

"Do you, um, know how?"

"I can do adding but not refracting." The pretty girl laughs politely into her hand. Instead of saving this conversation for later, I lower my whisper even further.

"No, do you know how to go to the bathroom?"

"Yeah, sometimes you aim and sometimes you push. It's not hard." The pretty girl digs in her purse with added vigor, the cop stares at the ceiling, both quaking with silent laughter. "I can show you how sometime."

The doors open on three. We step off with a gust of genuine laughter at our backs.

I have to explain my situation to the receptionist twice, then again to her supervisor, and one final time to an actual caseworker named Gustav. "So you had no idea you were the godfather?"

I shake my head, wondering how much of this is sinking in to the boy's head.

"So what do we do now?"

"I'm sure I don't know."

"Excuse me?"

"I don't think anyone's ever tried to, how shall we say, *return* a child before. I have no precedent, no procedure. I don't even have a form you can fill out. Do you at least have a copy of the will?"

"I'm working on it," I say, trying to remember what I did with Lucy's crinkled notebook paper.

"I'm afraid you'll need to speak with an agent in person. Or maybe your attorney."

"Well can you at least tell me what my options will be? I'm sure you can do that."

"I'd be guessing, of course," Gustav says, rubbing his goatee philosophically. "You could raise the boy yourself. Or we can enter him into the foster system."

I feel myself blanch, remembering the horror stories from Doug and looking to the boy to see if he's heard any himself. But he's content to keep on coloring.

Next Gustav produces a green lollipop and angles it toward the boy. "Say, what's your name?"

The boy shakes his head. I'm not sure if he's refusing the candy or the question. It appears Lucy trained him well when it came to strangers and candy. Gustav looks to me for help.

"It's okay," I say. "Tell the nice man your name."

He shakes his head again.

"That's okay to be shy," Gustav says. He hands the sucker over then turns to me. "I'd be happy to look into all this for you and give you a call. Just give me the boy's name and age and anything you can think of to help me in my search ..."

"Um, well, thanks. But I think I'll wait to talk to an agent."

I can't tell if the look clouding his face is suspicion or if it's just my imagination.

"Remember, Mr. Finneran. Life in foster care can be ugly, fraught with difficulty. But then again, maybe no worse than living with someone who doesn't want you."

Ozena

I'm still smarting from my embarrassing outburst in Reg's meeting when I turn the lock on my front door and see Lloyd Jr. at the dining room table fitting plastic warships into his Battleship game board.

I kiss my boy on the back of his head.

"Eugene?"

Something is amiss, but I can't figure out exactly what. There's a hint of perfume instead of bug poison. There's no sweating can of Coors opposite Lloyd's chocolate milk. And the biggie — Eugene hates Battleship. It's the one thing he will not indulge my son, claiming it promotes a "war mentality." As if a boy incapable of tying his own shoes will suddenly be inspired to take up arms and start shooting neighborhood communists. But *someone's* playing with him because my son never plays alone.

"Yoo-hoo?" I'm not typically prone to yoo-hooing, but the peculiar circumstance warrants it. "Eugene?"

Monday, Wednesday, and Friday are physical therapy days for Lloyd, which means Patti would have finished up around four thirty when Eugene got home from work and watched Lloyd until I got home.

I hear a toilet flush, then the sound of water running. The footsteps coming up the hall are too light, too quick together to be my brother. I don't realize I've fashioned the most ridiculous self-defense weapon — a fist clenched around a clump of keys, with one poking out like a jagged little dagger — until a familiar form emerges, humming softly and massaging lotion into her hands.

"Oh, hey Ms. Webb. I didn't hear you come in." She nods at my protruding key and laughs. "You're not going to poke me with that thing, are you?"

"Patti? Oh, sorry. I didn't expect to see you here."

"Your brother called to say he was running late. Said he was hoping you was home so he could pull some overtime. I told him me and Lloyd was about to finish up with therapy, and that I promised Lloyd a game or two for doing such a good job today."

"That's awfully sweet of you to stay, Patti. But he shouldn't have ..."

"Ain't *that* sweet. He offered me eight bucks an hour to stay till you got home." Patti beams at me, giddy and proud. "Told him I'd do it for ten."

It's no secret she needs thousands to finish her education. She shields her mouth with her hand and says, "Don't tell him this, but I would have done it for free after today."

"Did Lloyd have a breakthrough? Or did some cute boy ask you on a date?"

"Both! He asked me to marry him today."

"Who did?"

"He did." She points at Lloyd Jr., who then points at himself and starts rocking in his chair. I reach down and thumb a glob of peanut butter from the corner of his mouth. "Sweetest proposal I will ever hear. Ruined me for all other men."

She cups his face in her hand, then sits across from him and starts aligning ships on her game board. Lloyd throttles his rocking motion down, looking everywhere at once and humming in monotone.

This is a sweet moment, one I should slow down and savor, my son's first romantic crush. But I can already feel that first trickle of regret. Later, when I should be sleeping, my heart will become pregnant with it. I suppose this is a natural part of Lloyd's development, but there's no rule that says I have to like it. Is he even capable of romantic love? I almost hope not. I know how selfish that sounds, but sometimes love breaks the very thing it sets out to create. And I don't think I could bear a broken boy with a broken heart.

A new journal entry forms in my head — *love is a troublemaker, a bully with no conscience. It preys on the weak, then moves on to the next victim. And for all his bluster, no one can really remember him years later.*

"I hope you let him down easy."

Patti shakes her head sadly. "No worries. I explained all about fraternizing with patients. And besides, the world ain't ready for mixed marriages. Can you imagine the scandal?"

Lloyd shouts, "B – 4." Then he giggles and rocks violently in his chair at his unrelenting and "ambidextrous" joke — his pun works for both Battleship and Bingo, but not at all for me. Thankfully, Patti is a better sport than me and plays along.

"'B – 4' you marry me, you're gonna have to quit with all that drooling." She leans across the table and wipes his chin with her thumb. "Now what's your real guess?"

"D – 10 ... *shun* hall!" He laughs so hard he chokes.

Patti feigns dismay, then matches his volume and says, "Hit!" Which elicits a series of slurpy explosion sound effects from my deliriously happy son.

I pretend not to notice her moving her submarine to the spot Lloyd just guessed. I never let him win, not anymore. I used to — what mother wouldn't? He would squeal with delight, grinning his drooly grin, sometimes pounding the table and honking out self-congratulations until the neighbors called to complain. Around the time he turned ten I realized I didn't need to let him win any longer. He just figured it out. And what *I* eventually figured out was that what truly delighted him was not the winning itself, but outsmarting me. My sweet Lloyd Jr. will forever drag one foot behind him, float his gaze like a blind man, jabber in his incessantly slurred tenor, bark when he laughs, and cry for no apparent reason. He'll be prone to seizures and surgeries and may never see his fourth decade. But he's not stupid. He gets things, things like math and beauty and cartoons. The kid spouts NFL statistics like a computer but can't explain the rules. He spends hours doing play-by-play voices and acting out his clumsy versions of heroic touchdowns with his Nerf football. He carries his Bible everywhere, but only reads the red letters. Maybe I'm just a proud mother, but I know Lloyd's a smart kid. It may be disjointed and irrational, but there's more going on inside his head than people know.

Except Patti. She not only sees what I see, she sees beyond it. She sees potential. Patti is Lloyd's physical therapist, but she is convinced that between her work, future medical advances, and a "little bit of Jesus" my son will think and walk and act his age someday. I wish I had her optimism, or that I could even pretend. Instead I just feel like a heel for doubting her.

I put a pan of water on and watch it till it boils. Then I snap raw spaghetti twigs in half and drop them in the water. "Can you stay for dinner, Patti?"

"Thank you, no. Too much homework for a social life. Speaking of which … ?"

"Yes?"

"Who's this Levi character that Lloyd's all giggly about? Are you holding out on me, girl? Got some exotic new boyfriend stashed away someplace?"

"Only if you consider my brother exotic. It's Lloyd's new nickname for Eugene, based on his brand loyalty in blue jeans."

She musses my boy's hair and says, "You keep them creative juices flowing, you hear? Strong mind helps make a stronger body."

I fill a smaller pan with Ragu red sauce, then forage around the pantry for something green. If not for Lloyd, I'm not sure I'd ever eat another vegetable. Not proud of that, just stating it for the record. Once everything is simmering along, I lean on the counter and allow the happy voices to waft over me, mingling with the smells, haunting me with the sounds of family. I feel the dull stab of dread in my chest at the thought of losing Patti. This promotion is no mere luxury. I need it. Lloyd Jr. needs it.

Before the undertow of melancholy sucks me under, the phone rings. I check the caller ID, disappointed and surprised. My first thought was that Reggie was calling, maybe to apologize for this afternoon before asking me "a couple of things." Not that I actually want him calling my home. But who doesn't want to feel pursued? Then I thought it could possibly be Willy Finneran calling. I know it's a ridiculous notion. But I savor it a moment longer before answering.

"Hey, Sis."

"Next time ask, Eugene. At least if you want free dinner."

"Ask what?"

"What makes you think you can hire a babysitter without even asking me first?"

"But you love Patti. And she loves Lloyd. And she said yes."

"It's a good thing we're related."

"Glad you think so, cuz I'm not going to be able to make it for dinner."

"Working late?"

"Nope, hot date. You should try it sometime."

"Are you asking me out, little brother?"

"It wouldn't do any good."

"Brat."

"Spinster."

"Good night, Eugene."

* * *

I try to muster some of Patti's boundless enthusiasm as Lloyd and I marathon our way through Connect Four, Sorry!, and eleven games of War. But I can't. The good news is that Lloyd either doesn't notice or doesn't care. Patti is a treat, I'm familiar and safe. She's a bowl of ice cream, and I'm a bowl of lowfat grits.

Every night I have amazing plans and ideas for how I'll spend my two hours of alone time once Lloyd is tucked in and snoring. And every night I abandon them in favor of TV or a mindless novel or simply staring at the ceiling and wondering what might have been. The hard part, no, the really cruel part, is the fact that his mother's touch means nothing. Not to him, anyway.

But that doesn't stop me.

I drag myself up off the couch and to his room. I watch from the doorway as his chest rises and falls. I say his name once, then again more loudly. He loves to pretend he's sleeping, then scare me when I get close. I wait a moment longer, debating. Then I hear the lumbering footfalls outside my front door, followed by Eugene's atonal whistling and the sound of him throwing his own deadbolt. Now I can indulge myself; everyone I love is safe and secure and in their rightful place.

I take the four and a half steps to the edge of Lloyd's *Toy Story* sheets. I can deny it all I like, but puberty is about to explode in our lives. I hear Lloyd's bomb noises in my head and tear up at once. I crawl in behind my sleeping boy, propped on one elbow so I can stroke his hair and watch him sleep. After a time I slip down and cuddle with him, making believe that his cooing sleep sounds are because of, rather than in spite of, me.

Willy

Lucy's son is asleep in my bed, occupying roughly the same spot his mother used to. What he lacks in size he makes up for in mobility, shifting and sighing and jerking the covers to his side. I guess I miss Lucy's pointy elbows more than I imagined. Decorum gets the better of me and I end up sleeping on the couch, which is ironic because the last year Lucy lived with me she did the very same thing — started out in bed next to me, but she was never there when I woke up. As innocent as it may be, it's just too strange to share a bed with a small boy I met only a week ago. But no matter how many times I haul him back to my old bedroom, complete with new Lightning McQueen and Tow Mater sheets, he ends up padding back into my room, unable to go to sleep without me there next to him. So like an old married couple, we've carved our first shallow rut. I read a novel and he twitches and repositions himself to sleep. And it's tricky too; you can't just up and leave once his mouth relaxes into an O and his breathing levels off. He needs to cycle through a few contortions and drowsy mumbles first. If I get greedy and vacate early, his eyes pop open and oscillate like prison searchlights, all condemning and scary. Then it takes his suspicious little mind twice as long to fall asleep again.

I guess Shaq wore him out at the mission because tonight he's asleep in no time. I finished a collection of Lorrie Moore short stories ten minutes ago but can't bring myself to break away. The kid has snuggled up under the crook of my left arm and I can feel his warm breath through my T-shirt, his pudgy little fist resting on my tummy. Finally, he swivels and flops until he's lying sideways. And since the top of his head is pressing an instant bruise into my ribs, I get up and put some coffee on.

I toy around with the idea of writing something. But I know my mind is racing too hard to come up with anything good. My telecaster is draped across the sofa where I was entertaining the boy earlier with sloppy versions of Wiggles songs. I strap it on and noodle around for a bit until Doug knocks on my door. He thrusts a registered letter from the Stanley J. Jenkins Literary Agency into my hand, apparently retrieved from my inbox at the college. I toss it in the garbage unopened. Doug shakes his head and hands me a CD marked "special requests."

"It's from the bride and groom." He takes one look at my reaction and says, "You forgot, didn't you?"

"Yeah, I did. But I can't do it now anyway."

"You lose a finger or something?"

"It's more complicated than that."

"We can work around it. Whatever it is."

I motion for him to follow me to my bedroom door. I twist the handle silently, simultaneously pulling and lifting the door to prevent its aged moaning. Once the door is open I usher Doug inside to see the boy, blanket tucked under his chin and snoring softly in the middle of the bed I used to share with his mother.

"Looks just like Lucy."

He stirs under the sheet and we lower our voices to a whisper.

"Huh, I thought it was just me."

"Sorry, Will. Doesn't look a thing like you. Hope that's not a problem."

"No, the problem is much bigger than that."

"Which is?"

"Well ... actually, Lucy died a few days ago."

"Will, man. I'm so sorry. What happened?"

"A bad heart, of all things." I don't realize I'm massaging my scar until I see Doug watching me. "Guess she knew it was coming."

"And you didn't?"

I shake my head, ashamed that she couldn't trust me with her illness, assuming I was too weak to handle it. But I'd grieved the loss of Lucy years ago. I take one step toward the hallway, but Doug moves toward the boy as if magnetized. He puts his big palm on the boy's sweaty head, then brushes his hair up off his forehead. It's a tender gesture that fills me with envy. His big fingers graze the boy's cheeks then lift the back collar of his pajama top; he mouths the word *Michael* and nods his approval. Of course, why didn't I think to do that? Then he leans and kisses the sleeping boy where his hand just was. The boy sighs, then nestles further into his pillow and blanket.

Back in the kitchen I pour us each a cup of coffee and we sit on opposite ends of the table.

"So what's the story?" Doug says.

"According to Lucy's handwritten will, I'm his godfather too." I pause for the obligatory Brando impersonation, which thankfully never materializes. "So I guess he's staying with me until I figure out what to do with him."

For the first time in ages, Doug's grin falters. And I think I know why. "What are your options, Will?"

"Not sure. Lucy's parents died years ago. Her aunt wants nothing to do with him. No brothers or sisters that I know about. So I'll keep searching for extended family members, I guess. The state is trying to run down the father, but it's kinda hard when all they have to go on is 'a guy named Alvin who sent my dead wife an espresso maker as a token of his undying lust.'"

"So wait a minute. You already called the state?"

"I had to call someone."

"How do you know he's not yours?"

"Who?"

"The boy. Lucy was your wife, after all."

"I did the math."

"Yeah, but you suck at math."

"Trust me. That is not my kid."

"Sounds to me like he's your kid now, regardless of paternity." There's an edge in Doug's voice tinged by a decade of foster families. I've heard the stories, or at least the ones he can bear to tell. And even those gave me nightmares. He claims that his time in foster purgatory is what eventually led him to Jesus and Maggie and even me, but that's just Doug talking. "You are *not* considering turning him over to the state."

It's not a question.

"I don't know."

"Yes, Will." He pauses, waiting for me to lift my gaze from my coffee to his face. "You do."

"Well, he needs someone more responsible than me. I couldn't even remember the kid's name until you showed it to me on the tag of his pajamas."

"Why didn't you just ask him?"

"We're not all as smart and resourceful as you, Doug."

"Smart's got nothing to do with it."

"You don't even know the kid."

"You're right, Will. I may not know Michael's middle name or favorite kind of cookie. But trust me, I know *exactly* the kid he'll turn into if you force him into foster care."

"You can't save every kid from going through what you did."

"We're not talking about every kid."

"Look, I'm not making any decisions tonight." I grab a nearby deck of cards and begin to shuffle. "Can we just drop it and talk about something else?"

"You've been dropping things for way too long. And it's not working for you."

I shrug, noncommittal and not about to take the bait. As if on autopilot I begin dealing out a hand of solitaire.

"Stop it, Willy."

I ignore him, keep dealing, hoping he'll just go away but knowing he won't.

"You talk like you're afraid of dying, but I know better."

This looks like a good hand. I get two aces on the deal.

"You're afraid of what's going to happen if you keep on living. You're afraid someone else is going to leave you."

A red nine would create at least two plays. I remind myself to keep an eye out for that.

"Your parents, then Walter, then your grandparents, so you built this cocoon, like an insulated museum of the way things used to be."

Excellent. The nine of hearts, which frees a blank spot for a king. And the king of clubs is coming back around.

"Then Lucy."

I'm about to place the king in the empty spot, when I feel Doug's hand on mine. I push against him, determined to make this play. But he's too strong. When it's clear to him that I'm not giving up he uses his free hand to swipe the cards off the table. Everything goes quiet but the hum of the refrigerator. I won't look at Doug. And he won't stop looking at me.

"You *know* what it feels like, Willy. And I'm not going to let you abandon that little boy. He deserves better than that."

I sit there staring, wishing I was anywhere but here, resisting the urge to pick up the cards.

"You don't really have a choice here, Will. The fact that he's here in your home is no accident. God doesn't make mistakes."

I nod, but it's more of a surrender than a concession.

"If you let him go, you'll regret it the rest of your life."

"Point taken, Doug. All of them. So can we please talk about something else?"

"I need to get going." He stands and stretches, then moves to the sink to rinse his mug. "And you need to sleep on all this."

I still can't meet his eye but manage to say, "Anyway, guess I can't do the gig now. Sorry about that."

"Sure you can. Maggie can watch Michael or he can just tag along. It's a wedding gig, Will. Not a bachelor party."

"I don't know, Doug. I don't have a good feeling about this."

"Tell me something, when's the last time you had a good feeling about anything?"

I have to admit it's a good question. I want to say it was the last time I spoke to Ozena. But I'm pretty sure I don't say anything, rather I slip into some waking dream state. Finally Doug's voice hits me like one of Ronnie Cheevers's smelling salts. When I snap out of my reverie I see that Doug is standing, keys in hand.

"I swear, if I didn't know better I'd think you're in love with that broken espresso maker."

* * *

Eventually I'll end up in my customary spot on the couch. But for some reason I feel like being close to the boy. I won't be sleeping much tonight anyway. So I lie down beside him, arms laced behind my head, and stare at the ceiling. I try not to think about all the things Doug said. At some point I sense Michael stirring beside me in the bed.

"Why are you crying, Willy?"

"I'm not crying." If only Doug could hear me now, lying to the kid he thinks I should raise.

Michael continues in his thick, dreamy voice. "Is your heart broken? Like Mommy's?"

"Yeah, I guess it is." For once I have the truth on my side, and end-less piles of medical records.

The boy is quiet for a moment, then flops from one side to the next. Finally he ends up on his side facing me, inching so closer. The intimacy is unnerving, but not in a bad way. Not at all.

"Good, cuz mom says Jesus can fix broken hearts."

He then drapes his pudgy little hand over my chest and snuggles in tighter. He sighs once before his breathing evens out into tiny snor-ing sounds. Then, just like with his mother, my scar begins to tingle under his fingers.

* * *

10:07 a.m.

"Ozena, hey, sorry I'm late."

"No apologies necessary. It's not like we had a date."

"Well ..." I let this trial balloon of a syllable float.

"You said something before about having to deal with Lucy's kid."

"Yeah, his name is Michael."

"You sound very proud."

"I am." Of course my pride has less to do with the boy than the fact that I haven't forgotten his name again.

"So does this mean you have a son now?"

"Sort of."

"How do you sort of have a son?"

"I guess you could say I inherited him?"

"Are you always so vague?"

"What do you mean?"

"Everything with you is 'sort of' and 'probably' and 'maybe.'"

"Oh. I guess I'm just nervous."

She laughs again, and I realize I would pay obscene amounts for a CD of nothing but Ozena laughing. "Why on earth would you be nervous?"

"Never mind."

"Cryptic is not much of an improvement over vague."

"I'm sorry."

"Why don't you tell me — specifically — what makes this kid so special?"

I come up with a handful of answers, all either cryptic or vague. So I opt for the truth. "He needs me."

"That's ... an interesting way to look at it."

"Do you have a kid?"

"Lloyd," she says, then "Lloyd Jr., actually."

This obviously implies a Lloyd Senior, but I'm not about to ask. "Great, maybe you can give some pointers." She doesn't laugh or speak or anything, so I rush to fill the awkward silence. "Hey, maybe we need to schedule a play date or something."

While I'm patting myself on the back here for having worked the word "date" into the conversation without either fumbling the words or coming off sounding like a stalker, she goes even quieter.

"Something wrong?" I ask.

"Lloyd doesn't really play that well with other kids. He's, um, it's just ... never mind. It's nothing, really."

I try to analyze the ensuing silence. The saner of the two voices in my head tells me to just let it go, to change the subject, or go with my usual cop out and say something funny. Thankfully, I heed the other voice instead.

"But it's not nothing, is it? Not really?"

This silence is shorter, but way more severe.

"You love that Michael needs you. And I'm realizing how much I take for granted."

"Oh, I'm sorry."

She serves up another of her delicious laughs and says, "Don't be ridiculous. I should be thanking you. But it will have to wait."

"Why?"

"Break time is over."

"You're welcome anyway."

221

"Goodbye, Willy."

"How about 'see ya later' instead?"

"Talk to you soon, Willy."

"See ya."

Shaq

I'm pretending not to see Michael hiding under Prophet's cot when Willy announces it's time to clean up and get going. At first I think the whiny voice is coming from me, but it's the kid.

"Aw, but we're not done playing hide-and-speak yet."

"Sorry, pal. We need to go run a few errands."

"You go. I'll stay with Shaq."

Willy's face flushes with dread. And he does a lousy job of trying to hide it. "I don't mind, Willy. We'll be fine, just playing and stuff."

"Thanks, but no."

"Why not, Willy?" Michael is still hiding his face, but the rest of him juts out from under the bed. About as camouflaged as a shiny doorknob.

"I'm sure Shaq has better things to do. Grab your stuff and get moving."

"Really, it's no problem," I say. "And Father Joe will be in the next room."

"Actually, the errands we're running are Joe's, not mine."

Willy drags the boy out from under the cot and stands him up. He uses his shirttail to wipe a chocolate stain from the corner of Michael's mouth. That simple gesture tweaks something in me, another memory that feels old and borrowed. Together they stuff a few books and toys in a Spiderman backpack, then Willy ushers him off to the bathroom. He calls after him, "Don't dawdle in there. And wash your hands good, we're going for a ride."

"So that's it then?" I say when Michael is out of earshot.

"What's it?"

"Admit it. You're afraid to leave him with me. Afraid the home-less guy is going to let him play in traffic, teach him some bad words, maybe sell him into the sex trade for a bag of heroin?"

"Come on, Shaq. You know it's not like that."

"Whatever." I make an elaborate waving gesture, like I'm over it, like it doesn't matter, like I just don't care. But I overdo it, signaling just the opposite. And I think my bottom lip just began to quiver too. "He's not even your kid."

"Maybe not, but he's my responsibility now."

"Great. We all know how responsible you are."

It appears to take all of Willy's concentration to unclench his jaw. But before he can say whatever's on his mind, Michael comes bound-ing out of the bathroom. "Here," he says when he drops my crossword puzzle book in my lap. "You left this next to the potty."

I know better, but can't seem to stop myself. I ignore the boy and keep my eyes on Willy as I begin to shred the pages, slowly at first, then working my way into a frenzy of ripping.

"Stop it, Shaq." Michael's eyes grow impossibly wide as Willy pulls the boy closer to his side.

But I can't seem to care enough to stop. Willy keeps one protec-tive hand on the boy's shoulder as they disappear behind the closing door. That's when I kick the first cot over. It feels like I've ripped my big toenail off inside my shoe, but the pain just urges me to keep kick-ing things and making tortured howling sounds. I'm midway through yanking down the honeymoon suite shower curtain when Father Joe pokes his head in the door. He doesn't say anything, just stands there quietly, waiting on me to meet his gaze. But I refuse. Instead I slump to the floor and focus on my throbbing toe so I won't have to think about anything else. I can feel blood seeping into my sock. Or maybe I'm imagining it. Or maybe it's another taunting memory.

It's hard to say.

Finally Joe says, "Clean this place up, Shaq. We'll be back in an hour."

I listen to the muted sound of car doors slamming, the engine turning over and eventually fading. The replacement sounds are all in my head, mostly the angry rush of blood. My vision has as many black spots as my brain. But I can still see them, even when I close my eyes.

* * *

There is one spot on my memory I wish would stay black. But the harder I try to rub it out, the clearer it gets.

It was three years ago, maybe four, and about this time of year. I'd been at the mission only a short time because I still had my fancy belt. It was black on one side, the color of wine on the other, with a swiveling brushed nickel clasp. My fingernails were cropped short and my shoes were still black. Not shiny, but black enough. My beard was just coming in too. I remember how cool my tears were as they snaked between fresh whiskers. And how the room swiveled in a lazy arc, first one way ... then the other, the creaking sound of the leather belt much too loud in my ears.

I felt so tall too, for the first time ever, looking down on the world instead of the other way around. I'd finally found a way to make the wailing in my head subside, a way to dim the ugly pictures in my brain. The tradeoff was a burning in my throat and the taste of blood on the back of my tongue. But surely those wouldn't last much longer. I felt myself swelling, floating, a human piñata. I think this thought made me smile, can't be sure.

Before that night there were no black spots. It was more like a shutter that would click between the velvety darkness and the things I really couldn't bear to see or hear anymore. The blackness was too inviting, cathartic, holy.

I was just nestling in to this new, darker reality, weighing its permanence, when Father Joe came in and cut me down. He climbed the chair I'd toppled, held me by the waist with one hand, and sawed through my belt with the other. It was a gift, that belt, from my wife.

That's one thing that survived the shadows. Ironic, isn't it? How he saved me by destroying a gift from the one who is now destroying him?

But I can return the favor now. Father Joe Carter saved my life that day; three days later I arose from the dark place and he saved my soul. Or Jesus did. Father Joe saw to that.

Funny how I remember the belt was reversible.

Willy

Father Joe doesn't look so sad this morning as we pull away from the curb. Maybe it's the overly happy Wiggles guys singing about their big red car. Despite my great show of strapping Michael into his car seat, Father Joe still refuses to put his seatbelt on. I want to ask him if we're going to another hospital or the morgue, but I can't think of a way to do it without sounding glib.

But Father Joe pats the dashboard and says, "To the library, my good man." He gazes around the interior of the Rover with something like genuine awe. "How much did this thing set you back anyway?"

"More than I can count. It was supposed to be a gift."

"Didn't take?"

"My wife thought they looked cool, always pointing them out on the road and talking about how 'It must be nice ...' So when a decent royalty check showed up out of the blue, I decided to buy her one. Parked it in the driveway with a big bow on it and everything, then waited for her to get home from work."

"Wrong color?"

"Nope. She loved it. Until I handed her the keys and told her I bought it for her. She called me an idiot and didn't speak to me for over a week."

"So that's it? I thought you was a storyteller."

"Finances have never been my strong suit. I was so desperate to buy the house I grew up in, I ended up paying three times what it was worth. My novels had stopped selling and I didn't really have a job. 9–1–1 operators don't exactly make a great living either."

"Eyes outgrew your wallet?"

"Guess I got desperate."

"Yeah? For what?"

None of the answers in my head sound right. So I go with the simplest. "To keep her."

"You make her sound like a souvenir."

"It's not that. I just couldn't bear to lose anything else."

"She find a boyfriend?"

"Yeah, guy named Alvin." It's hard to properly despise my wife's ex-lover with Dorothy the Dinosaur's giggly falsetto punctuating the Wiggles' relentless invitations to dance.

"Your woman left you for an Alvin?"

"I'm pretty sure she left me for me. Alvin was a convenient excuse."

He marvels at the interior again. "So how much you owe on it now?"

"About three times what it's worth."

"At least you're consistent." We're about to pass the front of the Nashville Public Library when Father Joe raises both hands in front of him and says, "Don't park, just let me out here. You drive around the block and I'll be out in a second."

I thread my way through the city maze, watching people with purpose and jobs and hope, trying hard not to envy them. Even the road crews and valet parkers look like they belong in their own skin. I console myself with the fact that none of them look particularly happy. Except for the burly toothless guy wearing a tutu, pushing a shopping cart, and whispering nonsense to no one. He's painted blush marks and freckles on his cheeks and is sporting a Raggedy Ann wig. He's obviously taking a break from reality. But the strange part is that he *does* look happy, at peace with his madness. Stranger still, I find myself envying the guy. Surely there has to be some middle ground.

On my fourth pass by the library I see Father Joe at the curb. He scribbles something on a blue piece of scrap paper and tucks it into his breast pocket. This bothers me for some unknown reason.

I pull to the curb and reach across to open the door. But Joe is engaged in friendly banter with the beefy Raggedy Ann guy. My eavesdropping is shameless, as well as useless. I can't hear a word they're saying, only the dignity in Joe's voice. Before climbing in, he gives the man a powerful hug that ends with a loud slap on the back. The truck tilts under his weight as he gets in and slams the door.

"Did you guys have a fight or something?" I ask.

"What are you talking about?"

"Hugging? Apologies? Forgiveness?"

"You got it backwards, Willy."

"How so?"

"Nobody wants to touch a homeless man, much less actually hug one."

There's no judgment in his tone, merely a sad and simple truth.

"So," I say, eager to change the subject. "Where to now?"

"I think I want to try one of them fancy coffees. If you're still offering to buy, that is."

I turn, expecting a smirk. But he's squinting at some unseen puzzle in front of him. I navigate the one-way streets and traffic lights and head toward the Vanderbilt area. After a mile or so, I say, "I take it that had something to do with Shaq?"

"You guessed it."

"What's the story with him anyway?"

"Depends on the day, I guess."

"Is he okay? I mean, you know, in the head?"

"Shaq is one smart dude. But there's a wall in his head. And the two sides don't get along."

"He's quick on a computer."

"That's what keeps them from kicking him out of the library altogether. He works out glitches in their software that are too big for their budget. Instead of paying him, they overlook his, um, proclivities. But maybe not for much longer."

"Sniffing the women?"

"I think he thinks he's doing it for me."

"I think so too."

"He don't mean nothing. He calls it research. But I am going to have to rein him in before he gets arrested or stabbed in the eye with a nail file."

"Speaking of getting stabbed," I say, trying to sound lighthearted. "Do you think he's safe?"

"Shaq? He makes a lot of noise sometimes. But he's mostly harmless."

"He and Michael do play nice together at the mission."

He just stares straight ahead, lost in thought. I wish I could work up the nerve to ask him what he's thinking. Instead I glance at Michael in the rearview and click my turn signal into action. "Drive-through? Or you want to sit inside?"

He casts a wary gaze over the tops of luxury sedans and into the smoky glass. The bustle of the silhouettes inside seems to make him shudder. He points toward the drive-through and says, "You gonna order for me, right?"

I order two lattes and ease the car forward. "You know Shaq thinks we played in a band together."

"Not surprised. He has this thing for reminiscing with people he don't know."

"So it's not just me then?"

"One day he's the former mayor, another day he's a Viet Nam vet. He's been a pimp, a musician, an accountant, a garbage man, and supposedly the equipment manager on my college football team. And that's just in the last year."

"So he doesn't really know your daughter?"

Father Joe is quiet for a long time. Too long, long enough for me to start looking for places to hide if he does that inflating thing again. Finally, he shakes his head and I realize that it's not anger. He's probably so desperate to find his daughter that he's willing to entertain Shaq's clumsy notion of a love affair between his only daughter and a scatterbrained homeless man.

I'm not sure I've ever witnessed anything sadder.

"When he showed up at the mission he didn't sleep for three days, just off and on for like ten minutes at a time. Which means I wasn't sleeping much either. I had just about decided to ship him back to the nuthouse when I come up with the shower curtain thing. For some reason he needed to be by hisself at night. So I put him up in is own little cubby and it helped a little."

"Really, that cured him?"

"All's it did was calm him down for a bit so he could — "

The perky Starbucks lady hands over our frilly whipped cream drinks and says, "Y'all just have the cheeriest day ever, you hear?"

I put the car in gear and sip some of the frothy head of my latte. "Sorry, you were saying?"

But before he can answer, I hear Michael stirring in the back, then crying softly. I turn and say, "What's wrong, pal?"

"I think I peed myself."

Father Joe doesn't even try to hide his amusement. Nor does he offer to help as I struggle to clean Michael up using a combination of brown napkins, some hand sanitizer, and a leftover pair of Lucy's mittens. The process leaves both Michael and me raw, and on the verge of tears. Next I fashion a makeshift diaper using my own undershirt and a roll of duct tape.

When I finally manage to get the car in gear, Joe says, "You ever consider bringing a change of clothes?"

"Thanks, I'll remember that. Now what were you saying about Shaq and his shower curtain?"

"Oh that. Just that it calmed him down for a few days. Till he could figure out a way to kill himself."

3:01 p.m.

"I was wondering something personal."

"You can ask," Ozena says. "Just don't be surprised if I ignore you or change the subject."

"You mentioned something before, about what it was like when Lucy left me, that it probably *felt* like she was dead? I was wondering how you knew that."

"I just ... I don't know. I just did."

"You don't know? Or are you trying to be like me, all cryptic and vague?"

Her laugh is muted, more like a hard smile. But I'll take it. "I'm not really sure if I want to know."

"Or maybe you're not sure you want *me* to know?"

"No, Willy. For some strange reason I do want you to know things."

We listen to each other breathe a while, then she says, "We have eleven minutes left. You want to change the subject? Or do you want me to?"

"Do you have a boyfriend?"

At least she laughs for real this time. I think I'm becoming an addict.

"No," she says. And I can almost feel the heat of her blushing. "Do you?"

"I have this rather strict policy against dating guys."

"Yeah," she says. "Me too."

"Really?"

"Not if I can help it."

"Mind if I ask why?"

"Yeah, I do mind. In fact, I think it's downright nosy. But I feel myself about to answer anyway." She takes a deep breath. I can almost see her searching her office walls for where to begin. "I'm just not sure what the point would be."

"The point of what? Falling in love? Getting married? Making babies?"

"I thought we were talking about dating."

"Just trying to be clear."

"I've already done all that stuff. And I'm just not sure it's worth all the hassle."

"So ... hypothetically speaking ... are you saying love is too much trouble? Or that it doesn't even exist?"

"I've filled countless journals with 'Love is' phrases trying to figure that one out."

"So what did you come up with?"

"Love is a waste of time."

"You don't believe that."

"I've looked, Willy. Once with my heart, but it was broken. Since then I've been using my head, searching in theory, more like an archaeologist."

"So you're not looking for an actual living and breathing lover, just his bones?" She laughs again and I feel my heart pushing against the pink seam in my chest. In that instant, I'm finally ready to admit that I'm falling for Ozena—to myself anyway, not to her.

"Willy? You still with me?"

"I'm pretty sure love does exist, Ozena. In fact, I *know* it does."

"Oh yeah? What's your proof?"

"Hey, isn't your break about over?"

Ozena

I'm loading the dishwasher, listening to my brother cheat at Monopoly, and wondering how Willy Finneran spends his Wednesday nights. (Okay, that's not entirely true—I'm actually pondering how Willy spends his free time in a deliberate attempt to avoid thinking about our last conversation and how, in the span of about ten minutes, we veered into dating, marriage, making babies, my love journals, and Willy's vehement insistence that romantic love is alive and well in the world.) He doesn't strike me as a sports junkie or reality TV guy. I would like to think he spends his time helping elderly neighbors change light bulbs or reading great books. But that's probably because of the photograph on that book jacket that arrived in today's mail.

When I can't take it anymore, I drop a handful of silverware in its designated slot and say, "You know better than to cheat in his favor, Eugene. He's perfectly capable of running you into the poorhouse without any help from you."

Lloyd Jr. answers by rocking violently in his chair and making a loud cawing noise we recognize as laughter. It's a contagious sound, but the smile on my face feels heavy and unearned.

Why didn't I tell Willy about Lloyd's condition? Was I ashamed? Worried that he would somehow think less of me? Or maybe even quit calling? Shouldn't I give Willy a little more credit than that? So far he's proven to be anything but shallow.

Eugene says, "You can't win by buying up the utilities and railroads."

"You can't. But Lloyd can."

My son places his crooked index finger over his chapped lips and makes an exaggerated shushing noise that can be heard three doors down. "No fair helping, Mom!" Only three people on earth can decipher Lloyd Jr.'s muddled syllables — Eugene, Patti, and me. And that's probably enough.

I hear the thump of dice on cardboard, followed by more of Lloyd's laughter and his version of, "Reading Railroad. That's another seventy-five more bucks, please!"

"I knew we should have played Bingo," Eugene says. "Or maybe tackle football."

"Sore loser." I squirt detergent into the dispenser, then close the door and crank the knob. "Coffee, anyone?"

"I'll have a beer." Eugene says. "Maybe two while I can still afford them."

"Cocoa!" Lloyd says.

I start the coffee and cocoa, then hand Eugene a chilled can on my way to the sofa. But as soon as my head hits the pillow and I flip to the first page of *The Handyman*, I hear a knock at the door.

Eugene and I exchange wary glances. No one ever knocks on my door, not unless they're peddling timeshares or some deviant take on Jesus. I hoist my book up to the light and start reading again when there's another knock, more insistent this time. My plan was to keep on ignoring it until Lloyd says, "Door. Door. Someone's at the door!"

Eugene leans toward my son with a conspiratorial whisper, "Must be your mama's boyfriend."

"Yeah, Mama needs a boyfriend, huh Levi?"

I should just let it go, but I can't. "I have all the boyfriends I need in the two of you, thank you very much."

There's another knock. Eugene points at himself and raises his eyebrows. I wave him off and say, "Coming ..."

Once positioned in front of the door, I slide the tiny manhole cover off the peephole glass and stare at the distorted image of my boss's bald head and glasses.

"Reggie?" I hear myself say.

"Oh, hi Ozena." He waves at me; his voice is muffled through the door, but loud enough to drive my nosy neighbors to their own peepholes. "I'm sorry to barge in on you like this. I was just on my way home and ..."

"Hang on a sec."

I pat my hair uselessly while Eugene makes kissing faces at me and grins like a lunatic. Lloyd metronomes in his chair, humming a tuneless melody and waiting for his next turn. I catch myself smoothing the front of my jeans and pulling at the tail of my T-shirt, which I realize too late is just more ammunition for my already obnoxious brother. I crack the door just enough for me to squeeze through. Reggie's eyes widen, either because he's trying to see past me into the apartment or at the sight of me in jeans.

"You look really, you know, different. Because you're not in your work clothes. You're in jeans and all. Of course you already know you're in jeans." His gestures grow more intense, more aimless, as he continues to talk himself into a corner. "So anyway, I'm just saying, you dress down really well. Not that you're dressed down really. Just normal, you know? You look really great and normal and I like your jeans."

"Thank you, Reggie. I like your jeans too."

He looks down, as if shocked to see his own legs sheathed in denim. This makes his ears glow red again. I hear shuffling on the other side of my door, obviously Eugene watching through the peephole. I'm just praying none of my other neighbors are.

"Say, did you ever get your bug problem solved?"

"My what?"

"I was just wondering if all those fumigations actually paid off."

"Oh yeah, that. I think I'm in the clear." I try to ignore my rattling conscience, but it's no use. "And you know, I checked. Those spider larvae really and truly are the darndest things."

"Yeah, you said that before. I was just on the way home from my bowling league and was wondering if you wanted to go get some coffee."

"I'm sorry, I sort of have company tonight."

Reggie gapes at me, actually covering his mouth with his hand. "Oh, I'm sorry. I'll bet you have a man in there. I mean — well, you know what I mean."

"It's okay, Reg."

But is it okay? Did I just catch myself thinking of Willy Finneran? When I hear more shuffling behind the door, I thump it really hard with the heel of my hand. It must have worked because I think Eugene just said a bad word.

"Sorry. I — I didn't mean to intrude or make this awkward for you."

"You're fine, Reggie. I promise. So did you have anything in particular on your mind? Some burning question about work?"

"I did want to apologize for, you know, what happened in the meeting today with Sheila."

"That's okay, Reg. It was my own fault."

"Anyway, speaking of boyfriends …" He develops a sudden interest in an eroding section of grout.

My front door opens behind me, groaning on its hinges. Eugene says, "Hate to bother you, Zee. But Lloyd is kinda spazzing about his cocoa. Marshmallows or no?"

"Oh, um." This odd convergence of my two worlds has me more flustered than I would have thought possible. Eugene's macho, big brother posturing doesn't help matters. "Be there in a sec."

Eugene disappears and Reggie says, "I'll let you go."

"I'm sorry, Reggie. You were saying?"

His phone rings and he snatches it off his belt. He stares at the tiny screen, looking every bit as relieved as I feel.

"I'd better take this," he says. After saying hello, Reggie pauses in the hallway again and covers the mouthpiece. He stares at me through the half-open door and says, "You should try some WD-40 on those hinges."

Willy

I didn't even know Lucy had a church, but we find the small Presbyterian chapel tucked between two sprawling farms north of Nashville. The word that comes to mind is quaint, at least from a distance. Closer inspection reveals the need for fresh paint, a foundation in distress, and a severely fatigued steeple. Inside, every surface shimmers in the refracted glow of stained glass, but the carpet reeks of mildew.

I keep a guiding hand on Michael's right shoulder as we make our way up the aisle. When my eyes land on the open casket at the base of the pulpit, I stop, tempted to shield the boy's eyes. But he's waving at the white-collared man who's hunched over and approaching fast.

"Michael, Michael, it's so good to see you again this morning." The surprisingly young clergyman swallows Michael's small hands in his own, then musses his hair and pats him on the back, all while bent to the boy's level. "Will we have the good fortune of seeing you this Sunday too?"

The question is delivered to Michael, but it's aimed at me. Michael shrugs, all lopsided and heartbreakingly cute.

"And you must be Willy?" The man stands now, pumping my hand in both of his. He's about my age, although his cowlicks and grinning overbite make him appear much younger. "I'm sorry about the smell. I'm sure you're aware of Lucy's heroic efforts in spearheading our campaign to replace our leaky roof."

"No," I say.

"Lucy has said so many good things about you."

I'm tempted to say, "Oh yeah, name one, cause in all the years I knew her, I never once heard her say good things about me."

Instead I say, "And you are?"

"My apologies," he says, dropping his eyes. "My name is Paul. Paul Benjamin. I'm very pleased to make your acquaintance, even in this time of great loss."

I still have no clue what Michael understands and what flies over his head, so I simply let the "great loss" comment hang there, dissipating of its own volition. Benjamin rocks from heel to toe, looking from Michael to me. I attempt to avert my eyes — from the casket, from the rocking preacher, and from the sad little boy beside me picking his nose — but it's hard *not* to look all three places at once.

When I can't stand it any longer, I say, "Well, how about we take our seats?"

"Yes, yes, right this way."

Michael and I try to keep up as Benjamin ushers us to the front pew. I nudge Michael with my hip (a parenting maneuver I learned from Darnell) and sit nearest the aisle. It seems the least I can do is shield the boy from the big ornate box that holds the earthly remains of his mother. But before the pew can stop squeaking, Benjamin takes Michael by the hand and says, "Would you like to say goodbye to your mother now?"

236

I feel myself bristle, preparing to throw myself in front of the boy if need be, just whatever it takes to keep the ebullient minister from dragging poor Michael over to a dead body. But he just does that shrug thing again and follows along. After three steps he turns to me and says, "Aren't you coming, Willy?"

Under any other circumstance, my resolve would have rallied, at least put up a fight. But his blinking wet eyes, and the way his *L*'s get lost in his sweet Lucy mouth, saying my name *Wiwwy*, I'm up and holding his other hand before I even realize we're a few short strides from my dead wife. Or more accurately, this boy's dead mother. But when we get there, I see it's not Lucy at all. It's simply the place she used to live, all waxy and too made up. Of course I already knew this in my head, but this is the closest I've been to a deceased mammal since I last set foot in Aunt Mavis's funeral parlor over a decade ago. I bend to kiss Lucy's forehead, more than a little surprised to feel a tear fall from my cheek to hers. I may not have loved her properly, but I've always missed her perfectly. It's not like we didn't try to love each other, we were just terrible at it. Despite what she said, our sum *was* less than its parts, each lonesome and lacking, convinced we could patch the empty spots in the other. Apparently, hers was an Alvin-shaped hole. And for once I don't resent her indiscretion. I just pray he was able to do what I couldn't — make Lucy happy, even for just a little while.

But then that bout of sweet melancholy is followed by an over-whelming urge to frisk her for my missing toothbrush. That too passes when I feel Michael tugging on my pant leg. His tiny arms are aloft and I bend to lift him. I watch him watch the casket, waiting for recognition to bloom in his face.

Finally he says, "Is that my mommy?"

Benjamin cuts his eyes toward mine, merely adding to the panic roiling inside me.

"Your mommy is in heaven now." I don't realize I've phrased this like a question until I see the preacher nodding. "Her body is going to sleep now. But all the best parts, the parts you love the most, will be watching you from heaven."

I make a vague pointing motion, noticing the look on Benjamin's face. I give him my best *Hey, I'm doing the best I can here* expression.

"Goodbye, Mommy," Michael says loudly, as if trying to wake her from a deep sleep. A lady behind us starts to cry softly. Then another. "She can't hear me," Michael says.

"Sure she can," I say, ignoring Benjamin's silent protest. If he wants to plunge into a more nuanced discourse on the afterlife, he'll have to wait. "And you don't have to shout either. You can use your regular voice. Even the voice inside your head."

I watch Michael crane his neck for a closer look. Despite his squirming, he feels good in my arms; the weight of him grounds me. Satisfied with his search he turns to me and says, "You know what?"

"What?"

"She looks silly, Willy. The crying behind us grows louder. "That was my joke. Mommy says I make good jokes."

"Your mommy was right."

"Thanks, silly Willy."

I move to ease him back onto the ground, but he tightens his grip on me with his arms first, then his legs. As we make our way back to the pew, he burrows his head in my neck, sniffling. I feel something hot and wet there, and pray it's only tears. I'm surprised to see the number of onlookers scattered throughout, several offering somber nods and dropping their gazes as we pass.

At some point I realize there's organ music wafting about, then Benjamin is talking about Lucy and Jesus, then Lucy and Jesus together. His preaching voice is devoid of his previous, more rampant enthusiasm. Michael flinches slightly at the sound of his mother's name, but he never lets go of me. I think back to my To Do list, the part that says, "spend some meaningful time with a kid ..." I'm pretty sure this qualifies. But it's the second part that troubles me.

I'm still not sure if I've learned anything yet.

* * *

When the service is over, Benjamin asks Michael and me to stand and receive guests. I pry Michael loose and explain that we're going to shake hands and talk to his mommy's friends. But Michael wants no part of it.

Benjamin leans on his own knees and says, "It's okay, son, we'll stand right beside you."

He buries his head in my neck again and shakes it.

"Michael." The preacher takes a more stern approach, adopting that fatherly tone I've been striving for. "It's time to be a big boy and do as you're told."

Michael starts to whimper now. I realize I'm rubbing his back and telling him it's okay. But what's okay? Benjamin is turning pink now. When he says the boy's name again, it's through gritted teeth.

That's when I match his tone, keeping my voice just above a whisper. "Hey, lighten up, pal." I pause long enough for the lightning bolts to come crashing through the stained glass and turn me into a pillar of salt or a snake or something. When nothing happens, I continue. "If the kid doesn't want to stand up there, he's not standing up there."

The preacher and I glare at each other a moment longer, then he hurries to his spot by the pulpit and offers whispered condolences to a few people I recognize but don't know. I see a few of Lucy's colleagues from her 9−1−1 days. The other dozen or so must be people she went to church with. I realize Michael is patting my back lightly, as if he's comforting me now.

I ask Michael if he's okay and hear nothing. I ask a few more times and realize he's asleep, completely zonked out on my shoulder. It doesn't feel right to leave yet, so I stand around and watch people. I make a quick count. Not including Benjamin or myself, there are thirty-one people still milling about. Eighteen are women, which leaves a dozen men and one that could go either way. Of the dozen men, only half of those seem to fit the deranged images traipsing around my brain.

Even as I feel the word forming in my throat, I fire off synapses from my brain to keep quiet, to shut down the muscles in charge of making sound. But it's too late. I fix my eyes on an indiscriminate spot in the middle of the sanctuary so I can pick up any odd movements. I say the word, but it's muted in my clenched voice box.

"Alvin?"

Then I say it again, much louder than I meant to.

"Alvin! I know you're in here."

I sense movement, but not the guilty, wide-eyed head snap of a man caught climbing through a bedroom window. If my wife's former lover is in the room, he's too savvy for my sophomoric ploy. My voice is quiet now, calm, mostly defeated. "The least you could do is show yourself to your son."

The room goes silent as every head turns in my direction.

I turn and carry my sleeping boy to the car.

He begins stirring at the first stoplight we come to. I don't realize he's fully awake until I hear him say, "Willy, I'm sad now."

I catch his gaze in the mirror. Before I can think of a response, he says, "And hungry too."

"Sit tight, pal. I think I know just the place."

We arrive before the lunch crowd and get in line behind a pair of sleepy nurses. We hit the mother lode at the dessert counter. Between my tray and Michael's we have collected eleven small dishes of fruit Jell-O, some red, some green, all wobbly and inviting. Especially with the fake whipped cream on top.

"Are we gonna eat them all?"

"I usually do."

"Okay," Michael says as he spoons in the first bite.

"Hey, I think I saw some banana pudding up there." I think I'm holding my breath in hopes of finding even more common ground between this sad little boy and me. "Want some?"

"Nope." He doesn't look up. "Hate it."

"Yeah?" I swallow a cool glob of Jell-O and say, "Me too."

240

He ignores me, enchanted by the suction cup sound the spoon makes when it slices through the colorful gelatin.

Ozena

3:03 p.m.

I guess this makes me an addict. It's only three minutes after the hour and I'm already thinking Willy's late. My impatience this afternoon has less to do with Willy, however, than the peculiar vibe in the office. Reggie has been straining his neck all day to avoid making eye contact with me. He's obviously dealing with some residual embarrassment from his impromptu visit to my apartment. And the callers have all been either too cranky or too chatty. Twice already Sheila has popped into my office to interrogate me about fielding personal calls during non-sanctioned times.

So when the phone rings at six minutes after the hour, I can't grab it fast enough. It's Willy.

"Sorry I'm late. Had to make an appointment to see my boss tomorrow. And he likes to flex his superiority by keeping people on hold."

"Guess I need to do that myself."

"Put me on hold?" If laughter really is the best medicine, Ozena's could cure cancer.

"Schedule a meeting with my boss."

"That's right, the big promotion."

"Which might go a lot smoother if a certain someone would fill out that customer service survey for me."

"Right, sorry. I'll get to work on that as soon as we hang up. In fact, I'll have it to you by the end of the day."

"Thanks, Willy."

"So where do you live?"

"What? I'm not telling you my address."

"Why not? You have mine."

"That's different. You gave it to me."

"Okay, I see how this is going to work."

"How what's going to work?"

"This relationship."

"What relationship is that?" He does that silent thing again. But there's nothing sweet or introspective about it now.

"So you deny it?"

"Deny what exactly?"

"Your feelings for me."

"Who says I have feelings for you?"

"Not 'who' … 'what.'"

"What on earth are you talking about?"

"My Javatek 3000, the one with a wooden stake driven through its little heart."

Is he flirting with me? Of course he is, but why do I seem to like it so much? "That, Willy, is just stellar customer service, nothing more, nothing less."

"Don't kid yourself. You went above and beyond. That was way too much trouble for a lousy customer satisfaction evaluation. It seems rather *passionate*, don't you think?"

"Excuse me? Are you using my words against me?"

"Absolutely. I think you're too heavily invested in our little project. Not only that, I think this proves you have it too."

"Have what? Or do I really want to know?"

"Hope that love isn't just a waste of time."

"Yeah, right. My *hope* is that you'll hurry it up with that customer service review so I can get this promotion. There's even a comment section at the bottom where you can talk about how heavily invested I was."

"So you're going to sit there and deny your feelings for me?"

"No, Willy. I'm going to sit here and ignore them."

"Not for long."

"That's right, Willy. It's three fifteen."

Willy

Michael dozes in his car seat on the way to the university. I keep checking him in the rearview, his Play-Doh neck and shoulders slouched at impossible angles. I rehearse my speech in my head, confident that affecting just the right amount of contrition and respect will win Dean Langstrom over to my way of thinking. He doesn't like me, but surely he has a heart. I don't mind admitting I hope Michael will look especially pitiful this morning. Between the shameless use of Lucy's son and the threat of Doug staging some flamboyant protest, I feel like there's a sliver of hope I can keep my day job and start earning paychecks again.

Doug's Volvo is taking up two parking spaces in the faculty lot so I end up having to park along the curb on the street. Once I kill the ignition, Michael stirs in his seat. To head off any cranky outburst, I thrust his gnarled sippy cup (this seemingly innocuous contraption came in his suitcase; it took me a week to figure out how to use the little stopper) into his hands, then sit and listen to his sucking noises.

He tosses it on the floor when he's done and says, "I'm hungry."

I dangle a colorful box of animal crackers by its string, a shameless bribe. "These are for you if you're a good boy."

Once outside Michael drapes his blanket over his shoulder and grips my hand. Female students beam at Michael while the male students avert their eyes and make exaggerated arcs to keep out of our way. We arrive outside the dean's office exactly two minutes before our appointed time. I wait one minute, then knock, staring at our reflection in his pretentious door.

He then waits another three minutes before he says, "Come in."

The room is dim and cool, with one wall of windows, one wall of books, and two walls of diplomas, awards, and photographs of Langstrom's "family" — a Mercedes, a vintage Corvette, a sailboat named *Faulkner*, two giant poodles, three black cats, and what appears to be his mother. Without looking up he motions to a guest chair and keeps scribbling in his journal. I perch Michael in one squeaky leather chair, then ease into the other.

When Langstrom looks up, he blinks at us, alternating a rather dumb gaze between his two visitors.

"This is Michael. Michael, meet Mr. Langstrom."

"*Doctor* Langstrom. And it's a pleasure."

"What is?" Michael says.

"A pleasure to make your acquaintance."

Michael stares at him. I try to help. "He's only four."

"And a half!" Michael shouts.

"In that case," he says, offering Michael his most smarmy smile, "I'm sure your father can explain it to you."

"I'm not his father."

"Oh, well, I just thought … I mean, he looks just like you."

I want to rap my knuckles on the dean's forehead, asking if he's even looked at the boy, pointing out the obvious fact that he doesn't look a thing like me. I wonder if Langstrom sees everything in shades of distaste, banishing children and hack genre writers into the same leper colony in his pompous brain.

"All I meant," Langstrom continues, "was that I'm very happy to meet you."

"You don't look happy," Michael says. "You look like somebody swiped your diapers." Michael pauses for effect, then he eyes us expectantly, apparently baffled that we're not cracking up. I bail on my original bribe and hand Michael the box of animal crackers.

"Thank you for seeing me on short notice," I say to the dean. "I won't take up a lot of your time."

"That's correct. Because I don't really have a lot of time, given we've been working shorthanded around here the last few weeks."

"I'm sorry about—"

"Not to mention the bevy of negative publicity and letters from concerned parents. You've made this a most trying time, not only for me, but for your colleagues and the entire campus."

I suspect he's overacting—no, I'm sure of it—but I'm trying to behave. "Well I'd like to help out if I can. In fact I have a plan, a pretty good one I think."

Langstrom rests his chin on his hands and casts wary glances at Michael, pausing between loud chomps to make corresponding animal noises. Finally he says, "He's not going to soil that chair, is he?"

"No, he's a careful kid," I say, having no earthly idea how careful he may or may not be. "Anyway, I think I can still cover my classes, with one, maybe two exceptions."

"And how, may I ask, do you plan to accomplish that?"

"Mainly by swapping a few classes with Doug." I emphasize my friend's name, massaging the one syllable into three, then wait for apprehension to flicker in the dean's eyes. It flashes at once, then fades. I consider mentioning the petition rumored to be filtering through the student body on my behalf. But I can't help thinking that Doug would end up taking the fall for that too. "Then if we move my nine o'clock back a half hour and move my writing lab up an hour, I should have no problem making all my classes." I realize I'm rambling now but can't seem to stop. "The only other potential snag would be if I need to chauffer Father Joe around. But I think Doug has proven he can get pretty creative when it comes to covering for me."

"Absolutely not!" The dean practically leaps out of his chair, which at first makes me think he hates my plan. But he's ignoring me and pointing at Michael, who is now staging a demolition derby between a lion and a giraffe, spraying crumbs all over the suede armrest and thick rug.

Michael snaps his head up, his bottom lip quivering under the dean's glower. "I'm sorry."

"It's okay, Michael," I say. "Just try to be more careful."

"In point of fact, it is indeed *not* okay. I never realized I needed to post a "No Food or Drink" sign above my door."

Michael is crying in earnest now, a stream of brown cookie paste oozing from the corner of his mouth. I pick the boy up and put him on my lap.

"He's not a nice man, Willy."

As much as I want to agree, self-preservation wins out and I forge ahead. "So as you can see, I think it's a workable plan. A real win-win for everyone. And I can start tomorrow if you like."

Our staring match is cut short when Michael says, "I might frow up."

"Not in my office, young man." The dean's voice is shrill as he stands, panic burning his cheeks. "Please remove yourself from these premises if you're going to be sick."

I resist the urge to aim Michael's mouth at the dean and squeeze his percolating tummy. Instead I set him on the ground and square myself in front of the dean's desk. "Okay, fine. Have it your way. I quit."

Langstrom sputters some nonsense and I lean in close. "And don't you dare ever yell at my kid again."

When he opens his mouth to speak again, I snatch a handful of animal crackers and crumble them in my fist. Then I spread them like cremated remains all over his otherwise pristine desktop.

* * *

On the way out I ask Michael if he still feels sick.

"No, I maked that up."

"You did?"

"Yeah. I liked the funny faces it maked him make."

"Well, that wasn't very nice. You should always tell the truth, Michael." I know I sound ridiculous, clichéd, like a bad actor. But I can't seem to control this new parental impulse. "By the way, 'swiped your diapers'?"

"That's what Mommy always said." He pitches his voice high and says, "Why the long face, buddy? Somebody swipe your diapers?"

Speaking of long faces, I consider swinging by Doug's classroom to deliver the news of my resignation in person, but think better of it. There's no point spilling the whole story. It might prompt him to do something stupid. When I calm down enough, I'll type up an official resignation letter to the dean and send a copy to Doug.

Michael is asking for ice cream when I hear a familiar voice from my left.

"Professor Finneran?"

"Oh, hi Beverly."

She breaks away from a small group of coeds and sashays our way. Without thinking, I steer Michael by the shoulders until he's shielding me. I figure if she thinks I have a kid, that will surely break the spell I have on her. Romantic notions of a fling with her professor will shrivel and die in the face of such raw domesticity.

And if that doesn't work, maybe Michael will vomit on her shoes.

She winks at me, then bends at the waist until her face is even with Michael's. "And who is this handsome young man?"

"I'm Michael. This is Willy. He just quit."

"And I'm Beverly. It's very nice to meet you."

"Yeah, cuz you're smiling and everything." He looks up at me, jerks his thumb toward Beverly, and stage whispers, "Nobody swiped *her* diapers!"

She stands and regards me with renewed vigor. "That is quite a boy you have there, Mr. Finneran."

"Yeah, he's something alright."

"Ooh, and I got the note you sent me." Her tone is cryptic, carnal, and bordering on pornographic. Her warm hand has somehow landed on my arm, squeezing with intent. I have no clue what she's talking about until she adds, "And the check. Wow, my first paid writing gig!"

"Oh, that. Let me explain. I was under quite a bit of stress and sort of flipped out a little. Was trying to grade papers and pay bills at the same time and got confused. Just went a little crazy is all."

"I understand, believe me." Her voice is husky, exhilarated. Seduction is coming off her in creamy waves. I'm tempted to cover Michael's eyes. "I *so* know what it's like to go a little crazy."

"No, you really don't. Trust me, just ignore that whole thing."

She raises a silencing finger, then places it on *my* lips. I take one clumsy step in reverse, dragging Michael with me and nearly spilling us both into the bushes. Beverly grabs my arm again, this time to steady me. I'm marveling at just how strong she is when she pulls me toward her. Then I feel her lips warming my ear and hear her whisper, "And I think it's so sexy you have a kid."

"No," I say, sputtering now, just like the dean. "You don't understand. It's not my kid. I don't date students. I don't even work here anymore." I realize I'm pleading now but can't seem to shut up. "I'm a criminal," I say. "A bad kisser." I keep hitting my internal panic button, to no avail. "I'm gay. I hurt bunnies. I might even take up smoking."

But my ranting has fallen on deaf ears, or at least Beverly's. Michael is gaping up at me and the crowd of students that has gathered is all giggling. Beverly Ray has made her point and is now fully engaged in her dramatic exit. It appears she's taken my literary admonition to heart, to always leave them wanting more. It dawns on me that whatever Beverly lacks in discretion, she overcomes with audacity. I could stand to borrow some of that when it comes to Ozena.

As I'm loading Michael back into his car seat he says, "You don't really hurt bunnies, do you?"

"No."

"I think she likes you, Willy."

"Yeah, me too." Doug has somehow snuck up behind me. He and Michael exchange low fives. "How you doing, kiddo?"

"What's gay?" Michael asks him.

My best friend plants his fists on his hips and strikes a burlesque pose.

"Doug ..." I've *finally* attained that elusive fatherly tone. And it works.

"It means happy, Michael." As Doug lifts his gaze from the boy to me, it morphs from benevolent to betrayed. "It's the opposite of how I'm feeling about Willy right now."

"Come on, Doug. I was going to tell you." He just keeps looking at me, disgusted. "You don't understand. Langstrom gave me no choice."

"Whatever. A lot of people put their necks on the line to save your job. Then you just up and quit."

"Seriously, he provoked me."

"Yeah," Michael says. "And he made me cry!"

Doug blinks at the boy, astonished and confused. "He did?"

"Yeah, then Willy mashed cookies all over his desk."

"Oh, then tell him I forgive him then."

"He forgives you, Willy."

Shaq

I don't actually remember deciding anything, only that I know I did. And when that happens, it's usually better to just go with whatever I come up with than to try and second-guess myself. I have a vague, out-of-body image of myself sitting on the mission floor, thinking about my throbbing toe, imagining the blood oozing and soaking into my sock. That's when the black spots I was trying so hard to erase started filling in with color, or at least one of them did. It started out as a tiny stream of blood, then mixed with water and eventually thinned into a constant flow of clear liquid gurgling down some unseen drain. The old Father Joe would have twisted that into some spiritual lesson about the water that came pouring out of Jesus' side. Then he would blame my memory on my guilt and start talking about confessing and repenting and all that rot. But that's what scared me, what got me up off the floor and cleaning up the mission. It wasn't some spiritual epiphany; it was an actual memory, one of mine. And I couldn't bear to look at it. So I decided to do something about it.

Now every step feels like a dozen tiny spears jabbing into the place my toenail used to be. I try to focus on that. Otherwise I'll over-think my decision and start talking myself out of it.

It evolved slowly as I tried to clean up the mess I'd made at the mission. I wanted to gather all that anger swirling inside me and funnel it toward Willy. But there was just too much to go around. When I resituated the toppled cots, all I could think about was how Father Joe treats me like a child, how he seems to trust Willy more than me these days, and how he leaves me alone in the mission — when he *knows* I could find another belt if I set my mind to it. Makes me wonder if he's tempting me, or if maybe he's hoping I find one and finally put myself out of his misery. Rehanging the shower curtain just reminded me how Willy is bent on taking what's mine, from the honeymoon suite to Father Joe. How he takes Michael whenever he pleases. And how I'm certain he'll take Patrice as soon as he finds her.

I discover Michael's stuffed monkey, but even that doesn't help, what with the way the boy swells my heart one second, then breaks it again every time he chooses Willy over me.

But as much as I want to make this all about Willy, it's not. It's about Patrice. It's always been about Patrice. She's at the center of everything. The rest of us are simply in orbit around her, like spokes on a wheel going nowhere. Not only that, she can make the black spots go away. I know because that's what she does in my dreams.

It's simple. I just need to find her before Willy does. And that, I now realize, is going to take some money. It's called civil disobedience, like Rosa Parks and Martin Luther King Jr. Or maybe it's more like Jesus and Robin Hood, breaking a few laws for the greater good. Or maybe I'm just making stuff up so I won't feel bad about what I'm about to do. I take one deep breath, then another, before wandering into the Starbucks on Twenty-first Avenue.

The rich coffee smell is rife with too many memories to process, as if maybe I owned a coffee shop in my former life. I pause inside the door, waiting for some sort of new understanding about my time before the mission, but there's nothing there. The music is Thelonious Monk, the live version of "Well You Needn't," I believe. When the hippie behind the counter greets me, I get nervous and duck into the bathroom. But apparently my bladder only works at the mission. I splash cold water on my grizzled face. The mirror makes me look a decade older than the version of me in my head. I'm sure it's the *lack* of mirrors in recent years that are responsible for that unreliable image. Either way, I have a job to do and counting my wrinkles won't help.

On my way out, I'm forced into an awkward pardon-me two-step with a blond guy in a green apron that has the word "manager" on it. Before disappearing behind an office door, he does a double take, his wave petering out in midair, like he's realized too late that he's mistaken me for someone else.

I fill my mind with Robin Hood and Rosa Parks and Father Joe and humanity and the greater good and just whatever I can glom onto for inspiration. I imagine God smiling at the thinning spot on top of my head. But it doesn't help. I venture out to the pastry display case, stroke my thin carpet of beard, and pretend to mull my options. Monk's quirky piano musings make me feel light, capable, guiltless.

There's only three customers in the place, all oblivious to the shady character licking his lips and trying to make sense of the menu. The girl has her nose in a textbook. One of the guys is typing into his laptop, the other snoring softly in a leather chair. So far I've counted four employees on duty. The manager hasn't reappeared; the lady with the headset is adding whipped cream to some frothy beverage and talking too loud in the direction of no one. The girl that looks like a preppy witch ignites a loud coffee machine. And the military-looking guy catches my eye and says, "What can I get started for you today?"

The frenetic drum solo is making it hard to think.

I muster all my pent-up indignation and say, "Maybe you could start a campaign to rid your restroom of rodents!"

"Excuse me?" According to his nametag, his name is Todd.

"Yeah there's a big rat in the men's room. It's disgusting," I say, pleased to see at least two heads turn in my direction. "Not to mention a health hazard."

"I'm sorry, sir," he says. "Let me get your order and I'll get right on that."

"I'll have a coffee then."

"What kind?"

"Really hot, with lots of cream and sugar."

"Tall, Grande, Venti?"

For a second I think Todd's swearing at me, as if he's already on to my scheme and is making a preemptive strike.

"How about medium then?"

"Medium size or medium roast?"

"Yes," I say. "And you'd better get on that business with the rat in case another customer goes in there."

"Yes, sir. And just so you know, your coffee is on the house."

When he turns to pour my coffee, I take another quick inventory of the people in the room and the money in the tip jar. Seconds later, Todd's chaffed hand brushes mine as he passes me the coffee. The quick intimacy is unnerving. But then he's off to take care of the fictional rat in the men's room. As soon as the door clicks shut, I belly up close to the counter and reach into the tip jar. I remove every scrap of paper money and cram it into my front pocket. When no one shouts, "Stop thief!" I amble over to a revolving CD rack and pretend to browse the covers.

I'm about to make my getaway when one of Todd's aproned co-workers pours a refill for the laptop guy. She's like a doll, pig-tailed and freckled and utterly naive. I step to the counter again, bolder now, forcing myself to make eye contact, then ask her to break a five-dollar bill — the very one that rightfully belonged to her just a few minutes ago.

"Sure thing," she says.

"I'll need some quarters too, to make some calls."

She regards me with a funny face, not quite suspicious, but close. Probably hard for her to fathom a Starbucks customer who doesn't own a cell phone. As she makes change for me, I sip my coffee just to have something to do. I nearly scream out when it scalds my tongue and the top half of my esophagus. But somehow I manage to remain cool until all three one-dollar bills and eight quarters are mine again.

I thank her and exit onto the street.

When I hear the door swing shut behind me, my knees nearly buckle. I did it, took from the rich to help the poor. Or at least the poor in spirit. And I got away with it too. Then I feel a hand on my shoulder, squeezing. I hear teeth grinding even as I turn to lock gazes with the blond manager. I try to run but only manage to drop my coffee instead. The resulting splatter blisters my left ankle in the process. He grabs a fistful of my shirt and spins me around.

"I should call the cops," he says. "But frankly, I'm just too curious."

"I'm sorry. Here …" I make a frantic grab at my pocket, prepared to give the money back. But he just knocks my arm away.

"What's *happened* to you?"

I can't answer that. I'd like to, but I just can't.

"It's me. Randy." We're close enough for me to smell his gum, his cologne, even a hint of perspiration. But his eyes keep searching mine, helplessly and in vain, as if my face holds a secret.

"I think you've got the wrong guy," I say. There's no tingling spine or glassy mouth this time, just a sharp pain behind my left eye. And the longer I look, the more familiar he seems.

"I thought so too. But no, I can tell it's you."

"Who?" I can't believe how badly I want to hear his answer.

But Todd interrupts, propping the door open with his foot, asking if everything is okay.

"Yep," the manager says. "Just catching up with an old friend."

"Okay." Todd then makes a move to clean up my spilled coffee.

"Leave it," Randy says. "In fact, how about you run back inside and pour him a refill?"

"If you say so," Todd says. Then to me, "And just so you know, mister, I didn't find any rats in the bathroom."

When we're alone again, Randy loosens his grip but doesn't let go. I read his nametag again, then wait to see if it flips a light switch in my head. But I get nothing. He's pressing his right hand into my left, hard. There's something there, like balled up napkins maybe. I glance down, but he squeezes my hand again until I look him in the eye.

"Hard times or no, if you ever steal from me again, I'll chain your sorry butt to my fender and drag you to jail myself. Got it?"

I nod, then nearly keel over as he releases my hand and my shoulder at once. I can't help looking at the paper he placed in my hand before cramming it in my front pocket. It's a wad of twenty-dollar bills.

I mouth the words *thank you* as I back away.

"We're even now," he says. "Don't forget your coffee."

Todd steps forward and offers me a steaming paper cup. I take it, then turn and walk away, huddled and shivering like it's winter. I hear Todd ask, "You know that guy?"

I pause, praying he'll say my name.

"Nah, man. I just thought I did."

Ozena

I'm a prisoner in my own cubicle. But the simple fact is, I cannot avoid Reggie any longer. I did peruse the employee handbook and verify his "loophole": Management is indeed forbidden to fraternize with the worker bees, but there's no written prohibition of office romances when it comes to the upper echelon of Javatek executives. Thus if you have the word *president* or *chief* on the title line of your business card, you can date whomever you please. As long as they agree to date you back of course. They do still call that sexual harassment.

Regardless, there's no way I can continue to avoid Reggie *and* make my case for the promotion. According to the job posting tacked to the break room corkboard, the deadline for announcing the new Customer Service Manager is Monday afternoon. I could take the cowardly way out and send Reggie an email detailing all the reasons I'm more qualified than Sheila to run the department. But maybe Reggie needs to see the look on my face when I ask. I don't think I'll cry, but I did practice making earnest gazes in my bedroom mirror for an hour last night. When I whined again about how cheesy it felt to vie for this promotion, Eugene turned into a motivational speaker. Lloyd Jr. suggested we just pray about it. I had him do it.

Since the Javatek suits are meeting with shareholders until three, I have another forty-five minutes to bolster my resolve. I close my eyes and watch my imaginary self knock on Reggie's office door, whisk my way over the threshold, and win the promotion before my bottom warms the leather on his guest chair.

I try not to look at the clock. Ten o'clock has come and gone with no call from Willy. And I could really use his support this morning. I'm tempted to sulk, but instead I chide myself for becoming so dependent on his calls.

I hear another of Reggie's tuneless whistles. The meeting has adjourned early.

A wave of panic gathers around my neck and starts to squeeze. A dozen excuses assault my brain. Why not wait until tomorrow? Or until I finish updating the database project? Am I not just being greedy? Does God really want me to have this promotion? What if I have to work longer hours and miss spending time with Lloyd? But then Lloyd is the point, isn't he? His future, his health? And what if Reggie gets the wrong idea? Maybe I should prop my fat repulsive ankles on his desk to ward off any romantic notions he might have.

I look to the Whiteheads for help and nearly choke at their collective response. As if on cue, the entire family begins nodding their heads in perfect unison at my unasked questions.

It takes a second to realize that someone has bumped my cubicle wall, and that the resultant shimmying is what caused the nodding consensus of my fake family. It takes another second to realize it was Sheila who did the bumping. She's rubbing her elbow and wincing when she comes into view. She looks frazzled and out of sorts, her face pink in all the wrong places.

"Are you okay?" I ask.

"I'll live. Just in a hurry is all."

"Oh?" I ask a little too innocently as I gather my notes for the impromptu meeting with Reg.

"Yeah, I need to talk to Reggie before ..." Her eyes dart to the manila folder in my hand. "Never mind. I just need to talk to Reggie."

Was I really that obvious, to have filled my folder with my perfect attendance record and customer service reviews, then labeled it "Promotion Data"? "Come on, Sheila. Let's not make this personal, okay? We're both vying for the same thing. I say we give it our best shot and let the best man win. Right?"

"I say every man for herself."

I sigh like an untied balloon, taking an awkward stutter-step backward into my office chair. It swivels, bangs against the desk, then rebounds right back into my hipbone. The Whiteheads are still grinning, but shaking their heads now, as if warning me about flying off at the mouth.

"Look Ozena, don't take this wrong. It's not that I don't like you. You're just more qualified, is all. You're smarter, prettier, and people generally like you better. Which is why I don't understand why you're always trying so hard to outdo me in ... well, everything."

"But ... but ... I have the fattest ankles in the whole company." I thrust the left one forward for proof, just before I fully comprehend that I've actually said this out loud. And just how stupid it sounded.

Sheila stares at me and finally says, "You just don't get it, do you?"

"I guess not," and I mean it.

"Maybe it's all the vapors from your constant fumigations." Sheila's smiling now. "No one has that many bugs."

She turns and walks, head down now, toward Reggie's closed door.

I sit and stare at the Whiteheads. "That went well, don't you think?"

There's no nodding or shaking now. Just duplicitous grins all around.

* * *

I sit and stew, occasionally glancing up at Reggie's closed door. My mind conjures a reel of dreamlike snippets — Reggie and Sheila in a lovers' embrace, Reggie and Sheila tossing darts at a life-size headshot of me, Reggie and Sheila raising a bubbly toast as they compose the requisite paperwork to install her as my new boss.

These are the thoughts I'm tormenting myself with when Reggie buzzes me.

"Can I see you in my office?"

"Sure, give me two minutes."

I grab my folder and duck into the ladies' room. If I were the star of a movie, this is where I'd splash water on my face and stare at my reflection till I got my bearings. But then movie people don't have to worry about smearing eye makeup or reapplying lotion. I check my teeth, examine myself in the mirror (not quite approving), then walk stiff-backed to Reggie's office. My nerves steady with every step. If Reggie — or God, for that matter — wants me to have the promotion, I'll get it. I knock once and let myself in. I can't help but smile at the squealing hinge.

"Ozena, come in. Have a seat. I'll just be a minute."

He clicks his mouse a few times, his expression grim and proficient in the glow of his monitor. It's nice to see how well he's adapted to his new executive status. I want to tell him so but can't think of a way to broach the subject without embarrassing one or both of us.

"Listen," Reggie says at once. "I just had a talk with Sheila. And well ... frankly, I'm sort of running out of time here. I really do need to make a decision."

I'm experiencing a now-or-never feeling as I grip my folder like a security blanket. "Right, about that promotion ..."

Reggie blinks once, as if I've broken his train of thought. Then he continues, "Oh, right. Well as you know, my deadline for naming our new Customer Service Manager is Monday afternoon. There were only ever two real viable candidates, you and Sheila."

"Thank you, Reggie. I'm really flattered."

He makes a sour face, then leans forward and wrings his clasped hands together. Maybe it's my imagination, or just this oppressive case of jitters I'm experiencing, but Reggie really does look more at ease in his fancy suit. Not quite suave, but at least congruent.

"I wasn't really going for flattery, Ozena."

"What are you going for then?"

"I guess I want to know why you didn't want this job. It seemed like the perfect fit. Heck, you would've made a much better manager than me."

"You think I don't *want* it?"

"Well, it's been more than a little frustrating. Every time I've tried to bring it up, you make all these excuses and change the subject."

"What are you talking about? And when?"

"Around the office, at any one of the dinners you refused to go on, the other night while standing on your welcome mat."

"You mean all those times you were trying to get together for dinner, you really did want to talk about business?"

"Well, yeah ... mostly."

"Mostly?"

"Yes and no."

"I'm not sure I'm following you."

"To me it was a foregone conclusion that you'd get the job. It just seemed so obvious until I tried to talk to you about it."

"I'm sorry, Reggie. And more than a little embarrassed too. I thought you wanted ... you know ... to talk about more personal stuff? All that talk about loopholes and dating subordinates and stuff?"

"Well ..." His ears turn pink and he can't seem to focus on any one thing. "I did. I mean, I still do. At first I really wanted your input on ways to improve the department. Then, when this whole promotion thing landed in my lap I wanted to gauge your interest. And frankly, I did have a few more, um, delicate things I wanted to ask you about."

"I'm sorry, I'm still a little confused. Are you saying you wanted to offer me the job, then jump right into asking me on a date? I mean, pardon me for saying so, but that doesn't sound very professional."

"Wait, no. That's not right. I don't want to ask *you* on a date."

I'm surprised at how much this stings. No, I'm shocked. And it must be showing.

Reggie forges on. "I mean, sure I used to want that. But then I eventually accepted the fact that you weren't interested."

"Sorry, Reggie. I'm still a little lost here."

His eyes wander up and over my shoulder, all glazed and dreamy. "It's Sheila."

I turn toward the door, instantly humiliated. How much of this conversation has she heard? And how will I ever recover from it? But the door is still closed and there's no one there. Finally, I say, "What about her?"

"I wanted to ask if you thought she'd go out with me. You know, because you guys are so close and all. Maybe even help me plan our first date. If I could talk her into it, that is."

"Sheila?" I say, trying not to sound too incredulous.

"I know it's a long shot. But I really like her a lot. And, well, it's at least conceivable, isn't it?"

"Of course it is, Reg. It's more than conceivable. I think it's a great idea."

He nods like a dope. And it's adorable. All my relief comes gushing out in a burst of nervous laughter. This is doubly good news. Reggie gets Sheila and I get the promotion. But then I notice his face sagging, his dreamy eyes going gray and cloudy.

"Reggie, she's gorgeous, young, and never been married. She has no kids, a college degree, and a flawless driving record."

"Yeah," he says, sounding more deflated with each syllable. "She's something alright."

"She works out religiously and has perfectly thin ankles."

"Not sure I've ever noticed her ankles before."

He says this with faraway eyes, as if he'd like to dispense of this whole promotion nonsense and go check out Sheila's legs. I have to clear my throat to bring him back.

"So," he says, looking now like he might cry. "I guess I really screwed this one up."

"What are you talking about? This is perfect. You guys will make a great couple. And just to make it official, I'll take it."

"Take what?"

"The job, silly. Now stop wasting time and go talk to Sheila and tell her how you feel."

He makes a strange face and I realize my mistake. I've gotten too chummy with Reggie, too familiar. Management has no business referring to a VP as "silly." I'm about to apologize when Reggie simply says, "Oh, well, actually, I already talked to Sheila. I offered her the job."

"Oh …"

"I'm sorry, Ozena."

I am too. About everything. But I'm too stunned to speak.

Willy

Shaq is pacing on the sidewalk outside the mission, antsy and distracted, like a father on prom night. I can tell he wants to yell at me for being late. But when Michael calls his name, Shaq's apprehension seems to level off. And for the briefest moment I can see the man he was before he lost his mind.

I think I might have liked that man.

He's scrounged up some donated board games and mangy stuffed animals and piled them on the floor of the honeymoon suite. He's also changed and smoothed the blanket for an even playing surface. Michael chooses Hungry Hungry Hippos, and I duck into the kitchen to don my smelly apron and help Darnell with breakfast.

While I work I listen to the laughter and squeals and earnest conversation from the direction of the honeymoon suite. It's hard to tell Shaq's voice from Michael's. And it's impossible to gauge who has the longest face when I finally announce it's time for Michael and me to take off. Shaq seems like a natural with kids, except when his temper flares.

On the way out I ask him, "If I wanted to find somebody's address or home number on the Internet, how would I go about it?"

"You obviously know the name."

"Only the first name."

"Anything else? License number? Where the guy works?"

"It's a girl, actually. And she works at a place called Javatek."

"A girl, eh?"

Michael pipes in with, "Bet it's Zena. That's the only girl he knows."

I don't know why this embarrasses me, but it does. I'm ready to drop it when Shaq says, "I'll see what I can do."

* * *

My theory of yard sales lasted nearly three decades: namely, that yard sales are for losers. I get it — the potential goldmine of bargains as some lucky browser capitalizes on a New Year's resolution gone bad; and selling off the abandoned hobbies, orphaned gifts, inherited cuff links and golf clubs, and misguided impulse buys that are just taking up space. But half the fun of shopping is *not* having to paw your way through lampshades, mismatched croquet sets, and "As Is" stereo equipment just to find a rare John Coltrane album, only to discover later it's either scratched or warped as a result of sitting in someone's yard all afternoon.

Maybe my second-hand heart has something to do with it as well.

But that all changes on the way home from the mission today. I'm trying in vain to explain the concept of musical improvisation to Michael when we turn into my neighborhood and I spy a menagerie of plastic furniture in blinding primary colors. My hasty parallel parking job nearly takes out a mailbox. Michael showed up on my doorstep with one dingy suitcase, his frayed blanket, and a badly stained car seat. The poor kid needs some toys, some books with pictures, and maybe a few more long-sleeve shirts. A quick scan of my money clip reveals exactly twenty-three dollars. I debate leaving Michael locked in the car, but there's too many horror stories about that, and maybe even a law or two. I muster my sternest fatherly gaze and say, "We're going to pick up a few things here. But absolutely no begging or throwing fits, got it?"

"Okay, Willy. Ooh, I see a Buzz Light Year. And some Veggie movies. And a tire swing! Can we get a tire swing please?"

"They'd have to sell us an oak tree too."

"Okay, I like trees."

The lady guarding the moneybox eyes us through a haze of cigarette smoke as we browse the makeshift aisles of card tables, scarred bookshelves, and inverted cardboard boxes. I keep asking Michael to stop touching everything. He keeps agreeing, apologizing, then promptly forgetting and touching everything anyhow. It takes my full arsenal of self-control to keep from flipping through a bin of vinyl records.

Finally I hit the mother lode. "Hey, a baseball glove." I hold it up and wag it in the boy's face. "What do you say?"

"Okay."

"Just okay?"

He shrugs, then fingers a ceramic ashtray in the clumsy shape of a topless mermaid. I'm not sure if it's the germs or naked breasts that worry me most. Either way, I thrust the glove in his hands to distract him.

"Hold this. Every kid needs a baseball mitt."

"Do you have one too?"

"I used to, but a squirrel got it."

His eyes go wide, alternating between me and the big brown glove.

"Don't worry. Squirrels aren't really all that into leather these days."

It takes less than fifteen minutes to rummage our way through the entire inventory. All told, we end up with two Wiggles CDs, a night-

light, a dozen or so picture books, Rock 'Em Sock 'Em Robots, Battleship, Monopoly, a shoebox full of marbles and those tiny green Army
men, three long-sleeve shirts, a pair of corduroys, and a winter coat.
And of course the baseball glove, but (I realize too late) no ball.

I remind Michael to keep his hands to himself as we approach the
smoking lady behind the card table. When I ask if she happens to have
a baseball to go with the mitt, she says, "It's a yard sale, not Wal-Mart."
I ease my armful of purchases onto the table for her inspection. She
gropes and fumbles through them, making tally marks on a scrap of
paper. I redo the math in my head, confident that the total should be
twenty-two fifty. She taps her pencil on the table, squints through another long drag on her cigarette, and says, "Well?"

"That's it. I think we got everything we need."

"You gonna make me an offer?"

I'm distracted by the impossibly long amount of ash barely clinging to the end of her cigarette. The base of it glows orange and I'm just
positive it's going to topple into her cash drawer when she coughs and
start a fire. Then all at once I understand; she wants to haggle.

"Looks like I got some pretty good deals already, so I'd just like to
pay up and be on my way."

She shakes her head. "Sorry, don't work that way."

"You don't understand. I'm perfectly willing to pay the price on
the tags."

"No, *you* don't understand."

"You can't make me dicker if I don't want to."

"It's my yard, my sale, my stuff."

"You're telling me you won't sell this unless I make you some low-
ball offer?"

"Sure. You think I'm planning an early retirement from selling all
this crap? I don't play shuffleboard or watch soaps. So this is how I get
my kicks."

"Alright, fine. Would you take twenty-one dollars?"

She eyes her scribbled tally again, then looks at Michael with a *can-you-believe-this-guy?* expression.

"Your smoker is about to drop," he says.

"Thanks," she says, but not like she means it.

"You shouldn't do smokers. They make you sick."

"Michael," I say, trying again to make it sound like a threat.

"Run along now, sonny. Your daddy and I are conducting business."

He shrugs and turns and I remind him not to touch anything.

"Try again," she says to me.

"Okay. How about five bucks?"

"That's more like it." She's leering now. "But nope, no deal."

We stare at each other for a small eternity. When I can't stand it any longer, I say, "Aren't you supposed to make a counter-offer?"

"Nah, your low offer is just ridiculous. And you didn't leave me any wiggle room on the high end. Try again."

"Twenty?"

"That's better. But if you offer a ten or a twenty, you need to make like that's the only bills you got. Make up a sob story about how that's all you got in your wallet."

"But it's not. I have twenty-three dollars exactly."

"And you don't never tell how much you're holding. Now I'll be tempted to sell you up to your limit."

"Look, I don't have time for this. What about seventeen-fifty?"

"Much better. A reasonable offer with a hint of an excuse thrown in."

"Do we have a deal?"

"Nope. I think you can do better. And look …" She lifts the night-light off the table. "That thing don't even work."

"How about this? You keep the broken bits and I'll give you fifteen bucks. Either that or I'm out of here."

"There. Was that so hard?"

I reach for my money clip and see her eyes go wide. I hear Michael

264

say, "Uh!", followed by a series of tinkling sounds and a series of crashes, then, "Oh!"

By the time her perturbed gaze swivels back to me, I slap my money on the table and say, "Twenty-three bucks, take it or leave it."

Then I scoop up my new purchases and grab Michael's trembling hand. Before I can get him buckled in, I hear the smoking lady yelling at me to come back and clean up the mess my bratty kid made. I make my way around the car and wave at her before we drive off.

* * *

The resulting adrenaline rush from our narrow escape wears off quicker than I would have thought; it settles into lethargy. In fact, I can't believe how tired I am all of a sudden. Makes me wonder if this involuntary parenthood has my heart finally ready to throw in the towel for good. I'm barely aware of my head drooping to one side or the sharp snapping motion as I wake myself up and steer the Rover back into my lane. I sit up straighter and rub my eyes, considering a convenience store cup of coffee. But I only have a few miles left. I've already decided to skip Michael's bath, and am dreaming of turning in early, when I feel the rumble of gravel under the wheels. I jerk my head up again and gently steer from the shoulder back to the pavement.

Michael is giggling in the backseat, shouting "Do it again, Willy. Do it again!"

The CD blips over to the next track and that's when I realize my problem. The song was in E-flat. But by then it's too late. Blue lights are already flashing in my rearview mirror.

The grumpy policeman makes a great show of shining his flashlight in my eyes before requesting my license and registration. He inspects them silently, then explores the interior of my car with his miniature searchlight. After nodding at Michael, he looks back to me, disgusted.

"Please step out of your vehicle. And keep your hands where I can see them."

He then sits in his car for a small eternity. Michael and I improvise a hand-waving game through his window. When the lawman returns, he keeps his light trained on me and one hand on his revolver. Before I know it, he has me facing the car and is kicking my insteps out into a wide stance. Then he's frisking me.

I turn my head and say, "I think there's some sort of misunderstanding here."

"Shut up and keep still."

Another flashing cruiser pulls in front of my car. Two more serious looking cops get out and muscle-walk toward us, all business.

The next ten minutes are a flurry of surreal activities. I'm touching my nose and walking lines. And I'm all too eager to blow into their little Breathalyzer tube. And then I find myself seated in the back of a police car, straining to see through the cage-like material at what's happening with Michael. There's a lot of radio chatter but it makes no sense.

Finally the first cop returns and I ask him what's going on. He scribbles on his pad and I ask to call my lawyer. He ignores me some more and I have to resist the urge to kick the back of his seat or call him names.

"Look, if you don't believe me, just ask Joe Carter."

"The football player?"

"Yes, exactly."

"Sure thing. I have him on speed dial between Michael Jordan and Peyton Manning."

When he finally turns in his seat, I can barely hear him. Through the windshield of the cruiser I watch a female officer lift Michael out of his car seat, wide-eyed and searching. The officer is prattling on about unpaid parking tickets, revoked driver's licenses, parole violations, destruction of private property at a yard sale (that nicotined battleaxe actually got my license and reported me), counterfeiting, and my right to remain silent. But all I can hear is my pulse pounding in my throat and the muted pleading of a small scared boy outside my window.

Wiwwy?

Shaq

My plan yesterday was to take my newly found fortune directly to the nearest pay phone and start making calls. But the encounter with that Randy guy sent my brain into a tizzy and left my body drained. I sleepwalked home, skipped dinner, and turned in early. It took an extra cup of coffee to get me up and moving. Then playing with Michael this morning calmed my addled mind enough to think.

Now I set off on foot, heading north and trying to clear my head for the task at hand. At some point I find myself leaning against the window of a used record shop. I down the last of my coffee and fish out the bulky wad of cash that Randy forced on me. There's a twenty-dollar bill on the outside. I glance around before counting it again, then lose count after a dozen or so more. Amazing, I have twenty roommates who'd sell their eyes for a hundred bucks. It looks like a couple of hundred, at least. But even as I run my fingers across the bills again, I don't seem to care one way or the other.

The door to the record shop dings open and two yappy teenage girls emerge, all tinted and pierced and unnaturally pale. I slip the money back in my pocket and do my best to turn invisible. They don't notice me at first. But then the plump one raises a restraining forearm as the oblivious waif in the Guns N' Roses T-shirt nearly bumps into me. They pause, taking a quick inventory. And in that instant I can see me as they do — threadbare work pants, oversized wingtips, too tight sweater all frayed and out of season, nearly three weeks of stubble.

The skinny one digs into her jeans pocket and extends an open palm with what looks to be about twenty-eight cents. I don't mean to reach for it, but I do. That's when the heavy girl slaps her friend's wrist, catapulting the coins in every direction. One of the pennies hits my cheek. I'm shocked by how cold it is.

"Hey," the skinny girl squeals. "What the — ?"

"Don't let him touch you. Not unless you *want* leprosy or gonorrhea or something."

"What I wanted was to give the poor guy some change."

"Let him pick it up then. The exercise might sober him up."

"Look at him, he ain't drunk."

"If not drunk, then Looney Tunes." The big girl grabs a handful of her friend's shirt, likely to keep her from kneeling to gather the coins. "Either way, he's wasted."

They step off the curb and away from me. But not before the skinny Samaritan girl glances back to confirm her diagnosis.

"No, you're wrong. He's just sad."

I wish now I had another swig of coffee. To wash down the bulge forming in my throat. When the girls disappear into a vintage clothing store, I start moving, careful to step around the coins — and not just because I have a pocket full of money. I'm tempted to chase after the girls. I want to tell them I'm not what they think. I'm not really homeless because I have a home. Right now, it's the mission. And before that I had a regular home, just like them.

What I *don't* have right now is a past.

I fish the library printout from my pocket first, a single-spaced list of every *Patrice* I could find in a five-state area. There are twenty-three in all; more than half in Tennessee, the rest scattered among Georgia, Mississippi, Alabama, and Kentucky. My original plan was to dial the local numbers until I ran out of money.

I consider using the pay phone at the mission, but I don't want Father Joe to overhear me. Besides the library's closer. And the symmetry is nice since that's where I came up with the list in the first place. I slip my hand into my pocket and finger the wad of twenties. The fact that I can now afford the bus makes me feel like walking. It takes a half hour or more to get to the library. Yet even after thirty minutes I still have no idea what I'll say to Patrice when I finally get her on the phone. But she'll know what to say. She always does. Just outside the door I have to weave my way through an obnoxious band of skateboarders. They cut me off, call me names, ask to see my bottle and if *they* can borrow money from *me*. I keep my head down and a tight grip on my twenties and eventually step into the coolness of the library. After filling my lungs with conditioned air, I approach the circulation desk. The middle-aged librarian recognizes me but only as the pervert who smells the women, not as the volunteer computer repairman. Her eyes go wide behind her funky glasses when I produce a twenty and ask for change.

"I'm sorry, sir. This is not a convenience store."

"You don't sound sorry."

"I guess you'll have to take my word for it then. Why don't you try the bank around the corner?"

"No, ma'am. How about you help me out so I don't have to make a scene? You know, start yelling and moaning about how the mean library lady won't help the poor homeless man make change to call his wife and kid on the pay phone."

My own words bring me up short. Where did that come from? A kid? Was it just for effect, or do Patrice and I really have a child? My sinuses fill with that baby powder smell again.

"Very well," she says, eyeing the money like it's infected. Without touching it, she slides a ten, a five, and a bunch of quarters across the desk. "I just hope this wife of yours knows how you spend your time in the library."

"I'll be sure and remind her." I know I shouldn't, but I thrust my chin at her and make a loud sniffing noise. She recoils and I just know Father Joe is going to get another call.

I have my list of numbers and a pocketful of quarters, but still no idea what I plan to say when I get Patrice on the phone. So I log onto the library's computer and click around familiar websites trying to clear my head. At some point, I remember Willy's odd request about looking up some lady's number. Javatek is easy enough to find. And after scrolling through several pages I find the name closest to the one Michael mentioned. By the time I jot her information down, I realize I'm getting anxious. I know myself well; if I don't get busy calling for Patrice I might just chicken out.

Ironic or not, I can't help noticing the pay phone's receiver stinks worse than the one at the mission. I hold my breath and dial the first number with a 6 –1 – 5 area code. An answering machine picks up and I panic and hang up before leaving a message. My first fifty cents wasted.

The next number rings forever and the one after that tells me I have the wrong number. Finally, around the eighth or ninth call a man answers. Sounds like he's been drinking.

"May I speak to Patrice please?"

"Who is this?"

"I go by Shaq, since I sorta lost my real name awhile back."

"Sounds like you lost your marbles too. What do you want with Patrice?"

"I'd like to speak to her please."

"Mind if I ask why?"

"Just talking, that's all."

"Well I didn't figure you was gonna play badminton or split the atom together over the phone."

I should have thought this part through. "Look, I used to be married to a Patrice. I can't be sure, but I think I hurt her pretty bad."

"Me too, pal. Me too."

"So can I speak to her please?"

"Sure, if you can find her. And tell her Eric says hello."

Before he can hang up on me, I blurt out, "Wait, does she have a father named Joe?" The only answer is the mechanical clink of the pay phone digesting my quarters, followed by an obnoxious dial tone.

Instead of scratching through that number with the tiny pencil I borrowed from the library, I circle it. Then I drop two more coins in the slot and dial the next number on the list.

FOUR

Willy

Shaq is waiting at the police station when I get there. I was able to talk the arresting officer into one cell phone call on the ride here — I used it to ream Father Joe out for the charges against me that *he* allegedly took take care of with the judge. I guess his idea of apologizing is to send Shaq to bail me out — or just voyeuristically watch my incarceration.

I consider waving my cuffed hands at Shaq as I'm ushered through fingerprints, mug shots, and a lot of inane questions from grumpy lawmen. Once the booking procedure is finished I'm escorted to a holding cell by the nicest of all the cops. But there's a triangular booger dangling in his mustache. Along the way I inquire about my one phone call.

"That's just on TV." The crusty triangle wafts back and forth when he talks. I want to tell him, to save him the embarrassment of his fellow officers, but I can't figure out how.

"So I don't even get one call?"

"Didn't say that. Your cell has a pay phone. You can make as many as you want if you got quarters."

"Shaq?" I say, nearly shouting. "I need quarters for the phone."

Without a word, Shaq walks toward me shoveling coins from his pocket and dropping them in my cupped hands.

"Thanks, Shaq. I owe you."

The cop steering me by the elbow says, "That's gotta hurt."

"What's that?" I say.

"Grubbing coins from a wino. Bumming money from a bum."

Shaq looks up, blinking and unsure.

"He's no wino," I say.

"Whatever," the cop says, tsking and shaking his head. "You know what they say, if it walks like a wino and smells like a wino ..."

"You know you have a booger in your mustache."

I say this much louder than necessary, causing a couple of his buddies to laugh quietly at their desks. He dabs at his upper lip with the back of his free hand. Shaq doesn't even try to hide his smile.

Another cop says, "That's one tenacious little booger, Charlie."

I feel his thumb digging into my flesh, then he shoves me into the cell and slams the door behind me.

My first call is to check my messages. I have one, from Stan. My agent sounds more perturbed than sleepy, but I delete it anyway. Next I call Derrick. While his phone rings I torture myself with familiar warnings: Derrick telling me to keep my nose clean, Father Joe warning me about one more slipup, Dean Langstrom reminding me that someday soon I'll be revealed as a fake and phony and a hack, my grandmother telling me to wash behind my ears ...

By the time he answers, I'm sweaty and breathless. I explain, as best I can, what's going on. He's quiet when I tell him about my swervy driving and my accidental garage sale larceny.

"You stole from a garage sale?"

"Don't be ridiculous. I paid for the stuff."

"Then what's the problem?"

"Apparently I used a counterfeit bill."

Derrick's string of stilted questions ends with, "Where did you get counterfeit money?"

"From a couple of pot heads I know."

He adopts his most lawyerly tone and says, "I can't help you if you won't tell me what's going on, Willy."

"For once in my life, I'm telling the absolute truth. And I *thought* that was supposed to set me free."

"Look, just sit tight while I figure a few things out. Until then, your best bet is to see if you can get Father Joe to talk to the judge for you."

"That's it?"

"At this hour, yeah. I'm afraid it is."

"Thanks a lot, Derrick."

"But I didn't do anything yet."

"Exactly," I say, then slam the phone down. I try to clear my head of the dark, self-incriminating thoughts. But the picture in my head is one long line of dominoes, the first one teetering precariously toward the rest. Each represents something else I'm on the brink of losing forever — Michael, my job, my car, my house, whatever's left of my reputation, and anything I have with Ozena. Without a deck of cards I do the only thing I can think to do; I lift the receiver and call Information. I ignore all the voice prompts until a real live person comes on the line.

"Directory assistance." She sounds awfully chipper for an operator. "City and state please?"

"Nashville, Tennessee."

"What listing?"

"Um, Ozena."

She asks me to spell it. After a lengthy pause, she comes back on the line. "I'm sorry, sir. We have no business listing for Ozena."

"Actually, it's residential, not business."

"And what is the party's first name?"

"Ozena. That is the first name."

"Sir." She sounds decidedly less chipper now. And I don't blame her. "I'm afraid I'm going to need the party's last name."

"Can't you do a search on your computer? I mean, how many Ozenas can there be in Nashville?"

"I'm sure I don't know."

"Aren't you curious?"

"Excuse me?"

"You have to admit it's an interesting question. And I could really use the help. I'm desperate, calling from a jail cell actually."

"Is there anything else I can help you with?"

"Anything *else*? I'm still waiting on the first bit of help."

It's not her fault. I would have hung up on me too.

When I can't think of anything else to do I dial Javatek's toll-free number. I start speaking when I hear Ozena, forgetting for a moment that it's only her recorded voice. She begins by reminding me of

I get more than a little excited when she directs me to hit "2" for an employee directory. But my hopes are dashed when she asks for the first three letters of the party's *last* name. Guessing doesn't do any good either. After entering a few dozen combinations of letters I give up and just listen to Ozena's voice some more, wondering if there's some way to record her recording so I can listen to it at home or in my car.

I resist the urge to tell her things, at least out loud. But my internal monologue trips all over itself admitting what a wretched legal guardian I turned out to be, confessing an ignorant distaste for kids of all shapes and sizes, and owning up to just how much I miss Lucy's kid. I want Ozena to tell me I'm not crazy for wanting to storm the Department of Child Services and take him back.

Officer Charlie shows up again (sans booger) and unlocks my cell. I ignore him and focus on Ozena's voice some more. I especially love the way she says, "Otherwise, please stay on the line and the next available operator will assist you."

"Let's go, Finneran," Officer Charlie says. "The bum scrounged enough pocket change to post your bond."

That's when I realize I don't really care if I get out of here or not. That I'd rather sit here and listen to pretend Ozena than face the fact that I'm the world's worst excuse for a surrogate parent, that maybe Michael really would be better off in foster care than with me. That I had no business allowing myself to get so attached to him in the first place. I'm already picturing the smug look on Aunt Nadine's face when I hear for the third time today the two most blessed syllables in the English language.

"Willy?"

A female officer is holding Michael's hand. When I emerge from the bank of cells he breaks her grasp and runs toward me, head down and toddling hard. He hugs my thigh and I realize I don't even care if he's wiping snot on my pants. I stroke his hair, then meet Shaq's gaze.

Officer Charlie says, "Expect a call from Child Services in the morning."

"So we're free to go?"

"You are; your car's not."

He stares at me, unspeaking. When I can't stand it any longer I say, "Something on your mind?"

"Never seen nothing like it. You got bums posting bail and football legends pulling strings to get your license back and charges reduced."

I take one deep breath, another, and face the now disinterested policeman. "I'm sorry, you know, about the booger thing."

He blinks at me, then fingers the grip of his billy stick.

"Seriously, I was out of line." I spread my arms wide, take one clumsy step forward with Michael still clinging to my thigh, and attempt to hug Officer Charlie. He reaches for his holster, his crazed eyes darting back and forth between me and the "wino." "I said I was sorry, so how about a hug?"

The surrounding officers whoop and applaud and make catcalls. Officer Charlie offers his hand instead. I shake it.

* * *

As if my first trip to jail were not surreal enough, Shaq asks the sergeant to call us a cab, then informs me that he's paying. I resist the urge to ask him if Father Joe gives him an allowance. At least the cops had the foresight to retrieve Michael's car seat and hand it to me on my way out.

Shaq is unusually quiet on the drive; he's even ignoring Michael, just staring straight ahead. Then without warning he lists to one side and digs something out of his pocket. The next thing I know he's slipping a folded scrap of paper into my hand.

"What's this?"

"Paybacks."

"For what?"

"You take up for me sometimes. You don't freak out when I play with Michael."

I unfold and read the note. Under the word *Home* there's a phone number.

Before I can ask, Shaq says, "Coming up with the last name wasn't that hard. According to the website, she's been employee of the month three times."

"But this is her home number. Surely they didn't post that on the company website?"

Shaq shakes his head. "It's called a phone book, Willy."

* * *

The next morning Shaq seems as tired and distracted as I feel when we help get Darnell through yet another Saturday breakfast at the mission. We work by rote, efficient and mostly quiet (except for Michael shouting redundant questions over the sound of sizzling grease and clanking utensils — *What's that do? Why? Can I have another bacon? Why not?*).

When the last rack of dishes is put away I check on Michael and Shaq. They're coloring and giggling on the floor of the honeymoon suite. I find a nearby cot and collapse onto it, asleep in seconds.

In the dream I'm loading Lucy's Javatek 3000 with gunpowder and gasoline. Father Joe is there, along with Rufus and Bernie the Bass Player. The security guard from the hotel keeps placing me in a headlock and rubbing the top of my head with the sole of that miserable blue Puma sneaker. We're all on stage at the swanky Sheraton ballroom, the dance floor filled with homeless guys from the mission, all dancing with versions of Lucy. Alvin is there too, his arm around Ozena (something I know without knowing in that dreamy way). I concentrate on their faces, knowing I have no clue what either of them looks like in real life. Even in the dream I'm certain I'll wake later and realize I've transposed Alvin and Ozena with younger versions of Ronnie and Gladys Cheevers. I'm standing over the fuse, flicking my grandfather's

lighter into action when I feel a large presence looming over me. I open
one eye and see Father Joe sitting at the foot of my cot.

I'm watching him watch Michael and Shaq when it dawns on me
that Father Joe seems to have his own gravity that keeps pulling all
these dreary souls back night after night, despite the fact that he rarely
interacts with any of them. He's not even really that nice to us. Legally,
I'm the only one bound to this place. But even I can't help picturing
myself being drawn to the mission, even after I've served my time. I
think it boils down to the fact that we don't want to disappoint him.
And it's got nothing to do with pity or how unfair his life has been
(most of the regulars here either don't know or don't care about Joe's
past). It's not just his intimidating presence or his occasional bouts
of tenderness. Or even his fading celebrity. It's like we're all pulling
for him. We want him to like us. To see some glint of potential in us,
something we could never see ourselves, but something that makes us
worthy in his eyes.

Eventually I blink myself awake and sit up. I'm massaging my
eyelids when he juts his chin toward the honeymoon suite and says,
"They're something, huh?"

"Yeah, two peas in a pod. Maybe that's what Shaq needs." I pause
for comedic effect, then add, "A kid of his own."

"Maybe that's his problem. Maybe he already got one." I stare at
Father Joe to gauge if he's serious — he is. "Or had one."

We watch a while in silence. Then I say, "I hope you didn't come in
here to ask for a ride."

"I'll need one soon enough." He studies a scab on the back of his
hand.

"Meaning?"

"We'll be moving soon."

"Moving? As in packing up all your stuff and going to live somewhere else?"

He nods, then does that inflating thing again that makes my skin
prickle. "This'll all be over soon."

"What?"

"This, the mission."

"But why?"

"Judge Reynolds died in his sleep last night."

"That's terrible—but what's that got to do with closing down the mission? Isn't this like a state run thing?"

"Nope. He set the whole thing up as a personal favor to me. Pulled some strings, got the land donated and paid to have the building renovated out of his own pocket. He called in personal favors to get the cots in place, the food delivered every Tuesday morning, keep the lights and heat on. So it's all private run, not the government."

"Who owns the building then?"

"That'd be the judge."

"Yeah?"

Father Joe pulls a wrinkled fax from his hip pocket and hands it to me. I scan the enclosed document to get the gist of it. Now that the judge was gone, his two sons planned to divest the building in an upcoming estate sale.

"Judge said he was going to change his will, leave the mission to me. Guess he never got around to it. Kinda like me and them parking tickets. Sorry about that, Willy. Didn't mean to get you in trouble."

I start to speak, then stop. I open my mouth again, then snap it shut again.

"Something on your mind, Willy?"

"Any chance you could buy it?"

He laughs, but it's hollow and sad.

"I never see you spending any money, so I figure whatever they pay you could go to the taxes."

"Who is *they*?"

"I don't know. Whoever pays your salary, I guess."

"Ain't got no salary, Willy."

"Well then how do you afford food and the electricity and stuff?"

"Judge paid 'em."

I'm finding it exceedingly difficult to hang onto my grudge against Reynolds. "But what about the crutches? Darnell's glasses? Prophet's hearing aid?"

"We got some donations. And the judge gave me a few thousand a year. But that other stuff was God. He took what little social security I get and multiplied it."

"I thought you didn't have any use for Him."

"I don't. But that don't mean He ain't using me." He looks at his massive hands, then says, "Or you either."

I felt my mouth open and close several more times, like a wooden dummy with some unseen someone pulling my strings but failing to provide the words.

Shaq

"What's this?" I say when Father Joe hands me my old Army fatigue jacket.

"Saw one of the twins trying to make off with it. Besides, winter's coming. And we'll be leaving out of here soon."

"Leaving?"

Father Joe nods, almost. It's more like he blinked with his whole head. Then he notices Michael beside me and says, "Why don't you run along and see your daddy? I need to talk to Shaq for a minute."

I glance at Willy and can tell by the look on his face, he already knows what Joe is trying to explain to me.

"Leaving to where?"

This time he almost shrugs, just a whisper of a motion that implies a lot of the same stuff I'm feeling — confusion, loss, despair? Finally he says, "Someplace. Probably a hotel until I can figure something else out."

"But why?"

"Judge died."

It takes a second to sort it all out. The judge owns this place, or pays the taxes on it or whatever it is Joe told me he does for us. All I know is that now that he's gone, Joe won't be able to keep it up. And even while I'm processing all that, I can't help resenting the fact that Father Joe told Willy first.

"Shaq?" It's Michael tugging on my pant leg. Father Joe's news has blindsided me. All at once I'm oblivious and dizzy. "Are we still coloring?"

"Michael," Willy says. "Come on back here and let the grown-ups talk."

"But Shaq promised to color with me."

"You can color later."

Michael alternates his accusing gaze between Willy and me. He knows there's more going on than he can comprehend. I want to kneel down and hug him and tell him I understand that feeling all too well. But I'm still reeling from Joe's news.

"You run along and help Willy. We'll color in a few minutes, I promise."

I squeeze his shoulder once and nudge him in the direction of the kitchen. He offers a last suspicious scowl and trudges away. Father Joe watches the entire exchange in a distracted haze. He looks a decade older.

I stare at his face hard and say, "But I can't leave here."

"You got no choice. Don't none of us do."

"But you don't understand. This is all I know."

He regards me with an ironic expression, part glare, part grin, and all-knowing. And I get his unspoken meaning at once. This is really the only place he's ever known too, at least since prison. He doesn't drive or go to church or to the movies. His social life is as bleak as my memory. All he knows these days is helping the helpless and searching for his baby girl. And the inside of this mission.

As if reading my thoughts, he says, "Trust me, I do understand."

He thinks we're the same but we're not. Father Joe has a context. He understands how he ended up here. Tortured as it may be, *he has a past*. And it's not all bad. He has glory days and a mama who loved him, press clippings and trophies and even all those years in prison. They may have been awful, but they're his. They help complete his picture, put it in a frame, even if it's a bad picture with a splintered frame and cracked glass. Every day he wakes up in pain about his baby girl. But whether he knows it or not, some glimmer of hope drags him out of his bed and shoves him through the day. Even if his motivation is off, he can help people all day and hope that God will return the favor, even if he beds down every night with the same pain he woke up with, like it's there waiting for him.

But I've got none of that. All I have is my first hellish day in this building and every day since. Before that, there's nothing but unreliable pieces, like somebody else's scrapbook, with pages missing. My entire history, my whole biography resides within the walls of the place I'm now told I have to leave.

"Better pack your things," Father Joe says.

For the first time since I've known him I laugh in his face. Everything I own is already tucked inside a third-hand knapsack. I stay packed, just never dreamed I'd have to actually move. Finally, I ball up the fatigue jacket and hurl it at the ground, then stomp it like a child. Michael is still watching us from the doorway in the kitchen. I stare at him, hating the sound of my words before they leap from the end of my tongue. "What are you looking at, boy?"

The tears spring in his eyes at once. I can feel the heat of Father Joe's glare on my cheek as Willy looks up. I don't have to like the man, but at least he takes up for his kid. Then the most remarkable thing happens. I hear Michael taking up for *me*.

"It's okay, Shaq. Don't be sad. You can come and live with me and Willy."

Willy's eyes go wide and look to Father Joe for help.

"Thanks anyway, kid," I say to Michael. "But Willy doesn't want a dirty homeless guy hanging around his house."

"It's not that," Willy says. "It's just really, you know, small. And *already* dirty."

Father Joe finally intervenes and says, "Don't sweat it, Willy. I made some calls and we'll stay at the 8th Street shelter till something else comes along."

"8th Street?" Please. Even the homeless have standards. "That place is a dump. People always end up disappearing for days at a time, then come back with one more scar and one less kidney than the week before."

"You know that ain't true," Father Joe says. "Anyhow. Get your things together."

"We're leaving today?"

"Like I said, we got no choice."

Then something happens to my body. Pains and prickles break out in odd places like old memories. There's a painful bulge in my throat and a stinging in my eyes. Something warm, like rainwater, hits my cheekbone then cools as it trails down my face. I have a vague notion that these accumulated sensations equal crying. But as far as I know, I've never had anything to be sad about. I've not mourned a single thing since my life started over at the mission.

And the fact that I can't remember a single thing worth crying over makes me cry even harder.

My shoulders quake and I make futile dabs at my eyes. I sense movement before me, but it passes. Then I feel pressure on my waistband as I realize Michael is beside me, using me for leverage to hoist himself to a standing position on the cot nearest me. He tries to drape his arm over my shoulder but he's still too short. So I sit beside him on the cot and hug his puny little legs. He wraps his arms around me until I'm sniffling into his shirtsleeve, his head resting on mine.

"I guess ..." Willy clears his throat and starts again. "You guys could stay a few days. Until you figure something out."

"Thanks," Father Joe says. "But we'll manage okay."

"No, I insist. Michael can bunk with me. You take the couch and Shaq can sleep on Michael's bed."

Willy's offer is sincere enough. But you can tell he's holding out for some act of God to keep us out of his house, like Abraham with his boy on the altar. At some point Father Joe nods again. It may have been decided, but it's anything but settled. We all stand around, knee deep in our own inadequacy, wounded pride, and bad luck. Just when it feels like none of us will ever be able to look each other in the eye again, Michael says, "You need a shower, Shaq. Your head is really stinky."

No one laughs out loud. But it's funny enough to get us up and moving and making small talk again. Before he and Willy leave for the last time ever, Michael approaches me and says, "Here you go, Shaq." He's holding my Army jacket in a sloppy bundle. "I folded it for you."

"Thanks, kid." I snatch it from his hand and bend to cram it in my backpack, mainly so he won't see the tears welling in my eyes again.

Willy

Having houseguests will be a new kind of incarceration. Since this is my last day of freedom for the foreseeable future, I decide to spend my final few hours of privacy trying to find Ozena. My first call is to Javatek. But Ozena's recorded voice reminds me it's Sunday.

I hang up the phone, stare at her home number, and resolve to call her before I chicken out. But then I decide to make some tea first. After that I sort through the board games I picked up at the yard sale. It suddenly seems imperative that I teach Michael how to play Battleship, so I waste another five minutes positioning little gray ships on plastic grids. I decide again to call Ozena, but instead check the mailbox, tune my Les Paul, and watch Michael nap on my bed for a few minutes. I do eventually sit down and screw up the courage to start dialing, but I accidentally hit a four instead of a seven, then use that as an excuse to check my calendar. If I'm going to call and ask Ozena out on a real date, doesn't it make some sense to make sure I don't have a gig that night?

I keep staring at the calendar, but it makes no sense. I can't seem to focus on anything but the fact that Shaq and Father Joe could arrive anytime. And I know myself well enough to realize I could never ask

Ozena out with an audience. Instead of picking up the cordless hand-set, I give it a spin. The urge to procrastinate is so intense I find myself toying with the idea of returning my agent's call. As the twirling slows, I notice a rather alluring deck of cards. It takes all the self-control at my disposal to keep from dealing out the first hand of solitaire. I make a pact with myself, that I'll finally dial the number after I win just one game of solitaire, figuring that this would somehow put the timing in God's hands and maybe up my chances. Then I call myself an idiot and start dialing.

It rings two and a half times before someone answers. My thumb twitches once over the Off button, but I manage to blurt something out before disconnecting.

"Is Ozena there?"

"No, sir."

The voice is thick and throaty, a caricature voice, slightly more male than female, but hard to say for sure. There's another voice in the background, distinctly male, and wanting to know who's on the phone. After some loud breathing the tortured voice says he doesn't know who it is and wonders aloud if he should just hang up.

"My name is Willy Finneran," I say, a preemptive strike. "Do you expect Ozena home soon?"

"You mean my mom?"

"Maybe. Is your mom's name Ozena?"

"I just call her Mom. Not 'Mommy' cuz that's for babies or 'Mother' cuz that's for TV people."

Every sentence has a tail, a wet humming sound, almost like an urban preacher working himself into a lather. For some reason I'd pictured a much younger kid. Or maybe his speech impediment makes him sound older.

"So do you think I could leave a message for your mom?"

"Nope."

"Oh … how come?"

"Cuz I picked the phone up. You can only leave a message if the machine gets it."

"Could you just tell her I called then?"

"Nope."

"Why not?"

"Cuz I won't remember."

I listen for any trace of irony or sarcasm. But all I hear is devout sincerity and more of that wet humming. Then he coughs directly into the mouthpiece, loudly.

Before I can figure out my next move he says, "Do you like licorice?"

"I think so. Haven't thought about it in a while."

"I like it lot. The black kind. The red kind is not really licorice, you know. I like the Titans too. Keith Bullock is my favorite. He tackles hard."

"Is your name Lloyd?"

"Wow ... how'd you do that?"

"I think your mom told me one time. Maybe I should just call her back later?"

"I'd rather play a game. I like board games. Do you like board games?"

"Yeah, but that might be hard to do over the phone. Don't you think?" He goes quiet, which I now find excruciating. And before I know it, my tongue has betrayed me again. "How about Battleship?"

I'm not sure what I'm hearing next. A gasp? Clapping? Several small explosions? After a few more rummaging sounds he says, "Levi hates Battleship."

"Levi?"

"Yeah, he's here right now."

"Oh, is he a friend from school?"

"Nah, he's way too old for school. He's just drinking some beer and falling asleep on the couch. So can we play Battleship now?"

"Sure," I say, not quite able to square the image of Ozena hiring a babysitter who brunches on beer, then passes out when he should be watching her kid. So I do my best to just ignore it. "Let's go ahead and hide our ships."

"Okay … wait a second. How do I know you won't cheat?"

"That's a good question. How about if I promise not to?"

"Do you have some Bibles to swear on?"

"I only have the one right now."

"Okay," he says, as if that settles it. "I get to go first."

"Because you're the youngest?"

"No, because I'm retarded. That's what Levi says. But then Mom always punches his arm to make him say 'challenged.' But I don't mind 'retarded.' It's a medical condition so it's not a bad word, even if Mom doesn't like it. Okay, before …"

"Before what?"

"Gotcha! I mean in Battleship, B – 4. That's one of my jokes."

"Oh, you did get me."

"No, you have to make an explosion sound, then say 'hit.' That's how you have to do it."

I glance toward the bedroom, not quite ready to wake Michael up with fake war noises. After my best pretend detonation sound I ask, "So is Levi your mom's special friend?"

"Sure he is."

I move my ship on the board so it crosses the B – 4 space. I guess this is cheating, only in reverse, and not at all like I do in solitaire. This is for a good cause. Especially gauging by Lloyd's reaction. I have no idea how Levi can sleep through all this. I imagine a barrel-chested blue-collar type, surrounded by empty beer cans and snoozing on the couch while I stealthily assist Lloyd in sinking my submarine and aircraft carrier. Once I feel he's sufficiently distracted, I steer the conversation back to Ozena's boyfriend.

"So how long has your mom been with Levi?"

"Forever. D – 6."

"Hit. And forever, huh?"

"You didn't make the sounds."

"Sorry." I add some whistling missile sounds to keep things lively. "So does Levi live there too?"

"Oh yeah. He moved in a few months ago."

I should have known better than to get my hopes up. But then why would Ozena lie about all this? What possible motivation could she have? Unless maybe this is an old flame that's recently come back into the picture or something? But even that doesn't make any sense. I hear a few more background noises, then the familiar voice of Lloyd's mother. They exchange greetings, then I hear her ask who's on the phone.

"Uh ... I can't really remember." Then to me, Lloyd says, "Hey mister, what's your name again?"

I nearly blurt it out, but then hear a muffled exchange and the horrified voice of Ozena asking, "Who is this?"

But my hovering thumb presses the Off button. And every time I call back, I get a busy signal.

Ozena

It was like we were kids again. I slammed the phone down, made my way to the sofa, and used the fat part of my fists to wake my brother up. But that was only after I exhausted every effort to figure out who Lloyd was talking to. I dialed zero for the operator, who then proceeded to insinuate that I'm too *cheap* for caller ID or the Star–69 feature. I'm sure she was just retaliating because I yelled at her for not trying harder to help figure out what kind of pervert is calling my handicapped son and coercing him into playing games over the phone.

Eugene finally gets enough wits about him to put his arms up in defense. "Hey, cut it out."

"I thought you were watching Lloyd, not *Sportscenter* and the back of your eyelids!"

"You spilled my beer."

"Well, I paid for it. Just be glad I didn't want Lloyd to see me smashing the bottle over your head."

"What's gotten into you?"

"While you were napping some strange man called my son on the telephone and … and … *seduced* him into playing games with him on the phone."

I follow Eugene's gaze to my son, holding tiny ships in each hand and reenacting some famous sea battle or another.

"Who was it?"

"If I knew that I wouldn't be pounding on you, now would I? Or maybe I'd be using a steak knife instead."

"How do you know it was a man?"

"I heard his voice. And Lloyd called him mister."

"Why didn't you just ask him his name?"

"He hung up."

"Oh. Well I still think you're probably overreacting. It was probably that guy from work that you think you're too good to go out with."

I turn and approach Lloyd as calmly as I'm able. "Lloyd, honey? Look at me. Are you sure you can't remember the man's name on the phone?"

He shakes his head, then stares at his ships some more.

"Was his name Reggie?"

"No, not Reggie. And don't be mad, Mom. He was nice and we played Battleship. I love Battleship."

"I know you do, sweetie. Is there anything else you can remember? Anything at all that you talked about? Even a word he might have said more than once?"

"He wanted to know if I had a boyfriend."

At this point I feel myself grabbing the blue game board and hurling it at Eugene. Lloyd finds the hailstorm of red and white pegs hilarious. I spend the next hour and a half weeping in my locked bedroom. At some point Eugene knocks on the door and tells me he's going home, that he's left some spaghetti on the stove, that I shouldn't worry so much, and that I really needed to eat something too. I blow my nose louder than necessary and wait to hear the front door shut behind him.

I drag myself out to the kitchen for dinner, an hour of Sequence and Phase 10, then getting Lloyd ready for bed. I cup my sweet boy's face in my hands and kiss him on the cheek.

"I'm sorry I got so upset earlier tonight. I shouldn't have done that."

"It's okay. Just a little scary is all."

"You know I wasn't mad at you, right?"

He nods, not looking at me.

"But I do not want you talking to strangers again. Do you understand?"

"Yeah, but he's not as strange anymore."

"What do you mean?"

"I think I remember better now."

"Oh? What do you remember now?"

"He asked if you had a boyfriend, not me. I just got confused cuz you were yelling at everybody."

"I'm sorry. Do you remember anything else?"

He squirms under the covers, his gaze detached and wandering. "Only his name."

"Wait, you remember his name now?"

"Yeah, it's easy now. You're not yelling anymore."

"So are you going to tell me?"

"Yeah. It was Willy Fisherman. That's a funny name, isn't it, Mom? I'll bet that's why he likes Battleship."

My mixed bag of emotions bursts then. Relief comes first, followed by confusion, gratefulness, paranoia, then more confusion and paranoia before it all settles in the form of curiosity. It seems clear to me now, or at least makes some kind of sense, that Willy called and asked to speak to me. Then my persistent and sometimes engaging son talked him into a game of Battleship. That's at least plausible. But how did Willy get my home number? And how do I really feel about that?

It's naptime for Michael and I have to pee. Both of those are more complicated than they sound.

Willy was right about his house being tiny; cramped is more like it. The thin plaster walls are almost worse than no walls at all. At least at the mission you knew who was in your business because it was all out in the open. All except the bathroom, which was set apart by a short hallway and thick walls. Willy's bathroom is just the opposite.

I hear their voices in there now, Willy instructing the boy about his aim and washing his hands, Michael talking nonsense about our war games in the backyard. Now my bladder is like a fist, and I catch myself wondering if my bowels will ever move again. There's no way I'm going when everyone can hear me.

One major improvement over the mission is the grass. Michael and I spent the morning playing War in the backyard. He spent ten minutes deliberating over every fallen branch in the yard until selecting the two that would serve as our laser rifles. I never figured out what war we were reenacting, or even what century. It seems our battles borrowed elements and strategies from everything from Gettysburg to *Star Trek*. The picnic table was our primary transport vehicle whereas the various trees were enemy installations. The ramshackle aluminum shed represented an enemy planet with a name like an ice cream flavor. Michael insisted that we always fight on the same team. It was two against an unseen world of villains and soldiers and aliens. What seemed to bring him the greatest joy was getting shot and falling to the ground in slow motion.

My greatest joy was watching the boy. Michael's face has a way of making my memory flicker. In a good way.

The first time he goaded me into this pretend death, I didn't want to get up. Once my body landed in the grass, my mind leapfrogged back beyond my earliest real memory. This spongy sensation under my back, combined with the smell of soil and grass and the sound of a little boy laughing, tickled some faint recollection that filled me with equal parts fear and joy. By the time Michael dragged me up out of the grass I had two new sensations to deal with — a painful craving to keep calling the numbers on my list until I found Patrice and an even more painful desire to pee. So I told Michael to cover me while I went behind the rectangular aluminum planet with the funny name. I was just about to go when I heard him coming for me. As much as I hated to do it, I slammed my palm against the aluminum wall to scare him off. But it was too late, I'd lost my chance. When I eventually zipped up I found him sitting on the picnic table dejected, with tears drying on his dirty cheeks. Thankfully Willy called us in for naptime, which made him the bad guy. Or at least a worse guy than me for the moment.

I should have taken my opportunity to go behind the shed, but my pride got in the way. Guess I'd rather hold it than risk Willy catching me acting like an animal. The door shudders as Michael and Willy emerge. It seems Michael wants to nap in his old room — my new room — but Willy will have none of it. The argument ends when the boy stomps off to Willy's bedroom, his cheeks flushed and his mouth set in an angry pout. He'd be asleep in no time.

I get that glassy feeling again and tingle in my spine. Something about the way Michael balls his tiny fists and narrows his eyes makes me think back to my offhand remark to the librarian. About my wife *and* kid. A black spot emerges   painfully   at the front of my imagination, then fills with color. It's murky though, like looking through a fishbowl. The face is a delicate version of Father Joe's. Her slender hands resting on a swollen brown belly. Then she makes a harsh laughing sound, both painful and amused. "He's kicking again. Come feel, baby." I watch my hand moving toward her like it belongs to someone else. But the image fades before it gets there.

I get up and close the bedroom door with trembling hands, trying to be quiet, trying to forget. And it's not hard. The spots have all faded to black again. It's a good thing for me I brought my own cot from the mission. They all laughed when I packed it up, but I insisted. I don't expect them to understand, not even the boy. When your entire life history (or at least as far as you know) consists of only one bed, quality takes a back seat to familiarity. I tried sleeping in Michael's bed, hoping his smell would be enough. But it was just *too* comfortable. And eventually my own smell would overtake his anyway. It's true a real mattress might ease the pain in my lower back. But just like the mission and my cot and my flimsy pillow, my pain keeps me grounded in reality, my reality. I'd be lost without it.

The shrieking metal sounds impossibly loud as I unfold the legs of my cot. I glance at the closed bedroom door before inhaling my musty bedroll. To anyone else it reeks of unwashed hair and my own sour sweat. But to me it smells of peace and quiet and dreams of the life I had before this one. I can't remember a single one of them but the lingering sensations are all the proof I need. I flatten the thin excuse for a mattress. Once I pull my yellowing sheet and crusty blanket up to my chin, I reach over to Michael's bed and steal the pillow. I hold it, pretending I can smell him.

I know I'll fall asleep eventually. But it's hard without the snoring, the whimpering, the toilet flushing and crazed whispers and sirens outside. So I do my best to frame a mental picture of Patrice and count backward from a thousand. I only remember starting over twice before nodding off, then startling awake when the fickle black spots shimmy in my mind. I'm watching Patrice push our little boy in a baby swing, both of them laughing at something I can't see. The boy then turns and smiles his mother's brilliant smile at me. But that's when it dawns on me that I'm not looking at Patrice at all, but some white woman. And the boy has morphed into a miniature version of Michael.

Obviously it was only a dream, but it was way scarier than it should have been. I blame it on my angry bladder and set about quietly exploring Michael's room, or what used to be the guest bedroom. The closet is filled with winter clothes, mostly ladies' things. The nightstand drawer holds a spool of thread, a few pencils, and an old guitar magazine or two. Knowing Willy, I'm almost surprised there's no dirty magazines hidden in here. But I guess he had to clean up his act with the kid around. Or maybe he really has changed since our band days. I have to admit I'm having a hard time maintaining my intense dislike of the man, mostly because of the boy. I browse a few of his old yearbooks and find myself hoping it will trigger some memory from our shared past. Or at least a clue as to why we're here or what to do next. I hear Father Joe and Willy talking in hushed tones through the wall, then the front door open and close, followed by footsteps fading toward the kitchen.

I settle onto the bed with one of Willy's novels. But the writing seems so predictable, trite and completely unbelievable. A one-armed detective who has somehow invented a way to snap various attachments onto the end of his stump? In the first scene, this so-called Handyman is able to get out of a locked trunk with his reciprocating saw attachment, then connects the vacuum to clean up after himself before fleeing the premises. If he had a power saw on the end of his arm, how'd he get himself locked into the trunk in the first place? And where did all the sawdust he vacuumed up go? Up his sleeve? Into his bloodstream? And why the need to tidy up after making such a narrow escape? I put the book down and try to sleep.

When that doesn't work out, I get up for more exploring. Under the bed is a cardboard box filled with assorted gadgets. There are three alarm clocks (with their cords severed), a tape recorder, several coils of phone and cable wires, and an olive drab rotary phone. As quietly as possible, I slide furniture out from the wall looking for a phone jack. It's behind the toy box.

I root around in the box and find a section of phone cable and connect the phone to the wall. I fish my list of Patrices out of my pocket and stare at the numbers, half scratched-through, the other half yet to be called. The idea of running up a few long distance charges really appeals to me. So I lift the receiver, prepared for either a dial tone or complete silence. Instead I hear Willy talking to a woman. I cover the mouthpiece with a spare shirt from my duffel bag, then clamp my hand tight over it and try to breathe through my nose.

It's not the words that paralyze me, it's the sound of her voice. It reaches down inside me, grasps the dangling chain that hangs there, and tugs downward. I can feel the light about to go on when they say their goodbyes and hang up. My mouth turns to porcelain and the electric current in my lower back wraps around me like a belt before radiating out in every direction.

I'm not dreaming this time. I know that voice.

I don't need my list anymore.

Willy

I don't think I've been this nervous since the morning of my transplant. My insubordinate fingers refuse to get Ozena's phone number right and my hand-me-down heart seems to be beating in all the wrong places. I keep reminding myself that I didn't do anything wrong, that I simply called her number and was nice to her kid. But even I don't believe it. I nearly bail out and hang up when it starts ringing, but my shaky fingers can't even get that right.

"I guess I owe you an apology," Ozena says.

"Nah, just a simple misunderstanding."

"Oh, knock it off. I overreacted and you know it. And I'm sorry. I should never have said those things. Or allowed myself to think those things either."

"You were just protecting your kid."

"So do you forgive me?"

"I think maybe I could be persuaded. In fact, I find that I'm most forgiving over dinner. Must be a genetic thing."

"Sounds more like a birth defect."

"Come on, what do you say? Don't you think it's time for us to meet?"

"We've already met."

"I mean in person."

"Yes ..." she says. Relief floods my nervous system, followed by a small tsunami of panic. "... and no."

"Oh."

"I hate to break it to you, Willy, but I think you're addicted to the mystery. Every time you call Javatek is like pulling the wheel on a slot machine. If we meet, you'll have to figure out what to do with those buckets of quarters."

"I'll buy you roses and candy bars and a new hair dryer."

She laughs that beautiful laugh. "I don't know ..."

"Come on, give me one good reason why we shouldn't."

"For starters, my employee handbook prohibits fraternizing with customers."

"Technically, I'm not a customer. I'm not the one who bought that despicable machine. And if it makes you feel any better, I promise to never buy anything ever again from Javatek."

"Plus," Ozena says, as if she's really thought about it, "I don't think you're over Lucy yet. And I'm not all that into being your rebound girl."

"Nobody ever really gets over the hard stuff, not completely. You know that. But coping works better in pairs."

"Did you get that from Dr. Phil?"

"Fortune cookie. Didn't you tell me we can't just keep letting things go and expect them to get better?"

"Yeah, then you proceeded to lose your job and I didn't get the one I wanted."

"You didn't?"

"No, but we can't talk about it. At least not right now."

"Why not?"

"Because I said so. Now hurry up and change the subject before I start crying or something."

"Alright, you leave me no choice then. Do you *want* to go out with me?"

Nothing.

"Ozena?"

"I'm thinking."

Nothing from me.

"Do we have to call it a date?"

"You can call it whatever you like."

"Okay, yeah. And let's make it soon before I chicken out."

"I'll pick you up tomorrow at six then."

"I think I'd be a lot more comfortable if it were ten in the morning or three in the afternoon."

"But then we'd only have a fifteen-minute date."

"I really wish you wouldn't call it that."

"See you tomorrow, Ozena."

Ozena

I can't believe I said yes. But what choice did I have? Despite all my promises to the contrary and every molecule of stubborn common sense pinballing around my insides, I want to do this. I promise Lloyd a game of War, the most monotonous of all card games, then step out into the breezeway to swallow my pride and muster a little confidence. When Eugene answers my knock, he's in a towel. He props the door open with his naked foot and stands in the doorway as if posing for a Christmas catalog. I groan and cover my eyes.

"Please, go put some clothes on. I'll wait."

"It's not like you haven't seen most of me before, sis. We did used to share a bath."

"That was decades ago. And there wasn't so much of you back then."

He looks hurt but recovers quickly by patting his belly. "It's not quite a beer belly yet, thank you very much."

"I was talking about all that hair. But now that you mention it, maybe you should switch to lite beer? Or maybe water?"

"Whatever favor you wanted? The answer is no."

"What makes you think I needed a favor?"

"Your face is all stretched and your ears are pink."

Just like Reggie, I think. Which then makes me feel guilty for some insane reason. I decide to just blurt it out and get it over with. But my brother beats me to it.

"Wait a second. You've got a date, don't you?"

"No, I'm going to dinner."

"But with a guy, right?"

"I'm sure there'll be guys all over the place."

"Okay, I'll be a little more precise then. Is someone coming to pick you up?"

"I suppose."

"And who's buying?"

"We didn't get that far. Now are you going to do this for me or not?"

"I'm not babysitting until I get some answers here."

"Why do you need to know every little detail? You've been bugging me forever to develop some kind of social life. Why can't you just look at this as a baby step and be done with it?"

"Cuz if I do this for you, I'll have to cancel my own date."

"I can't ask you to do that. I'll see if Patti can do it."

"Nope, no way I'm missing out on this. I'll even play Battleship if I have to."

"You could bring your date over to my place if you want."

"So could you. We could double."

"Go put some clothes on."

Shaq

Michael and I are using a pair of straightened coat hangers to fish little green Army men out of the heating grate when I hear Willy approach Father Joe.

"Can I talk to you a second?"

"It's your house."

"I need a favor. For tomorrow night."

I can almost hear Joe stifling a grin from around the corner.

"You got a hot date?"

"Not sure how hot it is. But yeah, something like that."

"And you want me to babysit, that it?"

I can only assume Willy is nodding in the other room. Michael is tugging on my sleeve, anxious to get back to our rescue mission. I'm sure he senses how distracted I've been since I heard Patrice's voice on the phone. And I don't mean to, but I keep staring at him and comparing him to the visions in my head. It's a lot to process, actually, not just the familiar inflection in her voice, but the idea that Willy is about to go on an actual date with my wife, Father Joe's baby girl. I mumble something to Michael and lower my coat hanger into the furnace grate, clanking it around aimlessly. Finally, I hear Willy say, "Yeah, you and Shaq. If you guys don't mind?"

"What's it pay?"

"How about indefinite room and board and all you can eat?"

A moment later Father Joe yells, "Shaq? You got plans for tomorrow night?"

I try to answer, but can't. My throat feels tight and dry and unmovable. My plan was to follow Willy. Maybe even stow away or kidnap him if I have to. Whatever it takes, I just need to see for myself if the voice on the phone matches the one in my heart. But now all I can do is sit here and panic. Michael is making obnoxious machine gun noises when I hear Willy's footsteps.

"There you are," he says. "So you up for it, Shaq?"

"What's that?"

"Babysitting tomorrow night?"

Willy actually looks sincere, apologetic even, like he's trying to make amends for not trusting me before. It takes all the resolve I can muster to see through this act. It's simple really — he knows I can't follow him on his date if I'm stuck here watching the kid.

"Oh, I don't think so," I say. "Not this time."

"Really? Okay, suit yourself. Just thought I'd ask." He shrugs like he really doesn't care.

"Yeah," Michael says. "How come, Shaq?"

"Actually," I say, unsure of what comes next. So I say nothing.

We're all quiet for a moment, too quiet. I'm waiting for one of them to call me on my ridiculous excuse. I haven't had any real plans for nearly a decade. But when I venture a glance up at Willy he's just grinning stupidly at me and the boy. Finally he says, "Man, you guys look more and more alike every day."

"Who does?"

"You and Michael." Willy laughs, then smiles at me like I'm *not* crazy, which only proves what he's really thinking. Finally he winks and says, "Must be all that time you're spending together."

I'm suddenly desperate to stand up, but realize I can't. My left leg has fallen asleep. When Willy made that wisecrack about Michael and me, I just assumed he was taunting me. But then a big black wrecking ball of memories reduces my anger to a pile of rubble. I finally manage to push myself up off the heating grate. My leg tingles, then goes numb again, like a lump of driftwood. I drag it behind me into the bathroom and brace myself with both hands on the sink. I catch my breath, then search my reflection in the mirror for evidence, anything to support the voice in my head. Eventually I see through the wrinkles and patchy beard and see what Willy saw. I just pray it's not wishful thinking.

Willy

I change my clothes six times and my mirror is still not impressed. Not only that, I'm pretty sure I'm wearing the exact outfit I started in — an unremarkable brushed cotton long-sleeve, fashionably wrinkled khakis, scuffed loafers with dark socks.

On the drive over I rehearse casual questions, witty segues, and earnest gazes. But the questions end up being too personal, the segues overly self-deprecating, and my gazes deranged. I sound stiff and idiotic and breathless. My brain tells my body to calm down. But even that signal gets scrambled, especially when I realize Ozena's apartment is less than two miles from my house. So I have to circle the block a dozen times and hope no one calls the cops.

When it's finally time to knock on Ozena's apartment door I can barely keep my fist together. My first attempt is lame and soundless. Then I overcompensate and pound too hard, too fast, like the bass player in a punk rock band.

I hear footsteps on the other side and make one last stab at conjuring an image of Ozena. But nothing appears. The door swings open and I'm face-to-face with a slender man in coveralls. His skin is flushed and his sweaty bangs are pasted to his forehead.

"Come in, come in." I've never met the man, but he seems unnaturally pleasant. His greeting lands somewhere between giddy and downright fanatical. "Pardon the smell. Didn't have time to change after work."

"No problem," I say, all too aware that if a cartoon thought bubble appeared over my head it would feature a skull and crossbones. The air around him smells like a can of Raid. "I'm Willy Finneran."

He grips my spongy hand in his muscular one and shakes it hard. "I'm Eugene, Ozena's brother. And that big guy at the table there is Lloyd Jr."

A lanky boy of about twelve turns in his seat at the dining room table and waves at me. His face is slack, eyes meandering and unfocused, his chin glistening with drool. He's positioning little gray ships on a red game board when he says something that sounds like, "Up for another game of Battleship?" He ends his sibilant query by ramming two ships together in midair and making a familiar explosion sound.

"Sorry, I'll have to take a rain check." He looks at his uncle, clearly confused.

Eugene says, "Means he promises to play again later sometime."

"Promise?" he says.

"Yep."

He looks agitated, almost to the point of tears. "No, you have to *say* it."

"Oh, right. I promise then."

"Good. Cuz if you break your promises, or if you're not nice to my mommy on her date, then me and Levi are gonna sit on your belly and fumigate your face. Right, Levi?"

The boy peals with laughter; Eugene appears both conflicted and amused, but not surprised. Then a familiar voice emerges from the hallway.

"Lloyd!"

I doubt he even hears his mother's scolding over the wet chortling sound of his own laughter. It takes considerable effort to turn my head toward the sound of her voice. I cannot wait to see her, but I'm afraid to look.

At some point my eyes find Ozena's, then promptly get lost there. She's right there with me, as if we don't need to look any further. But eventually we have to and our steady gazes devolve into stiff and insecure gestures. So we stand there and fidget until I finally manage to say, "Hi." She counters with a soft "Hello" before we stall out again. I know I shouldn't stare. I just hope the grin on my face looks like it feels. I'm pretty sure it's the earnest one I couldn't quite muster in the car.

The spell is broken when Lloyd says, "Why are they just looking at each other like that?"

"They once were lost," Eugene says under his breath. "And now they're found."

He claps his hands once, all gregarious and paternal now, then suggests some photographs, forcing Ozena and me to smile and pose without actually touching each other. Our *not touching* becomes like another presence in the room, one we both recognize but refuse to acknowledge. Lloyd cracks himself up by making kissing noises on our way out the door.

There's another awkward moment at the mouth of her apartment

stairwell. Do I lead or follow? What is the etiquette here? No real gentle-
man would butt in front of her, but then I don't want her to feel like
she's on display either. After a couple of false starts we go down side
by side. This creates plenty of incidental contact that neither of us is
comfortable with, but maybe not for the same reasons.

Panic wells up inside me with each descending step. It's a ridiculous notion, one I'm sure will pass any moment. But even as I clear the
final stair, I realize I've completely forgotten how to drive.

Shaq

My plan, if you can even call it that, is to follow Willy in a taxi. Call it
a coincidence if anyone gets suspicious.

I rehearsed it all in my head and called the taxi while Willy was
outside doing some last-minute cleaning in his truck. Now, Father Joe
is watching *Wheel of Fortune* and mumbling wrong answers under his
breath, completely oblivious that his new landlord is off to have his
way with his precious baby girl. Michael is coloring at the table, and
I'm making two cups of hot cocoa with marshmallows and rehearsing
innocent-sounding leading questions when the phone rings. I pick up
on the first ring, hoping it's Patrice calling, but relieved when it's not.
There's a quick burst of chatter in the background before a grave voice
says, "Joe Carter please?"

"Hold on a sec."

I put the receiver down, say a quick and useless prayer on my way
into the TV room. I have to say his name three times to get his attention. Finally he looks up, blinking.

"It's for you."

He reads my grim face and matches it. "Morgue or the hospital?"

"I think it's the morgue."

His eyes close for what seems like days. When he opens them, he
looks small and afraid. By the time he pushes himself up he's managed
to replace his defeated look with his game face. He puts the receiver to

his ear, nods several times, then says thank you and hangs up. A car horn honks from the street. Father Joe parts the curtains enough for us to see Willy climbing into his truck and *my* taxi idling at the curb. That's when Joe realizes he'll have to leave me behind with Michael.

"You gone be okay here with the boy?"

"I had plans, Joe."

Joe looks at me hard, then shakes his head pitifully. "What plans you got, Shaq?"

I glance at Michael, still coloring, his tongue tucked into one corner of his mouth. "I need to meet somebody, that's all."

"Yeah? Who?"

Father Joe always preaches to us that telling the truth is the easiest thing in the world to do, even when it seems hard. But he's wrong. I feel the word on my tongue, floating around the inside of my skull, inflating my lungs, but I just can't say it. I want to tell him the truth, but I can't. Because if there's any hint of a chance that I'm wrong, it will break his heart all over again. But there's more to it than that too. He's afraid of what he'll find at the morgue. I'm afraid of what I'll find when I finally see Patrice. Or maybe I'm afraid of what I won't find.

We stand there quietly, listening to Michael's crayons scratching on paper. The sad reality is that I'll be fine. Partly because I feel relieved, like any good coward. It's just too much to process — the years of searching, all the failed memories, having no real idea what drove us apart, what she looks like, what she thinks of me. I'm afraid I won't know what to say. Or that if I say the wrong thing I'll lose her again.

I rationalize my fear with the fact that I now get to spend some alone time with my son.

"Shaq?" He's waving his big brown hand in my face. "You still in there?"

"Yeah, Joe. You go on."

"Look, I know you got something in your head against Willy. But he's a good guy. You got to ignore that paranoid voice in your head and just trust me on this one."

I nod, but only with my head. He can tell my heart's not in it.

"Shaq? Are you listening to me?"

The taxi horn honks again. "Yeah, I'm fine. And I'll take care of the boy. I'll do it for you and for me and for Michael, but not for Willy."

"Just be careful, Shaq."

"She won't be there, you know."

"Who won't?"

"Patrice. At the morgue."

He narrows his dark eyes at me, making the hair on the back of my neck prickle. But I stand my ground, hold his gaze, and say, "I know stuff, Joe. I'm not all the way crazy."

"I hope you're right, son." When he reaches for my belt I smack his hand away, defiant. "I'll be back in an hour, less if I can manage it."

Ozena

Although I appreciate that Willy is trying to respect my space, a steadying arm might be nice. And not just because of the way he looked at me that first time — all fascinated and afraid with a kind of dopey, underwater expression. (I do believe he actually gulped once. Or maybe he just swallowed his gum by accident.) And not because of the way I was forced to look at him either (which, once I got started, I found it hard to stop). It's not even the way he engaged my son, with only the mildest bit of shock and not even a whiff of pity. No, the reason my limbs won't cooperate is because of where I am and what I'm doing. I can deny it all I like, but my unruly heart tells me I'm on a real, honest-to-goodness date. And I swore to myself I'd never do that again.

I survive the stairwell without tripping and bouncing down on my butt. Then I manage to traverse the sidewalk without tumbling headlong into the bushes. Willy is saying something jokey about his driver's license. Whatever it is sounds confessional. But I miss most of it, as I'm too busy trying to convince myself that the current between Willy and me is the result of me having forgotten to use cling-free dryer sheets.

I have to squint at the sherbet sky as Willy leads me to a shiny black SUV, a Land Rover or Cruiser or some such nonsense. It takes him three tries to get the door open for me. It's obvious as soon as he climbs behind the wheel that the car doesn't fit the man. It dwarfs him, draining him of whatever natural grace he possessed even moments before. He sits too far forward. His every move seems studied. Even the shifter and steering wheel seem too big for his hands. Somehow, through a series of calculated yet clumsy maneuvers, he manages to start the car and get it in gear. Once safely in the flow of traffic, Willy turns to me and says, "We have a little time before dinner. Do you mind if I show you something?"

"Sure, mind if I ask what?"

"I'd rather just show you if that's alright. Hoping it'll help prove my sanity."

"Okay." I try not to sound like I just volunteered for a moonlight stroll with a known serial killer.

"It's just ... I have this bad habit of letting people assume things."

"So I've heard."

"I really don't want to do that with you."

"Good thinking."

Familiar landmarks blur together outside our windows as we exchange vital statistics — hometowns, college majors, our lack of hobbies, and even a few safe details about Lloyd and Michael. I've never been comfortable talking about my son or his handicap. And thankfully I don't have to delve too deep. The car slows, then eventually stops in a neighborhood that's at least twice as old as I am. Willy taps his knuckle on the window and says, "That's my house."

It's small and sensible, nestled between two identical homes, both exuding a reserved elegance that seems to have been charmed into existence rather than simply mowed, clipped, or painted. "Looks pretty sane to me."

The noise he makes sounds like laughter but seems to function more as a pressure release valve. Either way, it's a good sound. "That's the point."

On the way out of the neighborhood we cruise by Willy's elementary school. He shares a couple of embarrassing anecdotes and we're finally able to settle into an easy banter, now without the need to scrutinize every gesture or syllable. He seems cautious but not afraid, earnest yet determined, and best of all, vulnerable. Like he wants more than anything to get this right. I'd love to assure him he's doing fine, better than fine actually. But it's hard to think with him looking at me like that.

I don't realize how long it's been since I've been downtown until I see the skyline. Nashville's tallest building is also a punch line — affectionately referred to as the Batman building. The resemblance is so obvious that the first time Lloyd Jr. saw it he pointed up and launched into a slurpy rendition of *Da-na-na-na-na-na-na-na ... Bat! Man!* Willy has taken the 4th Avenue exit but seems to be going the wrong way. The citrusy sunset is bruising quickly as we drive through what could only be considered the projects. Everything seems more dense now — the foot traffic, the graffiti, the poverty and despair, even the air inside the car. After only a few blocks, Willy pulls alongside a nondescript box of a building. It's all white, even the plywood boards covering the places where windows should be. A cluster of what look to be homeless guys are huddled around a dice game, passing a brown paper bag around. Remarkably, an enormous African American man turns toward us, squints, then smiles when he recognizes Willy. For one horrific second, I'm convinced I'm about to become an accessory to trafficking narcotics on a mostly blind date. But then Willy waves at the man, his most casual gesture of the evening so far. "That's Darnell," he says. "He works magic in the kitchen."

"Interesting." And it really is. But I'm more interested in making sure the doors are locked.

"But you really don't want to hug him."

"I'll remember that."

Shaq

I can't explain why Father Joe leaving me alone with Michael makes me so nervous. But it does. It's probably Willy's fault. I know I make his job as a stand-in parent much easier by spending so much time with Michael, but he still doesn't trust me. It's not so much the way he looks at me, but the way he always looks *again*. Always doing double takes with that grim underbite and the big wrinkle between his eyebrows. And those seemingly innocent comments to Michael, the ones where he reminds the boy to be careful or mind his manners or some other fatherly nudge that is really aimed at me. Just like when I was a kid and my mother scolded my best friend Timmy *through* me to get his feet off the coffee table.

"Is something wrong, Shaq?" Michael wants to know.

"No, I don't think so."

"Then how come you look like you swallowed some scissors?"

"I think I just had a memory."

"Yeah, I get those too." Michael fingers the raised knobs on a bright yellow Lego brick. "Mostly of my mommy. I miss her a lot."

"I think I was just missing her too."

"You miss my mommy?"

"Yeah … I mean, no, I guess I was missing my mother just now."

"Did your mommy have a bad heart?"

"I really don't know. I hope not." I catch myself staring at the boy, ignoring the flood of questions I don't have the nerve to ask. Like what he remembers most about his mother? How he really feels about living with Willy? And if he would ever want to live with me instead? The one I ask surprises even me.

"Can I ask you something?"

"Sure," he says.

"Did your mommy ever mention the name Patrice?"

I hold my breath while his tiny features huddle up in concentration. But then he just shakes his head.

"Are you sure?"

"Yep, now can I ask *you* something?"

"Sure, whatever's on your mind."

"Can I listen to your heart?"

He doesn't wait for an answer, but instead wades noisily through a pile of Legos and puts his left ear against my chest. His pudgy hands feel warm on my shoulders. I know now that I love this kid. I guess I always have. But this sudden burst of intimacy is more than a little unnerving. I want to wrap him into a giant bear hug and cry on his little shoulder, but can't help imagining Willy bursting through the front door with a couple of cops, all accusing the homeless guy of lewd behavior with a kid. I make some half-hearted comment about picking up our mess.

Then Michael says, "Don't worry, Shaq. You have a good heart."

"Thanks, Michael."

My eyes get wet in a hurry. I'm about to change the subject to Nerf basketball or suggest another talking vegetable movie when Michael says, "I think it's time for my bath now."

"Who says?"

"Willy, that's who." And with that he turns and traipses off to the bathroom. He's already peeled his T-shirt off when I sit on the edge of the tub and start the water. I leave my hand under the stream, waiting for the water to heat up. Behind me, Michael is humming a tune and splashing pee around, some in the toilet water, most on the rim or the floor. I lean down to plug the drain when I start to panic. We shouldn't be doing this. It's not just what it would look like if someone showed up — a naked little boy splashing in the tub in front of a homeless man. I know it's innocent and that's enough. But there's something familiar and scary about it all. It just doesn't feel safe.

I pull the plug and shut the water off, then stand mesmerized by the funnel of water gurgling down the drain.

"What are you doing, Shaq? I didn't get my bath yet."

"Changed my mind. We're gonna build a Lego tower instead."

"We already did Legos."

"Yeah, well, we can do better. This time we'll make a humongous tower, taller than me even."

"But I need my bath."

I make a big show of sniffing the air around his head. "Nah, you smell great. Go get your pj's on and I'll find the blocks. I'm still sorting out what just happened in the bathroom as I dump the colorful blocks in front of the television. But a new sensation is crawling over me. It's fear.

Willy

Ozena turns in her seat and says, "So what is this place? And please tell me we're not getting out."

"Only if you insist."

I never considered how hard it would be to look at Ozena and talk to her at the same time. Despite the harsh surroundings, my eyes are enchanted. But my vocal cords are in revolt. Before tonight, Ozena had never laid eyes on me. All she really knows is that I have a vendetta against a coffee maker and that I can't keep a steady job. That my track record with relationships includes losing a wife to a guy named Alvin, allowing other people to assume she was dead, and that I'm trying to learn how to parent a kid I've already admitted I'd rather send back.

"It's called the Mercy Mission, basically a homeless shelter. I used to call you from the pay phone right inside that door there."

"So did you work here?"

I'm tempted to gloss over another technically true statement and let Ozena assume the best. "Yes I did. But only because I had to *live* here for a few months."

"Were you researching a new book or something?"

"Not on purpose. I was sentenced to two thousand hours of community service for running over Rufus the Lightning Badger in my SUV, then leaving the scene of the crime."

"The school mascot thing? That was *you*?"

"I'm afraid so."

"I think there was an office pool about how much time you'd have to spend in prison."

"My fifteen minutes of fame. Anyway, I just wanted you to see the place. You hungry?"

"Yes."

Her tone is more somber than I'd hoped. But at least she hasn't asked me to take her home yet. Less than ten minutes later we're safe in the neon glow of downtown Nashville. Somehow we find a spot in front of the newest, trendiest, most expensive steak house in town. (I can't really afford this place, but then I can't really afford to not get this right either.) To prove that chivalry is still limping along, I dutifully hold all the doors for her.

The inside of the restaurant smells divine and empty tables abound. I congratulate myself for getting here early, look the hostess in the eye, and proudly announce *Finneran, table for two.* Her face bunches up as she scans a list, then starts over again at the top.

"I'm sorry, sir. Could your reservation be under a different name perhaps?"

"I didn't make a reservation."

"Oh, well. You need a reservation."

I assume she's kidding, but her expression tells me otherwise. "But the place is half empty."

"We prefer to think of it as half full, actually."

I check to see if she's making an ill-timed joke. She's not. "How about if I make a reservation right now?"

Her face brightens as she flips the page on her calendar. "Wonderful, what day would you like?"

"Today, about fifteen minutes from now."

She seems unfazed by either sarcasm or common sense, quite possibly the most literal woman on earth. I'm about to try another tactic when Ozena tugs on my sleeve and says, "It's okay, Willy. There's plenty of places to eat around here."

"I know, but it's just the principle of the thing."

"I didn't come all this way to eat with your principles, silly."

Those last two syllables wrap their arms around my formerly orphaned heart, nuzzle its cheek, and plant a ticklish kiss on its dirty forehead. I can't explain why, but that one-letter substitution vaporized all my residual doubts. As much as I love the sound of my name on her lips, a *nickname* is the stuff of second dates, hand holding, and talking long into the night about absolutely nothing at all.

We set off down the street and I pepper her with questions about work. She has this knack for detailing her office foibles and misunderstandings without delving into gossip or slander. The beautiful thing is that it doesn't seem forced at all. I'm about to comment on this when she stops in front of a hotel and says, "Mind if I duck in here for a bathroom break?"

I stop short of following her inside when I realize where we are — the Harington Hotel, the scene of one of my many crimes. I hold the door for her, then hang back, making a lame (but true) excuse about needing fresh air. I scan the front steps for the security guard who chased me out of the back of this very hotel. Eventually I turn my back to the lobby and catch myself wondering how Michael and Shaq and Father Joe are making out until I hear Ozena calling from the top of the steps.

"Great news, Willy. Plenty of empty seats and no reservations required."

She looks so pleased I don't have the heart to tell her that our dinner might be interrupted with another chase scene through the kitchen and a trip to jail. Our hostess has a blinding smile, big white teeth, and even bigger pink gums. She gives us the litany of specials, but her southern accent is so syrupy I miss most of it. I'm too busy scanning the room for the beefy security guard anyhow.

"This is nice," Ozena says. "Not as stuffy as the other place. And the music's not as loud."

I'm about to respond when I sense a presence behind me. Ozena confirms this with a sweet smile and her hovering gaze over my left shoulder. I realize I'm cringing when I hear the waiter's voice. What are the odds? But it's him, the same guy that waited on Shaq and me. I keep my neck hunched and hide behind my menu. We both order ice water with lemon and our waiter promises to be back soon for our order. While Ozena paws through her shiny red purse in search of something, our hostess materializes and deposits our ice waters.

I squeeze my lemon and ask, "You don't happen to have any hang-ups about your ice cubes, do you?"

"What do you mean?"

"I was here once before when a fight nearly broke out because some guy wanted exactly two ice cubes in his water, no more and no less."

Ozena stops her search and looks at me, her eyebrows bunched as if she's trying to remember something important.

"Something wrong?" I ask.

"No, sorry. Just processing a distant memory."

"You care to share it?"

She pretends to really give it some thought, then says, "Nope, not really."

"Come on. I've been confessing my problems ever since we left your place. And I'm only halfway done."

She makes her thinking face again, apparently for real this time. "I suppose you're right." She slaps a handful of photos on the table. "You should really get a kick out of these."

I thumb through a series of family photos, an all-American husband, wife, boy, and girl, obviously vacationing someplace. Based on the tan lines and squinting into the camera, I'm guessing it's somewhere sunny. Finally, I say, "Should I recognize them?"

"Those are the Grinning Whiteheads. They keep me company in my cubicle."

"Are you related to them?"

"We do share the same last initial. It was a mix-up at the photo place. I got their photos and they probably got mine. But there was something about them I liked. Or maybe something I craved. Anyway, I tacked them up on my cubicle wall and they've been keeping me company ever since."

"So do the people you work with think they're your family?"

She ventures a begrudging grin just before our tuxedoed waiter appears. His face has that same look of practiced concern, but he doesn't seem to notice anything special about me. I only hope it lasts. He assures us that our identical orders of prime rib and salad are outstanding choices and promises to be right back with a warm basket of bread, emphasizing the word *warm* and looking right at me for the first time.

I point to the photos and say, "So where does the confession come in?"

"I talk to them about things."

"Do they talk back?"

"Sort of, but not like you might think. They're more of a sounding board. I bounce ideas and questions off of them, then scan the pictures until I find the answer I'm looking for. They just confirm what my common sense is already telling me. It's more like therapy than a Magic 8-Ball."

"So have you asked them about me?" Ozena looks caught in a trap. And I almost feel bad, but my curiosity outweighs any sympathy I'm feeling, so I press harder. "Come on now ... fess up."

"I brought them with me, didn't I?"

"What does that mean?"

"Maybe it means I'm asking them right now."

I move the photo of the kid crying in the sand to the bottom of the pile. I pick up a group shot — one with all smiles — and hold it up in front of Ozena. Then I slowly tilt it forward and back as if they're all nodding their approval in perfect unison. "I think they like me."

"No fair." She snatches the photo playfully and says, "That's cheating."

"So does that mean you're superstitious?"

"No, I don't think so. Unless Jesus counts."

My heart beats louder, but not faster. Another not-so-subtle reminder that I need to figure out which side of the door He's knocking from. And what about Ozena? Was that just a casual comment or is she fishing for something? Leading up to or away from somewhere?

"You believe in Jesus but not love?"

Ozena just smiles and I realize I may have the opposite problem. I watch her long fingers scoop the pictures up and put them back in her purse. I've already decided I could watch her fingers all day when she pulls her cell phone out and begins dialing. "Just gonna check on Lloyd."

As our food is delivered Ozena nods and playfully rolls her eyes at the sound of her son's voice. She's in no hurry either, hanging on every word and offering no apology when she hangs up. I want to compliment her on her patience, but can't think of a way to do it that doesn't sound dumb or offensive. I can't help feeling like I'm auditioning for the lead in some father-of-two drama, and I don't like it.

We eat in relative silence for a while. When I can't stand it any longer I say, "You mentioned Jesus before ... ?"

"Yeah, I did." She swallows hard, looks at me, and says, "And you made a really funny face."

"I've sort of been looking for Him for a while."

"You make it sound like you lost Him."

"I guess you could say that."

"I don't really think it works that way. Once you find Him, that's pretty much it. That's how it worked for me."

"So did you ask Jesus into your heart? Just like in Sunday school?"

"It was more like a breaking and entering. But He claimed squatter's rights and we eventually came to an agreement."

"So you really believe that? That our hearts are actually capable of emotion, and aren't just some fleshy muscle pumping blood all over the place?"

The waiter is back, pretending he didn't hear my last question. "So how is everything? More bread? More water?" We stop chewing long enough to thank him and assure him we're fine.

Ozena washes a bite down with water. "Wait, I'm lost. Are we talking about my 'Love is' diaries again? Or your searching for Jesus?"

"Both?"

"Okay, yeah. I think that's probably how it works. It all happens in the heart."

"That's what I was afraid of."

"This isn't about Lucy, is it?"

I shake my head, bracing myself for some embarrassing flood of emotion that never comes.

"Your transplant then?"

Before I even realize what's happening, I'm telling Ozena the whole story. How my brother Walter was on the run again for a string of convenience store robberies. About the night he called and learned about my downgrade to Status One and my dire need for a donor. How he tearfully told me goodbye and dialed 9–1–1 to turn himself in. Lucy took the call and my distraught brother made her promise to send EMTs to his girlfriend's doublewide, *And make sure they bring a cooler ...* this is where his voice supposedly cracked ... *with plenty of ice.* I describe how when the authorities arrived, they saw the curtains fall and heard the gunshot. They found him clutching his driver's license in one hand—the organ donor's side up—and his last will and testament in the other. It was a crinkled piece of notebook paper that read: *Give my heart to Willy.* I tell Ozena about the odd cravings and Walter's dreams and how sometimes I feel like I'm thinking someone else's thoughts.

But I knew about none of this until Lucy showed up on my doorstep and told me about The Call from Walter, and things began to fall into place. This new knowledge jigsawed with the pieces I already possessed. Lucy didn't convince me; I didn't need convincing. She just confirmed what I already knew. For all his faults, Walter was exactly the kind of guy who would lay down his life for his brother. I'd be lying if I said I wasn't grateful, but that doesn't help with the guilt.

"Of course, that's Lucy's story," I say. "Neither my mother, nor an entire legion of meddlesome surgeons would ever confirm or deny anything. There's privacy laws and the high probability that my brother and me wouldn't even be a match. Not to mention potential psychological issues for me. "

"So what do *you* think of Lucy's version?"

"I know she was never the same after she heard the gunshot. Other than that, I don't know what to think. I know what I feel though."

"Which is?"

"There's a reason I didn't want you to send me a new espresso maker."

"And?"

"I just can't handle any more replacements. I need the real thing." I realize I've cast an unwanted pall over the conversation. I'm scrambling for a safer subject when our waiter arrives and saves me again.

"So did you guys save some room for dessert?"

"It'll go straight to my ankles," Ozena says.

"Excuse me?" The waiter says, arching his back for a peek at her ankles. I sense movement under the table before Ozena brings her feet to rest next to mine, setting off an electrical storm in my shoes.

"Never mind," she says.

"And for you, sir? Could I interest you in a slice of pie? Or maybe a Hush Puppy?"

I feel my face go hot at once, my body slinking down in my chair, my eyes scanning the room for the burly security guard. Our waiter is dangling a grease-laden, left-footed suede shoe by its shoestring. "I thought I recognized you."

"You know," I say, sputtering words faster than my tongue can manage. "That was not my fault. The guy was supposed to be treating me to lunch, not stealing it for me. And I sort of panicked. But feel free to charge me for that meal too if you want."

"No need, my man. That one's already been paid for."

"It has?"

"Oh yeah. Some enormous black guy came in and paid it. Supposedly some famous football player, but I never heard of him. But he paid the tab and put in some extra for me. So we're good."

I give the waiter my credit card and give Ozena the *Reader's Digest* version of my lunch with Shaq and my near-death experience with the security guard. On the way out, she excuses herself to the restroom again. I hang around the bank of pay phones while I wait, wondering if I should call Father Joe and thank him. When Ozena emerges, she's still fiddling with the seal on a plastic baggie. Inside is her toothbrush. Before my stupid little brain has a chance to engage, I say, "Can I see that?"

"My toothbrush?"

"Yeah, I know it's weird. I just ... well, I sort of collect them."

"That might be the strangest thing you've said so far. But here you go. I'm warning you though, if you put it in your mouth I'm calling my brother to come and take me home."

I hold it up to the light, having no idea what I think I'm looking for and feeling a little stupid about the whole thing. I resist the urge to run my fingers across the bristles before handing it back to her.

"So," she says, "how many do you have?"

"What do you mean?"

"In your toothbrush collection."

"Oh, well. Just the one, actually."

"Not sure that qualifies as a collection, Willy."

I hold the door open for Ozena and follow her out. We both shudder at the cold while a mental skirmish breaks out in my head about whether or not I should put my arm around her. Less than a dozen steps later, a homeless man with blood drying on his lower lip steps out of a shadow, rubbing his hands together like carnival barker. Chivalrous thoughts fill my head, heroic visions of me rescuing Ozena from this panhandling cretin. But all I can manage is to position my body in front of Ozena like a shield, albeit a rather flimsy one.

"Excuse me," the man says. "Ya'll know what the most underprivileged nation on earth is?"

I shake my head, scooting my body to further shield Ozena.

"Do-Nation!" His punch line ends with his dirty palm up and an enormous lunatic grin.

Whatever canned comment my brain summoned up sputters out and dies on the tip of my tongue. Before I know it, I'm meeting the man's fanatical gaze, pitching my voice softly, and saying, "You hungry, brother?"

"Thirsty, mostly." His tone is conspiratorial.

"When did you eat last?"

Whatever flicker of light he had in his eyes goes out, more defeated than discouraged. He's staring at the sidewalk when he finally shrugs and says, "I don't know. Yesterday? The day before?"

"What's your name?"

"What's it matter?"

"It just does. You know it does. So tell me."

"Trevor."

"Come with me then, Trevor."

"Where to?"

I point to a snoozing hot dog vendor a half block away. I turn, careful to keep myself between Ozena and our new chaperone. Once we belly up to the gleaming, diamond-tread cart, the hot dog man rouses himself, then he winks at Ozena, pretty much ignores me, and sneers at Trevor. Eventually he deigns to ask what we're having.

"A hot dog," I say, then quickly add, "Better make it two." I turn to Trevor and say, "Drink?"

"Coke."

"We got Pepsi," the hot dog man says as he slathers mustard on.

"Make it a Pepsi then," I say. "A big one."

Trevor is shaking his head. "No way, man. I only like Coke."

The hot dog man chokes back a laugh and says something under his breath about beggars and choosers as he slops chili on the steaming dogs. I wait for Trevor to bristle beside me, but he just sighs instead. Inside my pocket, I finagle the top bill off my money clip, praying it's a five and not a twenty. Once liberated, I slip it into Trevor's crusty hand without looking at it.

Then to the hot dog man I say, "You calling me a beggar, pal?"

"No, him." He points at Trevor with a pair of tongs.

Like a bad actor I face Trevor and say, "Let's just see about that. You got money, Trevor?"

He blinks, thinking. And I find myself praying yet again that I haven't blown it. Trevor now has a fistful of money and is free to do what he wants. His face is bunched in concentration as his options must be dawning on him too. There's nothing in the world to keep him from turning his back on us and finding the nearest liquor store. Finally, he slaps the money on top of the sneeze guard and says, "My dogs ready yet? I ain't got all day."

I couldn't be more pleased to see Lincoln staring up at the stars. In one swift motion the hot dog man snatches the five and leaves two quarters clattering in its place. Trevor grabs them up, then waits until he has the hot dog man's full attention before dropping both coins in a waxy paper cup with the word *Tips* scrawled on it.

Trevor then turns and walks back toward the shadows, feasting on chili-laden pork, hopefully garnished with some tiny morsel of dignity.

Only then do I notice Ozena's arm threaded through mine.

Shaq

Willy doesn't have a microwave, so we have to pop the popcorn on the stove. Michael is fascinated, enough to almost make me forget about my nagging paranoia. Sure would be nice if Father Joe came back. I'd even settle for Willy at this point.

We adjourn to the den and watch an old *Tom & Jerry* VHS tape. I feel Michael's sleepy weight nestling into my rib cage. His breath catches once, then settles into a leisurely rhythm. I'm trying to decide whether to make him brush his teeth or just carry him to bed when someone knocks on the door.

I try not to move. I tell myself it's Father Joe. Then I tell myself that if it really is Father Joe, I can just wait for him to yell through the door for me to open up and let him in. The phone rings but I ignore that too. The last ring is cut short, followed by more urgent knocking.

Another familiar sensation washes over me. I realize I'm praying under my breath. Not for me though, nothing like that. Just praying for the boy, that God will protect him and keep him from harm. Or more specifically, keep *me* from harming him again. I can't help thinking this prayer is a memory too. It feels haunted, like I've said it before. Lots of times.

This time the knocking is followed by a voice. But it's not Father Joe or any of the boys from the mission. It's a woman.

I ease Michael onto his side on the couch, then make my way past the front door and peek through the blinds from the kitchen. The woman at the front door looks bored and ordinary. The two guys with her look like cops. The minivan at the door is littered with acronyms. My first thought is that something has happened to Father Joe and they're here to deliver the bad news. I scan the street for anything suspicious, then step to the front door and open it.

"My name is Agent Rachel Thompson with the Tennessee Department of Child Services." She flashes some wallet ID like a cop on TV. Then she steps across the threshold like she owns the place and says, "Is William Finneran here?"

"Nope, he's out."

"What about Michael Sharpe?"

I try to think, but it's hard with all those eyes boring into me. What would Father Joe do if he were here? I can't be sure so I opt for a half-truth.

"Sorry. I don't know anyone by that name. Why don't you folks come on back tomorrow and talk to Willy?"

"What is your name, sir?" She pulls out a little notebook and touches her pen to her tongue, waiting.

"Shaq."

"Your full name please?"

"That's it. Just Shaq."

The two cop-looking guys swap suspicious glances. Agent Thompson and I just stare. Finally she starts sniffing the air like a canine cop. "You having a party here tonight, Mr. Shaq?"

"No ma'am. Just a quiet night with movies and some burned popcorn."

I realize I'm in trouble when her eyes land on my fatigue jacket. She lifts it toward her face and I reach to snatch it from her. But she turns her body away from me, breathing deeply from the fabric. She frowns and says, "This your jacket, sir?"

"I can explain. That's …" It turns out I can't really explain it after all.

She reaches into one of the pockets and pulls out a small brick of marijuana. "That's probable cause, is what that is." That explains why the twins had my jacket.

"Shaq?" My heart stutters at the sound of Michael's voice. The agent is now looking past me, searching for the small boy who's wandered into the living room behind me. "Who's at the door?"

"Are you Michael?" the agent says, her voice calm and soothing.

"That's my name," he says, all innocent and playful. "Ask me again and I'll tell you the same."

All at once she pulls a cell phone from her belt and the cops push past me. One of them steps on my nail-less toe and I feel myself stumbling backward, then landing with a painless thud. I stare at the jacket splayed on the floor in front of me, vaguely aware of the shuffling feet and official sounding talk. I catch myself praying again, that this

323

will all stop. All of it, the reality spinning itself out in front of me and crippling memories running roughshod through my head. I pray that Michael will wake up and start screaming, that we're sharing the same bad dream.

And then he's gone and everything is quiet. Except for the zany orchestra music and sound effects from the *Tom & Jerry* cartoon in the other room.

Ozena

I'll admit it. I grabbed Willy's arm. I'm not sure if I was looking to protect him or the other way around. But either way, I decided I liked it there and left it. Once the ordeal is over with the uptight hot dog guy and Trevor the homeless man, Willy squeezes my hand tighter between his arm and his body, trapping it there. Then we wordlessly set off down Church Street toward the bustle of 2nd Avenue.

I resist one urge to put my head on his shoulder and another one to start making small talk. Something happened back there with Willy and Trevor, something he's still processing. And to talk about it might trivialize it somehow, rob it of whatever cathartic spell it cast on him. Besides, it's just nice not to have to say anything. Before I know it my mind is adrift, from wondering what Lloyd and Eugene are up to, to the realization that this is only the second first date of my life. I also have to admit it's a rather delicious thought. That is, until I remember how my last first date worked out. But that's just my inner cynic talking: *What makes you think this will turn out any better than that? Aren't these the very same giddy feelings you had about Lloyd all those years ago?*

Then I hear Willy saying, "Can I ask you something?"

"Only if you promise to quit asking permission to ask me stuff."

"Deal."

But then he goes quiet again as we watch a horse-drawn buggy filled with tipsy college girls cross the intersection. The light changes

324

and we step onto the crosswalk, finding ourselves in a grown-up version of Red Rover, or maybe a slo-mo battle scene, as a flank of a dozen or so pedestrians march right at us. That's when a precocious toddler breaks free from his mother's grasp and barrels his way between Willy and me, thus breaking the physical bond between us. And I know at once—we both do—that we won't muster the courage to get it back. Not unless another homeless man jumps out of the shadows. We keep walking, but the six inches between us feel like thirty-six. Finally, I say, "Weren't you going to ask me something?"

"Oh yeah, it was about your brother."

"Eugene? What about him?"

"I'm not so sure he's all that impressed."

"Impressed with what?"

"Me."

"You might be surprised."

"How so?"

"It's hard to explain."

"Try me."

"You remember when you picked me up? When I first came around the corner?"

"Kind of hard to forget that."

My neck heats up and I just know my ears are glowing pink. "I watched my brother watching you. You sort of won him over with that first reaction."

"Not sure I'm following you."

"He has this bad habit of sizing women up, like he's staring at a menu on an empty stomach. I know it's creepy, but he's my brother and I'm still working on him. And he has confidence issues too. So trust me, he was impressed. And if he gave you a funny look or something, I'm sure he was just jealous."

"I hope I wasn't gawking."

"Trust me, Willy. You have nothing to be sorry for. Nothing at all."

"Well, maybe there is *one* thing." He jerks his thumb toward the massive backside of his SUV. "We've made it all the way back to the car."

"Oh, no need to be sorry," I say, biting back an insatiable urge to giggle. "It's a nice car. A wee bit pretentious maybe, but nothing you need to apologize for."

He grins big and I'm not sure I'll recover anytime soon. Then he says, "I'm not ready to take you home yet."

I don't say anything. Not because I don't want to, just that I can't. I'd always heard that girls want more than anything to feel pursued, beautiful, and worth fighting for. Somehow Willy managed to hit on all three in a single declarative sentence. Finally, I say, "What do you have in mind?"

"Coffee?"

"I'm afraid it might keep me up half the night."

"Good, then it won't all be my fault."

"What do you mean?"

"I'm pretty sure I was planning to keep you up half the night anyway."

Willy

The coffee shop is brimming with clusters of high school and college students. We stare at the complicated menu and settle on chai lattes. Ozena insists on decaf, then excuses herself to call home again. I pay the cashier and try not to stare at the multiple piercings in his otherwise boyish face. I'm flipping through a rack of overpriced CD's when I feel a warm hand slip through my arm. I didn't realize until now that the spot never stopped tingling since the last time she rested her hand there. I am a bit shocked at how forward she's being, and wondering what prompted this sudden change.

But my confusion evaporates when I turn to greet Ozena and am instead staring into the face of Beverly Ray. She's caressing my forearm with her thumb. And she's close enough for me to feel the warmth of her breath on my face. And she hasn't even said anything yet.

"Oh, hi, Beverly. What are you doing here?"

"Having coffee. It is a coffee shop after all."

I try to pull my arm away, but she's stronger than she looks. I crane my neck in search of Ozena and try to think of some way to extricate myself.

"I've been thinking," Beverly says. "Now that you're not my teacher anymore, there's no reason why we couldn't, um, get to know each other a little better."

"Trust me, Beverly. There are plenty of reasons."

"Yeah?" She licks her teeth like some toothpaste commercial seductress. "Care to name one?"

"For starters," I say, "I'm on a date."

Somehow she interprets this as flirting, then counters with what feels like foreplay, her body getting much too close to mine. And of course that's when I see Ozena step out of the bathroom. And then she sees me. But instead of walking over, she scoops her cell phone out of her purse and starts dialing, no doubt calling her brother to come rescue her from the sleazy two-timing cad she so stupidly agreed to go out with.

Beverly giggles, but there's no humor in it. In fact, it's really kind of sad. Then she puts one finger to her lips and says, "So am I."

"Look, I have to be go—"

I feel her take my hand in both of hers, then something that tickles like mad. I glance down to see her inscribing her phone number onto my palm. Before she gets the last two digits done, I yank my hand away and trot off toward Ozena. By the time I reach her, she's snapped her phone shut and is all smiles. "Eugene says hello."

"Everything okay at home?" I say.

"Lloyd is sleeping and my brother's watching a game."

Someone yells out, "Big chai, little chai decaf!"

I grab the steaming mugs while Ozena claims a small table for two.

We sip our drinks and smile at each other a lot. Yet as much fun as I'm having, there's still that nagging Cinderella-like feeling that the dream will soon be over. Ozena must sense something is up.

"Something on your mind, Willy?"

"Why do you ask?"

"Because you've stopped talking and you can't seem to figure out what to do with your eyes. Or your fingers."

"Oh, sorry. Guess I was thinking."

"Care to share?"

"Nope." I spin my coffee mug a hundred and eighty degrees, pause to examine my work, then do it again. "But I probably will anyway."

"Good. I didn't want to have to beat it out of you."

"Okay, but it's a little embarrassing."

"More so than asking me to kill your espresso maker?"

"Good point."

"Or more than that sexpot coed hanging all over you?"

"Oh, you saw that?"

"Yeah, it was adorable." Ozena nearly spews hot tea at the expression on my face.

"Adorable?"

"Not her. You, silly."

"Why me?"

"Oh, I don't know, take your pick. The stricken look on your face. The veins popping out on your neck when you tried to pull your arm away. That little hip hop dance you were doing to try and see past her."

I groan, truly mortified.

"She is very pretty though." Ozena lifts her cup, ostensibly to sip tea. But I think it's more to cover the triumphant smirk on her face. She is relishing my embarrassment. And I guess I am too. Then she swallows quickly and sets her cup down hard. "So anyway, didn't mean to interrupt your train of thought."

"I was sort of hoping you forgot."

"Nope, sorry. Now out with it. I promise it won't seem nearly so embarrassing when it's out on the table."

I'm about to give my mug another spin when Ozena puts her hand on mine. I'm midway through a small prayer that she'll leave it there when she withdraws it, planting it under her chin like a pedestal.

"What I want more than anything," I say, "is for you to tell me I'm not going to die. I mean, I didn't use to care so much. I was just sort of marking time, waiting for my heart to wind down. But now ... I don't know."

Our collective silence invites that unseen presence back to the table. Only it's familiar now, stretching out and getting comfortable.

"You know I can't tell you that, Willy."

"Couldn't you just lie to me?"

"Sorry, I have a policy against that."

"That's really annoying, you know."

"Tell me about it. But I'll make it up to you by letting you ask me another favor. In fact, you can just keep on asking till we come up with one that's doable."

I'm fairly confident this is an invitation to ask for a follow-up date, but decide to make that my backup plan. I clear my throat, double-check my resolve, then say the words.

"Let's fall in love."

She laughs, making the most adorable snorting sound ever. "Excuse me?"

"Hear me out. People have survived arranged marriages for centuries. Societies have actually flourished that way. I even have a friend who married a girl he met online."

"How'd that work out?"

"She was rude to his pets and stole all his money."

"And that's your proof?"

"So that's not the most compelling example. Doesn't mean it's not a good idea though."

"Well, I'm just not sure it's the kind of thing we can sit here and decide."

"But are you sure it's not?"

"You don't know a thing about me, Willy. You don't know if I snore or whether or not I can cook. For all you know, I have Lloyd videotape soap operas all day so I can watch them every night while gorging myself on ice cream and value-sized bags of Funyuns. I could spy on my neighbors or have a gambling addiction or just anything. You don't know."

"I know you've got beautiful ankles."

To prove my point, I lean to one side for a look under the table. But I sense her feet retreating under her chair.

"They're awful and I forbid you to look at them ever again."

I lean to the other side, then glance up and watch her neck turn red.

"Besides," she says. "You still haven't come up with a good favor yet, one that I can grant with no hesitation."

I want to tell her I know it's late and that I shouldn't wear out my welcome. What I say instead is, "Can we make one last stop on the way home?"

"And this is your favor?"

I nod, almost wishing I could take it back already.

"Okay, but you at least have to tell me where first."

"We'll need to stop at my house on the way."

"On the way to where exactly?"

"The cemetery."

Ozena

If someone told me a week ago that I'd be on a real date, I would have laughed in his or her face. If that someone told me I would then allow this date to escort me up his darkened sidewalk after midnight, then follow him into his house unchaperoned, I would have had him or her custom fitted for a straight jacket. And if that same someone tried to tell me that my date and me were going to retrieve an espresso maker with a wooden stake driven through its electronic heart, then cart it off to the cemetery for some kind of impromptu funeral service, I would likely have punched him or her in the schnaz.

But it's all Willy Finneran's fault. He somehow manages to defy logic — or at least my logic anyway. It's like he tasered my better judgment into submission, leaving what's left of my discernment in a heap of impotent spasms on the floor. The cautionary voices are still there, duking it out in my head, asking, *How dangerous could this be? Especially with at least two other adults and a four-year-old child in the house? Of course, one of those adults was a convicted felon. And the other, by Willy's own admission, is more than a little deranged. So maybe I am too for not thinking this through a little better.*

But for some strange and completely irrational reason, I trust Willy. I'm just not sure how much to trust my own judgment right now. And I blame that — at least in part — on Willy's crazy suggestion that we just up and decide to fall in love.

But the really crazy part is, the more I think about it, the more sane the idea becomes. I mean, after years of trying to define love in my diaries — deconstructing it, probing its soft underbelly for clues, checking its teeth and kicking its tires — what have I learned? That love is a big scary pool. And you can't really tell how deep or how wide it is just by looking. And if that's true, what's actually crazier? Squeezing your eyes tight and falling blindly into it? Or rather baby-stepping, eyes wide open, with one hand gripping the edge of the pool for support?

"You okay?" he says.

"Yeah, why do you ask?"

"Well, for one thing, you're awfully quiet."

"Oh, sorry. I guess I was just thinking. What's the other thing?"

"You're digging your nails into my arm."

I release my grip at once, but am unable to pull my hand away. Willy has already anticipated my panicky retreat, covering my hand with his and holding it there. It's gentle but firm, and he doesn't let go until my fingers relax on his arm again. At least now he can't see my ears turning red with the porch light burned out.

Ascending the dark steps makes my knees wobbly. When Willy's key disappears into the slot I toss up a trio of quick prayers instead, one for wisdom, one for protection, and another for the return of my more boring, pragmatic self. My prayers take a more urgent tone as we step into the cold, concrete slab of silence of his home. Something seems terribly wrong to me. And Willy seems completely oblivious to whatever it is.

A man matching Father Joe's description is seated at the kitchen table, brooding, just like Willy said he would be. Willy introduces us, looking boyish and eager for the older man's approval. I pray a little harder still when Willy starts asking questions.

Their conversation is stilted, devoid of eye contact and like they're reading from two different scripts. Willy hears Joe's words but misses their real meaning. Not me. I sense Willy's despair before he does. It's obvious that all his pent-up passion for the boy will now be working against him. And I know exactly what that feels like, remembering details against my will. I want nothing more than to explain all this to Willy. But I can't shake that dreamy underwater feeling, where my brain knows exactly what to do but can't get the signal to my body. It seems I'm only capable of repeating his name over and over again.

Willy

I should be embarrassed to realize I forgot to replace the burnt-out porch light. But I'm finding it increasingly difficult to beat myself up with Ozena by my side, digging her fingernails into my forearm.

I stop and take a deep breath through my nose and can feel the oxygen tickle my sinuses, swirling downward, then frolicking a while in my lungs. It leaves a sweet taste in my mouth as it charges back through my windpipe and out onto the street. I'm wondering if this is what real love feels like when I realize Ozena is about to take that next intimate step across the threshold of my home. She's about to encounter my grandparents' old furniture, my ex-wife's son, and both of my homeless roommates. I'm not quite proud of all this, but I'm not quite embarrassed either. Mostly, I'm a little drunk with fascination of all things Ozena.

All that changes when we walk into my house. The air inside has that dense, recently abandoned feel to it, like the day Lucy left. So I'm more than a little relieved to find Father Joe at my kitchen table silently nursing a cup of coffee. He doesn't look up when we come in.

"Joe," I say. "This is Ozena. Ozena, Joe."

It hits me all at once, this ruthless need for Father Joe's approval. I feel blindsided by it, unprepared, and all too eager for one of his brilliant smiles. I wait for him to stand reverently, wrap Ozena's hands in his, and tell her how nice it is to finally meet her. Maybe even make some joke at my expense. But he just sits there. I don't start to worry until I sit down and see the blood drying on his lower lip.

"What happened to you?"

He touches the wound with the tip of his tongue, then says, "Shaq hit me."

"Guess that explains why it's so quiet in here. I suppose you buried him in the backyard?"

I check his reaction, then Ozena's. Neither one laughs. Joe just keeps staring at his coffee. I realize I'm staring too and am a bit startled when the smooth brown surface begins to ripple. It takes a second to realize the furnace just kicked on.

"So where is Shaq anyway?"

"He took off."

I wait for the rest of the story, but there doesn't seem to be any more. Joe seems content to just sit there, brooding and unforgivably rude. He hasn't even acknowledged Ozena yet. I decide to just grab the espresso maker and deal with Joe later. I am disappointed, but before it spirals into outright anger, I usher Ozena out of the kitchen and say, "Guess we'll check on Michael then."

"He's gone."

"Yeah, you just said that. That he just took off or something."

"I'm talking about Michael."

"What about him?" It's not a real question so I don't wait for an answer. Instead, I jog back to my bedroom. When I don't see him there, I begin calling his name and searching every room. I'm barely aware of Ozena repeating my name softly from the living room. For some odd reason this makes me call Michael's name even louder. Now I'm standing behind Father Joe, fists balled, seething and barely able to breathe. "Where is my boy, Joe? Tell me Shaq didn't take him. Please tell me that."

He shakes his head slowly. "Wasn't Shaq that took him. Fact, he's out looking for him."

My body tries to do the tipping hourglass thing again, but I stand my ground. "Who did then?"

"State of Tennessee, far as I can tell."

Ozena

I've devolved into a ridiculous schoolgirl, making any and all attempts at sleep pointless and frustrating. I know what needs to be done, but I just can't make myself get up and do it. Instead, I flop around under the covers, counting sheep, rambling through bedtime prayers, hugging pillows in an absurd attempt to recreate the feel of Willy's body pressed next to mine.

Less than two hours ago Willy walked me to Eugene's car, apologizing all the way about ruining our evening. The good news, for me anyway, is that his heart wasn't all the way in it. I simply assured him he didn't ruin anything, that I had a lovely time, and that getting Michael safely home was way more important than creating some storybook ending for our first date. He just kept shrugging, staring at the road, breathing in and out until my words registered.

"*First* date?" he said. "Doesn't that imply a second?"

"Yeah," I said, stunned by my own audacity. "And hopefully a third and a fourth."

"I really hate this, you know. I should be driving you home, not having to drag your brother and son out in the middle of the night."

"Nonsense. Eugene can't wait to start pumping me for details. And you need to find your boy. And Joe's right. You're in no shape to drive."

He nodded. Father Joe locked Willy's front door and was ambling down the sidewalk. My son and brother ogled us from the backseat. With at least four sets of eyes on us — and no threat whatsoever of a goodnight kiss — it was time for Willy and me to say our goodbyes. He shuffled, I fidgeted, then we sort of lunged at one another — me with open arms and Willy with an open hand. His aborted handshake morphed into a loose fist and jabbed my exposed middle between two ribs. It only hurt a little, but tickled like mad.

Willy looked too mortified to even apologize again. So he offered a half-wave and turned, head down, to meet Father Joe.

"I'd really like a hug, Willy."

He turned back and said, "You would?"

"It was a perfect evening, Willy. I can't let it end with you punching me in the stomach."

He almost smiled. It was close enough. We embraced then, not too tight, but enough to know we meant it. Willy tried to apologize but I shushed him into submission. When I asked Willy if there was anything at all I could do, Father Joe said, "Pray."

I promised Willy I would and he hugged me tighter. Seconds later we heard Father Joe clear his throat and say simply, "Willy."

I tug the covers up to my chin and pray for Willy now, just like I said I would. But I keep interrupting myself with thoughts of that hug. And I feel like God doesn't mind.

I don't mean to, but at some point I catch myself comparing the men in my life. Willy makes me feel lovely and desirable and most of all, pure. Lloyd did that for a while, but he liked to conquer things, then move on. He simply reached a point where he stopped caring. Then he just stopped trying. Reggie pursued me in his own way, but I was basically a convenient target for his clumsy affections. I'm afraid his paltry self-esteem requires the built-in advantage of authority. So if not me, Sheila. And if not Sheila, the next single girl in the office, so long as she's subordinate. My brother — and even my son — constantly remind me that I belong somewhere, that not only am I needed, but have needs. That I matter to someone. I feel myself wafting, slipping into some feathery, dream-filled void, when the thought of Willy Finneran comes boomeranging back at me.

"This is not working," I say to the slats of moonlight shimmying on the ceiling. And who am I trying to kid anyway? I suppose all this theorizing about boys is supposed to make me sleepy. But no matter what I try, I keep circling back to the same handful of delightful thoughts — not only is Willy insanely cute, I just love the way he looks at me.

After another fifteen minutes of not sleeping, I sit up and stare at my journal in the darkness. I consider turning the lamp on, but somehow it feels safer to write in the shadows. I use my teeth to uncap my pen, holding it there. Then I fondle the ribbony bookmark as I squint to make sure the page really is blank. When I can't think of any more excuses not to, I begin this entry like so many before it. The pen scratching on paper sounds more profound in the dark, but I'm sure it's just me.

I write, *Love is …*

I pause, waiting for the angst, the sarcasm, even the irony. My labored breathing whistles in the cap of the pen. I'm stalling.

I start over on the next line.

Love is … Willy Finneran.

But that's just too scary. So I quickly scribble in a question mark at the end of his name. Then I trace over it a dozen times for good measure.

Willy

We don't talk much on the way, mainly because we don't have to. For me, finding Shaq is a means to an end, a necessary link in the chain to finding Michael. I want to hear what happened, every detail, every word spoken, have him tell me about the look on Michael's face when they took him away. But mainly I want my boy back and figure that Shaq might be able to help in some way.

Father Joe's motivation is simpler. He's not worried about Michael being in the custody of the state. He has personal experience there, years of it, so he knows the boy will be safe enough. He just wants to find Shaq and make sure he's okay. For whatever reason, he feels responsible. In part, because he left him alone tonight with Michael, knowing full well that no matter how much Shaq seems to love the boy, the man is ill-equipped to deal with some bureaucrat with an agenda. In many ways, Shaq is a child in a man's body. And Joe's relationship with him is much like my relationship with Michael, more so than I ever realized. Neither of us asked to be guardians, but the children in our charge grew on us. Now we can't bear to think of anything bad happening to them. And when it's all said and done, we'd rather have them around than not. I've always assumed that Father Joe merely tolerates Shaq. It never dawned on me before that he actually loves the man.

We pull to the curb at the mission within seconds of a police cruiser, then another. I follow Joe to the front door and watch the cops bristle when he reaches into his pocket for his keys.

"Easy," he says, his voice measured and filled with authority. The young cop licks his lips, relieved when his partner recognizes Joe. "Put them guns away. This'll only take a minute."

Joe turns to the front door of the mission and the younger cop says something about trespassing. But then the older cop interrupts, saying, "Hey, aren't you Joe Carter?"

Father Joe nods once, then pushes through the door. I glance at the shrugging policemen and follow Joe inside. Shaq is snoring softly in the honeymoon suite, curled into a near-fetal position and hugging Michael's blanket to his chest. The cot squeaks when Joe sits on it, causing Shaq to stir but not wake up. Joe places his massive brown hand on Shaq's cheek. This uncages at least two strange thoughts in my head at once. One, I can't help thinking about the hand of God. Two, I'm jealous.

When he finally wakes up, Shaq is disoriented and teary but eventually allows Father Joe to lead him back out to the idling cab. I climb back in and wait. Through the open window I hear the older cop ask Father Joe for his autograph.

"Trust me," Father Joe says. "You don't want it."

Shaq

I guess I haven't spoken in a while. Since they found me crying myself to sleep at the mission. I can't tell if it's been two days or two weeks. All I really remember for sure is writing the note. And it's not like I've been counting my words either, just listening. Willy keeps asking Father Joe if I'm okay, almost like I'm not in the room. Joe replies the same way every time; he just looks at me. I'm not sure what he's thinking exactly. I'm not even sure I care. My only memory from what I now consider the longest weekend of my life is sneaking into Willy's bedroom. He was in the shower and Father Joe was snoring on the couch when I tiptoed to the big chest of drawers. It didn't take long to find what I was looking for. With one hand clamped on the buckle to mute the sound, I pulled the long leather strap through my fingers. I realized then I was smiling, but not the happy kind. A sound like a small earthquake erupted in the walls. It took a moment to recognize the violent knocking sound in the pipes as water hammer — Willy turned the shower off. When I turned back to close the drawers I caught my reflection in Willy's mirror. It was like a framed photo and it merely confirmed what I spend most of my waking hours trying to forget. It was a snapshot of an aging man, haggard and hollowed, caught in the act of stealing. Photographs exist for only one of two reasons — either for memories or for proof. And mirrors don't lie. The scariest part of that picture was the creepy smile on my face. And it had nothing at all to do with losing Michael or me having stooped to robbery again. It was simple, or maybe just ironic. Willy's belt is reversible too. I pinched it again, fingering the leather grain on either side, marveling at the different textures, wondering what it might mean. All I could come up with was more nothing. So I put the first belt back and dug around until I found one that wasn't reversible.

Willy's driving again this morning with Father Joe riding shotgun. I'm sure the only reason they insisted I tag along is so they wouldn't have to worry about me wandering off again or burning Willy's house down. No one speaks as we park outside the DCS. I take my time getting out. Then, when I'm sure no one is looking, I drop my note onto the passenger seat and climb out. We take the elevator up to the third floor. Willy paces, Father Joe leans against the wall, and I find a comfortable spot around the corner and slump to the floor. We hear muffled voices and the sound of people milling around behind the locked door. The sign says the Department of Child Services opens at nine. Willy just keeps on pacing; Father Joe and I are used to waiting.

Eventually the lock is tripped and the wooden door sighs open. Willy wastes no time pleading his case to some guy named Gustav. I hear snippets, enough to piece together how dismal the situation is. And it's much worse than I thought. The Agent Thompson lady who came and took Michael apparently filed a rather nasty report about what she found at Willy's house the other night — the drugs, the homeless guy, the smoldering popcorn on the unattended burner on the stove. Even Gustav makes her sound hardcore. And when you add that to Willy's recent criminal record, it doesn't sound good. Not for anybody.

Willy keeps saying, "But she came into my house and stole my kid."

"Please don't raise your voice at me, sir. If I recall, you didn't even know the boy's name last time you were here."

Things go quiet as I guess they come to some sort of understanding. I wish I could see Willy's face right now, but it's not worth getting up for. Then Gustav is trying to help. He calls the cops, his supervisor, and even a few of Agent Thompson's co-workers. Gauging by the long pauses, Gustav must be filling out some kind of report. He keeps peppering Willy and Joe with questions, but it's useless. The only things they have to go on are the ramblings of a suicidal homeless guy with blank spots on his memory. I finger the belt again, then the flesh of my neck. Whatever pangs of self-preservation I have left are fading fast. I'm a thief and a bum and can't remember things. I lost Patrice, now Michael. Not to mention the life I had before Father Joe cut me down. Now I'm losing my mind, or what's left of it. My last resort is to pray. But even God must agree with my self-assessment. Or maybe He's just in a mocking mood this morning. Because as soon as I call His name in my mind, it's replaced with the familiar scolding voice of the woman that came and took Michael away. I just assume I'm dreaming until I hear Michael too. And even in my demented brain, the boy sounds scared. That's all the answer I need. I resolve to push myself up off the floor, make my way to the mission, and finally finish what I started.

I'm halfway to a standing position when I actually see Agent Thompson, unwrapping a piece of Juicy Fruit with one hand while dragging Michael toward the open door of the office with the other. My heart tells my brain to spark my body into action. But I'm stuck here on the floor in a dreamy bog of apathy, disbelief, and fear. I watch as she balls up her gum wrapper and tosses it toward a hallway trash can. It hits the lip of the receptacle and bounces onto the floor. That's when I leap out into the hallway and hear a mad shrieking sound.

The shrieking is coming from me as I chase her into the office where Willy and Father Joe will be waiting. All I can think about is taking the boy. After that, I have no idea what I'm supposed to do.

Ozena

I was in the shower, my mind starting to play tricks on me, when Willy
finally called. As he left a message I was likely torturing myself with
images of that good-looking student with her hands all over Willy at the
coffee shop. But it only took one syllable to know something was still
horribly wrong. His message was disjointed and riddled with pauses.
He rambled about marijuana and some agent from the Department of
Child Services, but all I could comprehend with any certainty was that
Willy was hurting. I tried to call him back several times but there was
no answer. I debated whether or not to just go back to his house. But
Lloyd was already sleeping and Eugene was nowhere to be found.

After trying Willy a few more times I call Patti.

"Do you think you could watch Lloyd for me?"

"Sure, what time?"

"Now?"

"I have class."

"Oh …"

She must have heard something in my voice. "I'll be there, Ozena.
I need to work on cultivating more of a rebellious spirit anyhow. I'm
afraid all those straight A's and perfect attendance are starting to hamper my love life."

I thank her again and again. I alternate between rubbing my puffy,
bloodshot eyes and drinking weak coffee, while Lloyd spoons oatmeal
and recounts conversations he's had with Patti in excruciating detail as
I keep checking the clock on the microwave.

Finally, I hear footsteps on the landing and yank the door open
before Patti is finished knocking. I'm already shrugging into my coat
when I say, "You're a doll, Patti. I promise I'll find a way to make it up
to you."

"I'm way ahead of you." She thrust a stack of papers in front of me.
"I decided to take your advice. I'm applying to grad school and need
some references. So if you'd just fill out this section here for me?"

"Congratulations," I say, able to muster more enthusiasm than I'm feeling. I scan the pages, noting tidbits of information—her name, the long years of night school, the synopsis of her treatment of Lloyd. But then the words start to run together. "I'm sorry, can I take this with me? I'm in a bit of a hurry."

"'Long as you promise not to spill coffee on it. And to write nice things about me."

* * *

I know it's pointless, but I don't really know where else to start. Willy's house just *feels* empty when I knock on the door. I crank the Civic's ignition, then sit in his driveway and think. I decide to pray. But just between *Dear* and *heavenly Father* there's a knock on my window. I scream and slam on the brakes, a ridiculous move that only serves to hurt my shins, since the car is still in park. The pipe-smoking man in flannel takes a step back and makes a calming gesture with both hands. When the window is halfway down, we say roughly the same thing at the same time, "I'm sorry, didn't mean to startle you."

"I suppose you're looking for Willy?"

"Yeah, I think he needs some moral support. Have any idea where he is?"

"State building, round the corner from the capital. I'd check the Department of Child Services first."

"Of course, why didn't I think of that?"

"He grilled me and the missus about what we did or didn't see the other night. He's pretty tore up about losing the boy."

"I can imagine."

"I'm Ronnie, by the way." We shake hands through the open window. He smells wonderful, fragrant like a campfire. "You run along and see if you can help Willy."

I thank him, then tear out of the driveway backwards. The dashboard clock reminds me that I'm fifteen minutes late for work already. That's when it dawns on me that I should probably call Reggie or Sheila or somebody to let them know I'm not coming in this morning, which makes two missed days in less than a week. Minnie informs me that Reggie's in a meeting and Sheila's on the phone. Then I leave a few rambling voicemails and dial Information. It takes several very long minutes for the operator to help me narrow down the dozens of government phone numbers. I memorize the three best options and start dialing. Thankfully, I guess right the first time.

"Child Services," a young girl says, breathless and frazzled already. "This is Delores."

I adopt a stern, motherly tone. "I need to speak with Willy Finneran please."

"No one by that name works here."

"He's not an employee, he's ..." A what? A customer? Client? A delinquent legal guardian? A disgruntled recipient of someone else's kid? "I think your department recently handled a custody case involving a William Finneran."

The faint tapping sounds are punctuated by what sounds like distant shouting.

"I'm sorry," she says. "We don't have any — wait, did you say Finneran?"

"Yes, why?"

"Um, I'm not sure I can really say. Things are getting a little crazy around here at the moment. You think you could call back later?"

"No, I cannot! Is Willy there now?"

"I'm sorry, ma'am. We can't divulge personal information unless you're related or something."

I would like to say I blurted this next part out. That somehow my mouth jumped in front of my brain and the words that came roaring out of my mouth were in any way accidental. But then that would fly in the face of my abject devotion to honesty.

"Willy Finneran is my fiancé."

"Oh, in that case, hang on and I'll see if I can get him for you."

It sounds like a TV on in the background, some action flick with lots of scuffling and grunting. Finally she comes back on the line and says, "Sorry, he can't come to the phone right now."

"Is everything okay?"

"I think he just got in a fight."

Willy

I'm not sure who sees whom first, only that it's hard to think with the tortured bellowing emanating from the hallway. It's a two-part harmony, the louder of the two voices coming from Shaq. The other voice, softer but every bit as distinct, belongs to Michael. It takes my eyes a moment to catch up.

A sturdy-looking woman with a badge clipped to her belt is struggling to keep Michael from squirming out of her grasp. Behind them the doorway fills with color and sound. It's Shaq, or rather a mad, pinwheeling cartoon version of the small homeless man from the Mercy Mission.

I can only assume the woman is the DCS's very own Agent Thompson. She gapes at me, shoulders hunched as if she's preparing to take a blow to the back of her head. Her eyes expand to impossible widths as she tries to corral the boy and protect him from the perceived three-pronged attack of Shaq, Father Joe, and me. To her credit, she has no way of knowing that my goal is to protect her from Shaq, nor that Father Joe is trying to protect Shaq from himself. Whether she realizes it or not, Agent Thompson is probably the safest person in the room.

Shaq trips over his own feet and everything freezes, as if some unseen director suddenly yelled *Cut*. The chain reaction starts with the female agent. Her eyes thaw into the realization that we're all adults, not gang members. It's contagious, but not quite complete. We're all still a bit cagey, like compressed springs, eyeing each other warily and breathing much too hard.

"Good morning, Rachel." Gustav remains cool and composed, as if preparing to debate conflicting theories of intelligent design. Father

Joe calmly approaches the fallen Shaq, who is now pushing himself up off the floor. Michael yells *Willy* again and tries to break free. But any chance of civility evaporates when Agent Thompson wrenches Michael's arm hard enough to make him cry. When Shaq sees this, he ducks under Father Joe's outstretched arm and lunges for the stunned agent. Somehow I manage to close the distance before he does. I pounce on him, one hand on his forearm, the other with a fistful of his flannel shirt. He's stronger than I would have imagined and somehow manages to get his hands on Michael. The agent vaults her body between Shaq's flailing grasp and the boy. But Shaq is undeterred. He nearly pushes me off balance but I manage to shift my weight in time, allowing my right arm to slide up and loop around the back of his neck. I hook the bend of his knee with mine, then launch my leg upward as I push the top of his body back. For one split second we're airborne, then slamming onto the carpet.

I feel his lungs empty of air in one violent burst. I can smell the maple syrup he had for breakfast. When I finally open my eyes, I'm relieved to note the back of Shaq's head resting on my arm instead of the ground. Of course, my arm is now killing me.

I extricate myself from Shaq in time to scoop up the now-free Michael into a tight hug. Gustav is doing his best to help the agent make sense of the chaos. Father Joe kneels down beside Shaq, who is still flat on his back and wheezing, still trying to form words. But he'll have to wait for his lungs to refill first.

I'm only vaguely aware of Agent Thompson's battery of questions. Apparently Father Joe was able to get sworn affidavits from the twins that the drugs found in Shaq's jacket (and thus, *my house*) belonged to them. We both promise we'll be available to answer more questions if necessary, that we'll cooperate with whatever home inspections the department deems necessary, and that we promise not to leave the state. I nod along, agreeing with everything, more interested in kissing the top of Michael's musty hair.

Michael says, "I'm hungry, Willy. How about some Jell-O?"

"Sounds perfect," I say.

Father Joe keeps a wary eye on Shaq as he hoists himself up, his knees popping loud enough to turn heads. I plant one foot near Shaq and offer my hand.

"No hard feelings?" I say. But Shaq's gaze floats up and away, landing somewhere in the vicinity of the DCS doorway.

Ozena

There's a frenetic quality to the air when I step off the elevator. It's obvious whatever commotion was going on here is over. I pass a drowsy looking security guard talking to a uniformed policeman. There's another cop interviewing a balding man in a tie. He's scribbling notes and trying not to laugh. No one tries to stop me or even looks at me funny, so I keep moving toward the voices spilling out of the open door at the end of the hall. I must be more uptight than I realized, however. I hear Willy's voice, and that of a child. But it's the other voice that makes my knees give out. I grip the door frame with both hands for support.

My brain tries to tell my body to move, to poke my head through the doorway for proof that I'm just hearing things. But the only motor skills I can manage are wetting my dry lips and clinging tighter to the doorjamb. I hear the voice again and the world seems to tip forward. Or maybe it's me. Either way, I take one step forward and see what cannot possibly be there.

I'm too shocked to cry out. Or even cry. All I can think is that this must be the cruelest joke on earth.

I keep staring, soundless, willing myself into retreat. But before I can pull out of the doorway completely, I feel my throat constricting, my voice aiming at the other man, the one on his back, Father Joe at his side. That's when I see Willy reaching down to help the fallen man up. I don't mean to say it. I don't mean to do anything at all except run away and lock myself in a room. But it's too late. It comes out like a whimper, the kind of sound you would never hear unless it was your own name whispered in a crowded room.

"Lloyd!?"

He turns toward the sound, curious and disbelieving. He looks twenty years older instead of ten, grizzled and gaunt and still defeated. Then all at once recognition blooms on his face too and he too mouths a single word. I expect to hear my name. And if I had, I would have no doubt crumpled to the floor. But instead it sounds garbled as the elevator dings open behind me. I have a vague sense of heads snapping in my direction as I turn and run toward it. I yell for the officer on board to hold the door for me. I dash into the corner, breathing heavy and gripping the handrails along two walls. As soon as the door closes, the officer says, "You okay, lady? You look like you just saw a ghost."

Willy

Shaq whispers the name, Patrice. Then again.

My blurry eyes and overwrought brain conspire to play tricks on me as I follow his gaze. For a split second I would have sworn I saw Ozena in the doorway. I blink my eyes and try to focus. But there's nothing there but an empty hallway.

This temporary distraction is all Shaq needs. He rolls onto his stomach, bolts to a standing position, and darts out of the room. I make a halfhearted wisecrack about someone littering in the hallway, but Joe's not laughing. He twists his bottom lip between his thumb and forefinger and stares at the doorway Shaq just ran through.

"I think we'd better go check on our boy," he says. "And your girl."

"Wait. You saw her too?" My memory lobs an image at my wobbly heart, a ghostly one of Lucy at the class reunion.

Father Joe looks at me hard, like he does all the first-timers at the mission, like he's trying to assess just how crazy this one is. Unlike me, he's in no particular hurry to get to the Rover.

I'm fumbling with the buckle on Michael's car seat when I notice

Father Joe reading a scrap of lined yellow paper. It takes a second to recognize the writing as Shaq's. Joe just shakes his big head and mumbles the word *No* over and over again. He doesn't call it a suicide note. He doesn't have to.

We check the mission first. But there's no sign of Shaq. That's when Father Joe says, "I suppose you know the way to your girlfriend's house."

"I dropped breadcrumbs." I realize I'm trying hard to lighten the mood. But Joe ignores everything but the road in front of us. "You don't think he thinks Ozena is ... you know, *her*?"

"Hard to say."

Shaq

The black spots began to disappear at the sight of her. They didn't vanish so much as start to fill up. I don't wait for the elevator, but take the stairs instead. My feet hit every third or fourth step and I feel a blister forming as I use the handrail to propel me around the turns. On the ground floor, I have to lean against the metal door and wait for the dizziness to wear off. Then one piece at a time, the lost years begin to come out of hiding — cautious but hopeful, like the first faltering steps of tornado survivors emerging from shelters. I make it to the street in time to see Patrice climb into her Honda Civic and pull away from the curb. I start off on foot after her, but only make it to the end of the block before I'm hunched over my own knees and gasping. Guess I haven't recovered from Willy's wrestling move yet. But even as I stand there winded and confused, I feel a smile breaking out from under my beard. I don't have to follow Patrice. Instead I tilt my face toward the sun, close my eyes, and watch another black spot fade into a colorful map of my old neighborhood.

I walk along Commerce Street toward an idling taxi two blocks away. I climb into the backseat and wait for the cabbie to meet my eyes in the rearview. His widen, then narrow in suspicion. My homelessness must be showing.

"Can you pay?"

His accent is thick, but foreign to me. Even this little pun makes me giggle, either from the lack of oxygen making it to my brain or my rousing memory or maybe just the sight of Patrice. I dig one of the twenties out of my front pocket and toss it over the seat. The driver holds it up and squints at it. Then he shrugs and says, "Where to?"

"I'm not sure exactly. Just start driving."

"Did you rob someone?"

"No, of course not. I'm just in a hurry is all."

He shakes his head. "No, no games. I need an address."

"I don't have an address. I just know the way. Or I'll know it when I see it."

He reaches up and starts the meter, then we stare at each other in the mirror some more. He says, "I need a destination."

I remove my last twenty and wave it at him. He puts the car in gear and we follow the directions in my head.

Ozena

At least I had the foresight to call Patti and warn her. "Ozena? You okay?"

"I, um, no, I'm not okay." It's not that I don't want to tell her. I don't just know where to start. "I think I need a little time to myself, that's all."

"You want me to run a tub for you? Or put some tea on?"

"How about both?"

"Just drive careful. And don't you worry about Lloyd."

It takes a second to realize she's talking about my son and not the man I married. Then it takes another full minute for me to process what I think I just saw — Lloyd Davis Rogers Sr., my husband, the father of my child, the man I stayed with through his affairs, his alcoholism, his controlling family — only to watch him cowardly disappear after crippling our baby boy. And not only did I see him in the flesh after having divorced him and having him declared legally dead, but I saw him fraternizing with the only other man I thought I could trust with my heart. I pound the steering wheel in a lame attempt to dislodge the fury I so crave. I want to succumb to it, get lost in it, see what it feels like to rage. I've done my fair share of grief and pain and hurt. Now I want to skip all that and consummate my anger.

My apartment stairwell seems steeper than normal, taller too. I pause outside my door and stare longingly at Eugene's apartment. It would be so much easier to slip inside his place for an hour or two and not have to face anyone. But I need to see Lloyd — my Lloyd, not that bearded ghost in the state building.

My son doesn't turn around when I come in, a familiar and almost daily source of heartbreak when I get home from work. But the slow burn of his emotions are not his fault. His fuse is just too long.

He's moving Risk pieces around a map of the world when I hug him from behind. His body stiffens at the interruption, but I cling a little tighter. His hair needs washing. In fact he's stale all over, but I still can't breathe him in deep enough.

Patti meets me in the hall and knows better than to push too hard. She simply says, "You take your time, Ozena. Me and Lloyd will be fine."

I sit on the edge of my bed, suddenly too tired to stand and walk to the tub, aching from the inside out. The obvious antidote is to call Willy so he can cheer me up. But then I remember him standing there talking to a dead man. It doesn't even seem possible now. How could they possibly know each other? I suddenly remember Willy's seemingly innocent comment at dinner about his friend's insistence on two ice cubes and have to wonder: maybe the better question is, what kind of sick joke is he playing on me? I try distracting myself, but I'm unable to focus on anything but the tattered image of Lloyd and pinprick of anger inside me. I want to locate its source and stoke it, nurture it, climb inside and close the hatch on it if I can.

I hear someone knocking on the door. My heart leaps again at the thought of Willy, but I beat it back down, marveling again at just how ingrained he's become.

That will take some undoing.

The living room goes quiet, Patti no doubt shushing Lloyd so as not to disturb me. Then there's more knocking, louder, more insistent.

"You want me to answer it?" Patti is just outside my bedroom door, whispering. "Tell whoever it is to get lost?"

Whatever I was going to say is lost in the sound of more knocking. Before I realize it, I'm up and pushing past her. "No, thank you. I'll handle this."

I pause at the door, gathering whatever wits I have left. I'm vaguely aware of Patti pulling Lloyd down the hallway toward his room. He protests loudly, but it sounds like his idea of flirting.

I don't even bother with the peephole. As crazy as it sounds, I've heard this knock before. It's the desperate version, the one Lloyd used after one of our many fights, when he'd finally come home from a night of drinking or whoring or both. I pull the door open and there he is.

Up close, he looks even older, impossibly so. His scrawny frame and oversized clothes make him seem shorter too. It occurs to me just how much he looks like his father. I nearly say so, just to be mean. But I'm too busy watching his reaction.

His mouth opens with a wet popping sound, his eyes moist and searching. There's a familiar stirring in them, conjuring first dates and anniversaries and celebrating promotions and holding his newborn son for the very first time. When he raises his arms and steps toward me, I feel myself yielding once again.

He touches my face and whispers, "Patrice."

I recoil.

"What did you call me?"

"I can't believe it's really you."

"What are you talking about, Lloyd?"

He bristles, as if slapped. Then he blinks once and seems to deflate. The only visible tension in his body is the corners of his mouth floating upward, as if raised by pulleys. It's more than delight, more like rhapsody.

"So that's me, huh? Lloyd." He says his name again and again, swishing it around his mouth like a wine taster. It's obvious he approves, the way it sounds, the feel of it in his mouth. "I guess I'm Lloyd then."

Sympathy wells up inside me. But then he reaches for my face again.

"Oh Patrice," he says. "You have no idea how I've missed you."

"Why do you keep calling me that?" I step back and away, watching him. His eyes dart around inside their sockets, as if he's trying to process memories that aren't quite there. "And who is Patrice?"

"Your father ..." His features bloom, ecstatic now. And I have to wonder if he's on drugs. "He'll be thrilled to see you. Almost as happy as me."

"My father's been dead for years." I don't realize how scared I am until I hear the tremor in my voice. "You were a pallbearer, Lloyd. Don't you remember?"

He laughs, a sickeningly familiar sound. "Remembering is not my strong suit. At least not till now."

When he reaches for me again, I smack his hand away.

"Oh, I see." The edge is back in his voice. Lloyd never actually hit me, but this is the tone that felt like it. "I suppose you think you belong to Willy now."

"No, Lloyd. I don't *belong* to anyone. Not since you ran off the last time." I feel my vocal cords crumbling and just hate it. The last thing I want to do now is cry. "They said you were dead."

"Of course he'd say that. I'm sure he'd tell you anything to steal my sweet Patrice away from me."

"What do you mean steal? It's been ten years, Lloyd." He blinks, then looks down like he's calculating something. "Not since you ... you ... what you did to our son."

"I know, Patrice. And I felt terrible about losing him like that."

"Losing him? Is that what you call it?"

"Calm down, babe. It's all worked out now. Michael is safe and sound."

"Michael who?"

But the man impersonating my husband isn't listening. As if talking to himself, he says, "Of course we will need to figure out what to do about Willy now."

He sounds so confident, so familiar and soothing, that I find myself trying to believe it's somehow true. That we're actually a decade in the past on the tail end of one of our many ridiculous arguments, that my perfectly whole baby boy is indeed bouncing on my father's lap in North Carolina.

My reverie is cracked apart by his rough hands gripping both of mine. But then I realize these are not his hands, not really. The Lloyd I married had no calluses, would never abide facial hair or smelling like the bottom of a hamper. He was a meticulous dresser with a sharp and conniving mind.

"Come on, Patrice. I'm dying to hold you."

His arms open again and I practically flee toward the hallway. "Stop it, Lloyd. Stop touching me. And stop calling me Patrice. My name is Ozena."

I hear Lloyd Jr.'s door open and Patti ask, "Do you need me?"

"No, dear." I say, my voice choked with tears. "We're just talking."

"So why do ya'll keep calling my name?"

Before I can answer, my son comes rushing out of his bedroom holding a rocket in one hand and a dinosaur in the other. His clomping, off-kilter gait seems especially pathetic under the gaze of the man who caused it. And Lloyd Sr. can't seem to take his eyes off his son. I watch his face, eager to see any sign of recognition, but secretly hoping it never comes.

Finally, it dawns on Lloyd Jr. that there's a stranger in the room. He stops in front of his father and gazes up, matching his dumb expression feature for feature. It's excruciating to watch, both seemingly oblivious to the resemblance, much less the shared experiences or the identical blood filling their veins.

My son breaks the silence first. "Hello," he says.

The father waves awkwardly to his son, oblivious. His smile is tight and hurried and utterly unfamiliar. He's about to say something to me, when Lloyd Jr. takes two limping steps forward, wraps his arm around his father's waist, and rests his ear against his tummy.

I watch them together, wondering what my son is thinking. Or if he's thinking anything at all. Does he sense some deeper connection? Can he somehow see through the beard and wrinkles and match the face with old photographs of his father?

At some point Patti says, "You want me to call the cops?"

Lloyd looks up at Patti, startled by the sound. Or maybe by the word *cops*. He looks at me, mouths the word *Sorry*, then turns and runs away.

Again.

It only takes fifteen minutes or so to cry myself dry. Lloyd Jr. plays solitaire and seems unaffected. Patti has the good sense not to ask questions. Instead she holds my hand until the water boils. She's pouring our tea when there's another knock on the door. Patti looks at me and I look at the door. But it's not Lloyd.

"You want me to get that?" Patti says.

"No. Thanks anyway."

I take a deep breath, then another. Then one more before giving up and simply opening the door. At first all I can see is Willy. Probably because he's all really I want to see right now. Eventually I notice his hands resting on the shoulders of an adorable little boy. Father Joe is at the back of the pack. I step back and motion them inside, still not trusting my voice.

"Michael," Willy says, steering the boy toward me by the shoulders. "This is my friend Ozena."

"Hi, I'm Michael. I'm four." He raises one hand, then directs all his concentration to the task of bending his pinky in half. "And a half."

"It's very nice to meet you, Michael. Willy has said a lot of nice things about you."

"He did?" The boy looks up at Willy for confirmation.

"Yeah. I think it means he likes you a lot."

"Huh, Willy must love *you* then."

Patti is the only one who laughs. But Michael continues, undaunted. "I talk about chocolate because that's what I love. Do you have any chocolate?"

"I'll bet if you ask Patti real nice, she can find something." I don't dare look at Patti, certain that she's covering her mouth to keep from laughing. "And that's Lloyd at the table. He's my little boy."

"He's not so little," Michael says.

"I'm retarded," Lloyd says. "You want to play Battleship?"

Father Joe steps forward, grasps my hand in both of his, and says, "I'm sorry about the other night. Guess I was a little out of sorts. I'm Joe Carter. And I'm very pleased to meet you."

"Likewise," I say above the sound of Patti knocking around in the cupboards behind me. "And Willy's told me plenty of nice things about you too."

He winks, then flashes another of his almost-smiles. "Must be love then."

I feel my ears competing with my neck for blushing supremacy when Father Joe's face goes slack. His lips turn white and he steadies himself on the back of the couch. I realize I'm sorting through a jumble of CPR steps, just in case. Father Joe does put one hand over his heart, but it's not that kind of attack.

"Patrice?" he says.

The only sound in the house now is the inane rambling of two boys simulating a sea battle at my kitchen table. It's clear now that Joe's going to be okay. Better than okay. With two shaky fingers he unbuttons his breast pocket and removes a photograph. It's an old picture, trimmed on four sides with a white border, the color faded. But the big eyes and brown skin are unmistakable.

"Do I know you?" Patti says, clearly rattled by the sight of the big man with moist eyes.

There's no orchestra music, no slow motion sequences, and the heavens don't open up. Father Joe simply walks toward Patti, holding the picture feebly out before him, and says, "It's me, baby. It's Daddy."

Shaq

"How many is that?" Father Joe says.

I'm not startled because I heard the car doors slam.

"Three so far." I bounce the ball once, then again. "But my best is eight in a row."

"Not bad."

I try to ignore him and go through my pre-shot routine — eye the front of the rim, dribble twice with a slight hip waggle, tuck my tongue into the left corner of my mouth, and let the ball fly. The shot feels okay, good follow through, but I put too much on it. It hits the back of the rim, then the front, then takes a fortunate bounce and falls impotently through the net.

"Lucky shot, man." Joe is trying to sound playful. "You gonna count that?"

"You always did."

"Good point," he says as I retrieve the bouncing ball. "So tell me something. What happens when you hit ten?"

I shrug, preparing for my next shot. Father Joe lifts the tail of my flannel shirt. I can see his breath when he sighs.

"What if I'm not around to cut you down this time?"

"I didn't ask you to cut me down last time. You probably could have saved us all a lot of trouble if you didn't."

"You looking at this backwards, Shaq."

"Apparently my name is Lloyd."

"You're embarrassed cuz you think you messed up. But you're wrong. You led me right to my baby girl."

"Not on purpose."

"I disagree."

"Oh right, sorry. You probably think Jesus did it." And maybe he did, but I'm not in the mood to concede anything yet. "I looked in the wrong places, Joe. I wasn't even looking for the right girl."

"So what? We both been looking for Patrice ever since I met you. But in the end, it was you that found her, not me."

"Nice of you to say so." I dribble the ball once, then again. "But from where I'm standing, the woman I was married to hates me and it's my own fault my son is the way he is. Fresh memories continue to flood my brain, but they're all bad. Everything is scrambled and scary and makes my head hurt. So if you don't mind, I'd like to make my ten in a row and do what I need to do."

"What if I do mind?"

"I guess you can take my belt away from me. But I wish you wouldn't."

"It's not your belt."

I think he meant that to be funny. Or at least amusing enough to crack my resolve so I'd at least meet his eyes.

"Willy can have it back when I'm done with it."

I try to push past him, but he puts his hand on my chest, warming me from the outside in. "You know I'm not gonna let you hurt yourself, Shaq. As far as I'm concerned, you're mine."

Father Joe goes and stands by Willy. They watch me eye the rim, bounce the ball twice, and swish number five.

There's at least some truth to Ozena's story. I can feel it. There's even a few memories rattling around inside me that seem to confirm it. But they all seem dirty and used, like they belong to someone else. Whether they're mine or not, I can't say. But I do know that if I was that guy—the one in the memories—then I don't want to go back to being him anyway. I can tell Ozena deserves better than what she had in me.

I've now made nine in a row.

I repeat the routine one last time—the rhythmic dribbles, tongue touching, eyeing the front of the basket, the follow through. Any good coach would tell you to keep your eye on the rim, to not give in to the temptation of watching the ball. But this is a pretty shot and I know it's good when it leaves my hand. The chain net snaps, cradling the ball in a churning motion before dropping it to the pavement again. This time I let it roll to a stop near the goal. I won't be needing it anymore.

Willy's eyes grow wide as I approach him and say, "We need to talk."

I don't wait for an answer, just walk away. By the time I round the corner I hear Willy following behind. I pause at the front door of the mission and wait for him to catch up. He stops abruptly when I tug the tail of my shirt up and reach for my waistband. He even puts his hands up like he thinks I'm going to whip out a handgun.

"Here," I say, sliding the belt off in one quick motion. "I believe this is yours."

He kicks at a piece of gravel, looking conflicted, like he knows what he wants to say but isn't sure if he should, or how to get started. "Look, man. I know this is all messed up. You've got some things to sort through and I won't stand in your way, whatever you decide. But I won't lie to you either. I'm crazy about Ozena. And if I get the chance, I'm going to take care of her and Lloyd." Willy looks at me hard now, not quite threatening, but close. "Or at least make sure you do."

The relief almost makes my knees buckle, but I think I do an admirable job of not showing it. Hope so, anyway. And it's not just because I'm afraid of the unknown, or even that I'll turn back into who I think I was before. It's something in Willy's voice. He sounds like he's willing to fight for something, something that used to be mine, something

I abused. It's odd, this ability to know without remembering. I was a coward, and there's no reason to think that's changed. I'm not sure how much time elapses while we're standing there looking at each other. Finally Willy says, "So what do you say, Lloyd?"

"Man, you're as crazy as she is."

"What's that supposed to mean?" Willy looks offended, a good sign. He really is going to be good for her. And for the boy. Both of the boys. My boys.

"My name is Shaq, not Lloyd. And I need a ride."

Willy

I'll never get used to it. Stan the literary agent may sound like Eeyore, but he looks like the lead in a sports drink commercial, all sparkly and rugged and ready for a jog.

I introduce him to Ozena and they exchange pleasantries. I point them to a table in the middle of the dining room, then grab two moist trays and slide them toward the dessert area. Today I hit the mother lode — they have red, green, yellow, and orange Jell-O, cut into neat squares and laden with suspended pieces of fruit. The cashier is new, or new to me. At first she turns to see if a group of school children snuck in behind her. When I tell her they're all for me, her expression alternates between dubious and slightly terrified.

Ozena and Stan are laughing about something when I approach. Probably me, but that's okay. I distribute the spoons and napkins, then refuse to talk business until they both join me in a celebratory mouthful of colorful gelatin.

Stan looks queasy but manages at least three bites before pushing it to the side. He removes a sheaf of papers, clicks his pen into action, then asks me to sign and date the bottom of every page.

"So," Ozena says, swallowing hard. She looks startled, like she ate an entire grape. "You actually avoided your own agent for nearly a year?"

I nod.

"And it was good news?"

"How was I supposed to know that?"

"Easy." Stan licks his finger and turns another page for me. "You could have returned any one of my calls, opened one of the letters, or even looked for the smoke signals on a clear day."

Ozena shakes her head, but I can't tell if it's in disbelief or admiration. "And this is your 'serious' novel, right? The one you lost?"

"I didn't lose it. I just never made a copy."

My agent scans the contract once, then again. Satisfied, he tucks it into his briefcase and says, "I didn't even open it at first, since we don't take unsolicited manuscripts. But one of my interns had some down time, opened it up, and found the note from Lucy. When the intern finished the manuscript, she bounded into my office and said, 'Weren't you looking for Willy Finneran?' And I was, but only so I could resign as your agent."

"Thanks." I grab my third Jell-O and dig in.

"You weren't producing anything new. I was losing money simply by keeping you on our Christmas card list." He taps the official looking check with his fingernail. "Anyway, don't spend your advance money all in one place."

"Too late," I say.

"Oh yeah?"

"I'm think I'm going to help a friend buy back his home. Or try to anyway."

He motions toward Ozena. "Well you should at least buy the lady something nice."

I point to the uneaten bowls of colorful, jiggly Jell-O, and Ozena laughs her perfect laugh.

"One more thing." Stan reaches into his briefcase and removes a small metal case. It looks like my grandfather's lockbox, only newer and more durable. He places it gently on the table, then slides it toward me.

"What's this?" I say, feeling the cool metal surface.

"Lucy sent that too, about six months after the manuscript. My intern lost the note that came with it. But the gist of it was that she wanted me to hang on to this for a while. I was supposed to use my discretion and give it to you at some unknown point in the future. Figured now's as good a time as any, in case you decide to go into hiding again."

I stare at the box, clueless at first. But it doesn't take long. I know Lucy and I know how she thinks. I slide it back across the table. "I need you to hang on to this a little longer, Stan. Keep it in a safe place."

"You're not even going to open it?" he asks.

"Nope, I don't have to."

Ozena says, "What is it?"

"It could be nothing," I say. "Or it might be everything."

I imagine there are letters in there, probably a sloppy mix of confession and blame and maybe even some explanation. We didn't take a lot of photos, but I'm sure they're in there too. Of course, the bulk of it will have to do with Michael, some notes written to him and a few written about him. So I'll have to open it someday, just not today. And if that's all that was in there, I could handle it. But there's more; I know it. I sense them staring at me as I check the math in my head one more time, just to be sure. But I can't be sure, not all the way. And that's why I can't look in the box. It just proves Lucy knew me better than I know myself, even now. I don't have to look to know my toothbrush is in there, or that she would have wrapped it in inside a paternity test.

My borrowed heart taps calmly in my chest, as if sending a message in code. It seems obvious now who's knocking. And he's doing so from the inside, where he's always been. There's more to the message, most of which I don't understand, not yet. Maybe I'm not supposed to. But the part I do get with absolute certainty is that it takes more than DNA to prove fatherhood.

"So ..." Ozena says. She taps me on the forehead. "You still in there?"

I blink myself back into existence. Stan is already gone, as are a few bowls of Jell-O. "I guess I zoned out there for a bit."

"Quite a bit. You okay?"

"Well there is one thing we need to discuss."

"Oh?"

"Gustav mentioned something to me the other day and it's been troubling me ever since."

"Who?"

"The guy from Child Services."

Her face goes blank.

"Your conversation with Delores?"

"Who?" she says. Ozena fidgets and squirms and looks around the room, either for help or the nearest exit. "I'm not so good with names."

"Maybe this will help. She's the one who refused to divulge any personal information unless you could prove you were a family member?"

"Oh, *that* Delores," she says.

"She sends her congratulations, by the way."

Ozena begins gathering dishes and spoons, anything to avoid having to look at me. "Oh? Congratulating you for what exactly?"

"Not me, *us*." Ozena's breath catches and she nearly drops her tower of dirty dishes. "You're cute when you're conflicted."

"So you're saying I'm not cute when I'm not?"

"I would never say that. But I wonder what Delores could possibly be congratulating us for?"

"I guess she heard I got the promotion."

If Ozena was trying to derail me, it worked. Her lopsided grin is both proud and embarrassed, not to mention excruciatingly kissable. "You did?"

"Reggie and Sheila's first date was a raging success. Sheila's going to work for her dad to keep things from getting weird at work."

"Wow. That serious that quick, huh?"

"It's ridiculous, I know." Ozena stands and begins piling soiled dishes from a nearby table onto a tray.

"So I guess it was my customer service survey that tipped the scale in your favor, eh?"

"I'm not sure the execs were all that impressed with what a dreamy voice I have or the way my laughter nourishes your aching heart. And 'Herculean customer service' might have been a little over the top too."

"Did I write that?"

"But thanks for saying it anyway."

"Let me be the next to say congratulations."

"The next?"

"Yeah, right after Delores."

"Say, you never told me where you took Lloyd when you left the mission."

"Drove him to Starbucks so he could apply for a job. He claims there's a former business partner of his named Randy."

"Really? Randy?"

"That's what he said. Why? You know him?"

"If it's the same Randy. He and Lloyd were supposed to open a coffee shop."

"Weird ... now quit changing the subject."

She mimes an invitation toward the half-eaten bowl of Jell-O in front of me. I shake my head and she adds it to her collection. "I suppose he'll move into Patti's place for a while, with Father Joe?"

"Actually, he's staying with me for the time being."

"You? Really? That's awfully nice of you, Willy."

"Yes, it is."

"You know ..." Ozena is now wiping smudges off the table with a tattered napkin. "I say lots of things when I'm stressed."

"But you always tell the truth, right? So out with it."

"You already know what I said. Or else you wouldn't be, um, *badgering* me about it."

"Yeah, but I want to hear you say it."

She rises to her full height, the dishes teetering dangerously. She says, "Then I guess you'll have to call me sometime."

As she walks away, I ask, "What if I can't get through?"

"Then maybe it wasn't meant to be."

I watch her sort the silverware from the dishes. Then she loads trash into the mouth of the receptacle. But that's not the last sound I hear as Ozena disappears around the corner. I crane my ear just so and listen until her laughter slowly fades away.

I have to remind myself not to panic, that this is not like Lucy or Walter or anyone else who walked out of my life. Ozena *has* to come back.

Otherwise she won't have a ride home.

She doesn't look nearly as sheepish as I would have liked when she comes back and sits down across from me. I dangle my key ring in front of her, unabashedly smug, and say, "Forget something?"

"Nope. I just came back to tell you what's really wrong with your heart."

"Is that so?"

"Yep, I finally figured it out."

"Well are you going to tell me?"

"It's simple. You were boring it to death."

"That's some diagnosis. What do you prescribe?"

"You just need to give it something to do."

"Any ideas?"

"You could start a journal."

Ozena

Willy gets out first with the espresso maker, then offers me his hand to help navigate around a large glassy puddle. Once safely on the ground, I feel Willy's hand relax into a reluctant retreat. But I surprise us both by not letting go. His grin is boyish and sweet, and will no doubt inspire a hundred new *love is* ... entries.

We follow the pebbled trail up a steep hill, then veer off to pick our way through an assortment of headstones until we find Lucy's. I'm not sure if it's the chilled air or the cemetery itself, but I find myself pressing into Willy's warm body. I stop just shy of a genuine snuggle as we stare at the words on the headstone and I wait for him to speak. After all, this is about him.

Willy inhales like he's about to say something, then stops. He does this several more times, opening his mouth then closing it again. I have this sense that the words are in there, but they keep losing their way. Or maybe they're afraid too.

Sometime later, I do hear speaking. They're Willy's words, but colored by my voice.

"What I think Willy is trying to say, is that he forgives you, Lucy."

I check Willy's expression, suddenly desperate to know if I'm getting this right. He's biting his lip, blinking. Eventually he nods his approval, but I can tell there's more. I consider this for another long moment until I feel certain I'm not just guessing.

"And that he promises to look after Michael."

Willy places the espresso maker in the center of Lucy's grave. Then he stands upright, boldly takes my hand, and walks me back to the car.

Just before we get in, he clears his now ragged throat and says, "Thank you."

We climb in to the sound of both Lloyd and Michael making ridiculous kissing sounds.

Acknowledgments

I would first like to thank all the great people at Zondervan, in particular, the folks who have to put up with me on any sort of regular basis: Andy Meisenheimer, Becky Philpott, Karen Campbell, Karwyn Bursma, Beth Shagene, and Curt Diepenhorst. And to everyone else who has anything at all to do with allowing me the great privilege of writing and publishing books.

Steve Laube is not only an outstanding agent, but he makes me laugh too. Out loud. Thanks for everything. You really are the best.

And to my amazing family who indulges me this writing habit. I love you guys more than words can express ... so you're just going to have to trust me on this. Me mostest!

Lastly, but surely not leastly, to anyone who has bought, read, recommended, reviewed, praised, or panned my books ... THANK YOU! Writers barely exist without readers.

My Name Is Russell Fink

Michael Snyder

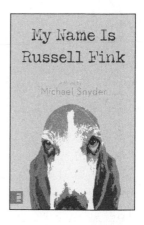

Russell Fink is twenty-six years old and determined to salvage a job he hates so he can finally move out of his parents' house for good. He's convinced he gave his twin sister cancer when they were nine years old. And his crazy fiancée refuses to accept the fact that their engagement really is over.

Then Sonny, his allegedly clairvoyant basset hound, is found murdered.

The ensuing amateur investigation forces Russell to confront several things at once—the enormity of his family's dysfunction, the guy stalking his family, and his long-buried feelings for a most peculiar love interest.

At its heart, *My Name Is Russell Fink* is a comedy, with sharp dialogue, characters steeped in authenticity, romance, suspense, and fresh humor. With a postmodern style similar to Nick Hornby and Douglas Coupland, the author explores reconciliation, forgiveness, and faith in the midst of tragedy. No amount of neurosis or dysfunction can derail God's redemptive purposes.

Softcover: 978-0-310-27727-9

Pick up a copy today at your favorite bookstore!

Share Your Thoughts

With the Author: Your comments will be forwarded to the author when you send them to *zauthor@zondervan.com*.

With Zondervan: Submit your review of this book by writing to *zreview@zondervan.com*.

Free Online Resources at

www.zondervan.com

Zondervan AuthorTracker: Be notified whenever your favorite authors publish new books, go on tour, or post an update about what's happening in their lives.

Daily Bible Verses and Devotions: Enrich your life with daily Bible verses or devotions that help you start every morning focused on God.

Free Email Publications: Sign up for newsletters on fiction, Christian living, church ministry, parenting, and more.

Zondervan Bible Search: Find and compare Bible passages in a variety of translations at www.zondervanbiblesearch.com.

Other Benefits: Register yourself to receive online benefits like coupons and special offers, or to participate in research.

ZONDERVAN®
.com